SELECTED FICTION AND DRAMA OF
ELIZA HAYWOOD

WOMEN WRITERS IN ENGLISH
1350-1850

GENERAL EDITORS
Susanne Woods and Elizabeth H. Hageman

EDITORS
Carol Barash
Stuart Curran
Margaret J. M. Ezell

SELECTED FICTION
AND DRAMA OF
Eliza Haywood

Edited by
Paula R. Backscheider

New York   Oxford

Oxford University Press

1999

Oxford University Press

Oxford   New York
Athens   Auckland   Bangkok   Bogotá   Buenos Aires   Calcutta
Cape Town   Chennai   Dar es Salaam   Delhi   Florence   Hong Kong   Istanbul
Karachi   Kuala Lumpur   Madrid   Melbourne   Mexico City   Mumbai
Nairobi   Paris   São Paulo   Singapore   Taipei   Tokyo   Toronto   Warsaw

and associated companies in
Berlin   Ibadan

Copyright © 1999 by Oxford University Press, Inc.

Published by Oxford University Press, Inc.
198 Madison Avenue, New York, New York 10016

Oxford is a registered trademark of Oxford University Press.

Library of Congress Cataloging-in-Publication Data
Haywood, Eliza Fowler, 1693?–1756.
[Selections.   1999]
Selected fiction and drama of Eliza Haywood /
edited by Paula R. Backscheider.
p.   cm. — (Women writers in English 1350–1850)
Includes bibliographical references
Contents: A wife to be lett—The city jilt—The mercenary
lover—From The fruitless enquiry—The opera of operas—From
The adventures of Eovaai—From The invisible spy—From The wife.
ISBN 0-19-510846-9; ISBN 0-19-510847-7 (pbk)
1. England—Social life and customs—18th century—Literary
collections.   2. Women—England—Literary collections.
I. Backscheider, Paula R.   II. Title.   III. Series.
PR3506.H94A6   1998
823'.5—dc21   97-48889

1 3 5 7 9 8 6 4 2

Printed in the United States of America
on acid-free paper.

FOR

LISA HOWE BACKSCHEIDER

CONTENTS

FOREWORD

Women Writers in English 1350–1850 presents texts of cultural and literary interest in the English-speaking tradition, often for the first time since their original publication. Most of the writers represented in the series were well known and highly regarded until the professionalization of English studies in the later nineteenth century coincided with their excision from canonical status and from the majority of literary histories.

The purpose of this series is to make available a wide range of unfamiliar texts by women, thus challenging the common assumption that women wrote little of real value before the Victorian period. While no one can doubt the relative difficulty women experienced in writing for an audience before that time, or indeed have encountered since, this series shows that women nonetheless had been writing from early on and in a variety of genres, that they maintained a clear eye to readers, and that they experimented with an interesting array of literary strategies for claiming their authorial voices. Despite the tendency to treat the powerful fictions of Virginia Woolf's *A Room of One's Own* (1928) as if they were fact, we now know, against her suggestion to the contrary, that there were many "Judith Shakespeares" and that not all of them died lamentable deaths before fulfilling their literary ambitions.

This series offers, for the first time, concrete evidence of a rich and lively heritage of women writing in English before the mid-nineteenth century. It grew out of one of the world's most sophisticated and forward-looking electronic resources, the Brown University Women Writer's Project (WWP), with the earliest volumes of the series derived directly from the WWP textbase. The WWP, with support from the National Endowment for the Humanities, continues to recover and encode for a wide range of purposes complete texts of early women writers and maintains a cordial relationship with Oxford University Press as this series continues independently.

Women Writers in English 1350–1850 offers lightly annotated versions based on single good copies or, in some cases, collated versions of texts with more complex editorial histories, normally in their original spelling. The editions are aimed at a wide audience, from the informed undergraduate through professional students of literature— and they attempt to include the general reader who is interested in exploring a fuller tradition of early texts in English than has been available through the almost exclusively male canonical tradition.

SUSANNE WOODS

ELIZABETH H. HAGEMAN

General Editors

ACKNOWLEDGMENTS

I would like to acknowledge the help and encouragement of a succession of research assistants, Elizabeth Cater, Hope Cotton, Nancy Naugle, and Patsy Fowler, who worked on this volume with energy, humor, and ingenuity. Karen Beckwith provided advice and practical help on editorial matters, and I thank her. Patsy Fowler deserves special thanks for formatting the volume and Elizabeth Cater and Jessica Smith for their tireless editorial work. My colleague James Hammersmith and the fine reference and Interlibrary Loan librarians at Auburn University, especially Glenn Anderson, Angela Courtney, and Linda Thornton, contributed generously and gave me new ideas; I am grateful to them. Robert D. Hume has been an invaluable resource. Nikki Graves checked material in the Emory University Library for me, and Catherine Ingrassia shared her specialized knowledge. Support for the work came from the Philpott-Pepperell Research Fund and Oxford University Press.

PAULA R. BACKSCHEIDER

INTRODUCTION

Eliza Haywood is a remarkable writer—how remarkable is yet to be fully explored. Still known primarily as the author of erotic seduction novels, she was also a deeply engaged political writer, a poet, a journalist, a translator, a dramatist, a literary critic, and the author of conduct books and essays. Her career as a writer extended over thirty-seven years beginning in 1719 with *Love in Excess*, the book that, with *Robinson Crusoe* (also 1719), opened eyes to the enormous potential readership for prose fiction, and concluding in the year of her death with *The Wife* and *The Husband*, two witty, wide-ranging collections of advice essays, and *The Young Lady*, a weekly periodical, the last number of which appeared less than two weeks before her death.

Haywood's place in literary history is equally remarkable and as neglected, misunderstood, and misrepresented as her oeuvre.[1] During her lifetime, the novel became a well-recognized and then respectable form, and her career spans that of Daniel Defoe, Samuel Richardson, and Henry Fielding. She was an actress and a playwright and in the 1730s an integral part of the radical and innovative Haymarket Theatre. She did all of the things that people bent on supporting themselves as writers did. Her work (like that of Defoe, Joseph Addison, Henry Fielding, Samuel Johnson, and now-forgotten "hacks" such as Charles Gildon) included translations, periodical essays, and political propaganda. Scholars are still discovering texts she authored,[2] and, partly because of her risky political involvement and partly because she herself was a publisher, there is general agreement that we may never identify all that she wrote.

---

1. There is no complete list of what we know Haywood to have written. The most authoritative is Eliza Haywood, *The History of Miss Betsy Thoughtless*, ed. Christine Blouch (Peterborough, Ontario: Broadview Press, 1998), 21–24.

2. Examples of works recently attributed to Haywood include *Memoirs of a Man of Honour* (1747) ascribed by Christine Blouch in "Eliza Haywood and the Romance of Obscurity," *Studies in English Literature* 31 (1991): 544; and *Dalinda: or, the Double Marriage* (1749) attributed by Thomas Lockwood in "Eliza Haywood in 1749," *Notes and Queries* n.s. 234 (1989): 475–76.

The Life

Haywood's life is still largely a mystery, and information about it is more likely to come from her competitors and enemies than from the neutral documents recording births, marriages, and business transactions. As recently as 1991, her burial in St. Margaret's parish churchyard on 3 March 1756 was discovered,[1] an addendum to an often overlooked confirmation of her death on 25 February 1756.[2] Haywood was probably born in 1693. By 1719 the marriage she described as "unfortunate" was over, and she had already performed on the stage of the most prestigious theater outside of London, Smock Alley in Dublin. While there, she worked under Joseph Ashbury, the manager reputed to be a preeminent teacher of acting. She made useful contacts there, including William Wilkes, younger brother of Robert Wilkes, one of the great stars of the London stage and co-manager of Drury Lane Theatre, who had sent William there to learn from Ashbury,[3] and William Chetwood, who would help her career later and print some of her books. She had moved to London, where she played Nottingham in *The Earl of Essex* (1673) at Lincoln's Inn Fields, one of the two royal theaters.[4] By 1730, she had two children, and some of her fiction, notably *The Rash Resolve* (1724) and *The Force of Nature* (1725), suggests she delighted in motherhood even as she engaged with such issues as the options of single mothers.[5] For example, in *The Rash Resolve*, published years before Samuel Richardson's dramatization of the limits of

1. Blouch, "Romance of Obscurity," 546n.1. Information about her life is from Blouch's article and the work of Catherine Ingrassia, to whom I am grateful for sharing the manuscript of her forthcoming *Paper Credit: Grub Street, Exchange Alley, and Feminization in the Culture* (Cambridge: Cambridge University Press).

2. Blouch notes D. M. Walmsley's discovery of an obituary ("Romance of Obscurity," 544, 552nn.54, 56).

3. William S. Clark, *The Early Irish Stage: The Beginnings to 1720* (Oxford: Clarendon, 1955), 149. Clark says that Haywood spent three seasons there, 1714–1717. Clark identifies William as Robert's nephew, but *A Biographical Dictionary of Actors, Actresses, Musicians . . .* , ed. Philip H. Highfall, Kalman A. Burnim, and Edward A. Langhans, vols. 1–16 (Carbondale: Southern Illinois Univ. Press, 1973–1993), identifies him as the younger brother.

4. Performed in April 1717.

5. Toni Bowers argues that Haywood addresses the possibility of autonomous female authority in these novels and a fiction in *The Female Spectator* and that she offers radical alternatives, including maternal empowerment through female community. See Bowers, *The*

maternal authority in *Pamela*, vols. 3 & 4, *In her Exalted Condition* (1741), Haywood has a heroine confronted with the superior rights of her child's father. Although the father has been unaware of this illegitimate son, he takes possession of his son and makes the child part of *his* new family. The mothers in her fiction, like Emanuella in *The Rash Resolve*, are groundbreaking characters who have managed to attain respectable, economic independence.

Haywood's first child appears to have been fathered by Richard Savage and her second by William Hatchett. She and Savage had plays performed within the same year at Drury Lane and shared the same circle of theatrical friends. He wrote a complimentary poem for her *Love in Excess* but satirized her later in *An Author to be Let* (1729) and *The Authors of the Town* (1725). Haywood lived with Hatchett for over twenty years, and exactly how their careers intersected and their work was influenced by the relationship is unclear. Haywood performed in a play attributed to Hatchett, *The Rival Father* (1730), and he has often been listed as a full collaborator on *The Opera of Operas* since Baker's *Companion to the Playhouse* did so in 1764. Hatchett is a shadowy figure who at least once was cited as delivering a seditious publication, *A Letter from H——G——, Esq.* (1750), to booksellers for her, and the two of them are intriguingly listed as having rented the Haymarket Theatre for one night each in the season it closed.[1] Hatchett is named as one of the co-defendants in an Exchequer Court case brought by John Frederick Lampe against his former partners in an English opera venture that included the first production of *Opera of Operas*.[2] Haywood's *Female Spectator* announced that she was ending the periodical

Politics of Motherhood: British Writing and Culture, 1680–1720 (Cambridge: Cambridge UP, 1996), 124–47.

1. See Thomas Lockwood, "William Hatchett, *A Rehearsal of Kings* (1737), and the Panton Street Puppet Show (1748)," *Philological Quarterly* 68 (1989): 315–23, and "Eliza Haywood in 1749," 475–77. Robert D. Hume reprints the list of people in John Potter's appeal to (probably) the Duke of Grafton in *Henry Fielding and the London Theatre, 1728–1737* (Oxford: Clarendon, 1988), 246. I agree that "Kaywood" is an error for "Haywood." Hume also speculates that *The Female Free Mason* was "possibly" by Hatchett and written "probably as a vehicle for . . . Haywood" (231). Hume reminds us that *A Rehearsal of Kings* is "a lost, anonymous work" and nowhere speculates that Hatchett wrote it (229).

2. Judith Milhous and Robert D. Hume, "J. F. Lampe and English Opera at the Little Haymarket in 1732–33," *Music and Letters* 78 (1997): 502–31. I am grateful to them for sharing their manuscript.

in order to "collaborate on a new magazine [*The Parrot*, 1746] with a gentleman friend," probably Hatchett.[1]

Among the unexplored aspects of Haywood's life is her place in various theatrical and literary circles. Aaron Hill, William Chetwood, John Rich, Henry Fielding, and others are shadowy presences in her life. In a time when connections and friendships were crucial for access to publication and production, Haywood could not have been the solitary, bedraggled hack peddling her works bookseller to bookseller that she is so frequently described to be. On the night before Prime Minister Robert Walpole brought the Licensing Act before the House of Commons,[2] Fielding's *Eurydice Hiss'd* (1737) and *The Historical Register* (1737) were performed at the Haymarket for her benefit, and she played in both; in *Eurydice* she was the Muse. Sarah Churchill, duchess of Marlborough, who appreciated Haywood's political writing, attended that performance. As unresolved as some details of Haywood's life are, her relationships—personal, professional, and literary—with Fielding and others in the company are more so. She was one of three actors to join Fielding's company in its final year, the year he began a push to own his own theater (Hume, *Henry Fielding*, 233).

The people to whom Haywood dedicated her work, some of whom she claims personal knowledge, comprise an intriguing group. *The Adventures of Eovaai* (1736), for instance, was dedicated to Sarah Churchill, with an anti-Walpole, Opposition-style invoking of the contrast between "some ambitious, or avaritious Favourite, void of Abilities as of Morals" and Sarah's husband, whose victories and political advice displayed "the Love of Liberty, Glory, Virtue" (iv). Her closing is unusually enthusiastic for her and for closings in general: "Your Grace's most Humble, most Obedient, and most zealously Devoted Servant." Sarah was, of course, in the thick of politics and political

---

1. Alvin Sullivan, ed. *British Literary Magazines: The Augustan Age and the Age of Johnson, 1698–1788* (Westport, Conn.: Greenwood, 1983), 1:121.

2. The Licensing Act had the effect of limiting play production in London to those theaters with a royal patent, specifically Drury Lane and Covent Garden, and institutionalized strict new rules for licensing plays by the Lord Chamberlain before performance. The date of the benefit was 23 May 1737.

writing throughout her life and presented monetary gifts, some quite generous, to writers who pleased her.[1]

Viscount Thomas Gage, to whom she dedicates *The Fair Captive* (1721) and to whom she gives credit for pitying her condition and helping her, had a reputation for supporting literature. He was a member of Parliament from 1717 to 1754, supported Walpole until the Excise Bill controversy,[2] and in 1747 became steward of the household to Frederick, Prince of Wales, who was often part of the Opposition to his father. In 1721, Haywood, who may have known him in Ireland, was commemorating two events and intended to flatter him at an auspicious time: in 1720, Gage had been made Viscount Gage of Castle Island, Kerry,[3] and his son, Thomas, was born in early 1721.

William Yonge, to whom *The Fatal Secret* (1724) is dedicated, was loyal to Walpole, had taken an active role in the impeachment of Alexander Pope's friend Francis Atterbury, and had just been made a commissioner of the Treasury.[4] Col. James Stanley, to whom *The Masqueraders* (1724) is dedicated, became the leader of the Court Tories; Haywood implied in the dedication that she knew his wife, Mary. Charles Howard, ninth earl of Suffolk and Binden, was a groom of the bedchamber to King George I and the dedicatee of *Lasselia*, 1723.

---

1. Frances Harris, *A Passion for Government: The Life of Sarah, Duchess of Marlborough* (Oxford: Clarendon, 1991), 297–300. This biography makes clear the Duchess's symbolic value.

2. The excise bill would have extended the kind of taxes on tea and coffee to wine and tobacco and was extremely unpopular. Information on Gage is from Burke's *Peerage* and John Richard Alden, *General Gage in America: Being Principally a History of His Role in the American Revolution* (Baton Rouge: Louisiana State Univ. Press, 1948), 4–8.

3. As early as 1729, Frederick was identified with the opposition to Robert Walpole, and groups of politicians attempted to widen the differences between them and build their factions.

4. Francis Atterbury, bishop of Rochester and dean of Westminster Cathedral, was sentenced to perpetual banishment in May 1723. Basil Williams, *The Whig Supremacy, 1714–1760*, rev. ed. C. H. Stuart (Oxford: Clarendon, 1962), 182–84. Yonge and Gage were attacked by Pope and other poets as "dunces of state," toadies of Walpole. Yonge's *Sedition and Defamation Display'd* (1731) attacked Pope's friend Bolingbroke's *Craftsman* as trivial and dishonest. In these dedications can be found the roots of some of Pope's antipathy toward Haywood. In 1735, Yonge was made Secretary of War, and he hung on to political appointments through several changes in government. In his Introduction to *Sedition and Defamation Display'd* (New York: AMS, 1997), Alex Pettit describes him as "the dedicated placeman forced by circumstance or temperament into dependency," (xii–xiii).

Haywood's Hanoverian and pro-Marlborough sentiments were also evident in her dedication of *The Injur'd Husband* (1723) to Lady Ruperta Howe, wife of the English envoy at Hanover who had returned to England in 1709 and was a friend of Sarah Churchill's. Lady Howe was the illegitimate daughter of the actress Margaret Hughes and Rupert, Prince Palatine of the Rhine. According to the *Dictionary of National Biography*, she carried on an "injudicious correspondence" with Sarah.

Haywood's fascination with the Churchill family continued, as she dedicated the first volume of *The Female Spectator* to Mary Godolphin Osborne, duchess of Leeds, the daughter of Sarah and John Churchill's daughter Henrietta and, legally, of Francis, second earl of Godolphin (though she was reputedly the daughter of William Congreve).[1] She dedicated the second and fourth volumes to two of Sarah's other granddaughters, Anne, duchess of Bedford, and Isabella, duchess of Manchester. Anne had been taken into Sarah's home as a child, and Isabella had been a great favorite of Sarah's but, probably unknown to Haywood, had quarreled with her grandmother and never saw her after 1742.[2]

In the 1720s, Haywood published most frequently with James Roberts and with Daniel Browne and Samuel Chapmen, often in conjunction with James Woodman and William Chetwood who had published *Love in Excess*. Chetwood and Chapman were pilloried in Pope's *Dunciad* (1728, 1729) for publishing Haywood's work and had published Savage's *Miscellaneous Poems and Translations* in 1726. Roberts tended to do her shorter works, and Browne and Chapman the multivolume novels such as *Idalia* (1723) and her collected works. Cheryl Turner has pointed out how women writers frequently benefited from sustained relationships with publishers. In the last decade of her life, Haywood published largely with Thomas Gardner, who had been an associate of the notorious, often-arrested William Rayner.[3] By then,

1. Harris, *A Passion for Government*, 338.

2. Ibid., 329, 334–35; see also David Green, *Sarah, Duchess of Marlborough* (New York: Scribner's, 1967), 256–57. The first volume has the only true dedication; the others are simply marked "Inscribed to" without text.

3. Cheryl Turner, *Living by the Pen: Women Writers in the Eighteenth Century* (London: Routledge, 1992), 86–87. Rayner published Haywood's *Opera of Operas*, which, like many

Gardner was associated with periodicals written and edited by the most prominent writers in England. *The Universal Visiter* (1756), for instance, was edited by Christopher Smart and Richard Rolt and included articles by Samuel Johnson, David Garrick, and Charles Burney, the most famous music critic of the time.[1]

Haywood established a new and formidable reputation and exploited her success as author of *The Female Spectator*, which was a notable success in the very competitive periodical market of the 1740s. Richard Holmes says the periodical established her as "a Society gossip,"[2] thereby pioneering a form of journalism that became the rage in the second half of the century. Both of her novels from this decade as well as *The Invisible Spy* (1754) were serialized in *The Novelist's Magazine* (1780–1789), as were the major works of Fielding, Richardson, Smollet, Sterne, Frances Sheridan, Mary Collyer, and many more. Some of her contemporaries believed that she had become a rich woman; for instance, the earl of Egmont believed she had "amassed, 'tis said, near 10,000 [pounds]" (Blouch, "Romance of Obscurity," 544).

Haywood died on 25 February 1756 after an illness she described as "incapacitating" and was buried in St. Margaret's churchyard, Westminster, on 3 March (Blouch, "Romance of Obscurity," 545, 546n.1). Why her death duties were unpaid and her burial unusually delayed have never been explained.

Career

A reconsideration of the early history of the English novel, a cameo of a unique moment in the life of the theater, and a portrait of the eighteenth-century print world await those who study Haywood's career closely. Her first known publication, *Love in Excess*, was modeled on the still-popular multi-volume French romances, and the names of

---

of his publications, carries the line, "Printed for William Rayner, Prisoner in the King's Bench." For an account of his offenses, see Michael Harris, *London Newspapers in the Age of Walpole: A Study of the Origins of the Modern English Press* (Rutherford, N.J.: Associated Univ. Presses, 1987), 87–107.

1. Sullivan, *British Literary Magazines,* 1:349–54.

2. Richard Holmes, *Dr. Johnson and Mr. Savage* (New York: Pantheon, 1993), 72.

two successful London booksellers, William Chetwood and John Roberts, who invested heavily and early in prose fiction appeared on her title page. Linking and interweaving stories of several couples' lives in the manner of Madeleine de Scudéry, Haywood creates an attractive, psychologically interesting hero, D'Elmont, whose involvement with a succession of women is the means of comparing and contrasting women's decisions, temperaments, and social conduct even as the hero grows and reforms, somewhat in the manner of Samuel Richardson's Belford in the later novel *Clarissa* (1748). The romance form depended upon the proliferation of "histories" of characters' lives, which invited evaluative commentary from the other characters and, incidentally, readers. Sensationally popular, *Love in Excess* would not be equalled in sales until Jonathan Swift's *Gulliver's Travels* (1726) and Samuel Richardson's *Pamela* (1740) were published.

Throughout the 1720s, the crucial, formative decade for English fiction, Haywood published a steady stream of entertaining, successful books. Although some modern critics treat them as repetitious and formulaic, they are experimental, revisionary, and ground breaking.[1] If they are marked by a tendency toward soft-core pornography, they are rich in social commentary and increasingly strike a critically observant note. *The British Recluse* (1722), her second original prose fiction, begins her movement toward imaginative combinations of the kinds of interpolated incidents and tales common to French romances with the short, often violent novellas translated from Spanish and Portuguese and imitated or adapted by writers such as Aphra Behn.[2] The use of

---

1. Jerry C. Beasley lists her as one of the writers who "By thus licensing the author's invention to play freely over its subject," laid the foundation for the "astonishing achievements of the 1740s." *Novels of the 1740s* (Athens: Univ. of Georgia Press, 1982), 166.

2. See Aphra Behn, *The Histories and Novels of the Late Ingenious Mrs. Behn* (1696), and Samuel Croxall, *A Select Collection of Novels* (1720). Although noted by critics such as Mary Anne Schofield, this topic is yet to be explored fully. See Mary Anne Schofield, *Quiet Rebellion: The Fictional Heroines of Eliza Fowler Haywood* (Washington: Univ. Press of America, 1982), 4–7. The relevance of texts such as Marguerite de Navarre's *Heptameron* have all but been ignored. The influence of French fiction on English writing has received considerable, excellent attention in recent years, but southern European contributions continue to be all but ignored. On French fiction, see Joan DeJean, *Tender Geographies: Women and the Origins of the Novel in France* (New York: Columbia Univ. Press, 1991); April Alliston, *Virtue's Faults: Correspondences in Eighteenth-Century British and French Women's Fiction*

these forms gives her fiction original, sometimes shocking twists and modernizes them. In *The British Recluse*, two women tell each other their life stories, which are tales of seduction and exile from society with the kind of "warm writing" that characterized *Love in Excess*. In this text, the double—and then triple and then proliferating—retelling becomes a critique of society and the value structure that confers power. Cleomira's story, told first, could be part of a romance, but Belinda's is told in the straightforward prose of the novel-to-be. Cleomira is the seduced, abandoned, helpless female; Belinda is the active agent determined to find a new life course. This doubling and tripling of characters, of couples, and of plots is one of Haywood's most characteristic and effective narrative strategies, and many of the texts in this collection display it. *The City Jilt* (1726) can be read as doubling in the same way: the old, familiar story of the seduced and abandoned Glicera is balanced by the actions of the Glicera who becomes a woman, like Defoe's Moll Flanders, by assuming agency and acting in a very modern world.[1]

After this book, the short novels—Samuel Johnson's "little tales of love"—multiply.[2] Some settings become more specific to London while others congenially use those of travel books, pastorals, or romances; some episodes become grounded in commercial, litigious London while others are deliberately constructed to suggest "any time, any place," "every time, every place." French fiction, shorter texts such as *La Princesse de Clèves* and the romances, and English sonnet sequences had explored the subtle, various moods of love, and Haywood integrated this focus in stories far more violent and explicit than her contemporaries' fiction. Some texts suggest that evil actions come from

---

(Stanford: Stanford Univ. Press, 1996); and Ros Ballaster, *Seductive Forms: Women's Amatory Fiction from 1684 to 1740* (Oxford: Clarendon, 1992).

1. See Catherine Craft-Fairchild, *Masquerade and Gender: Disguise and Female Identity in Eighteenth-Century Fiction by Women* (University Park: Penn State Univ. Press, 1993), 68–73; and my *Spectacular Politics: Theatrical Power and Mass Culture in Early Modern England* (Baltimore: Johns Hopkins Univ. Press, 1993), 137–48. Craft-Fairchild's argument that Glicera masquerades, creatively enacting femininity in order to manipulate others, uses masquerade theory well to illuminate an aspect of Haywood's revisionary art.

2. In his *Dictionary of the English Language* (1755), Samuel Johnson defines the novel as "a small tale, generally of love."

traditional sins—avarice, lust, jealousy, pride, anger—but others, as the later novel will do, concentrate relentlessly on society, capitalism, and social forces. A few tantalizingly portray the warping of the human spirit, the development of a monster within a good and decent person, as *The City Jilt* does. The conventional types of women in *Love in Excess* become the means to explore women's sexuality, intelligence, and alleged "nature." The poles that are Amena and Alovisa and Melantha and Melliora give way in part 3 to the rich variety of Ciamara, Camilla, Violetta, and more. The problems, personalities, desires, and destinies are repeated, reconfigured, developed, and explored in the fictions that follow, among them *The Injur'd Husband* (1723), *Idalia; or, the Unfortunate Mistress* (1723), *The Rash Resolve* (1724), *The Masqueraders* (1724), *Fantomina* (1725), *The Mercenary Lover* (1726), *The City Jilt (1726), Cleomelia* (1727), and *Philidore and Placentia* (1727).

In this same magic decade, Haywood began writing the kind of political "scandalous memoir" associated with Delarivière Manley but as old as Procopius's *Secret History* (ca. 565 A.D.).[1] These fictionalized exposés, usually presented as written by a high-ranking servant and confidant, allege to give an inside look at the private lives of the famous and influential and the ways their private alliances and maneuvers influence the public sphere. Both *Memoirs of a Certain Island* (1725) and *The Secret History of the Present Intrigues of the Court of Caramania* (1727) prove Haywood's ability to write in this sensational political form, and they are yet one more way that she criticized the social classes that believed themselves above the law and used the private sphere for public gain. Here and elsewhere she assumes that power and avarice in one sphere will be mirrored in the other and that the sexual libertine is the unscrupulous politician, businessman, or trustee. In *The Adventures of Eovaai*, for instance, she writes,

> An elevated Station is therefore chiefly to be desired, as it is a Sanction to all our Actions, indulges the Gratification of each luxurious Wish,

---

1. Procopius was the private secretary to Belisarius and wrote the official military history of Justinian's reign. Known as the *Anecdota*, "Unpublished Things," by the Greeks, *The Secret History* was not published until after Procopius's death (G. A. Williamson, ed. and trans. [London: Penquin, 1981]).

and gives a Privilege, not only of doing, but also of glorying in those things which are criminal and shameful in the Vulgar:—Bound by no Laws, subjected by no Fears, we give a Loose to all the gay Delights of Sense. . . .

Other texts draw upon the conventions of mythology, legends, and folktales in groups of tales told by a single narrator or by members of a group in the manner of Boccaccio. Among these are *The Fruitless Inquiry* (1727) and the translated *La Belle Assemblée* (1724–1726).

A large number of eighteenth-century writers earned at least part of their income translating Continental books, and the exercise expanded the horizons of their understanding of literary possibilities, specifically of forms of fiction, plot structures and outcomes, presentation of characters and dialogue, and prose style. That women writers in particular learned from this work is beginning to be recognized and documented. Among Haywood's translations in this decade are *Letters from a Lady of Quality to a Chevalier* (1721), *Love in its Variety* (1727), and *La Belle Assemblée*. In *La Belle Assemblée*, *The Fruitless Inquiry*, and other texts by Haywood, the ideology of heterosexual love and notions of happiness are displaced, deconstructed, and finally, and often with a "once-upon-a-time" air, reinserted. As Sally O'Driscoll says, *La Belle Assemblée* "examines almost every possibility of inappropriate, unsanctioned love and sex/gender behavior." She continues: "As a whole, the dizzying sequence of terrible possibilities makes it clear that all kinds of sexual behaviors are thinkable," and "that the narrative resolution backs away from them every time does not make them disappear."[1] Much modern formula fiction delivers its satisfactions by exercising and then containing a culture's anxieties, and these Boccaccio– or, more accurately, southern European–style stories work this way.

In fact, Haywood's fiction makes it clear that all kinds of behaviors—violent, vicious, gentle, loving, self-sacrificing, impulsive, and, of course, erotic—are possible. It could be argued that a strong, unidentified influence on Haywood is Aphra Behn, who late in her career published a number of short fictions in the southern European nou-

---

1. Sally O'Driscoll, "Outlaw Readings: Beyond Queer Theory," *Signs* 22 (1996): 39.

velle tradition. Some were close to their sources in every way while others were original creations. Certainly the obsessive erotic drives, sudden outbursts of fiendish behavior, and sustained villainous conduct of many of the male protagonists in both Behn's and Haywood's texts were common to these stories, as were the seduced heroines whose grief, rage, pathos, and despair created a repertory of conventional behavior such as hair- and ruffle-tearing. What Haywood did that was original was find a ground between the extremes of the southern European stories and the subtle panoply of carefully nuanced emotions in French fiction. Combined with her increasing use of London or other familiar and "realistically" rendered settings and props and her developed use of doubles, this middle ground delivered the "pleasures" of the other forms but also some of the experiences that we associate with the modern novel's power to create immediacy and even identification. Although Glicera in *The City Jilt* delivers the fascination of watching a cobra's hypnotic sway with the inevitable swallowing of its prey, she is also an intriguing social and psychological creation. This fiction depends upon a knowledge of fashionable pastimes and the inner workings of contemporary mortgage and loan transactions, and leaves the reader with a gritty view of the upperclass "way of the world."[1]

About the time that she published *Love in Excess*, Haywood wrote to a potential patron for her first translation, *Letters from a Lady of Quality to a Chevalier* (1721),[2] that the stage had not "answered her expectations" and that she had been forced to "turn [her] Genius another Way." She was probably able to capitalize on her new fame not only with this translation but also with her *Fair Captive* (1721), a play manager John Rich gave her to make stageworthy. Rich had pur-

---

1. David Oakleaf, in a quotation that applies to Haywood as well as Defoe, has pointed out that "Defoe's heroines are no more predatory than, say, the schemers in Congreve's *Way of the World*, but Congreve's devious plotters (and plot) are fixed by the genealogical and financial certainties symbolized by the black box containing the definitive contracts. Free of the constraints . . . that define a more stable class, Moll Flanders and Roxana by contrast can choose the characters they will support" and fixed expectations are thwarted. See Oakleaf, "Marks, Stamps, and Representations: Character in Eighteenth-Century Fiction," *Studies in the Novel* 23 (1991): 304–5.

2. Also published by Chetwood, this book attracted 309 subscribers.

chased the play from Captain Robert Hurst, and Haywood describes some of the revisions she made in the "Advertisement to the Reader" and mentions in the dedication that she now must depend on her pen for her livelihood. One of the popular Turkish plays with the heroine confined in a harem by a lascivious, autocratic grand vizier, it includes speeches on power, jealousy, erotic desire, and prejudice typical of Haywood. The play ran three nights plus a fourth as a second benefit for Haywood.[1] Her first original play, *A Wife to Be Lett*, was performed in 1724, and she played the part of Mrs. Graspall. In 1802, Ann Minton published a two-act adaptation of the play, *A Wife to Be Lett; or, The Miser Cured.*[2]

It was in the 1730s, however, that Haywood's involvement with the theater—and national politics—was most intense. In 1729, her second original play, *Frederick, Duke of Brunswick-Lunenburgh*, was performed at Lincoln's Inn Fields. The play was written to honor Frederick Louis, who had just arrived in England and become Prince of Wales and who would become a center of opposition to the Walpole ministry.[3] Haywood soon became part of the Haymarket Theatre circle, which became a hotbed of Walpole opposition in 1737. Robert Walpole, a long-time member of Parliament, became Chancellor of the Exchequer in the wake of the stock market crash called "the South Sea Bubble." Prime minister from 1721 to 1742, he became, in Jerry Beasley's words, a "public obsession" and commanded "rapt attention" whenever he was sighted. As Beasley says, Walpole became "an almost mythological figure of frightening power and gross indecency"[4] and the subject of numerous publications. Partly for political purposes, Haywood adapted Henry Fielding's *Tragedy of Tragedies* into her *Opera of Operas*, acted a number of parts—some in quite subversive plays—and wrote *The*

---

1. See Valerie Rudolph's discussion and Haywood's "Advertisement to the Reader" in *The Plays of Eliza Haywood* (New York: Garland Publishing, 1983).

2. David D. Mann and Susan Garland Mann, with Camille Garnier, *Women Playwrights in England, Ireland, and Scotland 1660–1823* (Bloomington: Indiana Univ. Press, 1996), 358–59.

3. See my "The Shadow of an Author: Elizabeth Haywood," *Eighteenth Century Fiction* 11 (1998): 79–102.

4. Jerry C. Beasley, "Portraits of a Monster: Robert Walpole and Early Eighteenth-Century Fiction," *Eighteenth-Century Studies* 14 (1981): 416.

Adventures of Eovaai, Princess of Ijaveo, her most sensational scandal chronicle. *The Opera of Operas* was her greatest hit; eleven productions over nearly four weeks beginning on 31 May 1733 and publication of the text show that it was successful from the beginning.[1] Set to music by John Frederick Lampe and Thomas Arne, it opened on 31 May 1733 at the Haymarket and, in the fall, played another eighteen nights there as an afterpiece adapted by Arne. Lampe revived the full production at Drury Lane in November. This time the Prince of Wales and "a vast concourse of nobility" attended.[2] Records of the parts she acted are the most complete for this decade, and at this time she wrote *The Dramatic Historiographer* (1735), her survey of plays with comments on the "usefulness" of the theater and what it ought to be and do.

In the 1740s, she engaged anew with prose fiction and the evolution of the English novel. Her *Anti-Pamela; or, Feign'd Innocence Detected* (1741) joins a number of other books, including Fielding's *Shamela,* that attacked the improbabilities and social implications of Richardson's *Pamela (1740)*. Her Syrena Tricksy has been bred to believe "that a woman who had Beauty to attract the Men, and Cunning to manage them afterwards, was secure of making her Fortune" (261). Syrena, however, is better at spending money than amassing capital and, like the wife in *City Jilt*, threatens men with economic ruin. Haywood's first full-length conduct book, *A Present for a Servant-Maid; or, The Sure Means of Gaining Love and Esteem* (1743) when read with *Anti-Pamela*, is a fascinating look at how she could profit from a contemporary, popular topic and from championing first one sex and then the other through cautionary advice, as she does in *The Wife* and *The Husband* at the end of her life.

In the decade of the forties, she published *The Female Spectator*, her

---

1. Milhous and Hume reproduce the record of receipts, which show that £347.5.d. were received for the eleven-night run. See their "J. F. Lampe and English Opera," 524–25.

2. Wilbur L. Cross, *The History of Henry Fielding* (New Haven: Yale Univ. Press, 1918), 1: 147, gives the date as 6 June; see Rudolph, xviii–xx. On 4 June, Prince Frederick's sister Amelia and her husband attended, and on 8 June the other sisters came.

best-known periodical and one that Ann Messenger describes as energetic and even impassioned.[1] In it, she took stands on public issues, including the effects of the Licensing Act.[2] *The Adventures of Eovaai* was reissued in 1741, the year before Walpole's fall from power, as *The Unfortunate Princess: The Life and Surprizing Adventures of the Princess of Ijaveo. Interspers'd with several curious and entertaining Novels.* In this decade, she became an independent publisher and, for a short time, had her own shop at the Sign of Fame in Covent Garden.[3]

The long novels of this decade—*The Fortunate Foundlings* (1744) and *Life's Progress through the Passions* (1748)—and those of the 1750s show Haywood's ability to shape and adapt to the changing tastes of her readers and have considerable importance for the history of the novel. *The Fortunate Foundlings*, for example, shows a few similarities to Fielding's later *Tom Jones* (1750). The children are discovered and reared by Dorilaus, who is eventually discovered to be their father. They show the kind of natural good breeding that Tom does, one that hints at their gentle birth, and their experiences are more developed examples of the gendered spheres and possible, contrasting plots for men and women than Fielding's are for Tom and Sophia Western. *The Fortunate Foundlings* also has a stronger, more threatening incest plot, but still reminds the reader of that in *Tom Jones*.

In this period, a time marked by productivity and creativity at least as striking as that of the 1720s, she turned to journalism, and both *The Female Spectator* and *The Parrot* are still highly readable, revealing records of the time and of Haywood's opinions. *The Female Spectator*

---

1. Ann Messenger, *His and Hers: Essays in Restoration and Eighteenth-Century Literature* (Lexington: Univ. Press of Kentucky, 1986), 108–47. Patricia M. Spacks is editing *Selections from the Female Spectator* for the Women Writers in English series, forthcoming from Oxford University Press.

2. In a letter dated 21 October 1744 in *The Female Spectator*, she speculates about how the "licence-office" really works and expresses amazement and dismay that James Thomson's *Edward and Eleonora* and Henry Brooke's *Gustavus Vasa*, "founded on the most interesting parts of history . . . and illustrated with all the strength and beauty of language," were not more successful (2:69–84; quotation 74–75). All quotations from *The Female Spectator* are from the first collected edition (London: T. Gardner, 1745).

3. Catherine Ingrassia's forthcoming book discusses Haywood as bookseller.

had considerable longevity, as it was published in eight editions between 1747 and 1775. She also completed *Epistles for the Ladies* (1749),
a translation, *The Virtuous Villager* (1742), and a conduct book that
treated a serious contemporary, social problem openly, *A Present for
Women Addicted to Drinking* (1750). Several of these books invoke her
successful publications in order to attract readers and raise sales. *Epistles
for the Ladies*, for instance, carries on its title page "*By the Authors of
The Female Spectator,*" and *The Wife* reads, "By *Mira*, One of the
Authors of *The Female Spectator.*" In fact, depending on how she is
identified on the title page, Haywood or her bookseller seems to have
provided her readers with a sort of guide to the content. Her plays
and her amorous and scandalous fictions, such as *The Rash Resolve* and
The Unfortunate Princess (the 1741 title of *Eovaai),* are "By Mrs. Eliza
Haywood," while the more bourgeois moral publications cite the "authors" of *The Female Spectator.*[1] Other title pages remind the reader
of especially successful publications and are of the same or closely
related literary kinds; for instance, *The British Recluse* invokes *Love
in Excess,* and *The Fruitless Inquiry* and *The History of Jemmy and
Jenny Jessamy* are "By the Author of the History of Miss Betsy
Thoughtless."

Haywood's prolific 1750s began with the book many consider Haywood's best, *The History of Miss Betsy Thoughtless* (1751), which devel-
ops one of the stories in *The British Recluse* and reworks the wife-
lending episode in *A Wife to Be Lett. The History of Jemmy and Jenny
Jessamy* (1753) followed. Apparently often in poor health and with fail-
ing eyesight, Haywood returned to easier writing, specifically collections of short tales framed creatively, as *The Invisible Spy* (1755) is.
Always a slippery, teasing narrator, she opens this four-volume work
by taunting the reader: "I have observed, that when a new book begins
to make a noise in the world, every one is desirous of becoming acquainted with the author; and this impatience increases the more he

---

1. In the persona of the editor of the *Female Spectator,* Haywood described the group that
she brought into her enterprise and who "wrote" essays for her: Mira, the happily married
wife of a gentleman who was "descended from a family to which wit seems hereditary"; a
"Widow of quality"; and Euphrosine, daughter of a wealthy merchant and as cheerful and
sweet as the goddess of the same name (1:4–5).

endeavors to conceal himself. . . . but whether I am even a man or a woman, they will find it, after all their conjectures, as difficult to discover as the longitude."

Contributions

The generation before ours knew Haywood primarily as the object of scurrilous attacks by Alexander Pope and others; today's students and scholars know her differently. As David Oakleaf says, "appallingly cruel satire was almost the routine tribute to success."[1] The ad hominem attacks aimed at Defoe and Alexander Pope are not read the way those directed at Haywood have been, and the alternative readings suggested by new work on Haywood are useful correctives.[2] Few today would quarrel with the observation that Haywood throws useful light on how writers in the first half of the eighteenth century supported themselves in the new—and distinctly modern—print culture. Irrefutably, she is an important example of an early woman writer's navigation and reception in that world.

Fielding cast Haywood as the Muse and as Mrs. Novel in his plays, and she was, indeed, the epitome of the novel until Richardson published *Pamela.* Exploration of all of the ways this statement is true and of her contributions to the genre is scarcely beyond the embryonic stage, but her place in literary history is clearly and rapidly undergoing drastic revision. Margaret Doody, for instance, points out that Haywood made a number of notable contributions to the formation of what we now call the mainline English novel. She argues that Haywood "established the seduction novel as a minor genre in English fiction, and it is to that genre that Richardson's work ultimately belongs."[3] In *Novels of the 1740s,* Jerry Beasley calls her "a seminal writer"

---

1. Introduction to *Love in Excess* (Peterborough, Ontario: Broadview Press, 1994), 5.

2. See, for example, Ballaster, 160–67; and Catherine Ingrassia, "Women Writing / Writing Women: Pope, Dulness, and 'Feminization' in the *Dunciad,*" *Eighteenth-Century Life* 14 (1990): 40–58, esp. 50–54, where she explains how Haywood "threatened Pope professionally, offended him personally," and even, in some ways, "controlled him textually" (51).

3. Margaret Anne Doody, *A Natural Passion: A Study of the Novels of Samuel Richardson* (Oxford: Clarendon, 1974), esp. 144–50, quotation 149. Katherine S. Green reasonably points

and one who helped generate the great novels of Richardson and Fielding. This familiar argument has recently been recast by William B.
Warner, who argues that the male novelists "disavowed rather than
assumed their debt" to her and "absorbed," "erased," and "sup-
planted" her fictions and those of other early women writers.[1] As John
Richetti and I have said elsewhere, "She, Penelope Aubin, and Daniel
Defoe dominated prose fiction in the decade of the 1720s, and she
may have done more than the other two to set the course of the
English novel."[2]

Important recent books by feminist critics have pointed out Haywood's contributions to the art of the novel and offered new ways of
explicating her texts. For example, Jane Spencer credits her with the
introduction of interior monologues and with an ability to portray
growing self-knowledge that is better developed in her novels than in
Richardson's and Fielding's. In an important argument, Spencer points
out that Haywood is primarily responsible for the genesis of a sub-
genre, one "begun by women and almost exclusive to them: the mistaken heroine who reforms." Calling *Betsy Thoughtless* "the paradigm
of the central female tradition in the eighteenth-century novel," she
points out how the form furthers both the "realistic" and psychological
elements of the form we call novel and concludes that Haywood "truly
ancipates the moral art of Jane Austen."[3]

Ros Ballaster devotes an entire chapter of *Seductive Forms: Women's
Amatory Fiction from 1684 to 1740* (1992) to Haywood and argues persuasively the "pragmatic political and ideological reasons" for Hay-

out, "The question of influence . . . is as appropriately posed in relation to Haywood's on
Richardson as to Richardson's on Haywood." *The Courtship Novel, 1740–1820: A Feminized
Genre* (Lexington: Univ. Press of Kentucky, 1991), 25. Warner has an intriguing comparison
between *Pamela* and *Fantomina* in his "The Elevation of the Novel in England: Hegemony
and Literary History," *ELH* 59 (1992): 585–88.

1. William B. Warner, "Licensing Pleasure," in John Richetti et al., eds., *The Columbia
History of the British Novel* (New York: Columbia UP, 1994), 6–7; see also Warner's "The
Elevation of the Novel in England," 577–96.

2. Paula R. Backscheider and John J. Richetti, eds., *Popular Fiction by Women 1660–1730:
An Anthology* (Oxford: Clarendon, 1996), 154.

3. Jane Spencer, *The Rise of the Woman Novelist: From Aphra Behn to Jane Austen* (Oxford:
Basil Blackwell, 1986), 141, 143–44, 147–53; quotations 141. I would amend this statement to
recognize earlier novels, such as Mary Davys's *The Reformed Coquet*.

wood's choice of fictional forms. She joins the other recent critics in finding Haywood a revisionary, path-breaking contributor to the history of the novel. "I would argue," Ballaster writes, that Haywood's amatory novels "mark the beginnings of an autonomous tradition in romantic fiction" (158). Warner hypothesizes that Richardson and Fielding find the early women's novels to represent "threatening rivals in a zero-sum struggle to control a common cultural space" ("The Elevation of the Novel," 580). The debate over whether Haywood's novels are an integral, indispensable part of the history of the English novel or part of a counter or rival tradition continues and plays a major part in firing the current proliferation of "stories" of the history of the novel.[1]

Regardless of which story of the novel we accept, Haywood cannot be ignored. She has come to stand for the nexus *and* the point of tension between a number of things—the transgressive, outspoken woman and the modest woman writer, amatory fiction and the new fiction, the romance and the modern novel. Haywood's novels remain controversial and revisionary because integral to them are the most serious dangers that novels posed. Written by the underclass, the excluded, and even oppressed,[2] novels display markedly different attitudes from the prestige genres and, thereby, expose for critique, or at least reevaluation, things taken for granted. The accepting humor directed at men like *The Spectator*'s Will Honeycomb, who has honor "where Women are not concerned" (no. 2, 2 March 1711) dissipates in the light thrown on the conduct of upperclass men who seduce, rape, and abandon, or who band together to cheat women of their fortunes. Crowds who dare not intervene watch kidnap attempts, and good women tell younger women that "it is ever thus," as happens in

---

1. Other examples are Homer O. Brown, "Why the Story of the Origin of the (English) Novel is an American Romance (If Not the Great American Novel)," in Deidre Lynch and William B. Warner, eds., *Cultural Institutions of the Novel* (Durham: Duke Univ. Press, 1996), 11–43; and J. A. Downie, "The Making of the English Novel," *Eighteenth-Century Fiction* 9 (1997): 249–66.

2. Many of the early fiction writers were Nonconformists, such as John Bunyan, Defoe, and Elizabeth Singer Rowe; Catholics, such as Penelope Aubin and Jane Barker; clearly bourgeois, such as Richardson; or women. Most, therefore, lacked legal and cultural rights and privileges.

The City Jilt. When women characters such as Glicera or Fantomina step onto the playing field with a rake, the stakes are high and the games fairly desperate; but, win or lose, the woman has brought to light how male privilege is assumed and society implicated. And the writers are likely to be criticized for malice and impudence, as Haywood and Defoe frequently were.

The assumptions and values of a commodity culture undergird all of Haywood's writings. Everything has market value, especially women, and everything is assumed to be for sale. Over and over, Haywood tells an initiation story—an innocent woman who believes she is a person is taught that she is merely a sign, a representation, of her economic value. In a startlingly modern way, Haywood writes about use value, exchange value, and even cultural-commodity value.[1] She writes and rewrites the initiation and plays with possible ways for women to cope with this world. Within a variety of forms—the nouvelle, the novella, the travel-adventure tale, the general history, the history-at-large—she exposes the ugly machinery that drives her society. For example, in contrast to *The City Jilt*, *Philidore and Placentia*, a fiction long familiar because it was included in William H. McBurney's *Four Before Richardson* (1963), relies upon the conventions of the older, travel literature form and depends upon lucky accidents to resolve the lovers' estrangement. Yet for those who look hard at the apparently satisfying, romantic, order-restoring conclusion, the double standard that the tale exposes and critiques is merely painted over and is still "a morality of the marketplace" that "says personal merit when it means cash."[2]

Haywood's experimentation led to an expansion of the techniques

---

1. Things with "use value" have a utility and fill human wants, as in providing the necessities of life such as food; those with "exchange value" can be traded for commodities, cash, or credit and accumulated. As societies evolved, they began to specialize and produce items for exchange, and capitalism developed. Cultural capital—education, acquisition of works of art, ritual displays of finery (Ascot)—demonstrates that social inequality is determined not only by differences in income or economic capital but also by the relative ease with which a person is perceived to be a part of the dominant culture.

2. The phrases are from Michael McKeon's discussion of *Philidore and Placentia*; he devotes two pages to Haywood in *The Origins of the English Novel, 1600–1740* (Baltimore: Johns Hopkins Univ. Press, 1987), 261.

and subjects that make the novel a powerful social and moral force. Among these techniques is the use of "expanded doubles," characters or tales that mirror or repeat or offer nuanced, small variations on each other. Anticipating the feminist position that "there is absolutely no degree of grandeur that protects against woman's frightful condition,"[1] in texts such as *The Fruitless Inquiry* Haywood constructs groups of characters whose age, wealth, beauty, and social status form a wide continuum that illustrates a line from her *Wife to Be Lett*: "to what Fate are wretched Women born!" Simultaneously, there is a denial that conventional categories can define or explain. Such categories as "heiress," "servant," "wife," and especially "seduced and ruined" fail to contain characters and plots.

Even as she depicts the shared oppressive situations of women, she contests a number of major conceptions about the nature and destiny of women.[2] Many of her characters, like Glicera and Miranda (*Mercenary Lover*) are roused from victimhood and naiveté to independence, "citizenship," or even revenge.[3] Haywood questions representations of women's capacity for action and agency, their sexuality and intellectual abilities, and their dissatisfactions with marriage and men and often offers characters who counter or deconstruct existing paradigms. As she interrogates the sexual ideology of her time, she examines the role it plays in identity formation and in the exercise of power and privilege.

Among the most subversive powers of the novel form is its ability to construct reader positions that encourage identification with the

---

1. Claudine Herrmann, *The Tongue Snatchers*, trans. Nancy Kline (Lincoln: Univ. of Nebraska Press, 1989), 32.

2. In a speech presented at the annual meeting of the American Society for Eighteenth Century Studies, Carolyn Woodward noted that feminist work is about "Woman, women, and gender" (Nashville, Tenn., 11 April 1997). Polly Fields argues that "the masculine myth of the female runs head long into the truth of women's reality" and that Haywood shows "her central characters with other women collectively oppressed by the system, albeit acting autonomously." Fields, "Manly Vigor and Woman's Wit: Dialoging Gender in the Plays of Eliza Haywood," *Compendious Conversations: The Method of Dialogue in the Early Enlightenment* (Frankfurt: Peter Lang, 1992), 259.

3. I say "citizenship" because during this period in literature and in parliamentary hearings women were asking, "Do I not have the rights of an English citizen?" See my "Endless Aversion Rooted in the Soul: Divorce in the 1690–1730 Theater," *Eighteenth Century: Theory and Interpretation* 37 (1996): 99–135.

resulting possibility of sympathy evolving into belief and even action. Theorists today are deeply interested in the part the novel (and the culture's other dominant narrative structures) plays in the construction of reality, and Haywood contributed a female reader position from which male perspective and ideology could be challenged. She frequently invites the reader, especially the female reader, to assume the roles of judge and jury and assent to the outcome of episodes or conclusions in her fictions. She encourages identification with herself and some of her characters by including her women readers in important statements that purport to describe women's feelings and common actions. In the novels, and especially in texts such as *The Adventures of Eovaai,* she joined writers, including Behn, Manley, and Defoe, who developed an ideological position that despised the ethos of the hypocritical world of fashion and defined noble leisure as vicious[1] and as infallibly carrying over from the private sphere into the public.

There is evidence that Haywood joined her contemporaries in believing the novel to be a potentially dangerous and especially unpredictable influence on individuals and society and, like her fellow writers, incorporated addresses to its perceived dangers in her texts. Clitander in *The Mercenary Lover* encourages Althea to read Ovid, Rochester, and books of "more modern Date" (contemporary fiction immediately comes to mind) that "insensibly melt down the Soul, and make it fit for amorous Impression." This sexually arousing aspect of fiction, one John Richetti has explicated persuasively, seems to have been taken for granted at this time. Examples of rakes and would-be seducers reading such texts and cases in which a seducer leaves a young woman alone with, for instance, a novel by Aphra Behn, occur.[2] At the end of the eighteenth century, Clara Reeve wrote about the effect of fiction on women's hopes and expectations in her important treatise on reading, *The Progress of Romance*: "If a plain man addresses her in rational terms and pays her the greatest compliments,—that of desiring

---

1. This sentence plays on one in Richetti, *Popular Fiction before Richardson*, in which "hypocritical" is "hypothetical" (197).

2. Philander in Mary Hearne's *Lover's Week* has *The Histories and Novels of the Late Mrs. Behn* on the table in the room where he locks Amaryllis. Reading and its effects was a lifelong concern of Haywood's. See, for instance, *The Female Spectator* 2:44–46.

to spend his life with her,—that is not sufficient, her vanity is disappointed, she expects to meet a Hero in Romance." Seventy-five years earlier, Haywood had made that the plot of several of her fictions and is more convincing about the pleasures of marriage to such a man than, for instance, Richardson is with Hickman and Anna Howe in *Clarissa*.

Critics have begun to warn us of the price of omitting Haywood from the history of the novel. Warner notes, "The exclusion of the novel of amorous intrigue—with a current of writing about sexuality, desire and love that is the British novel's most direct link to the renaissance and continental literature of love—has long term consequences."[1] When a genre begins to wear itself out, to become less relevant and satisfying to the culture, it begins simultaneously to adapt and to deconstruct itself. Such periods are marked by rapid and fascinating experimentation and revisionary writings, and Haywood's works are an indispensible part of one of these times. This recognition explains to a great extent the complex and even contradictory responses to her work. Ballaster reminds us that "Haywood's name . . . was synonymous with the most extreme excesses of romance" (158), one of the signs of the deconstruction of a form. Her novels were also the signs of the new romance, an enormously popular form still and one that attracts critics of the stature of Janice Radway[2] who study its cultural and literary roots and the personal and social needs it meets. Janet Todd points out that Haywood amended her "cautionary" voice and created a moral one of "teacher and chaste author."[3] Indeed, Haywood wrote at the moment the novel was becoming the culture's chief

---

1. William B. Warner, "Licensing Entertainment." I am grateful to him for sharing his in-press book manuscript, *Licensing Entertainment* (Berkeley: Univ. of California Press, 1998).

2. Janice Radway's pioneering book *Reading the Romance: Women, Patriarchy, and Popular Literature* (Chapel Hill: Univ. of North Carolina Press, 1984) began the serious modern study of the formula descendent of Haywood's love stories and of the satisfactions the form delivers to readers. A more theoretical, still useful early study is John G. Cawelti, *Adventure, Mystery, and Romance: Formula Stories as Art and Popular Culture* (Chicago: Univ. of Chicago Press, 1976); Laurie Langbauer's *Women and Romance: The Consolations of Gender in the English Novel* (Ithaca: Cornell Univ. Press, 1990) has a useful bibliography (it does not consider Haywood).

3. Janet Todd, *The Sign of Angellica: Women, Writing, and Fiction, 1660–1800* (New York: Columbia Univ. Press, 1989), 147.

vehicle for moral and social instruction, and her technical innovations were part of this foundation.

Beasley argues that "it is important to acknowledge that the major novels of the period—the works we think of when we try to define the form as it emerged—were written, published, and read within a context of popular fiction-writing that included [political] tales" like *The Adventures of Eovaai*.[1] This text was indeed part of the landscape, an important manifestation of the rich experimentation with prose fiction and its possible uses that helped determine that the novel would be the literary form with the most contact with the zone of immediate reality. Taken together, Haywood's texts offer new possibilities in form, both in modifications to old and in creation of new ones, and demonstrate the novel's potential to be a serious site for political, moral, and social inquiry and a new hegemonic apparatus.

This Volume's Selections

We need a standard edition of all of Haywood's works—her poems, her plays, her novels, her nonfiction prose, her periodicals. Choosing among her works is very difficult, and after trying many combinations I offer what I consider a representative selection of most of the forms she used and from every decade of her career. With the texts that are available and immediately forthcoming in a number of other editions, there may now be enough of her work easily available for large numbers of scholars and students to see how incomplete our understanding of her work is and to begin to address our limitations.

This volume includes in chronological order two of Haywood's plays, two complete novellas, and excerpts from four of her other texts. *A Wife to Be Lett*, her original comedy; *The City Jilt* and *The Mercenary Lover*, examples of her short novels; and *The Fruitless Inquiry*, a south-

---

1. Jerry C. Beasley, "Portraits of a Monster," 408. William B. Warner lists the "secret history" type of prose fiction as one of the three categories of "prior instances of novel writing" [prior to Richardson and Fielding]. "The Elevation of the Novel in England," 579–80.

ern European–style collection of unified adventures, are all from the magic decade of the 1720s. In spite of major differences in form and perspective, they share emphases on personal identity, relationships between the sexes, and the nature of human happiness. *The Opera of Operas* and *The Adventures of Eovaai* were among her most successful and original publications and represent her political and dramatic activity in the 1730s. *The Adventures of Eovaai* was reissued in 1741 as *The Unfortunate Princess*. This edition concludes with excerpts from two works from the 1750s, *The Invisible Spy* and *The Wife*, both of which return to many of the personal, social, artistic, and political concerns of Haywood's earlier work even as they break new ground and show more comprehensive understanding of her milieu.

A Wife to Be Lett, like the first work of many playwrights, tries to combine a few too many of the most popular elements of the fashionable comedies of the day. Two plots turn on forced marriages, another has a deserted beauty in a breeches part, and the third, perhaps influenced by Aphra Behn's *The Luckey Chance* (1686), is the story of Graspall's attempt to "let," or rent, his wife to Sir Harry Beaumont and the clever trick intended to make him an ideal husband. There is also a subplot reminiscent of one in William Congreve's *Way of the World* (1700) in which servants trick an eager-to-be married widow. The play is filled with action, interesting characters, and Haywood's themes and opinions. Part of its interest comes, in fact, from its reading of what audiences enjoyed.

The two novellas, *The City Jilt* and *The Mercenary Lover*, are among Haywood's most shocking. Both stories feature the kind of feckless, unprincipled male common to much of Haywood's work. Such men are motivated by ambition, avarice, lust—desires they have no wish to control. Both texts have an innocent, charming heroine who becomes the victim. Yet both belong to a fairly large group of revenge fantasies, and each has plot twists that show the man "in the power of one from whom he neither could, nor ought to hope for Mercy" (*City Jilt*). In *The City Jilt*, Glicera is shockingly successful, and in *The Mercenary Lover* Clitander is hideously effective, and Haywood supplies two endings rich in irony. In these tales as elsewhere, Haywood, like Defoe, made few assumptions about the gender styles of any human being or group of humans.[1] Members of either sex could be victimized or commit monstrous acts, and both are depicted in scenes of strong sexual enjoyment. Feminine power is almost always problematic but is given striking expressions, and qualities usually praised in women—gentleness, innocence, constancy—often allow unscrupulous men to take advantage of women.

The Fruitless Inquiry, an important example of Haywood's southern European–style fictions, begins with the portrait of one of Haywood's confident, mature women. Miramillia rears her son from age six, and Haywood writes without fanfare that she refused to remarry because she could not trust a man to manage her son's inheritance as well as she. When Adario disappears, the lesson so often voiced in her fiction and that of her contemporary Defoe, begins: "But alass! on how weak a Foundation do all humane Joys depend, and how little ought we to triumph in the transient Blessings of Fate, which in a Moment may vanish, and in their Room as poynant Ills arise." To gain his return she is sent on a quest she believes not too difficult—to obtain a shirt made by a person with a completely contented mind—but one on which she finds a succession of horrors. This text demonstrates her ability to adapt the popular Boccaccio-style tales for femino-centric purposes. The excerpt included here exemplifies the book's technical sophistication and Haywood's ability to create suspense in domestic settings.

The Opera of Operas was produced in 1733 near the end of Walpole's attempt to extend the excise tax and at one of the peaks of the Opposition's demand that England declare war on Spain.[2] Using Henry Fielding's text for *The Tragedy of Tragedies* with its satiric lament for how diminished the English court and its concerns are in comparison to the time of King Arthur, the collaborators (Haywood, Lampe, Arne, and Hatchett) convert his play into a comic opera but also increase

---

1. See Don Akenson, "Theory and Fiction: The Author Comments on *At Face Value: The Life and Times of Eliza McCormack/John White*," in James Noonan, ed., *Biography and Autobiography: Essays on Irish and Canadian History and Literature* (Ottawa: Carleton Univ. Press, 1993), 239.

2. A brief account of this time and these issues is given in W. A. Speck, *Stability and Strife: England, 1714–1760* (Cambridge, Mass.: Harvard Univ. Press, 1977), 203–38.

the ridicule of the inflated egos of the principal characters.[1] The text of *The Opera of Operas* is very close to that of Fielding's play. Some of the thirty-three songs that they added in order to convert it into a ballad opera are based on witty or satiric analogies in *The Tragedy of Tragedies*. Air 1, for example, expands upon the lines describing Tom Thumb, "So some Cock-Sparrow in a Farmer's Yard, / Hops at the Head of an huge Flock of Turkeys" (1.1.13–14), and Air 4 celebrates Tom: "While others brag of Mac's and O's, / Let England boast of *Thummy*" from Fielding's "Let *Rome* her *Caesar's* and her *Scipio's* show, / *Ireland* her O's . . ." (1.3.80–84). Many of the songs appear to illustrate the actions, motives, or emotions of the characters but also universalize them to implicate the audience and society. As the familiar conclusion of *Tragedy of Tragedies* winds down, Sir Crit-Operatical and Modely interrupt in the manner of Fielding's *Author's Farce* or *Pasquin* and a new, happy ending is substituted.

The Adventures of Eovaai, one of the prose fictions that demonized Walpole into an embodiment of evil, corruption, and depravity, was first published in 1736, about the time Prince Frederick became especially hostile to Walpole and his father and as Walpole was losing control of the crucial parliamentary Committee on Elections and Petitions, the committee that rather arbitrarily, and certainly with partisan sentiment, decided petitions from defeated candidates. In one of her most sophisticated literary works, Haywood weaves a strong defense of the contract theory of government into a tale of magic, corruption, and romance-come-true. Ideas expressed in the earlier fictions are played out in the public, political arena. For instance, her lifelong belief in the absolute identification of the public and private, civic and physical, is most fully expressed in the intensity with which Ochihatou wishes to possess utterly (and, in this tale, completely corrupt) Eovaai as ruler and as sexual woman.[2]

---

1. It is common opinion that *Opera of Operas* is a cut version of Fielding's play. This impression may be the result of not recognizing how many of the airs are Fielding's lines set to music; in fact, few lines are eliminated. Innumerable minor revisions in his lines, both prose and verse, have been made.

2. Beasley points out that Haywood's erotic scenes are standard in the anti-Walpole fiction and, indeed, other texts such as the more obscure *A True and Impartial History of the Life and Adventures of Some-Body* (1740) much more obscene. "Portraits of a Monster," 426–27.

A remarkable variant on the seduction story, *The Adventures of Eovaai* has Ochihatou, like Clitander in *The Mercenary Lover*, use a variety of cultural means to seduce Eovaai physically, but, just as much, he wants her kingdom and to convert her to his ideology of power. It is important to see that parallel to the plot of kidnapped and threatened Princess Eovaai is the plot of the education of Eovaai as a ruler and the explication of an ideal form of government. Beginning with her father's lecture, substantial sections of the book are dissertations and dramatizations of forms of government, and the ending suggests the ideal order a good monarch who holds the right philosophy brings to a fortunate nation. The excerpts in this volume (about 16 percent of the whole) provide examples of the various kinds of writing—political essay, narrative, scandalous memoir—that Haywood used to create her highly original book.

The final two selections, excerpts from *The Invisible Spy* and *The Wife,* have distinctive, strong narrative voices and include some of Haywood's strongest statements about contemporary social mores and events. *The Invisible Spy* brings together Haywood's fiction, journalism, and extensive experience in the highly capitalistic literary marketplace. This almost unknown work of hers is about the power of print—ethical, economic, and political. As she did in *The Fruitless Inquiry*, Haywood creates a highly imaginative, somewhat supernatural element: the Invisible Spy has received two gifts from an enchanter: the ability to be invisible, and thereby collect material (both public and private) unavailable to others, and a magic tablet that transcribes verbatim what is said. The first "report" is the moving life of Alinda, another reworking of the courtship story in the contract society of modern London. When lawyers, moral suasion, money, and appeals for pity fail Alinda, the narrator becomes the instrument of discovery and punishment. Haywood echoes Pope's stance:

> Yes, I am proud; I must be proud to see
> Men not afraid of God, afraid of me
> Safe from the Bar, the Pulpit, and the Throne,
> Yet touch'd and sham'd . . . [1]

---

1. See Pope's *Epilogue to the Satires, Dialogue 2* (1738), ll.208–11.

The next excerpt comments upon a news event, the saga of Elizabeth Canning. Like Robert Walpole, Canning was a public obsession. During one of the trials, the prosecuting counsel observed:

> There have been accounts published, which have gone all over the kingdom; and, I believe, I may with truth say, all over Europe. I do not believe there is an individual in this great city that has not heard of this affair, nor hath a company met for one single evening where this was not a subject-matter of conversation.[1]

Canning was a tiny, small-pox-scarred, underdeveloped servant girl who disappeared on 1 January 1753 on her way between some relatives' house and her employer's home. She appeared at her mother's on 29 January in wretched condition and with a story that even her friends recognized as tainted with improbabilities. Allegedly, she had been accosted on the road and dragged to a house, later identified as that of Mother Wells, a woman reputed to be a procuress.

Canning was brought before Henry Fielding, then a magistrate for Westminster. Canning identified Mary Squires, a tall, "remarkably swarthy" gypsy with a huge nose and a lower lip swollen and disfigured by scrofula, as the woman who had tried to make her a prostitute, abused her, and then locked her in an attic, where she had been imprisoned with only a little bread and water for twenty-eight days. Squires and Wells were tried and convicted at the Old Bailey on 26 February, but a controversy over evidence had begun to rage. Wells was convicted of "well-knowing," "guilty knowledge" (meaning that she had awareness of a crime but did not attempt to prevent it or report it) and was sentenced to six months' imprisonment and branded on the thumb. Squires was sentenced to hang for assault and theft.[2]

---

1. Quoted in Henry Fielding, *An Enquiry into the Late Increase of Robbers and Related Writings*, ed. Malvin R. Zirker (Oxford: Clarendon, 1988), xcv n.2.

2. A number of detailed, scholarly accounts of the Canning saga have appeared recently. The fullest is Judith Moore, *The Appearance of Truth: The Story of Elizabeth Canning and Eighteenth-Century Narrative* (Newark: Univ. of Delaware Press, 1994); others worth consulting are Malvin Zirker's introduction to *An Enquiry into the Causes of the Late Increase of Robbers*; and Kristina Straub, "Heteroanxiety and the Case of Elizabeth Canning," *Eighteenth-Century Studies* 30 (1997): 296–304. Descriptions of the principals, which come from contemporary documents, are from Moore, 13–14, 40. Gascoyne's description of Squires quoted in Straub, 299.

Squires and Wells were tried before the Lord Mayor, Sir Crisp Gascoyne, who happened to be running for parliament in Southwark. Between the end of the trial and sentencing, he wrote to a Dorset clergyman about Squires's alibi. When the answer finally came in March, it supported the gypsy's story.

At that point, the case took on remarkable importance in the minds of a surprising number of prominent and influential people. On 20 March Henry Fielding's *A Clear State of the Case of Elizabeth Canning* appeared and was one of "some 40 pamphlets" to appear on the case in the next year (Zirker, cxi). Among other statements about the case, Gascoyne published *An Address to the Liverymen of the City of London . . . Relative to His Conduct in the Case of Elizabeth Canning and Mary Squires.* Fielding had listed many improbabilities but answered them and concluded with the hope that the government would "authorise some proper Persons to examine to the very Bottom, a Matter in which *the Honour of our national Justice* is so deeply concerned."[1] The battle was joined to some extent on just those grounds. Allan Ramsay, for instance, described it as "an inquiry into the nature of moral evidence" (quoted in Moore, 17). Even before Fielding's pamphlet, newspapers and other publications had taken sides, and advertisements and *The Case of Elizabeth Canning* (10 February 1753) appealed for donations for Canning (Zirker, xcviii, 293; Moore, 216–17). Fielding had objected to the establishment of "a kind of Court of Appeal from this Justice in the Bookseller's Shop" (285), and that is what happened.

Gascoyne decided that his political enemies were behind Canning, and he continued to bear the costs of investigating the case. He lost the election in April 1754 and continued to fume over the part the Canning case had played. On 29 April Elizabeth Canning was tried for perjury. Twenty-seven witnesses appeared for Canning and over forty for Squires.[2] On 7 May, the jury found her guilty of perjury,

---

1. Emphasis added. The list of improbabilities with answers is reprinted in Zirker's edition, 288–95; quotation, 312.

2. This is an extraordinary number; in the eighteenth century, a single jury served for an entire session of the court, and it was common for it to hear and decide several trials a day. A detailed account of the trial is in Moore, chapter 3.

"but not wilful or corrupt." Dissatisfied, the judge sent them back, and they returned with the desired verdict: "Guilty of wilful and corrupt perjury." A motion for a new trial was denied. Eight members of the Lord Mayor's court voted for a light sentence of six months' imprisonment, but it was outvoted. Canning was sentenced to transportation and sent to Connecticut in August 1754.

By the time Haywood wrote about Canning in *The Invisible Spy*, she was in a position to comment reflectively, and her interest is as much in the way the case was used as in Canning. In the excerpt, she shows us some contemporary uses of print but also dramatizes the ways unscrupulous people can abuse its power. This section is an illuminating picture of the way the print world works and provides one of the period's most vivid and delightful snapshots of newspapers and their coffeehouse readers. Haywood's comments were in the forefront of the reaction Tobias Smollett describes in his *Continuation of the Complete History of England* (1760). He remarked that the "frenzy" would be an embarrassment, for it was a dispute of "little consequence" and Canning was "an obscure damsel, of low degree" with an "improbable and unsupported" story. Indeed, public opinion did dismiss her.[1] In our own time, however, critics have read the Canning story as deeply revelatory. Kristina Straub, for instance, places it within the anxieties and the successful attempt to construct and control feminine sexuality. She and Judith Moore agree that it was "a test case for the encompassing neutrality of English Justice"; Moore recognizes additional "gendered judgments" but concludes that Canning's "servitude," not sexuality, determines the case and makes Canning the threatening Other. As she points out, "All of the writers on the Canning case belong to the class that 'gives' a character to a servant," and Canning, like Mary Carleton before her, became a fascinating site of cultural struggle.[2]

Finally, the excerpts from *The Wife*, a collection of essays and tales,

---

1. Quoted in Moore, 194, who says that opinion turned decidedly against Canning with a margin of 3 to 1 in printed sources.

2. Mary Jo Kietzman offers an intriguing way of reading such trials in "Publicizing Private History: Mary Carleton's Case in Court and in Print," *Prose Studies* 18 (1995): 105–33.

include a witty look at marital disharmony that features a couple with exaggerated political loyalties and a survey of fashionable London entertainments. Again, the selections invite comparison with the work of Addison, Steele, and Fielding. *The Wife* is purportedly written by "Mira," one of the most respectable of the fictional contributors to *The Female Spectator*—the happily married wife of a gentleman who was "descended from a family to which wit seems hereditary." The essays printed here give a taste of the range of Haywood's interests and abilities, her periodical talent, and her keen, critical view of her contemporaries.

This Oxford collection represents the variety of Haywood's work. It shows something of the degree of her political engagement, of the power of her observations and opinions about society, and of the diversity of genres, modes, and styles at her command. Among the works are those that use old forms conventionally, those that are serious revisions and experiments with familiar forms, and those that create new forms, some that could accurately be called avant garde. The selections show a variety of treatments of recurrent subjects and themes, including her attention to topical events and the *uses* of them by her contemporaries. Indeed, it could be argued that we have failed to recognize Haywood's experimentation with the power of print, and, once noticed, it becomes pervasively visible. Perhaps, above all, this collection suggests the need for continued study, discussion, and mastery of Eliza Haywood's work.

Selected Bibliography

Backscheider, Paula R. *Spectacular Politics: Theatrical Power and Mass Culture in Early Modern England.* Baltimore: Johns Hopkins Univ. Press, 1993.

Backscheider, Paula R., and John J. Richetti, eds. *Popular Fiction by Women 1660–1730: An Anthology.* Oxford: Clarendon, 1996.

Ballaster, Ros. *Seductive Forms: Women's Amatory Fiction from 1684 to 1740.* Oxford: Clarendon, 1992.

Beasley, Jerry C. *Novels of the 1740s.* Athens: Univ. of Georgia Press, 1982.

Blouch, Christine. "An Annotated Critical Bibliography." In *Eighteenth-*

Century Anglo-American Women Novelists: A Reference Guide. Ed. Doreen Saar and Mary Anne Schofield. New York: Macmillan, 1996. 263–300.

————. "Eliza Haywood and the Romance of Obscurity." *Studies in English Literature* 31 (1991): 535–52.

Bowers, Toni. *The Politics of Motherhood: British Writing and Culture, 1680–1760*. Cambridge: Cambridge UP, 1996.

Craft-Fairchild, Catherine. *Masquerade and Gender: Disguise and Female Identity in Eighteenth-Century Fiction by Women*. University Park: Penn State Univ. Press, 1993.

Doody, Margaret Anne. *A Natural Passion: A Study of the Novels of Samuel Richardson*. Oxford: Clarendon, 1974.

Haywood, Eliza. *Love in Excess, or the Fatal Enquiry*. Ed. David Oakleaf. Peterborough, Ontario: Broadview Press, 1994.

Holmes, Richard. *Dr. Johnson and Mr. Savage*. New York: Pantheon, 1993.

Ingrassia, Catherine. *Paper Credit: Grub Street, Exchange Alley, and Feminization in the Culture*. Cambridge: Cambridge Univ. Press, forthcoming.

Messenger, Ann. *His and Hers: Essays in Restoration and Eighteenth-Century Literature*. Lexington: Univ. Press of Kentucky, 1986.

Moore, Judith. *The Appearance of Truth: The Story of Elizabeth Canning and Eighteenth-Century Narrative*. Newark: Univ. of Delaware Press, 1994.

O'Driscoll, Sally. "Outlaw Readings: Beyond Queer Theory." *Signs* 22 (1996): 30–51.

Pearson, Jacqueline. *The Prostituted Muse: Images of Women and Women Dramatists, 1642–1737*. New York: St. Martin's Press, 1988.

Richetti, John J. *Popular Fiction before Richardson: Narrative Patterns, 1700–1739*. 1969. Oxford: Clarendon, 1992.

Rudolph, Valerie C. *The Plays of Eliza Haywood*. New York: Garland Publishing, 1983.

Schofield, Mary Anne. *Quiet Rebellion: The Fictional Heroines of Eliza Fowler Haywood*. Washington, D.C.: Univ. Press of America, 1982.

Spencer, Jane. *The Rise of the Woman Novelist: From Aphra Behn to Jane Austen*. Oxford: Basil Blackwell, 1986.

Todd, Janet M. *The Sign of Angellica: Women, Writing, and Fiction, 1660–1800*. New York: Columbia Univ. Press, 1989.

Turner, Cheryl. *Living by the Pen: Women Writers in the Eighteenth Century*. London: Routledge, 1992.

Warner, William B. "The Elevation of the Novel in England: Hegemony and Literary History." *ELH* 59 (1992): 577–96.

————. *Licensing Entertainment: The Elevation of Novel Reading in Britain, 1684–1740.* Berkeley: Univ. of California Press, 1998.

Williamson, Marilyn L. *Raising their Voices: British Women Writers, 1650–1750.* Detroit: Wayne State Univ. Press, 1990.

Note on the Texts

The texts are from the first London edition; all editions published in Haywood's lifetime have been collated. Haywood made no revisions in the 1736 *The Adventures of Eovaai*, although the title was changed to *The Unfortunate Princess* in 1741.

As is conventional with this series, obvious printer's errors in the texts (e.g., "little" for "litte") have been silently emended, but eighteenth-century variants in orthography have been retained. Decorative initials or following capital letters have not been retained at the beginning of chapters, and the long *s* has been regularized. Variants in punctuation have also been retained with the exception of quotation marks, which have been modernized or added for clarity. Abbreviated names of speakers in the plays have not been changed although they are sometimes inconsistent. Haywood's notes have been incorporated into the footnotes with bracketed markers indicating their provenance. In cases where Haywood placed markers for her footnotes before the word or phrase, the markers have been moved to follow modern conventions.

A

WIFE

To be LETT:

A

COMEDY.

As it is Acted at the

THEATRE-ROYAL
in DRURY-LANE,

By his MAJESTY's Servants.

Written by Mrs. ELIZA HAYWOOD.

LONDON;

Printed for DAN. BROWNE *jun.* at the *Black-Swan*
without *Temple-Bar;* and SAM. CHAPMAN, at the
Angel in *Pall-Mall.* M.DCC.XXIV.

(Price I *s.* 6 *d.*)

An approximation of the title page from the 1724 edition.

PROLOGUE,

Spoken by Mr. THEOPHILUS CIBBER.[1]

The Tragick Muse, to merit wish'd Applause,
From fancy'd Misery, real Caution draws;
Her flaming Strokes display some purple Crime,
The Passions feel, and the Soul swells Sublime.
The Comick, all this Pomp of Woe declines,
Softens her Light, and rather smiles, than shines;
She but your known familiar Follies shews,
Prudes, Misers, Cullies, Fops, Coquets, and Beaus:[2]
With her, as at some poor Man's Feast, you meet,
Where, what the Guests contribute, makes the Treat.

Criticks! Be dumb to-night—no Skill display;
A dangerous *Woman-Poet* wrote the Play:
One, who not fears your Fury, tho prevailing,
More than your Match, in everything, but Railing.
Give her fair Quarter,[3] and whene'er she tries ye,
Safe in Superior *Spirit,* she defies ye:
Measure her Force, by her *known Novels,*[4] writ

---

1. **Theophilus Cibber:** son of Colley Cibber, who was an actor, playwright, co-manager of Drury Lane Theatre, and poet laureate. Theophilus Cibber's play *Apollo and Daphne* and his adaptation *King Henry VI* were performed in the same year as *A Wife to Be Lett.* Although he played Toywell in Haywood's play, he does not speak here in character. At the time of this play he was co-manager of the summer company only, but for a twenty-one year old he had considerable influence.

2. **Prudes . . . Beaus:** popular stage types that satirize human follies. **Cullies:** simpletons, dupes, those easily fooled or taken advantage of. **Fops:** vain, affected dandies. **Coquets:** flirts, the female equivalent of rakes. **Beaus:** flirtatious men excessively concerned with fashionable, courtly conduct.

3. **Fair Quarter:** a fair chance, forebear quick judgment.

4. **Her known Novels:** By the time this play was produced, Haywood had published a number of successful novels, including *The British Recluse* and the best-seller *Love in Excess.*

With manly Vigour, and with Woman's Wit.
Then tremble, and depend, if ye beset her,
She, who can talk so well, may act yet better.[1]

Learn, from the opening Scene, ye blooming Fair,
Rightly to know your Worth, and match with Care;
When a Fool tempts ye, arm your hearts with Pride,
And think th'Ungenerous born to be deny'd:
But, to the Worthy, and the Wise, be kind,
Their *Cupid*[2] is not, like the Vulgar's, blind:
Justly they weigh your Charms, and sweetly pay
Your soft Submission, with permitted Sway.

---

1. **She, who . . . better:** a pun on the fact that Haywood acted the part of Mrs. Graspall.

2. **Cupid:** Roman god of love usually depicted as a beautiful winged boy, blind-folded and carrying a bow and arrow.

DRAMATIS PERSONÆ[1]

MEN.

Fairman.	Mr. *Boman*.[2]
Mr. Graspall.	Mr. *Evans*.[3]
Sir Harry Beaumont.	Mr. *Wilks*.[4]
Captain Gaylove.	Mr. *Bridgewater*.[5]
Courtly.	Mr. *Oates*.[6]
Toywell.	Mr. *Cibber*.[7]
Sneaksby.	Mr. *Parler*.
Shamble.	Mr. *Harper*.
Tim.	Mr. *Peplow*.

WOMEN.

Widow Stately.	Mrs. *Willis*.[8]
Mrs. Graspall.	Mrs. *Haywood,* the Author.

---

1. **Dramatis Personæ:** The following cast list appears in the published edition of 1724; only actors filling major roles are noted.

2. **Bowman:** As a singer, John Bowman was a court favorite who entertained both Charles II and James II; as an actor, he generally played either the fop or the kindly friend roles. Although he did perform in serious roles, comedy was his specialty during his sixty-year career.

3. **Evans:** a young member of the Drury Lane Company; Robert D. Hume and Judith Milhous believe that he is the same man who went on to be a dancer, actor, and singer at Drury Lane and Goodman's Fields.

4. **Wilkes:** William, nephew of Robert Wilkes, the manager of Drury Lane. He, like Haywood, had been trained at Smock Alley Theatre, Dublin.

5. **Bridgewater:** Roger, known as both a comic and tragic actor; his roles included Mirabel in *The Way of the World,* Horner in *The Country Wife,* and roles in numerous Shakespearean tragedies.

6. **Oates:** James, an actor, singer, and dancer whose career spanned more than thirty years; he spent brief stints in the summers managing fair booths with Fielding and others.

7. **Cibber:** Theophilus, an experienced actor of minor parts at Drury Lane. His first play, an adaptation of Shakespeare's *Henry VI,* had been performed in the summer of 1723.

8. **Willis:** Elizabeth, a well-known actress and occasional singer and dancer whose prolific career covered more than fifty years; she was very much a utility actress whose roles included Foible in *The Way of the World,* Lady Pride in *The Amorous Widow,* and Callis in *The Rover.*

Celemena.	Mrs. *Tenoe.*[1]
Marilla.	Mrs. *Lindar.*[2]
Amadea.	Mrs. *Brett.*
Dogood.	Mrs. *Davison.*

---

1. **Tenoe:** Theodosia Teno, an experienced Drury Lane actress and dancer; among her parts had been Damaris in *The Amorous Widow,* Mrs. Hartshorn in *The Wife's Resentment,* and Lucy in *The Old Bachelor.*

2. **Lindar:** A member of the Drury Lane company from 1715, she had been noted for playing the parts of young boys, but by the time of this production she played leading roles; she was a major attraction and an excellent singer and dancer.

A Wife to Be Lett

A Comedy

ACT I. SCENE I.[1]

Enter Captain Gaylove, Courtly, *and* Shamble.

COURTLY. I little thought when I went out to take the Air this Morning, to be so agreeably surpriz'd with the sight of my old Companion, and Friend—but I hope no Misfortune of yours has occasion'd me this Happiness, which I confess would be much more compleat, but for that Doubt.

GAYLOVE. While Fortune has a Being, we must all expect to find Vicissitudes—but nothing of my own Affairs can take me up so much as to make me forgetful of my Friends.—May I yet wish you Joy? Art marry'd? Or do you still set *Hymen*[2] at defiance?

COURT. No, *Charles,* I am not yet so happy.

GAY. Happy! Is it possible you can term the Loss of Liberty a Happiness? You, who of all Mankind seem'd most averse to it.

COURT. My Eyes, at last, are open'd, *Charles,* and I now court those Bonds as a Blessing, which I once look'd upon as galling Fetters.

---

1. Early eighteenth-century plays did not mark scene changes, but the entry and exit of characters indicated scene changes.

2. **Hymen:** Greek god of marriage, usually portrayed carrying a torch and a veil.

GAY. Poor *Ned*—I pity thy Change—But pray who is the Lady whose Charms have wrought so wonderful a Transformation?

COURT. I will not go about to describe her, because I am certain you'll look on her real Character as an extravagant Encomium;—but she is the Niece of Mr. *Fairman,* whom you have often seen with me in *London.*

GAY. If I remember the Man, he's of a downright sincere Temper, affable and obliging; but I believe loves Money.

COURT. You read his Character:—His Brother was a positive, hasty, old Gentleman, and consider'd Money as the Source of all Happiness—left an only Daughter, whom, on his Death-bed, he oblig'd to swear she should marry the Man he propos'd to her, (one who is, without exception, the greatest Fop in nature, but has 3000 *l.* a Year, which was an irresistible Motive to him:) You cannot but have seen him either at *London* or *Bath;*[1] his Name is *Toywell.*

GAY. O! I know him perfectly.

COURT. This Wretch, who has no Sense of what is truly valuable, and esteems *Marilla* only for her Fortune, makes me despair of Happiness: for she seems so religiously bent to keep her Vow, that all my Applications hitherto have been ineffectual to obtain any thing more from her than a bare Complaisance.—But prithee, dear *Charles,* give me leave to be impertinent, and enquire what drove you to *Salisbury?*[2]

GAY. Why faith, *Ned,* you know in what manner I us'd to live;—the Consequence of which was a certain Equipage of People call'd Duns,[3] whose daily Attendance was no way pleasing to me.—In short, my Creditors having no Patience, my Father no Compassion, and I no Money, I was oblig'd to leave *London* in compliance to my Trades-

---

1. **Bath:** city in Somersetshire built by the Romans and a fashionable resort city throughout the eighteenth century; its warm mineral baths were believed to be restorative, to cure infertility, and to heal a wide variety of mental and physical ailments.

2. **Salisbury:** city in Wiltshire noted for its cathedral and its Salisbury Whites, long cloth manufactured for sale in Turkey and the Near East.

3. **Duns:** bill collectors, often professional.

men—fearing I should put them to the expence of providing a Lodging for one,[1] who thought himself too far engag'd to 'em already—therefore selling my Company in the Guards, I bought in one of these Regiments.[2]—But prithee, *Ned,* give me some little Idea how you spend your time here.

COURT. As they do in most Country Towns—the Men in Hunting, Hawking, and Drinking—the Women in Cookery, Pickling, and Preserving—not but there are some more elegant among us, to whom I shall make it my business to introduce you.

GAY. I shall think myself infinitely oblig'd to you.

COURT. Of the Number of those I Last mention'd, is Sir *Harry Beaumont;* who, tho' he chuses to live retir'd in this Country at present, where he has a vast Estate, has been a very great Traveller, and from all the different Courts where he has been, brought with him every thing worth the wearing of a fine Gentleman.—In short, I know nothing of his Character that a Man of the strictest Honour wou'd not be proud of—then for his Wit and Conversation, 'tis such as I'm sure you'll be infinitely charm'd with.

GAY. The Description you give of him is no more than what he merits—I knew him about a Year ago, he then made his Addresses to a Relation of mine—I never heard what occasion'd their breaking off—I thought him a most accomplish'd Gentleman, and I am glad to hear his late Accession to his Uncle's Title and Estate has not taken from him that easy Gayety and Freedom of Behaviour, which is one of the greatest Charms of Conversation, and without which the brightest Wit wants relish.

COURT. You shall anon[3] renew your Acquaintance with him—he has engag'd me to dine with him to-day, your Company will add to the Pleasure of the Entertainment, and in the Afternoon I will carry you to visit some Ladies.

---

1. **fearing . . . one:** his creditors would have him imprisoned, thereby providing lodging for him.

2. **bought . . . Regiments:** Commissions in the army could be bought and sold.

3. **anon:** soon.

GAY. May I ask you who they are?

COURT. I believe you never saw either of 'em—one is my Mistress, the other is Daughter to Mr. *Fairman,* whose Name is *Celemena.*— She is speedily to be marry'd to a very Blockhead, one *Sneaksby.*—She is a Woman of a world of Life and Spirit in her Conversation, and has as much Wit as her intended Husband wants it; I am certain you will be pleas'd with her Acquaintance.

GAY. I were stupid else, if she be what you represent.—But, *Ned,* I have heard of a mighty fine Woman you have here, since my coming into these Parts, one who bears the Bell[1] from all the rest—I think they call her Mrs. *Graspall.*

COURT. She is extreamly handsome indeed, and virtuous they say;— but I never visit there:—She is marry'd to the most covetous miserable Wretch that ever was; he denies her the Privilege of any Company, not out of Jealousy, but for fear she shou'd be at any Expence in entertaining 'em.

GAY. And how does she endure a Restraint so disagreeable to her Youth and Beauty?

COURT. With a Resignation, which is surprizing to all who know her: —But come, we'll take a little Walk, and then to dinner.

GAY. With all my heart.

Exeunt.

Enter Dogood, *and pulls* Shamble *back.*

DOGOOD. 'Tis he for certain! Harkye! harkye! 'Squire *Sancho,* you have follow'd your Don *Quixote* long enough—to take upon you the Protection of a distressed Damsel[2]—without any Infringement, I hope, on the hardy Knight—your Master.

---

1. **bears the Bell:** takes the first place, wins the prize; from the custom of awarding a gold or silver bell to the winners of contests. Also, the cow or sheep that led the rest of the herd or flock was said to "bear the bell."

2. **Don Quixote . . . distressed Damsel:** Don Quixote, hero of Miguel de Cervantes's satirical picaresque novel, believed himself to be a knight with the duty to perform such knightly actions as rescuing women in trouble.

SHAMBLE. Faith, Lady, I know you not;—and if you have any Commands for me, I shall be more at leisure, and in better humour after Dinner.

DO. Well, I find the Proverb's false, which says, Custom is a second Nature[1]—or the want of a Dinner would not put the accustom'd Mr. *Shamble* out of humour.

SHAM. Ha! by my Veracity, *Jenny!*

DO. Ay, by my Maidenhead[2] (as terrible an Oath) the very same; but I wonder thou could'st forget me in so short a time.

SHAM. Why how was it possible to know thee thus metamorphos'd, fine Lace Pinners[3] transmogrify'd into a round-ear'd Coif[4] and a high-crown'd Hat[5]—a Gold Watch into a Pincushion, and a Tweezer into a Scissar-Case[6]—Prithee on what Design art thou thus equipt?

DO. Why, faith, *Shamble*—I found Trading in publick grew somewhat slippery, and now deal all in private.

SHAM. What, kept?

DO. Not for the purpose you mean—In short, being weary of the Life I led in *London,* I resolv'd to take up, and live retir'd—I found means to be recommended to the Service of one of the richest Widows in this Country, with whom I now live as a Housekeeper—not but I have a great deal of spare Time for the service of my Friends.

---

1. **Custom is a second nature:** "Custom is almost second nature," Plutarch, *Rules for the Preservation of Health,* 18.

2. **by my Maidenhead:** an obscene or blasphemous oath, "By my virginity" or, possibly, "by the face of the Virgin Mary"; the latter was obsolete in Haywood's time.

3. **Lace Pinners:** a close-fitting hat with long flaps on the sides that could be pinned down tightly; primarily a fashion of women of rank.

4. **round-ear'd Coif:** a close-fitting cap with flaps that could be tied under the ears, thereby covering the hair completely. Although women of all classes wore caps, this style was usually associated with the country and often worn under a bonnet by women working outdoors.

5. **high-crown'd Hat:** straw hat with a high crown shaped like the haystacks that the people who wore them built; they were worn by country people, often with a scarf or bonnet underneath. Low-crowned straw hats, called bergère or shepherdess hats, were fashionable among upperclass women.

6. **Scissar-Case:** scissors case.

SHAM. Ha! say'st thou so? Why then methinks 'tis greatly in thy power to oblige my Master—thy Assistance may be needful in a Place where he has so little Acquaintance. The Company of a kind She would not be unwelcome to a man of his Constitution—and as his Affairs stand at present, a rich Widow or Heiress would be an excellent Cordial to his sinking Fortune.

DO. O! I thought you would be glad to own me—Why my Mistress is a Widow, and exceeding rich; but, duce on't, her Age and Affectation will never down with thy queasy stomach'd Master.

SHAM. Prithee what, who is she?

DO. The Relict[1] of a Country Mercer,[2] who, dying, left her an immense Sum of Money, besides a good Estate he had purchas'd in Land—She has no Child, but a foolish Nephew is look'd upon as Heir—he is speedily to be marry'd to a young Lady of a great Fortune, and a celebrated Beauty—I could wish thy Master were in his place, but that's impossible to be effected.

SHAM. But has this old Lady of yours no Suitors?

DO. Yes, enow—but she is all for a Title; a Man of her own Station she looks upon as unworthy of her. As soon as this Marriage is over, she designs to go to *London,* and lay out her whole Estate, rather than want a Bargain of Knight's Flesh.

SHAM. I have a Thought come into my Head, which may prove a lucky one—Dost thou not think if I were equipt accordingly, I might pass for a Knight?

DO. A Knight, ha! ha! ha!

SHAM. Why, I have seen as bad a Face in a gilded Chariot.

DO. That's true; and now I think on't, 'tis not the Man, but the Title that must charm her—I don't know, but with my Management, such a thing might be possible.

---

1. **Relict:** widow.

2. **Mercer:** dealer in textiles and cloth.

SHAM. If it cou'd, *500 l.* are thine out of her Money—besides a Premium[1] [is] better than any Jointure[2] I can make her.

DO. O Goodman[3] Promiser! as if I were not acquainted with your Abilities—make but the Money secure to me, and I'll give you a Discharge from all other Demands.

SHAM. Well, but harkye, I suppose with your Change of Habit, you have also shifted your Name—by what must I call you now?

DO. *Dogood,* at your Service.

SHAM. A very good Name, and I hope prophetick to us both—but come, shall we step into some House, and consult about this Affair.

DO. Ay, I have an Acquaintance just by.

Exit.

Enter Mrs. Graspall, *and* Amadea *in Boys Cloaths.*

WIFE. Very unaccountable—that neither at Home or Abroad, I can one Moment get rid of this little troublesome Impertinent.—Have you any Business this way, Sir.

AMAD. No other, Madam, than to wait on you; now the Camp's so near, 'tis unsafe for Ladies to walk alone.

WIFE. I am much obliged to you—but I apprehend no Danger. I cannot harbour so ill an Opinion of the Gentlemen of the Army, as to imagine any of them wou'd offer an Affront to a Woman, who, I hope, looks not to deserve it—and as for the Meaner Sort (Thanks to the good Discipline they are under) they are oblig'd to follow the Example of their Leaders.

AMAD. Were it so, which yet I can't allow—there is another Danger

---

1. **Premium:** sum additional to interest or other fixed remunerations; a bonus.

2. **Jointure:** provision of land or income contracted in the marriage settlement for the wife should she survive her husband; some expired at the woman's death, but others were property she could bequeath.

3. **Goodman:** respectful title used to address men, often elderly, who were below the rank of gentleman.

not less imminent, tho' perhaps more pleasing than what I have mentioned—A certain Gentleman who lives not far off, and very much frequents this Walk, carries a kind of Spell in his Eyes and Tongue, which has been fatal to many of your Sex.

WIFE. Ay; pray who is that?

AMAD. I fancy, Madam, after what I've said, 'tis needless to repeat his Name—however, for your Satisfaction—

WIFE. My Satisfaction! what means he?

AMAD. Ha! she blushes—then my Suspicions are too just.—Yes, Madam, since you take pleasure in the Sound, Sir *Harry Beaumont.*

WIFE. Was ever such an Insolence—I take pleasure in the Sound! What is Sir *Harry Beaumont* to me, or I to him?

AMAD. Nay, if you are angry, Madam—

WIFE. Have I not Reason? What Act of mine has ever justify'd this Rudeness—but I guess by whom you are set on; and if it were not more Love of myself, than my Husband, I wou'd be reveng'd even in the way he fears.

AMAD. Nay, now I understand you not—but if you think your Husband—

WIFE. Yes, I know you wou'd not dare, unless authoriz'd by him, to treat me in this manner—Ungrateful Man! have I submitted to the hard uncoveted Condition of his Wife, to be at last suspected of Dishonour—O! to what Fate are wretched Women born! Condemn'd to Slavery, tho' conscious of superior Merit, and bound to obey the severe Dictates of a very Fool, when e'er the Name of Husband gives 'em Force.

AMAD. Transport not thus your self with causeless Rage, but listen patiently, while I confess I am alone the Offender—your Virtue appears fair, your Conduct blameless, to the fond Eyes of your admiring Husband—but the judging World, which takes delight in finding something to condemn, watch all your Actions; and as I so freely have begun, I will take the liberty still to remind you, that the frequent Visits of Sir *Harry Beaumont* are most pernicious to your Character.—

WIFE. 'Tis well—then this is your Surmise.

AMAD. If mine, why not others?

WIFE. No, bold Adviser—my Reputation is too well establish'd—no Malice ever attempted to sully my unblemish'd Fame, till thou, for what base End I know not, hast presum'd to tax me—but I despise whatever thou can'st say, and secure in my own Innocence, defy thy Malice.

AMAD. But one word more—if to receive the Addresses of a Man, whose utmost Wit can find no Form to make 'em look like honourable—and varnish o'er the vile Design they are made for; if this, I say, be not a fault to Vertue, I have done.

WIFE. Oh Heav'ns!

AMAD. If you are free from this, then I confess my Accusation false— but if charm'd with Flattery, your Sexes bait to ruin, you still encourage the Deceiver's Hopes, you wrong yourself, not I. I leave you to reflect on what I've said; and, as you want not Sense, entreat you to exert it on an Occasion which requires it all—think, 'tis your good Genius warns thro' my Lips, immortal Honour, Fame, and Peace, attend to crown the glorious Conquest—Eternal Infamy, Disgrace, and those worse Racks the Stings of Conscience, watch to seize your Soul, if you persist to listen to the undoing Vows of faithless *Beaumont.*—Madam, farewel, and rest assur'd, whatever my Thoughts are, my Tongue, but to yourself, shall on this Theme be dumb forever.

Exit.

WIFE. His Words, methinks, have open'd all my Heart, and fill'd it with a Horror, till now a Stranger to me—O Vertue! if I in aught had swerv'd from the strict Precepts, I shou'd not wonder at these Starts, and Tremblings—but as I have held, and still will hold my Honour dearer than my Life, why am I thus alarm'd? Why, arm'd with Innocence, did I not hear, unmov'd, the audacious Monitor? O 'tis too true, I've been to blame: tho' resolute never to yield to what the Tempter sues for, I have, perhaps, with too attentive Ears, listned to his Persuasions—and 'tis a Crime to Vertue, ev'n but to hear what loose Desires suggest—were I unmarried—cou'd I with Honour receive Sir *Harry's* Love, how happy were my Lot?—For sure, of all Mankind, he is most form'd to charm, and bless a Woman's fondest, softest Wishes—but as I am, tho' hard my Fate, I must be blind and deaf to all his Worth, and place my sole Felicity in Duty.—That Creature here!

Enter Toywell.

TOY. She's here, and alone—now will I accost her with such Phrases, as she shall not be able to withstand.—Stay, Madam, fly not your adoring Slave—who long has languish'd for this Opportunity, to tell you that he dies for you.

WIFE. What means the Wretch? are you mad, Sir?

TOY. If Love be Madness, I have wondrous Cause—for from the first Moment I beheld that Field of Beauty, I have done nothing, but wish and languish, burn and bleed, with Passion and Desire.

WIFE. Hold, Sir; if you really are in your Senses, let me tell you, you are guilty of an Assurance, which you will not find me easy to forgive.

TOY. No matter for that, I know she's pleas'd with it—Ah, Madam! as the inimitable *Otway* says, Who can behold such Beauty, and be silent?[1]

WIFE. Wretched Animal—If I did not think that all Advice was lost upon you, I wou'd give you this friendly Caution—to know to whom you speak.

TOY. Ha! Perhaps I've been too grave—Gad, I'll try another way. [*Aside.*]—Why, Faith, Madam, I believe I know you, and I am sure I know myself—there stand you, Mrs. *Susanna Graspall*—without Exception, the most agreeable Woman breathing—married to an old

---

1. **Who . . . silent:** Thomas Otway, *The Orphan* (1680), 1.1.305; Polydore is speaking to Monimia. Otway was the author of three successful tragedies, including this one, and of several other plays.

decrepid, miserly Curmudgeon—who debars you from all the Pleasures of Life; and here am I, *Jack Toywell,* in free Possession of full three thousand Pounds a Year—with Youth, Vigour, and some other tolerable Qualifications, ready with my Person and Fortune to make you happy in all those Enjoyments your Husband's Age and Avarice denies.—Gad, I am mighty florid to-day.

WIFE. Since you oblige me to be more serious than I thought at first your ridiculous Addresses merited, I must tell you, that you are an impudent pretending Fop—that I despise and loath you; and if you dare to trouble me again with such impertinent Discourses, my Husband shall be acquainted with the Character you give of him.

TOY. Come, Madam, egad I like you ne'er the worse for this dissembled Coldness—it whets the Edge of Appetite, and gives a double Relish to those Raptures your yielding will bestow.

WIFE. Nay, if you grow rude—

TOY. No Rudeness, Madam, but what you will one day pardon:—A Lover must begin with humble distant Sighs, but when the ice is broke, and he has once ventur'd to say he loves, then he proceeds by swift Degrees to greater Freedoms—your Hand, your Lips.—

Offers to kiss her.

WIFE. Impudent Villain. [*Boxes his Ears.*] But here's Company—if ever thou dar'st affront me thus again.

Enter Beaumont.

BEAU. Ha! so free!

TOY. Sir *Harry Beaumont*—dear Sir *Harry,* I am your most obsequious humble Servant.

BEAU. Yours, yours, Mr. *Toywell*—a good day to you, Madam, I see you are taking the Benefit of the fresh Air this Morning—I doubt not but you have been agreeably entertain'd in the Conversation of so polite a Gentleman as Mr. *Toywell.*

WIFE. I shall not envy you that Happiness, Sir *Harry,* therefore leave you to enjoy it—your Servant! Oh the Difference of Men!

Exit.

BEAU. Madam, your most humble—methinks, Mr. *Toywell,* the Lady seems displeas'd—what have you done to her?

TOY. O Sir *Harry,* you and I know the World too well, to think a Woman's Anger, in some Cases, worth regarding; I dare swear it has escaped the Observation of neither of us, that they are frequently most pleas'd, when least they seem to be so.—

BEAU. What! then you have been making Love.

TOY. Why, Faith, she is look'd upon as one of the finest Women in the County—and having had of late a pretty deal of idle time on my hands, I took it into my head to make her some Offers, which, I believe, when she has consider'd on, she'll scarce refuse.

BEAU. Conceited Coxcomb![1] but she has the Reputation of a vertuous Woman.—

TOY. Vertuous! so they are all till they are try'd—and I don't remember to have heard that before me, and Man of Figure has attack'd her—

BEAU. Intolerable Fop!—A Man truly deserving of a Lady's Favour, Mr. *Toywell,* seldom discloses his Design on the Woman he admires, but to herself—for anything you know, Mrs. *Graspall* may have been Proof against the most elegant Addresses.

TOY. 'Twas then for want of a right method in applying them—for my part, I never yet had the Mortification to engage with any Woman, silly enough to hold out above three Summons.—

BEAU. You are a happy Man indeed—but methinks 'tis a little odd you dare venture to make an Attempt of this nature so near your

---

1. **Coxcomb:** conceited fop.

Marriage—for I hear your Wedding with the fair *Marilla* is to be accomplished in a day or two—Suppose she shou'd hear of it.

TOY. Psha! 'tis so long ago since we were contracted, that for a great while we have regarded each other with an absolute Indifference.—I lik'd her well enough indeed at first, but the Certainty that she must one day be my Wife, has set her in the self-same View as she wou'd have appear'd after seven Years Possession. But now I think on't, I promis'd her Uncle to dine with 'em to-day—prithee, Sir *Harry,* go along with me, I shall be so dull else.

BEAU. I wou'd willingly accompany you, Mr. *Toywell,* to such agreeable Conversation, if I were not engag'd at home with some Friends, who I believe by this time expect me.

TOY. Phoo, Pox—well then I must take my leave; 'tis pretty near One, and they dine consumed early.[1]—Sir *Harry,* your Servant.

Exit.

BEAU. Your Servant, Sir.—Fool! Heavens, how strange a Creature is a Lover!—I am asham'd to think the Rivalship of such a Wretch can give me Pain, and yet it does—which proves more strongly than I e'er knew before, the Violence of my Passion—Yes, I find I love to such a height, that if unlicens'd Enjoyment be a Crime, 'tis here excus'd by the Necessity—but be as it will, wou'd I promise it myself at any rate—but Hope is not so vain; yet she has heard my Suit, and still continues to admit my Visits—confesses an Esteem, and if so, 'tis the first Step to Love—A constant Assiduity, in time, perhaps may loosen the strict Bonds of galling Duty, and make the Charmer mine.

> Ne'er let the Lover of his Wish despair,
> Whose Vows of Passion reach th'attentive Fair:

---

1. **early:** The ordinary time for dinner, the main meal of the day, was between 5:00 and 6:00 P.M.; because the working classes tended to eat dinner around 12:00 or 1:00, this observation carries class overtones.

Tho' bent to follow Vertue, 'tis her Fate
At last to yield, if once capitulate.

END OF THE FIRST ACT.

ACT II. SCENE I.

Enter Celemena *and* Marilla.

CEL. Prithee, good Cousin, take a Friend's Advice, and cast off this obstinate Humour of marrying the Man who slights you, and slighting the Man who loves you. *Toywell* has indeed a great Estate, but *Courtly* knows how to use what he has handsomely, and is withall very easy in his Circumstances.—Can any thing, that has not taken an entire leave of her Understanding, persist in a Resolution of throwing herself away in this manner?

MAR. Allowing all that you have said—the religious Observance I owe to the Vow I made my dying Father, leaves me no choice.

CEL. If the Dead cou'd tell what we Living are doing, I am apt to believe the old Gentleman wou'd quit his Grave a while, to forbid the Banes,[1] and save his Daughter from so visible a Ruin.—Besides, the Vow you made was forc'd, and consequently not binding.—Heavens! it provokes me to see you act so contrary to Reason, nay, to your own Inclination too; for I am sure you love *Courtly.*

MAR. How came you so well acquainted with my Thoughts, good Cousin?

CEL. Prithee, none of your Airs! I know you have sense enough to distinguish a Man of Parts from a Fool.

---

1. **Banes:** archaic spelling of banns, the proclamation or public notice of the intention to marry. They were to be read or published on three successive Sundays.

Enter Servant.

SERV. Ladies, Mr. *Courtly* and a strange Gentleman desire to know if you are at leisure.

CEL. Show 'em up. [*Exit Servant.*] Now let me see you use him as you us'd to do, and I protest I'll disclaim Kindred with you.

MAR. You will—but I fancy I shall put it to the venture.

CEL. I wonder who he has brought with him.

Enter Courtly *and* Gaylove.

COURT. Ladies, I hope you will pardon my introducing a Gentleman whose Conversation will hereafter make his own Apology.—This, Captain, is Mr. *Fairman's* Daughter; this, his Niece.

CEL. We are too well acquainted with Mr. *Courtly's* Delicacy, not to afford a ready Welcome to any whom he calls Friend. Such Entertainment, Sir, as furnishes a homely Country Cottage, you may expect.

GAY. He must be covetous indeed, could form a Wish beyond what here is to be found.

CEL. This Fellow has something in him prodigiously agreeable, I can't help liking him.—[*Aside.*] Well, Mr. *Courtly,* I have been labouring for you, you must now e'en speak for yourself.

COURT. If all that can betoken a sincere and ardent Passion, cou'd influence the fair *Marilla* to pity what I feel, she would not thus cruelly resolve to make my Rival happy.

MAR. If you have any value for my Quiet, you will forbear to urge a Suit, which, were my Inclination otherwise, is not in my power to grant; and consider me not as Mistress of myself.

COURT. Shou'd the Man you purpose to bless, not know the Value of the Treasure you bestow, I do assure you, Madam, 'twou'd give me an Uneasiness almost equal to the Loss of you.

MAR. That's generous indeed, but—

COURT. Yet give me leave—Your pardon, Madam! [*To Cel.*]

They walk apart.

CEL. O Sir, you will have it, if your Friend will as willingly forgive your leaving him to the Conversation of a raw Country Girl.

GAY. Now have I a great mind to tell you the pleasure he does me, but fear of disobliging, stops my Mouth:

> But Eccho shall so oft repeat your Name,
> You'll learn my Sufferings, and reward my Flame.[1]

As my Passion is more than common, my Style, Madam, ought to be no less than Heroick.

CEL. But had I an inclination to give ear to it, you have more Modesty, I hope, than to make love at first sight—But now I think on't, perhaps you may imagine, that the Apprehension of the fine things may be saying yonder, makes me wish I were capable of inspiring the same; however, to shew you I have vanity enough to believe I've made a Conquest, when I have found the Bark of every Tree carv'd with the cruel *Celemena's* Name, and you have sigh'd away some seven Years—

GAY. I find, Madam, you're like to be pretty reasonable.

CEL.

> When Cooing Doves the shady Cypress shun,
> And hide their Heads, to find their Plaints outdone;
> When sympathizing Grief o'erspreads the Plains,
> And Shepherds mourn your Fate in rural Strains;
> When my Disdain's the Theme of every Song,
> And Celemena hangs on every Tongue.—[2]

---

1. **But Eccho . . . Flame:** verse probably by Haywood based on the Roman myth of Echo, a nymph in love with Narcissus; her love was unreturned, and she pined away until nothing but her voice remained.

2. **When . . . Tongue:** probably by Haywood.

GAY. For Heaven's sake Madam! have you no Compassion?

CEL.

> When cruel Nymph thro' Hills and Valleys flies,
> And distant Eccho *cruel Nymph* replies—[1]

GAY. Dear Madam, come to a Conclusion.

CEL. I have done—and here give you permission to spend the following seven Years in the same manner; then come to me again, and I perhaps may allow you my Hand to—Kiss.

GAY. Truly, Madam, I can't but say your Demands are extremely moderate—But can't you as well suppose all this past?—I have lov'd you very passionately these seven Minutes, and, according to Modern Calculation, they appear so many Ages.

CEL. No, I can't suppose one word on't—nor can I admit of your Modern Calculations—'tis impossible the Man can love me, who would hesitate on starving, hanging or drowning, on my account— much less in passing a few Years in so sublime a Despair, as I have enjoin'd you—

GAY. But, Madam—

CEL. A word more—and I'll not allow of you as a Servant, till you have kill'd Lions, and made Monsters tame.

GAY. There's no talking to her—she will be too hard for me. O! here comes a Relief.

Enter Fairman *and* Toywell.

TOY. So, Ladies and Gentlemen, Wit and Beauty are inseparable here, and, let me Blood,[2] I am so pleasant myself, I am like a Fish out of Water, in dull Company.

---

1. **When . . . replies:** probably by Haywood.

2. **let me blood:** "blood" was a term often used in oaths and ejaculations, a vulgar adage; "letting blood" refers to the common medical practice of drawing blood as a means of purifying the body of impurities. Here it is probably a conflation of the two.

FAIR. O' my Conscience, this Nephew of mine that is to be, grows every day a greater Fop than ever. Your Servant, Gentlemen. Daughter, pray invite this good Company to your Wedding.—I expect 'Squire *Sneaksby* to-night, and tomorrow shall make you one.

CEL. Heaven forbid—'Tis very sudden, Sir.

FAIR. His Aunt, Child, the Widow *Stately,* is a fickle Woman; if she happen to marry again, or should change her mind, there is not such another Match in the County—You don't consider, she is to settle best part of her Estate on him: and the Fortune I'll give you, will set you on a foot with the Nobility—

MAR. Now, *Celemena,* 'twill be my turn to wonder how you can submit to be the Wife of a Fool—But, Uncle, this *Sneaksby* is accounted exceeding silly.

FAIR. He is good-natur'd, Niece, and rich; two things a young Woman ought to prefer to a full Head and light Purse.

TOY. Nay, Sir, you would not marry my Cuz to a Fool—Why, Sir, she'll never enjoy a happy Minute with a Fool—

FAIR. Hum! then you think a Fool can never make a good Husband.

TOY. Certainly.

FAIR. Ha! then if you have any value for the Fair Sex, shew it, by laying aside all Thoughts of marrying.

TOY. The old Gentleman is mighty testy, methinks.

FAIR. Well, *Celemena,* I expect your Compliance.

CEL. Sir, my Duty obliges me not to dispute with your Commands— But I may find some way to evade 'em.

Aside.

FAIR. That's my good Girl, and to-morrow thou shalt have my Blessing in a Bag of ten thousand Pounds—But come, I have some Business with you; your Servant all.

Exit.

TOY. *Marilla.*

MAR. Sir!

TOY. Prithee, my Dear, e'en let our Wedding be to-morrow.

MAR. Sir, you know my Obedience to my Father submits my Will to yours.

TOY. To-morrow then, if you please; 'twill save Expences.

COURT. Heaven! that she can bear this Usage—Dear Madam, have some compassion for yourself, if you have none for me.

GAY. Pardon a Stranger's Freedom, Madam, if I say, not only my Concern for my Friend, but also the sincere Esteem your Character has fill'd me with, makes me wish you could avoid this Marriage.

MAR. I thank you, Sir—but alas! you speak the Charms of Liberty to a Galley-Slave.

GAY. But suppose some lucky Means should offer, would you then bless my Friend?

MAR. There is not a Possibility, unless the Dead could be restor'd to Life, and give me back my Vow—but if there were, I'd promise nothing.

COURT. I do not ask it—May your Fate be happy—my own I leave to your Dispose.

MAR. 'Tis kindly said—and I, perhaps, should not be found ungrateful—But I'll order Tea, you'll follow.

COURT. Immediately, Madam. I fancy, *Charles,* this is a good time for our Design.

GAY. Ay, ay, let me alone—Poor Lady, I pity her.

COURT. So do I, for he had all her Fortune in his hands—But I am strangely surpriz'd; he was reckon'd one of the most substantial Men in *London:* I fear his breaking[1] will involve more than *Marilla* in his Ruin.

TOY. Ha! what's that? Pray, Sir, who is the Gentleman you speak of?

GAY. Mr. *Trusty,* Sir, a Banker in *Lombard street.*

TOY. Ha! Mr. *Trusty!*

GAY. Yes, Sir; a Statute was taken out against him two days before I left *London*—But you seem concern'd, Sir; I hope it will prove of no Prejudice to you.

TOY. Me! hum! no, Sir—I had no Dealings with him, but I know the best part, if not all of *Marilla's* Fortune was lodg'd in his hands—I must find some way to break with her—This was lucky News, a Day more, and it had been as unfortunate. Gentlemen, your Servant.

Exit.

GAY. Come, chear up, *Ned,* who knows how this may work.

COURT. His Mercenary base Nature gives me some hopes.

GAY. If we could as easily contrive some Stratagem to defer *Celemena's* Wedding; for I confess I feel something here that will give me Disquiet to see her marry'd to another.

COURT. How! *Charles,* I thought you were proof against Love and Matrimony.

GAY. Why, will you allow nobody to repent of their Mistakes but yourself?—*Celemena* has Wit, Beauty, and Good-nature—and I heard her Father express himself very prettily to her—10000 *l.* would make a Convert of one more Reprobate than your humble Servant.

COURT. 'Tis a receiv'd Article[2] indeed—but let's in, the Ladies wait.

---

1. **breaking:** going bankrupt. A statute was granted his creditors upon their complaint.
2. **receiv'd Article:** standard, well-accepted clause in an agreement or contract.

GAY. Allons.[1]

Exit.

Mrs. Graspall *discover'd reading at a Toylet.*[2]

WIFE. How small a Relief can Books afford us when the Mind's perplex'd?—The Subject that our Thoughts are bent upon, forms Characters more capital and swelling, than any these useless Pages can produce—and 'tis no matter on what Theme the Author treats; we read
it our own way, and see but with our Passions Eyes—*Beaumont* is
here in ev'ry Line—*Beaumont* in all the Volume—I'll look no more
on't—These Opticks[3] too are Traytors, and conspire with Fancy to
undo me—To what shall I have recourse?

Enter Beaumont.

BEAU. The Door happening to be open, and nobody in the way, I
presum'd to enter without Ceremony.

WIFE. Ha! catch'd in this Confusion of my Soul! when all my
Thoughts were unprepar'd and hurry'd! Unlucky Accident!

BEAU. You are disorder'd, Madam—I hope my Presence has not offended.—

WIFE. Sir *Harry,* you can be guilty of but one Offence—forbear to
talk of Love, and you shall ever be most welcome here.

BEAU. O too severe Injunction! you know this is the only Command
I could refuse to obey you in—and yet, unkind and cruel, you rate
the Price of my Admittance at an Impossibility. The Language of my
Eyes you have long since understood and pardon'd, why then is it
greater Guilt when told you by my Tongue?

---

1. **Allons:** come on.
2. **Toylet:** dressing table.
3. **Opticks:** literally the science of sight.

WIFE. The Crime in both is equal—and since with Innocence I can admit of neither, have resolv'd—

BEAU. On what?

WIFE. Never to look on you, or hear you more.

BEAU. What have I done to merit such a Sentence?

WIFE. How shall I answer him, or how disguise the real Reason of my Change of Temper, for much I fear he will not think it Hate?— That I no sooner did forbid your Visits, was because I hoped you would endeavour to overcome a Passion which, I think, I never err'd so far by any Words or Actions to encourage—and wish'd I might with Honour have preserv'd your Friendship.

BEAU. Are Love and Friendship then at such a distance they ne'er can meet? O! wou'd you but rightly weigh their Likeness, you'd find the Scale so even, you'd think them Twins—Friendship is Love refin'd, and Love is Friendship of a warmer Soil—There's such a Sympathy between 'em, the Breast that harbours one, can never be a Stranger to the other.—

WIFE. I must not harken to such Sophistry—Hark! I think I hear somebody coming, and have reason to believe that of late I have had Spies upon my Actions—Step into the Closet while I see who 'tis.—

Exit Beaum.

Enter Toywell.

Toywell! what means this Intrusion? Did I not bid you trouble me no more? Or if I had not, were there no Servants in the way to keep down such Impertinents?

TOY. No, faith, Madam, all your People are in the middle of the Street yonder, crowding about a Pedlar's Pack—and chusing Nick-nacks; and so, Madam, Passage being free, I took an opportunity to, to, to—come in, Madam.—

WIFE. Very well—but I shall call 'em to guard it better, and show you down a nearer way than you came up, unless you leave me immediatly.

TOY. I don't think you have so little Understanding—Besides, I am come to make a new Proposal—I have heard some news, which will certainly dissappoint *Marilla* in her hopes of marrying me—I can now settle a whole Heart upon you.

WIFE. Peace, thou despicable Fop—if you fancy this Gallantry, as 'tis possible you may be weak enough—I pity your Simplicity—But if your Designs are as base as your impudent persisting in this Behaviour intimates, once more I tell you, I have Virtue to arm me against the Assaults of your whole Sex, and Value enough for my Husband, to let him know the Favour you would do him—Who's there?

TOY. Nay, Madam, if I part with you so, you may justly suspect my want of Parts[1]—Women often pardon Actions when they will not Words; a little Companion gives 'em an Excuse.—Come, come, you will not be always cruel.

WIFE. Unhand me, Villain—help—

TOY. Nay, nay, I can stop your Mouth—[*As they struggle, she falls against the Closet Door, which opens, and discovers* Beaumont.] 'Sdeath, Sir *Harry Beaumont!* why who the devil thought to find you here? I beg ten thousand Pardons, if I have been the Cause of your Imprisonment—Let me blood, I must banter him a little—he dares not resent it, for fear I should tell.

WIFE. O! I'm undone—my Reputation's ruin'd! For Heaven's sake, Sir *Harry,* how came you there?

TOY. I suppose, Madam, Sir *Harry* offer'd this as a Piece of Gallantry; but I hope your Goodness will pardon him, for all the vain Attempts he may make on a Virtue so impregnable as yours—ha! ha! ha!

BEAU. Give over your ridiculous Mirth, or—

TOY. Fye, fye, Sir *Harry,* that's no proper Weapon to be us'd in a

---

1. **Parts:** intelligence, abilities.

Lady's Chamber—But, Sir *Harry,* you forget the Lady desir'd you to tell her how you came hither.

BEAU. Madam, I heartily beg pardon for the Surprize I have occasion'd you—but having some Business with Mr. *Graspall,* and finding nobody at home, I took the freedom to step into the Closet, which I knew to be well furnish'd with Books—designing no more than to amuse myself till he came home—I happen'd to meet with one which so agreeably entertain'd me, that till the opening of the Door, I had forgot where I was.

TOY. Hum! Mr. *Graspall* has indeed an admirable Collection—but Age has somewhat impair'd his Eye-sight, poor Man! I believe he seldom reads—And I must own 'tis a great Conveniency for a Gentleman, who has not Books of his own, to have the liberty of so fine a Library.

BEAU. Sir, I wish you either cou'd, or wou'd explain yourself—But if you harbour a Thought to the Prejudice of this Lady's Character, cou'd I discover it, I'd make such an Example of you, as should be a Terror to all talkative Coxcombs.

TOY. Who I, Sir *Harry?*

WIFE. The Aspersions of this Fool are intolerable—tho my Innocence should make me despise his Malice, and my Character not fear it, yet those of his own Stamp may believe the mean Reflections he may cast on me.

TOY. You see, Madam, what Inconveniencies attend Ill-nature; when you are kind, I'll—

WIFE. Peace, Screech-Owl—

Exit.

BEAU. Come, Sir, the Lady is now gone; and since I am the unhappy Cause of her Uneasiness, it lies upon me to vindicate her Reputation— A Fool's most dangerous Weapon is his Tongue, and I find there is no way to stop yours, but by cutting it out—Draw, Sir.

TOY. I don't like his Looks—Gad, I wish I had not been so witty—

Draw, Sir *Harry!* why I hope you are not in earnest—What draw on your Friend for a little harmless Rallery?[1]—if you have no more value for me, I'll shew you I love you better.—

BEAU. That shan't do, Sir.

TOY. Why, Sir *Harry,* I was but in jest as I hope to live—I vow to Gad I believe the Lady as chaste as the Moon, and her Virtue as conspicuous as the Stars in the Firmament—Draw quoth'a! What draw upon my Friend—Sir *Harry Beaumont!*—All the World shan't make me draw upon my Friend.

BEAU. Harkye, Sir, your Cowardice shan't skreen you another time— if ever I hear a word injurious of this Lady, assure yourself I shall justify her Honour with my Life.

Exit.

TOY. Pox! who would have thought he had lov'd fighting so well?— I'm glad I'm well off tho'—I'll trouble myself no more about her— there are as fine Women to be had without venturing one's Life for 'em. Now if I could but find some plausible Pretence to break with *Marilla,* I should be the most easy Man in the World; for

> When her Fortune's gone, the loveliest Woman
> In this wise Age is a fit Wife for no Man.

END OF THE SECOND ACT.

ACT III. SCENE I

Enter Captain Gaylove, Courtly *laughing, and* Shamble *very fine.*

GAY. Ha! ha! ha! how sawcy the Rogue looks?

COURT. Why he tells you his Grandeur must charm the Widow.

---

1. **Rallery:** raillery, jesting, teasing.

SHAM. Ha! ha! I have quite forgot my Dancing for want of Practice—but Business, State-Affairs, Intrigues, and one Hurry or another takes up all my time—Ha! ha! Pray Gentlemen stand by—Do you know who I am? Won't this do, Sir?

In an affected Tone.

COURT. Rarely!

Dancing in an awkward manner.

GAY. Excellent! if he can but keep up to his Character.

SHAM. O! Sir, there is no one thing in the World so soon learnt as the forgetting what one really is, in the Appearance of another—Humility is a Lesson few study with much Pleasure, and all, at some times, are truant from. Then why may not I, Sir *Tristram Shamtown,* forget I have been your Honour's Pimp and Serving Man.

COURT. Sir *Tristram.*

GAY. Aye, that Name was of my inventing. But pray, good Sir *Tristram,* don't so far forget your self, as to neglect the main Chance—take care to put the Widow off settling any Part of her Estate on her Nephew.

SHAM. No, no, Sir, never doubt it, I shall retain that Principle of Honour, to serve my Friends, when in so doing I doubly serve myself—If I marry the Widow, depend upon it not a foot of the Estate shall be parted with.—In that I go a great way in breaking off the designed Match between her Nephew and *Celemena.*

COURT. A great way—all in all! for I am satisfy'd Mr. *Fairman* will never sacrifice his Daughter to such a Fool as *Sneaksby,* without a Certainty of the Widow's Land for her Jointure.

GAY. Well, faith, I have a strong Opinion we shall succeed—prithee *Shamble* tell honest *Jenny,* Mrs. *Dogood* I think you call her now, that if she has not quite forgot past Kindnesses, she must lend her Assistance in this Affair; and to refresh her Memory, let her know 500

Pieces more are at her Service, the Moment *Sneaksby* quits his Pretensions to *Celemena*.

SHAM. I'll warrant you, Sir—but 'tis about the time she order'd me to come.

GAY. Come, shall we walk? Mr. *Fairman*, you know, was so obliging to desire we'd pass the Evening there.

COURT. With all my heart—tho' it is feeding me with the Fare of *Tantalus*[1]—I ought to shun the Sight of what I must desire, and yet am hopeless of enjoying.

GAY. Never despair, our Design on *Toywell* may have more effect than you imagine.—Farewell *Shamble,* good Luck attend thee—if anything happens, I shall be here, or at Mr. *Fairman's.*

Exit.

SHAM. I have a good Stock of Impudence, and that often carries the day.

> And they went to a Widow's House,
> And she was dancing naked,
> And all the Tunes the Piper play'd,
> Was take it, Widow, take it.[2]

Exit.

Enter Sneaksby *and* Tim.

SNEAK. Come, *Tim,* let's go close together—I can't abide to be out when it grows towards dark, now here be all these Soldiers come down—they are plaguy mischievous, they say—.

---

1. **Tantalus:** child of Zeus and Pluto who gave away the secrets of the gods and whose punishment was to be bound in the river Hades. Whenever he tried to drink, the water receded; and whenever he tried to reach the succulent fruit, it remained out of his reach. Thus, he was tantalized but never satisfied.

2. **And they . . . take it:** unidentified.

TIM. Ay, Sir, my Mother us'd to tell me terrible Stories of 'em.

SNEAK. 'Twan't well done of Aunt, so 'twan't, to turn one out as soon as ever one come—She might have made one eat a bit of somewhat first, methinks—what did I care if I did not see my Mistress till to-morrow, we an't to be marry'd to-night.

TIM. Mayhap, Sir, she thought 'twou'd not look respectful enough.—

SNEAK. What did I care, I have paid respect to her long enough, I think—besides, is not she a going to be my Wife, and as long as we know one another's Mind, what signifies making such a to do about it?

TIM. Why, Sir, you told me you had never ask'd her the Question yet.

SNEAK. What then? Aunt has, and Father-in-law that must be, and that's as well—Oh here he comes.—

Enter Fairman.

FAIR. Your Servant, Father-in-law—Mr. *Sneaksby* your Servant—how happens it your Aunt is not with you—I expected her.—

SNEAK. Why, Aunt gives her Service—but she has some great Visiter to come to-night belike,[1] for all the House is stuck with Candles, and she is woundy[2] fine.

FAIR. An humble Servant, it may be.

SNEAK. Mayhap so, I never ask Questions.

FAIR. I wish I had the Writings seal'd tho'.

Aside.

SNEAK. 'Tis nothing to me, you know she has promis'd me the Estate.

FAIR. If she should marry, I much question whether she'll keep her word——I must be satisfy'd.

---

1. **belike:** most likely, probably.
2. **woundy:** very, extremely.

[*Aside.*] But come, Sir, let's go in, my Daughter expects you.

SNEAK. Ay, Father-in-law—but I wish you'd let me have a bit of somewhat first, for *Tim* and I are plaguy hungry, and Aunt wou'd not let us stay to eat a bit.

FAIR. You shall command anything my House affords.

Exit.

Enter Dogood *and* Shamble.

DO. Well, now I think 'tis almost impossible our Plot shou'd fail— the Widow is half distracted in Love with you, before she sees you.

SHAM. My Person cannot but secure the Conquest.

DO. You wou'd have laugh'd if you had seen how greedily she swallow'd the Bait—but you must be sure to strut and look big, and not lose an Inch of your Grandeur.—

SHAM. O, you need not fear—none look so proud and scornful as your new made Gentry.

DO. I have told her, I waited on a Sister of yours in *London;* that you have a good Estate in Possession, and another in Reversion;[1] that you are of a most ancient Family,—

SHAM. And my Name is—

DO. Sir *Tristram Shamtown*—of *Shamtown-Hall*—but I hear her coming, step into the next Room, and you shall hear a little of her Humour.

Exit Sham.

Enter Widow.

WID. And did Sir *Tristram* tell you he'd be sure to come?

DO. I warrant you, Madam, he'll not fail; for tho' I say it, he had always a great Respect for me.

---

1. **Reversion:** a future interest in real property, that part of the grantor's estate still retained by him when he conveys away an estate smaller than he has; Susan Staves, "Glossary," *Married Women's Separate Property.*

WID. I long to see him—how do I look, *Dogood?*

DO. Perfectly amiable, Madam.

WID. I think I am bloated to-day—[*Pulls out a Pocket-Glass.*[1]] Here, pull this Ribband a little more to my Face—so, there, 'tis well enough now—well, I don't like myself, 'tis impossible a Man of his Quality shou'd take a fancy to me.

DO. 'Tis rather impossible he shou'd not, Madam. But hark, somebody knocks—'tis he for certain.

WID. Well, I vow, I believe something will come of this, for I never had such a Palpitation since the Day I first saw Mr. *Stately.*

Enter Servant.

SERV. A Gentleman enquires for Mrs. *Dogood;* he told me his name, but 'tis so hard a one, I have forgot it.

WID. It must be he—this Blockhead is us'd to nothing but the Vulgar—but if he continues with me, he must improve his Understanding.

DO. Desire the Gentleman to walk up.

WID. And do you hear, Loggerhead, be sure you pay him a great deal of Respect. [*Ex. Servant.*] I leave thee to receive him—I'll step into the next Room, and settle myself a little, and then return as if I did not know anybody was here.—

DO. Very well, Madam—and in the mean time, I'll be giving him a Character.

WID. That's my good Wench—and I'll reward thee.

Exit.

DO. They say good Actions reward themselves—but if my Project goes on as luckily as it begins, I am like to have Rewards from all Sides.

---

1. **Pocket-Glass:** small mirror.

Enter Shamble.

So, you have nothing to do, you see, but to summon the Governour, the Fort's ready to surrender.

SHAM. Egad, and I like the Situation of it extremely, it seems to want no Fortification.

DO. You see but the Outworks,[1] there's a Magazine[2] within, of Plate,[3] and Jewels, and old Broadpieces,[4] that have not seen the Sun these forty Years, enough to set the whole Country in a Blaze—But I hear her coming—now to your part.

SHAM. Ay, ay,—And your Lady is so fine a Woman you say, Mrs. *Dogood*?

Enter Widow.

DO. She's here, Sir *Tristram*.

WID. *Dogood!* bless me! I did not know you had anybody with you—

DO. A Gentleman you have often heard me talk of, Sir *Tristram Shamtown,* Madam.

WID. Oh Heav'ns! Sir *Tristram Shamtown!* I am asham'd to be caught thus in my Dishabillé[5]—and the House, O gad, the House is not fit for anybody to come into, much more a Gentleman of Sir *Tristram Shamtown's* Quality.

SHAM. Madam, 'tis impossible that anything can be more elegant than the Oeconomy[6] of ev'ry thing about you—I was perfectly charm'd

---

1. **Outworks:** detached, advance fortifications such as trenches.

2. **Magazine:** stock of ammunition.

3. **Plate:** silver and gold utensils and tableware of all kinds; trays and salt cellars are examples.

4. **Broadpieces:** common name for the "unite," the twenty-shilling coin, because it was thinner and broader than the guinea, which the government began minting in 1663.

5. **Dishabillé:** dressed in careless way, not fully dressed for the day.

6. **Oeconomy:** management.

with your House, till the Appearance of your Ladyship made me forget all but you.

WID. O Sir *Tristram!*

SHAM. O Madam!

WID. You are such a Courtier—

SHAM. You are such a Beauty—

WID. So full of Gallantry.—

SHAM. So full of Charms—

WID. Nay, Sir *Tristram*—

SHAM. So all over engaging, that it wou'd puzzle a Logician to define your Brightness.

WID. This is too much, Sir *Tristram.*

SHAM. Madam, everybody that has Eyes must admire you—what a Shape—pray, Mrs. *Dogood,* did you ever see so exact a Symmetry of Body?

WID. O fye, Sir *Tristram!* you make me blush to death—

SHAM. What a Foot! Mrs. *Dogood,* pray look at your Lady's Foot— there's a Foot proportion'd to the Body; the Body suited to the Grandeur of the Face; and the Air of the Face bespeaks the Grandeur of the Soul—

WID. I vow, Sir *Tristram,* you quite confound me—but you Men of Quality are so used to Rallery—[1]

SHAM. How, Madam! another such a word you'd make me curse my Stars, grow mad, and die—Is there any need to say I adore you, after having seen you?—

WID. Alas, Sir *Tristram,* I have nothing in me worth the regard of a Man of your Quality—

---

1. **Rallery:** raillery, banter, repartée.

SHAM. Ah, Madam, you cannot be ignorant of the Pow'r of your Charms, and but say this because you think me undeserving of your Favour—

WID. I protest you wrong me, Sir. Sir *Tristram Shamtown* cannot but know any Woman wou'd be proud of his Addresses.

SHAM. If you receive 'em, Madam, let all your Sex besides think as they please—Mrs. *Dogood,* you know I cannot flatter; help me to convince your Lady of the Sincerity of my Passion—for my Stock of Speeches are almost exhausted.

DO. What do you think of him, Madam?

WID. O charming! but dost thou think he really admires me so much as he says?—

DO. I never saw a Man so much transported.

WID. What a difference between a Man of Quality, and the Vulgar!— Mr. *Stately* never courted me in this Manner.

SHAM. Speak, Madam, what must I do to prove myself your Beauty's Slave—Will nothing but my Death suffice?

WID. O Heaven forbid, Sir *Tristram!* I wou'd not do so much Injustice to the World, whose chief Ornament you are.

SHAM. Your Goodness is equal to your Beauty.

WID. Will you favour me so far, Sir *Tristram,* as to take part of a Collation,[1] just what the House affords.

SHAM. A Sallad, with your Ladyship, is preferable to Ortelans[2] in any other Company.

WID. *Dogood,* lead the way, and see if ev'ry thing is ready.

DO. Yes, Madam—

---

1. **Collation:** a light meal.
2. **Ortelans:** scraps, leftovers.

Exit.

WID. Sir *Tristram!*

SHAM. Exquisite Hand!

WID. Nay, Sir *Tristram.*

SHAM. Madam, I obey.

Exit.

Enter Celemena, Marilla.

MAR. Sure never any two were so nearly ally'd in their Misfortunes as ourselves—Was there ever such a Wretch in Human Kind, as *Sneaksby?*

CEL. Never, unless it be Mr. *Toywell;* but if I had no more to fear from the Resentment of a living Father, than you have from a dead one, I shou'd not think my Condition very deplorable.

MAR. You talk strangely; were mine alive, I might hope by Prayers and Tears to move him, or that the Sight of *Toywell's* Indifference might change his Mind; but as he's past the Knowledge of all this, and has my Vow, nothing remains for me, but Patience in my Sufferings.

CEL. Well, I find there's no persuading you—but for my part, I'm resolv'd—

MAR. On what?

CEL. Never to be a Wife to *Sneaksby.*

MAR. But how will you avoid it?

CEL. Nay, that I can't tell.

Sighs.

MAR. Here comes one may inform you, for if I know anything of the Language of the Eyes, you understand one another's already.

CEL. Psha!

MAR. Farewell, I'll be no Interruption.

Enter Gaylove.

CEL. Why, *Marilla, Marilla.*

GAY. Whither in such haste, Madam?

MAR. Your Pardon, Captain; I have Business.

Exit.

GAY. Have you told her our Design on *Toywell?*

CEL. No, nor I would not have you—I know not but she may be whimsically nice enough to disapprove the Means, tho' she would bless the Effect.

GAY. 'Tis not impossible—but methinks, Madam, you stand here prodigiously indolent and degagée[1]—I fancy you forget to-morrow is your Wedding-day——What, no Preparations? Spouse that must be, is arriv'd, I see—but I think, at present, he seems more inclinable to pay his Addresses to a good Supper, than a Mistress—As I came thro the Hall just now, I saw him lay about him, like a Man of Mettle,[2] at a piece of cold roast Beef, and a Tankard of Ale.

CEL. 'Tis ungenerous in you, Captain, to insult.

GAY. Who I, Madam? I protest the farthest from it in the World—Why I thought you had been infinitely pleas'd with the Match—and that no Discourse could have been so agreeable as that which mention'd Mr. *Sneaksby*—And without doubt the Squire will make you prodigiously happy in a Husband—

CEL. Well, Captain, well.

GAY. If your ready Compliance with your Father's Commands, had

---

1. **degagée:** relaxed, casual.
2. **Mettle:** spirit, courage.

not assur'd me 'twas your own Desire, I had a Project in my Head, which would certainly have left you at your liberty.

CEL. For Heaven's sake, what?

GAY. No, Madam no; far be it from me to separate Hearts so strictly join'd—Marry, Madam, the lovely beloved Youth;

> Enjoy th' unenvy'd Title of his Wife,
> While I at distance languish out my Life.

CEL. I hate your Rallery—when one has a mind to be serious—But tell me what you mean, and I'll forgive it.

GAY. That won't do, Madam; I have you in my power now, and you can't blame me if I follow your own Example in making use of it.

CEL. Duce take you—Well, but what must I do to bribe you then?

GAY. Why faith, Madam, no less than cancelling all the Injunctions you laid me under this Morning; that you will immediately, on the breaking off of this Match, put me in possession of the same Title your Father designs to give *Sneaksby*.

CEL. O the impudent Demand! So to escape one Slavery, I must throw myself into another, which, for ought I know, may be as bad.

GAY. Nay, if you think so—

CEL. Stay, have you no Conscience?

GAY. You hear the Price, Madam.

CEL. I thought a Lock of my Hair, or my Picture, had been a Reward, the greatest your Ambition could have ask'd for the highest Obligation.

GAY. No, no, Madam—Knight-Errantry has been a long time out of fashion; I shan't bate an Ace[1] of what I told you—but see, here comes your Doom, if you persist in Obstinacy.

CEL. Cursed, teazing, charming Devil.

---

1. **bate an Ace:** abate in the slightest, decrease by a jot or tiny bit.

Enter Fairman *and* Sneaksby.

SNEAK. I hope, Father-in-law that must be, you have told her every thing, for I hate a great many Words. An' she were a Man now, I should know what to say to her; but mayhap she mayn't like my way.

FAIR. Well, well; she knows your Mind.

SNEAK. Why that's well enough—Your Servant, Mistress.

CEL. Your Servant, Sir.

FAIR. Captain, if you please, we'll walk into the next Room.

GAY. I wait upon you, Sir. You'll remember the Conditions, Madam.

Exit.

CEL. Hang you—Won't you please to sit, Sir?

SNEAK. No, I thank you, I'd as lief stand[1]—What must I say now? I wonder what made 'em go away?

CEL. I hope he has not Courage enough to be impertinent.

SNEAK. I suppose, Mrs. *Celemena,* you know that Aunt and your Father think it convenient our Wedding should be to-morrow.

CEL. 'Tis so design'd, Sir, I hear.

SNEAK. Nay, as the Saying is, as long as 'tis to be, the sooner 'tis over the better—for my part, I have nothing to say against it; have you?—

CEL. Not that I know of, Sir.

SNEAK. Why then, I may go to the Company again, mayn't I?

CEL. With all my heart, Sir—

SNEAK. Nay, do you go first; I an't so unmannerly neither.

---

1. **as lief stand:** just as soon, it would be just as acceptable to stand.

CEL. O intolerable! Heaven grant the Captain be in earnest—or I shall lose my Senses.

Exit.

Enter Graspall *and* Wife.

GRASP. You know, Spouse, the Duty of a Husband is to love and provide for his Wife; and, in return, the Wife is oblig'd to obey the Commands, and study the Interest of her Husband.

WIFE. I don't know that I have given any occasion for this Recital of a Wife's Duty.

GRASP. Far be it from me to accuse thee—I mention Obedience to a Husband, not that I believe thee to have err'd in it, but that it being fresh in thy Memory, thou might'st not boggle at anything which tends to the enriching thy Husband.

WIFE. To what purpose can this Harangue be made? Sir, let me know what you expect from me, and I shall answer with a ready Compliance.

GRASP. Indeed thou'rt very good, and thou would'st not scruple anything for thy old Lovy, ha! *Pudsy?*[1]

WIFE. I hope you can command me nothing I can make a Scruple of obeying you in—But why all these Precautions?

GRASP. Well, well, I ha' done—I ha' done—But remember that Obedience to a Husband ought to be the *Primum Mobile*[2] in a Woman—Here, *Pudsy,* read this.

WIFE. Heavens! a Letter from Sir *Harry.*

GRASP. Read, *Pudsy,* it's prettily turn'd—Come, I'll read it for thee.

---

1. **Pudsy:** adjective meaning "plump"; usually a term of endearment for babies.

2. **Primum Mobile:** prime mover; in Medieval astronomy, the primum mobile was the tenth sphere of the universe and was thought to make the other spheres revolve around the earth with it.

Madam,

What I feel in the Contemplation of your Cruelty this Morning, is not to be express'd: I beg you will be at least, so just, as to let me know to what I owe so great a Misfortune.

Your Everlasting Admirer,
Beaumont.

Now, *Pudsy,* you shall see if I had not a tender Regard for your Youth, and a just Consideration of my own Age. I fitted him with a Letter in your Name.

WIFE. I am undone—O! Sir, I beg you on my Knees, whatever Appearances may be against me, you will not think me guilty of Dishonour; for on my Soul—

GRASP. Rise prithee, I am not jealous—Hear what I writ to him—I have the Copy—O here 'tis.

WIFE. What will this come to?

GRASP. Now, *Pudsy,* you shall hear.

Sir,

The Satisfaction you require of me shall be made you, if you will give yourself the trouble to meet me in the little Field behind our Garden, at four a-clock this Afternoon—

Your Humble Servant,
Susanna Graspall.

WIFE. And did you send him this impudent Letter in my Name?

GRASP. Have patience—Condemn me when you have reason, *Pudsy.*

WIFE. I know not what to think.

GRASP. The appointed Hour, and the Lover, came together; whom I accosted with, *Sir* Harry, *your humble Servant,* and so forth.

WIFE. Heavens! how I tremble?

GRASP. And then it seems, said I, by this Letter, which accidentally fell into my hands, that you have some Affairs to negotiate with my

Wife. Now she being under Covert-Baron,[1] can transact nothing without by leave; for which reason, and believing my Age and Experience might enable me to treat more effectually with you, I answer'd your Letter—Nay, Sir *Harry,* said I, don't blush (for he did look cursedly confus'd, that he did) a Sword and a Wife, said I, are both useless to me; and as I wear one for the Ornament of my Dress, so I marry'd the other as a Grace to my House—

WIFE. Where will this end?

GRASP. Now, Sir *Harry,* says I, whoever has the use of my Sword, it's but reasonable he pay for the furbishing[2]—and if you really have so violent a Passion for my Wife, as your Letter intimates, pay the Money down she has expended me in Clothes, and allow me some Consideration for the Pity I have of your Sufferings, and I here give you free Ingress, Egress and Regress[3]—I was some time before I could persuade him that I was in earnest.

WIFE. In earnest, Sir!—

GRASP. Ay, *Pudsy;* for a good while I could not make him believe I really design'd him the Favour of paying me 2000 *l.* the Price I set for giving him the liberty to—visit thee now and then, that's all—But I convinc'd him at last, and he immediately sent the Sum propos'd to my House, in a strong Box, with Condition only of keeping the Key, till you set your Hand to the Covenant. Now, *Pudsy,* if thou hast any Love for thy old Hubby, never let such a Sum depart the House, by a foolish Denial—if thou dost, it is as bad as robbing me, for whatever I have in my Custody, I always look upon as my own.

WIFE. Is it possible you can have so mean a Spirit?—Or do you

---

1. **Covert-Baron:** literally, covered by a husband; the condition and position of a married woman, who could not transact certain kinds of business unless premarital contracts had been signed to give her power over property. At this time, a married woman was so much under the "influence and protection" of her husband that she was not responsible for debts and also could not be prosecuted for some property crimes.

2. **furbishing:** cleaning, polishing.

3. **Ingress, Egress, and Regress:** the formulaic sequence of terms of access and use in property law documents.

believe, if you have so sordid and groveling a Soul, that I can, regardless of[1] my Fame, and lost to Vertue, yield to such a detested Bargain.

GRASP. Dear, dear Pudsy—don't be too hasty in resolving—consider, will Fame ever get the 2000 *l.* Remember, Pudsy! two thousand Pounds! when I think what a Sum it is, I sweat at the Apprehension of Vertue.

WIFE. And would you be a Cuckold?

GRASP. Two thousand Pounds, *Pudsy*—

WIFE. Despis'd and pointed at.

GRASP. Two thousand Pounds.—

WIFE. Become the publick Scorn, and all for Gain, a little trifling Trash.

GRASP. A little, dost thou call it? I wish thy Vertue has not flown into thy Head, and turn'd thy Brain—Why what dost thou value thy Vertue at?

WIFE. The World cannot repair the loss of it.

GRASP. Ah! to be sure thou art a little touch'd, but don't think that I'll be fool'd out of the strong Box—if you are mad, I am not; and you had best consent quietly to what I desire, or I shall make you— 'Sbud[2] I've been too humble—

WIFE. No Husband's Power extends to force the Execution of unlawful Commands—But sure you cannot be so dead to Shame, to wish it seriously.

GRASP. Seriously! why there 'tis now—Don't I tell you that 2000 *l.* are in a strong Box, and that I have that Box in keeping—and that there is nothing hinders me from being Master of it, but your refusing to perform Articles.

WIFE. Monstrous Stupidity! not to be believ'd!

---

1. **regardless of:** without regard for reputation.

2. **'Sbud:** short for "God's blood," an oath or strong affirmative ejaculation.

GRASP. But you'll believe it, I hope, when you find Sir *Harry* tells you the same thing—I have appointed him to come this Night—I'll give you half an Hour to consider on't—but would advise you not to be a Fool, nor think to make me so—

Exit.

WIFE. Thou mak'st thyself a wretched, wicked Fool: Was ever anything like this?

Enter Amadea.

AMAD. Start not, Madam, I have overheard all, and know not whether my Admiration of your Virtue, or Amazement at your Husband's base Intention, most takes up my Thoughts.

WIFE. Expos'd to him—Heav'ns! this Story will be the Jest of the whole Country—Whatever are my Husband's Faults, is not your business to examine—and 'twas unmannerly to listen to our private Conference.

AMAD. I doubt not of your Pardon for this and many other Actions, which have seem'd impertinent, when you shall know my Reasons for Curiosity; which now, fully convinc'd of your Virtue, and confident of your Good-nature, and Compassion, I shall make no scruple of revealing—I am a Woman, Madam.

WIFE. A Woman!

AMAD. My Name *Amadea*—descended from a Family I need not blush to own—blest with a Fortune equal to my Birth, and bred in expectation of the fairest Hopes—Sir *Harry Beaumont* once was not asham'd to own to all who knew him, he thought me worthy of the tenderest Passion.—

WIFE. A Woman! and Sir *Harry Beaumont*'s Mistress—

AMAD. His Wife, if Vows can make me so—therefore in such a Circumstance, you cannot wonder I took all Opportunities to dive into the Secret of his coming hither—You shall hereafter be inform'd of all the Particulars of my Story—but the time allow'd you for Consideration is so short, I must defer it, and only beg you (for in your power alone it is) to help a wretched Woman, and save me from eternal Ruin and Despair.

WIFE. Alas! what can I do?

AMAD. Seem to consent to what your Husband asks, and leave the rest to me.

WIFE. How will that serve you?

AMAD. You shall know anon—In the mean time, I conjure you to dissemble a Compliance—your Virtue shall not suffer by your Charity to me.

WIFE. Well, you shall persuade me.

AMAD. —

> Heav'n will reward the generous Aid you lend,
> And the soft Wishes of my Soul befriend:
> Since, true to Virtue, my Endeavours aim
> Only the dear false Rover to reclaim.

END OF THE THIRD ACT.

ACT IV. SCENE I

Enter Dogood, Shamble, *and* Widow.

WID. Indeed, Sir *Tristram*, this Offer of your Sister for my Nephew convinces me the most of any thing of your Affection—I wish there were a way for me to get off with Mr. *Fairman*.

SHAM. Madam, the Passion I have for you makes me study your Interest, which I think you ought to prefer to Ceremony—My Sister's Fortune, which is 5000 *l.* more than Mr. *Fairman* proffers with his Daughter, is in her own hands, and I'll undertake she shall be content with only her own Money settled on her.

WID. That is obliging indeed—I was certainly bewitch'd when I agreed to Mr. *Fairman's* Proposal—But alas! I did not think of marrying then, nor am I sure I shall yet.

SHAM. How, Madam! not sure of marrying? You have undone my Quiet—drove me to Despair, and without you retract those cruel Words, you shall very soon see the fatal Consequence.

WID. Nay, Sir *Tristram,* I only said—

SHAM. O you have ruin'd me! Farewel Board-Wages[1] and Lace'd Liveries![2] Farewell all Joy, all Peace of Mind, all Happiness—Welcome ye solitary Groves and baleful Yew, ye purling Streams and cooing Doves; behold the unhappy *Shamtown* oppress'd with Grief, and sunk with sad Despair, joins in your Moan! the cruel Stately scorns my Passion.

WID. Sir *Tristram,* won't you hear me?

SHAM. Oh! can I bear a Doubt of that Happiness I so ardently desire, and yet live? No, no, Death will soon ease me of these Pains—I will rip up this faithful Breast, and shew my panting Heart.

WID. Sir *Tristram,* I did not say that—

SHAM. Was it for this you gave me hopes? Did you raise me up but to make my Fall the greater?

WID. Why, Sir *Tristram!* Lard,[3] I think he's run mad indeed—What shall I say to him, *Dogood?*

DO. Tell him you'll marry him this minute—Say any thing.

WID. Then, Sir *Tristram,* to show you—

SHAM. What unhappy Destiny drove me here, or first fix'd my Eyes on that lovely cruel Woman—Oh that I could forget I ever saw you!

---

1. **Board-Wages:** wages allowed to servants for buying their own food.

2. **Liveries:** commonly, the suit of clothes given servants and designed with distinctive colors and trim so that they could be recognized as employed by an individual or family. The term sometimes meant the provisions, cloth, and allowance given to servants, including actors and actresses in the royal companies.

3. **Lard:** Lord.

WID. Why, Sir *Tristram*, to convince you that I am not cruel, send for a Parson, and make me my Lady *Shamtown*.

SHAM. Ha! do you mock my Grief? Nay, then Death must be my Portion.

Offers to fall on his Sword.

DO. Ah!

WID. Ah! for Goodness sake, Sir *Tristram*, I am in earnest, I vow and swear—I will marry you this minute, if you please.

SHAM. Can it be possible—But I'll not believe I am so happy.

WID. Then follow me, and put it to the proof.

Exit.

DO. You'd make a rare Actor.

SHAM. Send for a Parson, lest some unlucky Accident should prevent us—I'm quite out of breath.

Exit.

Enter Celemena *and* Gaylove.

GAY. Well, Madam, what think you of my Plots? You see, as near as your Cousin *Marilla* thought herself to *Hymen*, my Contrivance is in a fair way to make her lose sight of him.

CEL. I can't but say you are like to be successful enough, and I should be very apt to employ you in the same Business, if you were not so exorbitant in your Demands.

GAY. Good Workmen, Madam, will have good Prices—I would fain do your Business once for all—If I should be compassionate enough to hew off this Rub in your way for little or nothing, who knows but another may start up—No, no, let me see you at your Journey's end—

Lodge you safe in Matrimony, and I'll trust to your Management afterwards.

CEL. You are very confident of your own Abilities, I find—But suppose you should be mistaken—Many a Woman has been glad of a Fool after Matrimony, that she would have despis'd before.

GAY. That's because then she has a Husband too wise.

Enter Courtly.

COURT. Dear *Gaylove,* I am infinitely oblig'd to thee—*Toywell* is grown so insolent to *Marilla,* that if she should still persist in her Resolution of marrying him, I think 'twould cure my Passion.

CEL. 'Twas almost come to a downright Quarrel, when we left 'em.

COURT. Nothing to what is now—Here they come, pray observe 'em.

Enter Marilla *and* Toywell.

MAR. I wish, Mr. *Toywell,* you'd forbear your Visits, unless you could behave yourself with more good Manners—You play the Husband too soon.

TOY. And to deal plainly with you, Madam, I think you play the Wife too soon.

MAR. If I never give you leave to call me by that Title, your Usage would almost excuse my Breach of Vow.

TOY. Why really, Madam, I believe, of all Womankind, your Charms have the least effect on me—and I don't think 'twould be the death of me, if you should refuse me that Blessing of calling you my Wife— If that's your Desire, pray let me know it, probably I may have Tenderness enough for you, to give up my Pretensions on very easy Terms.

MAR. Say on what? say on any—Leave me but a Competency[1] for Bread, and take the rest of my Fortune.

---

1. **Competency:** enough; sufficiency enough for comfort.

TOY. Which is little enough, if she knew all—Look ye, Madam, tho you are so cruel as to tax me with Indifference, to shew you how vast a Regard I have for your Ease, I will forego all the Happiness I propos'd in the Possession of so much Beauty, and now swear from my Soul, in the Presence of these Witnesses, that upon no account will I, *John Toywell,* ever be the Husband of you, *Marilla Fairman.*

MAR. I thank you, and with Joy receive my Liberty.

COURT. Now, Madam, may I not hope?—

MAR. The Usage I have receiv'd from him, is sufficient to make me hate all Men.

Exit.

COURT. Yes, Madam.

Exit.

GAY. Why, are you in earnest, Mr. *Toywell?* really quitted your Pretensions?

TOY. Really! Ay, Captain—'twou'd have been carrying the Jest too far, to have marry'd her without a Portion.[1]—There stands one, and a good agreeable Woman—Egad, I think I'll make Love to her.

GAY. But you know she's to be marry'd to *Sneaksby.*

TOY. It's no matter for that—do you think she'd be such a Fool to refuse me for him?

GAY. But you have affronted her Cousin, don't you believe she'll resent it?

TOY. Psha! I'll tell her 'twas for her Sake.

GAY. Nay, you may try: Madam, here's a Gentleman is fallen desperately in Love with you on the sudden—

---

1. **Portion:** dowry.

CEL. Who? What do you mean?

GAY. That he must explain.

TOY. Madam, I long have ador'd you; 'tis impossible to tell you with how much Ardor; that, your Glass must inform you, because nothing else can give you any just Idea of your Perfections.

CEL. The Fool's distracted sure; or is it your Contrivance too?

GAY. No, faith, Madam, 'tis all his own—

TOY. Till this happy Moment, Madam, I was not at my own Disposal—but was oblig'd to smother all the Transports of my Soul, when I beheld you—

GAY. Hold, Mr. *Toywell*—take care—here's a Rival approaching, trebly arm'd with Mead,[1] Syder,[2] and Metheglin.[3]

TOY. What, *Sneaksby* drunk! O the Putt![4]

Enter Sneaksby *drunk.*

SNEAK. Adod![5] Father-in-law keeps good Liquor; but 'tis plaguy heady—who's here? O Mistress! Wife that must be, here, tie my Neckcloth[6]—

CEL. Oh hideous! really Sir, I don't know how.

SNEAK. Not know how! you are very fit for a Wife indeed! mayhap you'll never learn.

CEL. 'Tis possible.

TOY. O the Brute, how he smells! sure, Madam, you cannot consent to bury your Youth and Beauty in the Arms of that Wretch—

---

1. **Mead:** alcoholic beverage made from fermented honey.
2. **Syder:** cider, then a beverage made from fermented fruit juice, not always apple.
3. **metheglin:** spiced mead, originated in Wales.
4. **Putt:** ignorant, awkward clown; country idiot.
5. **Adod:** Ah, God!
6. **Neckcloth:** cravat, scarf.

CEL. Whatever he is, I prefer him to a Fop—Mr. *Sneaksby,* you are not apt to be jealous, I hope—Mr. *Toywell* is making Love to me—How do you approve of it?

SNEAK. Making Love to you—ugh!

TOY. Well, Sir; and what then, Sir? what if I do, Sir—Egad I may bully him.

GAY. I don't know but these two Coxcombs might afford some Diversion—if we had time to work em to any Pitch.

SNEAK. Ugh—why then, mayhap, you may make me a Cuckold—

TOY. And what then, Sir?

SNEAK. Ha! ugh! what then Sir—why then? mayhap I may break your Sconce,[1] I'll tell you but that.

TOY. How, Sir! gad I'll charm her with my Courage. Do you see this, Sir?

Draws.

SNEAK. Why Mistress, do you stand there and see your Husband that is to be—murder'd—but he shall kill you first, I'll tell you but that.

GAY. O Sir! he'll do you no hurt—Come, put up, Mr. *Toywell,* put up.

SNEAK. Nay, you shan't stir.

CEL. Out, filthy Creature!

SNEAK. What's the Matter—ugh—

CEL. Oh insufferable! Captain, help me.

GAY. Ha, ha, ha—come Mr. *Toywell,* you see your Antagonist is not *se defendendo*[2]—'twill be generous to lend your Arm to help him in.

---

1. **Sconce:** head.

2. **se defendendo:** legal term for "in self-defence."

CEL. Oh, I am poison'd!

Exit.

TOY. In Complaisance to you, Capt.—fough! how he stinks.

SNEAK. Ugh! What are you doing—Murder, Murder!—where are you carrying me? Murder!

Enter Servants.

I SERV. Murder! What's the Matter?

GAY. Why, your young Master that is to be, as he says, is a little overtaken, that's all.

I SERV. O, the Squire's drunk.

SNEAK. Murder, Murder!

GAY. There; there lug him in—

Exit.

Enter Beaumont *and* Graspall.

BEAU. Well, my kind Sollicitor,[1] what Hopes? shall we enjoy our Mistress, or not? Here's the Key, old *Mammon*,[2] gives you Admittance to your Yellow Beauties—methinks thy Looks foretel Success, and say, your Wife gives ear to Reason—

GRASP. Ah, Sir *Harry,* what Pains have I taken?

BEAU. But to what purpose, my old *Plutus?*[3] What's the Success; is she still cruel? and must I send for the Box?

GRASP. When the Box goes, your Suit ends, good Sir *Harry*—Ev'n

---

1. **Sollicitor:** instigator, partner, lawyer.

2. **Mammon:** god of this world, a lover of wealth and material things; Sir Epicure Mammon in Ben Jonson's *The Alchemist* (production 1610; publication 1612) is a worldly sensualist.

3. **Plutus:** Greek god of riches; Jupiter blinded him so that he would distribute wealth to both the just and the unjust.

Jove had been repuls'd, if a Show'r of Gold had not introduc'd him[1]—
my Reasons had, I hope, some effect, and I left her—

BEAU. How, my dear *Graspall*?

GRASP. Like the Sea after a Storm, tho' the Winds are laid, there yet
remains some Swell—which must have time to settle—But the Key,
Sir *Harry*.

BEAU. Nay, I must have some Assurance that I don't part with such
a Sum for nothing, the Minute your Wife consents—

GRASP. Consents! 'sbud she had as good meet a hungry Lion, as pro-
nounce the first Letter of a Denial—I'll have the Letters *N.O.* struck
out of the Alphabet, except to poor Rogues that come for Money, and
there, Self-preservation makes it lawful.

BEAU. Farewel.

Exit.

GRASP. I'm in the House, if you want Help—Since I can't persuade
him out of the Key, I'll force the Box; let him take the same Method
if he pleases, with his Mistress.—Bless me! that Sir *Harry*, esteem'd a
Man of Wit, can part with such a Sum, for such a Bauble as a Woman!

Exit.

Enter Mrs. Graspall, Beaumont.

WIFE. And is it possible then, Sir *Harry*, that you can have join'd with
my Husband in an Attempt at once so ridiculous and base—but tho'
your Gold has had this Influence in his sordid Nature, know, I despise
the Man who dares believe 'twill bribe me out of my Honour.

BEAU. Far be it from me, Madam, ever to have harbour'd such a

---

1. **Jove . . . him:** another name for Jupiter, supreme Roman deity, lord of heaven and prince
of light. He desired Danae, who had been locked in a tower by her father, and entered her
chamber as a shower of gold.

Thought; and as the Proposal was made by your Husband, 'tis he alone you shou'd condemn.

WIFE. But you agreed to't.

BEAU. If I had not, you might have believ'd I had thought so small a Sum more valuable than your Favour.

WIFE. You have taken a very wrong Method to obtain it; But as for him, base, mean-spirited, and sordid as he is, he is my Husband still— nor will I wrong him, tho' by his own Consent.

BEAU. Can you have so much value for a Man, who, tastless of your Charms, and ignorant of the Treasure he is master of, wou'd barter it for Trash—if no Compassion for my Sufferings wou'd move you, methinks the Injury he does you, shou'd prompt you to revenge.

WIFE. What you call revenging Injuries, is being accessary to 'em.

BEAU. Your Husband has transfer'd his Right to me; and if deaf to Arguments, has giv'n me Pow'r to seize—

WIFE. Which if you dare attempt—

BEAU. Be not frighted, Madam; I never gave you cause to think I'd be a Villain—Honour has always been the Guide of my Actions— and 'tis that now whispers me, No Epithets so vile, as that of Ravisher.

WIFE. And does it not inform you too, you ought not to ask of me what Honour forbids me to grant—you look confounded—Oh, Sir *Harry!* how forcible is Truth, tho' ne'er so plainly utter'd?—Not all your Learning, Wit, or Artiface, can form an Answer in Contradiction to this short Demand.

BEAU. Madam, I will not answer on this Theme—because I know that all the Arguments I cou'd bring, wou'd, to a Woman of your Temper, appear too weak to convince you that all those Conversations, which the World calls criminal, are not also really dishonourable in themselves—nay, I will own to you, that I cou'd wish there were a Possibility for me to love you less, unless my Passion cou'd appear in a more noble Light.

WIFE. 'Tis generously confess'd—but why will you then persist to urge a Suit your Reason does condemn?

BEAU. Ah, lovely Creature—you may as well ask Madmen why they rave—but do not mistake me; when I say I wish I lov'd you less, 'tis not because my Reason tells me 'tis a Fault, but because it is not in my pow'r to give you so convincing a Proof as I wou'd do, of my sincere Affection: the Flame I feel for you, is in it self so pure, I grieve it shou'd appear in any Likeness with those unconstant Fires which base Desires create; I tremble when I approach you; and tho' I'd forfeit Life to touch that Hand, so fearful am I to offend, I dare not ask it— Consider, Madam, and justly weigh the difference between us.—Did *Toywell* treat you thus?

WIFE. That Wretch's Impudence was owing to his Folly—if I look into your Designs, they are the same; and you, but with more Art, wou'd ruin me.

BEAU. By Heav'n I wou'd not—your Reputation shou'd be sacred and unblasted—the dear, the happy Secret safe lodg'd within my Soul, shou'd take no Air, nor let in the least room for a Conjecture—then for your Fears, those little Fears, which all your Sex are prone to, and which the Inconstancy of ours too frequently gives Cause for, I'd follow you, as now, with Sighs and Pray'rs, and ardent Vows of everlasting Passion.

WIFE. Then you'll allow that Constancy's the only Test of true Affection.

BEAU. Most sure it is, the only certain one.

WIFE. How am I then secure of yours, till I have purchas'd the Experiment at a Rate too dear—I must resign my Honour, my Vertue, and my Peace of Mind, before I can promise myself the least Assurance I have not done all this for an ungrateful Man—

BEAU. There are a thousand Marks by which you may distinguish which Passions will be lasting, and which not—and if repeated Vows and Imprecations can have Force—

WIFE. No, Sir *Harry;* I know with how much ease you men absolve yourselves the Breach of Vows in an Affair of this nature—but since you have confest that Constancy's the only Proof of true Affection, answer me, did you ne'er love before?

BEAU. Suppose I did; if I hereafter shall love none but you, the former Errors of my Fancy may be forgiv'n.

WIFE. But tell me if you did; and I conjure you, speak with the same Sincerity as you wou'd answer Heav'n—

BEAU. What can she mean? few Men, Madam, I believe, who have travell'd so far as I have done, had such Variety of Conversations, (some of which perhaps have not been over-nice) and seen such Numbers of fine Women, can boast an entire Continency.[1] I do not deny but I have met Temptations in my way, which Youth and Inadvertency, at some unguarded Hours, have yielded to.

WIFE. I speak not of those slight and transient Passions, but of a Flame which bore the show of Honourable—did you not—answer without Equivocation, did you not, (neglecting all the rest) never address one Favourite Fair?

BEAU. Ha! But whate'er she aims at, I scorn the Baseness of a Lye— Yes, Madam—I confess, I once before, and ne'er but once, knew what it was to love—But why this Question, and with such Earnestness?

WIFE. You shall be told—Pray who was she?

BEAU. She was a Woman, Madam, whose Deserts[2] might well excuse my Passion—But why this Enquiry?

WIFE. But one thing more, and you shall know. Since so belov'd, and so deserving, why are you disunited? Grew she unkind?

BEAU. I am so confounded, I know not what to say. O *Amadea!* now thy Image rises to my View, and brings my broken Vows to my Remembrance.

WIFE. What say you, Sir? Did she prove false? or is she dead?

BEAU. Neither, Madam—but, pray no more—This Talk is foreign to the kind End your Husband brought me for.

WIFE. Stand off, perfidious Man! by your own Mouth you are con-

---

1. **Continency:** abstaining from sexual activity.
2. **Deserts:** merits.

demn'd—since, as yourself confess, Constancy's the only Proof of Love and Honour, how can you be justify'd by either?—You own you lov'd, where both Desert and Kindness join'd to engage—yet, full of your Sex's Falshood and Ingratitude, that Conquest gain'd, you offer to another your prostituted Heart, and think a little idle Flattery can win me to accept your violated Faith.

BEAU. I have lost her by my Plainness—What you speak of, Madam, happen'd a long time ago, we now are separated—Forgive what is past—your Beauty, as it justifies my Change, will also be your own Security for my future Constancy.

WIFE. I'll hear no more—nor is it my Business to judge either your past or present Actions—Come forth, *Amadea*—

BEAU. *Amadea!*

Enter Amadea *in her own Clothes.*

WIFE. If you can obtain a Pardon here, mine will not be long with-held.

BEAU. 'Tis she indeed!

AMA. Turn not away confus'd; I shall believe you never knew the Force of Love, if you can doubt my Readiness to pardon—You wrong me more by this unkind Delay to meet my stretch'd-out Arms, than e'er you did in your Addresses there.

BEAU. Can there be so much Generosity in Nature!

AMA. Come, Sir *Harry,* look on me, and as you just now said, forget what's past: By Heaven! your future Kindness will more than expiate all you have done, or would have done to wrong me.

BEAU. Excellent Woman! may I then believe thee—Can it be possible that thou (who, I perceive, art well acquainted with my Crime) can'st wish to pardon it, and again receive me to that soft Breast, that lovely Mansion of eternal Truth?

AMA. I now am fully recompens'd.

BEAU. Thou Prodigy of Goodness—to find thou hast left *London,* thy Father, Friends, Relations and Acquaintance—to meet thee here— here in this Scene of guilty Wishes, so strangely, so unexpected, fills me at once with Shame, with Joy, and Wonder.

AMA. Could *London,* my Father's House, or the Society of any Friends, bring Comfort to me, when I saw not you? 'Twas enough to know that *Beaumont* was in *Salisbury,* to wing the Feet of *Amadea* hither— Besides, you may remember the News of your Uncle's Death took you away so suddenly, I scarce had time for one short Adieu—You writ to me indeed, and made me hope a quick Return; but in a little time (tho I'm unwilling to mention past Unkindness) you left off even that distant Conversation—I writ, and writ again, but had no Answer—at first I thought my Letters had miscarry'd—but long Expectance at last grew weary, and I resolv'd to know the Truth of what I then began to fear; and to that end left *London* in Disguise.

BEAU. In Disguise!

AMA. I dress'd me in a Suit of my Brother's Clothes, which happening to be out of Town, he had left behind him, and came down here in the Stage-Coach—At the Inn where I alighted, I met Mr. *Graspall,* who hearing me enquire for Lodgings, made me an Offer of a Chamber in his House, where I have been ever since; and by that means had an Opportunity of finding out that Secret, which now you are so good to acknowledge as a Fault.

BEAU. And ever shall—Nor will this Lady think me unmannerly, when I declare, I ought to have been blind to every Charm but yours.

WIFE. Sir *Harry,* I rejoice in your Conversion, and I hope you are too sincerely touch'd with a Sense of your late Errors to repeat 'em.

BEAU. O never! This unexampled Tenderness and Generosity has charm'd my very Soul—nor will we ever be divided more; but as by solemn Vows we have long since been one, my Chaplain to-morrow shall ratify the Contract.

WIFE. I heartily congratulate the Happiness of you both; but not-withstanding the real Pleasure it gives me to see every thing so well answer the End I propos'd by this Meeting, I cannot find in my heart to forgive my Husband's base Design upon me, and have thought of a way to be reveng'd, if you'll vouchsafe me your Assistance.

BEAU. I dare answer you may command us both.

WIFE. This Lady must put on her Men's Clothes once more.

AMA. Most willingly, they have been fortunate to me.

WIFE. Within I'll tell you my Design—please to walk—

BEAU. We'll follow, Madam.

> Ye false-name'd Pleasures of my Youth farewel,
> They charm'd my Sense, but you subdue my Soul.
> Tho fix'd to you alone, I've pow'r to change,
> While o'er each Beauty of your Form I range.
> Nor to those only need I be confin'd,
> But changing still, enjoy thy beauteous Mind.

END OF THE FOURTH ACT.

ACT V. SCENE I

Enter Graspall *and Wife.*

WIFE. Nay, you won't be so ungrateful to deny me so small a Request, when I have broke thro all Objections to oblige you.

GRASP. I would deny thee nothing, *Pudsy;* but thou dost not consider what an Inconvenience, as well as an Expence, this will be.

WIFE. Inconvenience! where can be the Inconvenience of having a few Friends to be merry with you?

GRASP. A few! why thou hast nam'd half the County, I think—but prithee, let me hear them over again.

WIFE. Why in the first place, Sir *Harry Beaumont;* you won't grudge him a Dinner out of his 2000 *l.* sure?

GRASP. If he is not satisfy'd with the Meal you have given him, he should e'en fast till Doomsday for me—But go on—

WIFE. Mr. *Courtly;* he is Sir *Harry's* Intimate, and 'twill be rude to leave him out.

GRASP. Well! who else?

WIFE. The Widow *Stately*—She is our next Neighbor, you know, and must be invited.

GRASP. So—to the rest.

WIFE. Mr. *Fairman,* his Niece, and Daughter, and their two Lovers, Squire *Sneaksby* and Mr. *Toywell;* and if you find any Company at their House, as they seldom are without, they must be ask'd.

GRASP. Very well—and these you call a few—besides a Retinue of Servants at the heels of 'em, of more than twice double the Number— A Pack of romping, tearing, hungry Hounds, that will eat me out of house and home, tho I had laid in for a Siege. 'Sdeath, how can you be so inconsiderate?

WIFE. Well, I'll never ask you any thing again—but remember, that if ever you make any more Bargains for me, your Unkindness has given me a very good Pretence to refuse making 'em good.

GRASP. Ha! let me consider—she'll be spiteful enough, that's certain, and who knows, but among these Blades[1] I may find a Fool as willing to part with his Money as Sir *Harry?*—I have a good mind to let her have her Will for once. Well, *Pudsy*—suppose I should oblige thee in this, thou wilt never be refractory hereafter, wilt thou?

WIFE. Not when 'tis for your Interest, *Tony.*[2]

GRASP. I shall never ask any thing of thee, *Pudsy,* that is not for the Interest of us both.

---

1. **Blades:** good-natured, happy-go-lucky, even reckless men.
2. **Tony:** simpleton, fool.

WIFE. But since you have consented to have this Company here to-day, 'tis time they were invited.

GRASP. Well, I'll go—but, *Pudsy,* dear *Pudsy,* prithee bate[1] me the Severity of one Article.

WIFE. What's that?

GRASP. Give me leave to desire they would not bring their Footmen with 'em.

WIFE. Fye! you would not make yourself so ridiculous.

GRASP. Well, for once—

Going.

WIFE. Stay, *Tony*—I protest I had like to have been guilty of a piece of Ill manners I should never have forgiven myself—

GRASP. What now?

WIFE. I am told there's a Baronet lately come down, I can't think of his Name, but he's at the Widow *Stately's*—you must be sure to entreat the Favour of his good Company.

GRASP. The Devil!

WIFE. You must not omit him by any means.

GRASP. No, no—Was ever Man thus plague'd?

WIFE. Well, go about it then, while I prepare for their Reception. Be sure not to forget.

GRASP. No, no, no—if I stay much longer, she'll remember as many more.

Exit.

WIFE. I'll fit you for your Bargain, Sir.

Exit.

---

1. **bate:** abate.

Enter Gaylove *and* Celemena.

CEL. 'Tis now no time for Dissimulation, Captain; I freely own nothing is so terrible to me as the Thoughts of being *Sneaksby's* Wife—therefore, if in earnest you can find any way to disappoint my Father in his design of marrying me to that Idiot, I give you leave to hope, I may one day have the Opinion of you, you wish.

GAY. That is not sufficient, Madam; I must have an immediate Security for your Performance of Articles, before I undertake any thing.

CEL. Why, I hope you have not seriously the Confidence to think of gaining me so soon—Do you think it reasonable, that a Woman, who believes herself in some measure agreeable, should lose the pleasure of seeing her Lover tremble at her Approach, and by his Sighs and Melancholy betray the Passion he has for her to all who know him, admire all she says, and cry up all she does, and threaten to poison, stab, or drown himself to pacify her, whenever she happens to be in the humour of giving Pain.

GAY. But, Madam, I believe 'Squire *Sneaksby* never read Romances, and will perhaps think it an unreasonable Request, should you desire him either to poison, stab, or drown himself—Therefore, Madam, since all these Preludiums, one way or other, must be cut off; you had e'en as good venture on me, and imagine that if there was time for it, I would willingly come into all these Methods to obtain you.

CEL. But do you consider what you ask? Tho my Father proffers *Sneaksby* 10000 *l.* to take his Daughter off his hands, I question whether he may be in the same Humour when *Gaylove* has me.

GAY. It is you, not your Fortune, that I am ambitious of. My Commission will keep us from want, if your Father gives you nothing; when mine dies, his Estate, for the greater Part is intail'd[1] on me: and without being romantick, I shall think it but a poor Purchase for my *Celemena.*

CEL. Well, let me consider—Here's a Coach and Six with my Father's

---

1. **intail'd:** settled on him and his direct heirs.

Commands, and 10000 *l.* to back it—On the other hand, 16*s.* a Day, and the Title of a Captain's Lady, with a reasonable Suspicion of being turn'd out of doors with never a Groat[1]—But then, on this side, I've a Fool—on that, a Man not disagreeable, and of allow'd Sense—One marries me upon Compact, the other generously runs the risque of a Fortune—Well, *Gaylove,* I think you carry the day—I'll lay aside the Woman for once—Here's my Hand.

GAY. My Future Carriage shall show my Gratitude for the Blessing, and—

CEL. Come, no Raptures—you are a Man of Honour, and I expect you'll keep your Promise—I can't bear this Coxcomb's Impertinence—Prithee banter him a little, while I retire to think on what I've done.

Exit.

Enter Toywell.

TOY. O Captain *Gaylove!* are you here? You have serv'd me finely!

GAY. As how, good Sir?

TOY. Why did not you tell me that Mr. *Trusty* the Banker was broke? and I saw a Letter from him just now, which says, he's in as good a Condition as ever.

GAY. Is he so? Faith I'm glad on't.

TOY. O! but you have ruin'd me, I have lost *Marilla* by it.

GAY. Why what's *Marilla* to *Trusty?*

TOY. Why he has her Fortune in his hands—and if he had fail'd, she had been no Wife for me—So, upon what you have told me, I broke off, and releas'd her from all Ties.

GAY. Why 'tis none of my Fault—Did I advise you to't?

TOY. No; for that matter, 'twas all my own doing—But I'll go and throw myself at her feet, and if she has any Compassion—

---

1. **Groat:** Medieval coin that was worth four pence and ceased to be issued in 1662; slang for a very small sum or nearly worthless.

GAY. You may spare yourself the pains, for to my certain Knowledge, there's a terrible ill-natur'd Fellow, with a Sword like a Scythe, pretends a Right to her—

Sings.

> With whom you cannot grapple,
> For at one Sup,
> He'd eat you up,
> As Boys do eat an Apple.[1]

TOY. Gad's Curse! So I am to lose my Mistress for an old Song?

GAY. His Name is *Courtly,* do you know such a Man?

TOY. *Courtly!* Pho, I've a better Estate than he has.

GAY. But he understands a Sword better than you do—Come, take my Advice, and be merry—and when you see *Courtly,* wish him Joy, with an Air of Indifference—for they are, by this time, marry'd; seem pleas'd with what you can't help, for to my knowledge you'll get little by Resentment.

TOY. Psha! I don't care this Pinch of Snuff, and since she's gone—let her go.

GAY. Ay, this becomes you—it shows you are a Man above Disappointment—But here they come—now let me see you bear your Misfortunes like a Man untouch'd by 'em.

TOY. You shall see me accost her with the Unconcern of a tir'd Keeper.

Enter Courtly, Celemena, *and* Marilla.

MAR. Your Importunity, Mr. *Courtly,* incenses me as much as Mr. *Toywell's* Indifference; and if you think to teaze me into a Compliance, you shall find yourself deceiv'd.

---

1. **With whom . . . Apple:** lyrics from a broadside ballad commonly called "The Dragon of Wantley" (1685); a version appears later in Henry Carey's and J. F. Lampe's burlesque opera of the same name in 1737.

GAY. How's this?

TOY. Ha! I find things are not so bad as I thought.

COURT. Heav'n is not displeas'd with Prayers and Adorations—'Tis with the most awful distance I pursue you, the tenderest Passion, and sincerest Vows.

MAR. Perhaps I'm fix'd never to marry—and if so, shall no more endeavour to force my Inclinations, than you to govern yours.

TOY. O! Madam, can you forgive my Rashness, occasion'd by the Violence of my Passion, for a belief I was not so well in your Esteem as I desir'd to be?

GAY. What a devil! have you a mind to have your Throat cut?

MAR. O! Mr. *Toywell,* do you repent? Then I'll soon put an end to Mr. *Courtly's* Importunities.

TOY. Ah Madam! how shall I requite your Goodness?

MAR. Hold Sir! thank me when I deserve it—Mr. *Courtly,* you have given me daily Uneasiness, haunting me from place to place, scarce leaving me a moment, and endeavouring by your Constancy to merit me; answer me, Guilty, or not?

COURT. Guilty, Madam.

MAR. You, Mr. *Toywell,* on the contrary—

TOY. Ay, Madam.

MAR. Always shunn'd the Places I frequented, never discover'd your Passion by either Words or Actions, or hoped by Assiduity to gain me.

TOY. Not I, Madam, upon my Soul—I carry'd myself so, that no Man on Earth would ever have thought I had valu'd you in the least, not I—I had more Sense—Poor *Courtly,* how he looks! he's finely fobb'd.[1]

GAY. What will this come to?

---

1. **fobb'd:** cheated, tricked.

MAR. Know then, that I resolve to give myself to him who most deserves me.

GAY. That's easily distinguish'd, Madam—

TOY. Ay, Captain, so 'tis—faith I pity *Courtly*—But the Lady must follow her Inclinations, ha! ha! ha!

GAY. 'Sdeath, leave your Impertinence—Prithee how came you and I so familiar?

TOY. Lord, you are as crafty as a sickly Miser to a Depending Heir. Come, Madam, I want that poor Gentlman should be put out of suspence.

COURT. Sir!

MAR. Nay, no quarrelling—Mr. *Courtly,* from this time forwards, I desire you will lay aside all Hopes, and Fears, for I now discharge you as my Servant.

GAY. 'Sdeath!

CEL. Why, Cousin, are you mad?

MAR. Have Patience—I give you now my Hand, with it my Heart, and make you now my Master.

COURT. Health to the Sick is not more welcome, I receive you as the greatest Blessing Heav'n had in store.

TOY. Fire and Brimstone!

GAY. You are out of Suspence now, Sir.

CEL. Joy to you, *Marilla,* I'll be bound you've made a worthy Choice, and done Justice.

GAY. I wanted but this to make me compleatly happy.

TOY. Sure, Madam, you are not in earnest.

GAY. You are only fobb'd, Sir.

Enter Fairman, *dragging in* Sneaksby.

FAIR. An impudent Villian! to make a Brothel of my House!

SNEAK. How did I know 'twas your House, when I was so drunk, I did not know myself—beside, you need not make such a to do about it; I did no harm as I know of—

GAY. What's the matter, Sir, that your intended Son-in-law is in this Condition?

FAIR. No, no, Captain, I'll have no such drunken lewd Wretches in my Family—Sending just now to look for him, to know what was the reason his Aunt did not come to seal the Writings, where do you think he was found? but in the Cockloft, where it seems he had lain all Night with the Wench that feeds the Poultry.

CEL. A blessed Husband you had chose for me truly, Sir!

FAIR. I was wrong indeed, in believing thou could'st be happy with such an Idiot—and rejoice I have made this Discovery before it was too late.

SNEAK. Marry what care I—I can have a Wife I warrant you; but Aunt shall know how you have us'd me—mayhap she may tell you your own.

GAY. Here's another fobb'd too—Come, cheer up Man, you see you have a Companion in Tribulation.

FAIR. Pray leave my House, and tell your Aunt there's no occasion for the Writings now.

GAY. I believe you may spare yourself that Trouble, Sir, for I expect her here every moment, with her new Husband.

FAIR. Husband! why, is she marry'd?

GAY. Yes, faith, and to one, who, I'll engage, will take care not a Foot of her Estate shall descend to this Gentleman.

FAIR. I'm glad on't—tho' this News yesterday wou'd have been a very great Disappointment to me.

Enter Graspall.

Ha! who have we here? a Stranger indeed! Mr. *Graspall!*

GRASP. Ay, truly, Mr. *Fairman,* I don't often visit—but my Pudsy has taken a Fancy to be mighty merry to-day, and I love to humour her—so if you, your Niece, and Daughter, and all this good Company, will take a Dinner with her, ye shall have a hearty Welcome.—As for the rest of her Entertainment, let her answer, I never trouble myself with those things.

FAIR. Miracles are not ceas'd, I find!

GRASP. What say you, Sir, will you do us the Favour? I hope he is engag'd.

[*Aside*].

FAIR. Sir, 'tis a Favour you so seldom ask, that I believe nobody will refuse it you—Gentlemen—Captain, you hear the Invitation—can you go?

COURT. O! by all means, Sir.

GAY. I'll wait upon you, Sir.

TOY. Am I in the Number of your Guests, Sir.

GRASP. Ay, ay, all of you, if there were a hundred—I shall expect you soon—your Servant, and I wish the first Dish may choak you.

Exit.

FAIR. There must be something extraordinary has happen'd to occasion this Fit of Generosity—let us go.

> If that which is most rare is counted best,
> We cannot want it in a Miser's Feast.

Exit.

Enter Beaumont, *and* Graspall.

BEAU. Ay, now I like you Mr. *Graspall*—this is done like a Man who knows how to use his Fortune—I look on Hospitality to be the most pleasurable of any Vertue, and when you have once try'd it, I don't doubt but the whole Country will very often find the Effects of it.

GRASP. You'll find yourself exceedingly out in your Politics, if you do think so, that I can tell you.

BEAU. Once or twice a Week at least, I suppose, one may expect to find good Company here.

GRASP. 'Sdeath! he wants to take out his 2000 *l.* in Board, I believe. [*Aside.*] As often as I can, Sir *Harry*—but, alas! I am infirm and crazy—very crazy—and sometimes can't bear the Sight of a Fire, or the Smell of dressing Meat for a Quarter of a year together.

BEAU. Poor Man! but you need not incommode yourself with that—a cold Collation, with three or four Dozen of *Champagne* and *Burgundy* will serve well enough—Your Friends will excuse the rest on account of your Indisposition,

GRASP. They shall when I give it 'em. [*Aside.*] But, Sir *Harry,* I can't endure a Noise.

BEAU. As for that, you have a large House here, and may easily retire into some remote Part of it, where you won't be disturb'd—Your Guests will be contented to spare you, provided you leave your Wife, and the Fiddles to entertain 'em.

GRASP. That wou'd be fine indeed—'Sbud! I'll sell my House, and live in *Wales* among the Mountains, where nobody will attempt to come near me for fear of breaking their Necks.

BEAU. I think you look ill now—I am afraid you won't be able to let us have your Company to-day—if you find yourself out of Order, pray don't hazard growing worse by an Over-Complaisance—I'll answer for it, nobody will take it ill if you shut up yourself all day.

GRASP. The Devil I will—no, no, Sir *Harry,* I am mighty well—mighty well as can be, and so all my good Friends shall find—Here they come.

Enter Gaylove, Courtly, Toywell, Fairman, Marilla, *and* Celemena.

You are welcome, Sirs, heartily welcome all—

FAIR. Sir, we thank you.

COURT. We are all oblig'd to you—Sir *Harry,* your most humble Servant—

BEAU. Yours, Sir—Ladies, yours—but where's your Wife, Mr. *Graspall?* your fair Visitors will think themselves unwelcome while she is absent—.

GRASP. I'll go and see for her.

BEAU. I'll save you the Trouble, if you please, Sir—you know I am free here.

Exit.

GRASP. Ay, and so shou'd they all be on the same Conditions. Come, Gentlemen—Mrs. *Celemena,* Mrs. *Marilla,* pray sit down—you'll excuse me, I don't love much Ceremony—but pray be merry.

FAIR. Wine, Sir, gives a Life to Conversation—after Dinner, when the chearful Glass goes round, you may expect we shall be heartily merry.

Wife *within.* Murder! Murder!

FAIR. Ha! what's this?

COURT. Murder cry'd!

FAIR. Your Wife's Voice.

Enter Beaumont *and* Amadea *fighting,* Mrs. Graspall *following.*

BEAU. Villain! to abuse so worthy a Man! but from my Arm thou shalt receive the just Reward of thy Treachery.

AMA. I fear you not.

WIFE. Part 'em, part 'em.

COURT. What's the Matter, Sir *Harry?*

BEAU. Base Villain! and thou, ungrateful Woman!

WIFE. Oh! Sir *Harry,* you will not be so barbarous to expose me?

GRASP. Why? what's the Meaning of all this?

BEAU. Not expose you, Madam! yes, to the whole World—you that cou'd wrong so kind, so tender a Husband.

GRASP. Ha! how's this?

BEAU. So good, so true a Friend, so worthy a Man, and one so infinitely fond of you, shall receive no Pity, no Regard from me—You must know, Gentlemen, that going to seek this Lady, for whom till now I had the greatest Respect, I found her in the Embraces of that young Gallant—They started when they saw me, and tho' my Sword was in a moment ready to revenge my injur'd Friend, his was not tardy in Defense—but tho' you have prevented me at present, I shall find a time to make the Villain smart.

COURT. I'm amaz'd.

FAIR. She that was esteem'd so vertuous!

TOY. They are all so till caught.

GRASP. And hast thou done this? Hast thou made a Cuckold of thy old Hubby—Ah Cockatrice![1]

WIFE. I see Surprize in every Face, and know my Reputation has been hitherto so fair, that I believe some here scarce credit what they hear; but I disdain to be a Hypocrite, nor will deny the Truth—This lovely Youth, this Darling of my Soul, has indeed receiv'd whatever Favours he cou'd intreat, or Love prompt me to grant.

CEL. Monstrous Impudence!

MAR. I never heard the like.

GRASP. And do you own it then? have you no Shame?

WIFE. You taught me to despise all the Sense of Shame, when laughing at that Notion which the World calls Virtue, you forc'd me, contrary to my Nature, to my Inclinations, to the Principles my Youth was

---

1. **Cocatrice:** mythical serpent hatched from a cock's egg; has the power to strike dead with a look.

bred to observe, to yield myself a Prey to your insatiate Avarice, and his base Desires.

FAIR. How!

WIFE. Did you not sell me? let me out to Hire, and forc'd my trembling Vertue to obey—Did I not kneel, and weep, and beg—but you had receiv'd the Price you set me at, and I must yield, or be turn'd out a Beggar.

FAIR. What! let his Wife for Hire.

COURT. Agree for Mony to his own Dishonour!

TOY. Egad, if I had known that; I'd have been a Customer—prithee what dost thou demand, old Lucre?[1] ha!

GRASP. Fop! Fool! Oh that I were dead!

WIFE. Since you have taught me, I'll now experience that Charm Mankind's so fond of, Variety—I'll give a Loose to each unbounded Appetite, range thro' all Degrees of Men, nor shall you dare to contradict my Pleasures.

GRASP. Pray kill me—will nobody kill me?

GAY. Why truly, Sir, as the Case stands, I think 'tis the greatest Kindness can be done you.

WIFE. But do not imagine you shall ever reap any Advantage from my Crimes—I have broke open your Closet, and the 2000 *l.* Sir *Harry* paid you for seducing me, I have bestow'd on this dear Man.

GRASP. Oh! Oh! the Money gone too!

WIFE. You shall find what 'tis to have a vicious Wife—Do you not now repent what you have done, and wish I cou'd resume my Vertue—tho' it shou'd cost you twice as much as you receiv'd for my renouncing it?

GRASP. I do indeed, I see my Error now 'tis too late—Oh damn'd, damn'd Avarice!

---

1. **Lucre:** money; greedy materialist.

WIFE. You wou'd not tempt me then, were it again to do.

GRASP. No.

WIFE. Not for the greatest Consideration.

GRASP. Not for the Universe—but do not plague me, I shall not live to endure it long.

WIFE. Stay, Sir, your Sorrow moves me; if I may believe your Penitence sincere, I can return to your Embraces a true; a faithful, and a vertuous Wife.

GRASP. What new Invention to distract me more?

BEAU. She tells you Truth by Heav'n—that seeming Gentleman with whom I fought, and who you think has injur'd you, has not the Pow'r—Appear, my Love, without Disguise—See, Sir, a Woman and my Wife.

OMN. How!

GAY. *Amadea!*

AMA. The same, dear Cousin—much happier than when you saw me last, by the addition of Sir *Harry's* Love confirm'd.

GAY. I wish you Joy.

GRASP. May I believe my Eyes?

BEAU. They do not deceive you, Sir—this Plot was laid on purpose to cure you, if 'twas possible, of that covetous, sordid Disposition, which has ever been the Blot of your Character—and a little also to revenge the Contempt you seem'd to have of so good a Wife—when you were willing to chaffer[1] her for Gold—

COURT. 'Twas handsomely contriv'd—

CEL. I am glad to find she has brought herself off; for I protest I trembled for her two Minutes ago.

BEAU. Come, Sir, if you have any Consideration of Honour, and the

---

1. **chaffer:** bargain, trade.

eternal Infamy and Disgrace she has preserv'd you from, you will admire her Vertues, and entreat her Pardon—

GRASP. *Pudsy,* dear *Pudsy,* can'st thou forgive me.

WIFE. Rise, Sir, this is not a Posture for a Husband—I form'd this Design only to make you worthy of that Name, and shall ever make it my Study to prove myself a most obedient Wife.

FAIR. This is a happy Conclusion, indeed; but here's more Company, Mr. *Graspall*—

Enter Widow, Dogood, Shamble.

WID. Your Servant, Gentlemen, your Servant, Ladies; I beg pardon for my long Absence—but, but—a—I cou'd not rise to-day, I think.

GAY. Sir *Tristram* play'd his part then pretty well, last Night, I find.

FAIR. Joy, Madam—you have stole a Wedding, I hear.

WID. People of Quality never talk of these Affairs till they are accomplish'd, Mr. *Fairman*—Sir *Tristram* here was so pressing.

COURT. And your Ladyship so easy—

GRASP. Sir *Tristram!* why are you all mad? why, this is *Jonathan Shamble*—sure I know *Jonathan Shamble;* he was Footman to a Nephew of mine about four or five Years age, when I was last in *London.*

ALL. Ha, ha, ha! a Footman!

GAY. Well, well, Mr. *Graspall,* he's a man of an Estate now, and 'twill be unmannerly to rip up[1] Pedigrees.

WID. I am not cheated, sure—what's the Meaning of all this?

SHAM. Why, faith, my dear Wife, since the Truth must out, I only borrow'd my Quality to make myself agreeable to you—

WID. Villain! Rogue! I'll tear you to pieces.

---

1. **rip up:** bring up, open up.

SHAM. Hold, hold, good Lady, Passion—have mercy on my Cloaths, for they are none of my own.

GAY. Patience, Madam, Patience! Boxing does not become a Woman of Quality.

WID. A Footman! a Footman! but I'll have him hang'd, he's a Cheat, he has marry'd me in a false Name; but you shan't think to carry it so—I was not born Yesterday: I'll go to a Lawyer immediately.

GAY. Hark ye, hark ye, Madam—your Anger will do you but little Service—he has wedded you, bedded you, and got your Writings, and if you consider calmly on the Matter, you'll find nothing can be done in this Affair for your Satisfaction—you had better therefore quietly forgive the Imposition; and as you have a good Estate, turn part of it into ready Money, and e'en buy him a Title[1]—such Things are done every day in *London*—and when once you have made a Gentleman of him, ev'ry body won't know by what means he came to be one.

WID. Why that's true, indeed.

GAY. You'll find it your best way.

WID. Well, since there's no Help, I'll sell all I have, and away to *London*.

GAY. You may be happy enough—I dare swear he'll make you a good Husband.

WID. That's all I have to hope.

GAY. Well, I think I have been very busy in endeavouring to settle the Happiness of others—'tis high time now to consider my own, which lies only in your pow'r, Sir, to bestow.

FAIR. Sir, Mr. *Courtly* has just now acquainted me with the Kindness you have for my Daughter—I know your Father, and I approve of your Character—therefore if she is of the same Opinion (for I will

---

1. **buy him a Title:** An occasional scandal was the creation of new titles, sometimes to change the voting marjority in parliament, as done during the reign of Queen Anne, and sometimes to increase the treasury.

never go about to force her Inclinations more) she is yours, with the same Fortune I design'd to give the Squire—what say you, *Celemena?*

CEL. I shou'd have endeavour'd to obey you, Sir, ev'n where my Nature was most reluctant—but in this, I confess, you've chosen with my Eyes.

FAIR. Why, then bless you both—I think poor Mr. *Toywell* is the only unhappy Man among us.

TOY. Faith, Sir, I am positively easy: I'll e'en trip to *Bath* this Season, and I don't doubt but I shall there find an Opportunity with some kind Damsel to repay my Loss in *Marilla.*

BEAU.

> How simply Politic is foolish Man!
> How poor, how vain, our deepest laid Designs,
> To the all-seeing Eye of Providence!
> Like those weak Webbs by *Æsop*'s Spider[1] wrought,
> To stop the swift-wing'd Swallow in her Flight;
> Who, with Contempt surveys her fruitless Pains,
> Her Folly pities, and her Rage disdains;
> Baffles her Wiles, breaks thro' the tender Snare,
> And, uncontroul'd divides the yielding Air.

FINIS.

EPILOGUE,[2]

Spoken by the Author.

We Women, who by Nature love to teaze ye,
Will have it, that the newest things best please ye;

---

1. **Aesop's Spider:** the fable of "A Swallow and a Spider" in which the spider, angry with the swallow for catching flies, attempts in vain to catch the bird in a web. The moral of the fable is "A wise man will not undertake any thing without means answerable to the end."

2. **Epilogue:** In the first printing, the epilogue appeared immediately after the prologue and before the play.

Sure then, to-night, our *Graspall* claims *Compassion,*
For ne'er, since Bridal Antlers[1] were in fashion,
Heard ye of one, who to a Beauty married,
Wou'd fain have been a Cuckold[2], and miscarry'd.
This Man's of *Novelty,* a Proof most *ample!*
Had ye but Grace to *copy out* th' Example;
Each well comply'd with by his kinder *Fair-One,*
Wou'd own that *Graspall's* Fate's a *new* and *rare one.*

    Well, we have shown ye *Av'rice* to the Life,
A rich old Miser, *melting* down his *Wife,*
Not into *soft Desires,* and amorous *Puling,*
He, *sober Thinker!* Was for no such *Fooling.*
Tho many a sparkling Jewel grac'd his *Honey,*
He thought no Gem, *about* her, worth that Money:
Two Thousand Pounds, he judg'd, would *soften* Satyr,[3]
And *weigh* against the *heavy'st Horns* in Nature.
Strange Bargain! but since *Husband* wish'd to strike it,
What Whim could work with *Madam*—not to *like* it!
'Twas this—she shun'd, when 'twas her *Husband's* Tasking,
What her *own Bounty* would have given for *asking.*
Women, however *stirring* in their Way,
Are ne'er too active, when they move *t'obey;*
They rather would (if I can *understand* 'em)
Not *do* at all—than *do* as Spouse *commands* 'em.

---

1. **Bridal Antlers:** antlers were the symbol of the mock stag hunt or skimmington. A folk custom surviving in the West Country and some rural parts of England, it was intended to humiliate and punish a person or couple believed to be guilty of sexual or marital misconduct. The skimmington is now often called "rough music" or, in the United States, a "shivaree." The person representing the miscreant wore antlers and acted the part of a hunted stag; given a few yards headstart, he was pursued by the villagers dressed as huntsmen and hounds, pulled down at the house of the offending person, and, with much shouting, horn-blowing, and raucous noises, is "killed" on the doorstep. In earlier times, the villagers often carried bladders of blood, which they poured around this final scene. In addition to marking an adulterer or cuckold, it shamed people who broke proprieties by, for instance, marrying too quickly after the death of a spouse or by marrying someone strikingly different in age. Richard Leighton Greene, "Hamlet's Skimmington," 2–5, 10–11.

2. **fain have been a Cuckold:** wanted to be cheated on by his wife, willing to have his wife commit adultery.

3. **Satyr:** Satire.

But to be grave—the Heroine of our Play
Gains Glory by a hard, and dangerous Way:
Belov'd, her Lover pleads—she fears no Spy,
Her Husband *favours*—and her *Pulse* beats high.
Warm glows his Hope—her Wishes *catch* the Fire,
Mutual their *Flame,* yet Virtue quells Desire.

Safe th' *Untempted* may defy Love's Call,
Why should the *Unencounter'd* fear to *fall?*
Virtue must pass thro Fire to prove its Weight,
And equal Danger make the Triumph great.

THE

CITY JILT;

OR, THE

Alderman turn'd Beau:

A SECRET

HISTORY.

Virtue now, nor noble Blood,

Nor Wit by Love, is understood;

Gold alone does Passion move;

Gold monopolizes Love.

COWLEY [1]

LONDON:

Printed for J. Roberts, near the *Oxford-Arms*
in *Warwick-Lane,* MDCCXXVI

An approximation of the title page from the 1726 edition.

1. **Cowley:** Abraham Cowley, "Upon Gold" from *Anacreon, Done into British out of the Original Greek* (1683). Cowley was a diplomat, Royalist spy, and an influential poet; many of his innovative combinations of content and verse forms were imitated, and his odes were especially influential.

The City Jilt

or, The Alderman Turn'd Beau: A Secret History

Glicera was the Daughter of an eminent Tradesman; the Reputation
of whose Riches drew a greater Number of Admirers to his House,
than the Beauty of his fair Daughter's Person; tho' she was really one
of the most lovely and accomplished Women of the Age. The most
favour'd of all who made Pretensions to her, was young *Melladore*, the
Son of a near Neighbour; he was handsome, witty, well made, and
seem'd to have an infinity of Affection for her. With all these Endowments therefore, join'd to an Equality of Birth and Fortune, 'tis not
to be wondered at that he was well received by the Father of *Glicera*,
as well as by herself. Nothing happening between them but what is
common to Persons in the Circumstances they were, I shall pass over
in silence the Days of their Courtship, and only say that their mutual
Affection encreasing the more they knew each other's Temper; and
every thing being agreed on by the Relations on both sides, a Day was
appointed for the Celebration of their Nuptials.

Now did this enamour'd Pair think of nothing but approaching
Joys, all the delightful Visions with which the God of Love deludes
his Votaries, play'd before their Eyes, and formed a thousand Day-
dreams of an imaginary Heaven of Pleasure—with equal Ardour, equal
Languishment did both long for the happy Minute which was to
crown their Loves,—the impatient Youth with fierce and vigorous
Wishes burn'd, the tender Maid in soft Desires dissolv'd.—Alas! she
knew not yet the meaning of those tumultuous Agitations, which at

every Kiss and fond Embrace she received from the amorous *Melladore*, made her Heart flutter with disordered Beatings, the Blood flow fast through each throbbing Vein, and a wild Mixture of Delight and Pain invade her every Faculty:—But he, more experienced, was not ignorant what it was, for which he sigh'd; scarce cou'd he refrain taking those Advantages which her Innocence and Love afforded him, to make him Master of the supremest Bliss that Passion can demand, or Beauty yield; and the Agonies of suppress'd Desire would sometime rise to such a Height, that nothing but the extremest Respect could have enabled him to endure them, rather than be guilty of the least Action which might shock the timorous Bashfulness of her virgin Soul.

In this Position were their Hearts, while those necessary Preparations were about, for the rendering magnificent that Ceremony which was to put an end to the Lover's Impatience, and the Virgin's Scruples. There now wanted but one Day of that which was to be the happy one, and 'tis difficult to say whether *Melladore*, or his intended Bride, felt the greater Satisfaction at the near Approach. But to what Vicissitudes are the Transports of Lovers incident! The Father of *Glicera* was taken suddenly ill, and that with so much Violence, that in a few hours time his Life was despaired of; Night brought with it an encrease of his Distemper, nor did the Morning afford any Abatement; not all the Prescriptions of the best Physicians, who were sent for on his first finding himself disordered, had the least Effect on him; and at the close of the second Day he paid that Debt to Nature, to which all who live must submit.

Here was now a sad Change in the Affairs of *Glicera*, her bridal Ornaments were exchanged for mournful Black; and at the time when she expected to have received the Gratulations of her Friends for her happy Nuptials, she had only the Consolations of them to regard. The Society of her dear *Melladore* was however a considerable Alleviation to her Sorrows, and as he scarce ever left her but in those Hours in which Decency obliged him to retire, he easily persuaded her to a Forgetfulness of *the Dead*, in the Comforts of *the Living*; and if Fate exacted the Life of one, she thought it yet a less terrible Misfortune to lose her *Father* than a *Lover* who was so dear to her, and by whom she believed herself so sincerely and tenderly belov'd, that she should know no want of any other Friend. Ah! how little is Youth sensible of what it owes to Age, and how far are we unable to conceive what is due to the Care of a tender Parent, or how greatly we suffer in the loss of such a one! But soon was this fond Maid made sensible of her Error; soon, alas! did sad Experience convince her of the Difference between natural Affection and the Vows of Passion.

Many People, who while they live make a very great Show, when once Death exposes to the World the truth of their Circumstances, are found vastly inferior to what their Appearance had promised: At least it here so happened, the Father of *Glicera*, reputed one of the richest Citizens of his Time, left behind him little more than would serve to defray the Expences of his Funeral, and pay the Debts he had contracted; and the fair Subject of this little History, instead of a hundred thousand Crowns, which was the least that was expected for her Portion,[1] had scarce sufficient left her to maintain her one Year in the manner she had been accustomed to live. *Melladore*, however, had enough for both; and fully depending on his Love and Constancy, she regarded not this Fall from her high-rais'd Hopes, nor once imagined that the Loss of her Wealth would also make her lose his Heart: for this reason, as well as that her Youth had not yet learned Hypocrisy, and scorn'd the Baseness of a Lye, she endeavoured not to conceal the reality of her Affairs, but frankly let him know that her Love and Virtue were her only Dower. They were sitting in an Arbour at the end of the Garden, so shadow'd o'er with Trees, that scarce could the Sun's Beams at the height of Noon penetrate the Gloom, much less those of the pale Moon, who then shone but with faint and sickly Fires, when first she related to him this surprizing News; so that unhappily for her she perceived not the shock her Words had given him, nor the Disorders which that moment overspread his alter'd Countenance; and being far from guessing at his Thoughts, prosecuted her Discourse without expecting any Reply from him till he had time enough to recollect himself, and have recourse to Dissimulation.[2] And

---

1. **Portion:** dowry.

2. **Dissimulation:** concealing feelings or intentions; feigning an appearance in order to deceive.

then he did not fail to tell her, that her adorable Person was of itself a Treasure infinitely beyond his Merit,—that he look'd on her as a Blessing sent from Heaven to make him the happiest of his Sex—that he rather rejoiced than the contrary, at this Opportunity to prove the Disinterestedness of his Affection,—and a thousand such like Expressions of Tenderness and Truth, which she hesitated not if she should believe, because she wish'd it so, and had before set down in her own Heart for Truth, all that he now professed.

So artfully did he deceive, that for many Weeks she had not the least reason to suspect, but that as soon as Decency for the Death of her Father would permit, she should become his Wife: But vastly different now were his Designs, the real Love he had was to the Wealth of which he expected she would be possess'd; but that being lost, his Passion also vanish'd, and left behind it only that part of Desire which tends to Enjoyment;—the nobler Inclinations all were fled, and brutal Appetite alone remained:—In an unguarded Hour, when most he found her melted by his Pressures, and wholly incapable of repelling his amorous Efforts, did he attack her with all the ruinous Force of fatal Passion—He told her, that since their Hearts were united too firmly to be ever separated, 'twere most unjust to themselves and the soft Languishments which both confess'd, to make their Bodies observe a cruel Distance:—That Caution between them now was needless, and tho' in regard to Custom, and that Decorum which enslaves the World, the Ceremony which was to authorize Possession had not yet passed; yet might they in secret indulge those Wishes to which Marriage hereafter would give a Sanction.—By such kind of Arguments, accompanied with unnumber'd Vows, Sighs, Tears, and Implorations, was she at last subdued, and fell the Victim of his lawless Flame.

O'erwhelm'd in Tenderness, and lost to every Thought but that of giving Pleasure to the dear Undoer, was she for a time content with what she had done, nor once imagined how despicable she was now grown in his Eyes for that very Action which she had yielded to but to endear him more: while lull'd, by his continued Ardours into a Belief that he was all Sincerity; how tranquil was her State! But when Indifference came, and cold Neglect, how much beyond the reach of dull Description were the Agonies of her distracted Soul!—To enhance the Misery of her Condition, she found herself with Child; with Child by a Man who was already tired with her Embraces, despised her Tenderness, and from whom she had not the least hope of receiving any Reparation for the Shame to which he had reduced her.—Now was she touch'd with a just Sensibility of the Crime she had been guilty of to Heaven, and to herself:—Now did Reflection glare full of Horror on her affrighted View:—Now did the sharpest Stings of late Repentance torture her afflicted Soul, and drive her to Despair.

Concealing, however, as much as possible, how far she had discovered his Ingratitude, she let him know the Consequence of their unlicensed Joys, and press'd him to marry her in Terms so moving and so tender, that had he not been abandoned by all Sense of Honour or of Justice, he would, indeed, have fulfill'd what he so often, and so solemnly had vow'd: But he had now obtained his wanton Purpose, Desire was satiated; and of that stock of Fondness and Admiration which his Breast lately glow'd with, there scarce remained a common Pity for the ruin he had caused. When first she mentioned Marriage to him; he evaded the Question, and seem'd but to *delay,* not absolutely *deny* what she required; but soon he threw aside Hypocrisy, and plainly told her he had other Views: that it was not consistent with his Circumstances to take a Wife without a Portion, and that his Father had before his Death exacted from him a Vow never to marry, but where at least an Equality of Fortune afforded him a prospect of future Happiness. Mild, and gentle as he had ever found *Glicera,* he now perceived her Soul could change as well as his had done. Never was Rage carried to a greater height than hers,—she seem'd all Fury—and distracted with her Wrongs, beholding the cruel Author of them rather exulting than any way compassionating her Misery, she said and did a thousand things which could not be reconciled to Reason:—Impossible is it to describe her Behaviour such as it was, therefore I shall only say that proportioned to the *Love* she had born him while she believed him *true,* was her *Resentment* when she knew him *false.* With an Indifference the most stabbing to a Lover's Soul did he listen to her Upbraidings, and coolly telling her that if he stay'd much longer, she might be in danger of railing herself quite out of breath, made a scornful Bow, and took his Leave.

Some perhaps, into whose hands this little Narrative may fall, may have shar'd the same Fate with poor *Glicera;* like her have been betrayed by the undoing Artifices of deluding Men; like her have been abandoned by the Perfidy of an ungrateful Lover to Shame, to late Repentance, and never-ending Griefs; and it is those only, who can conceive what 'twas she suffered, or know to compassionate the labouring Anguish of a Heart abus'd and inspir'd in this superlative degree. The happy *Insensible,* or the *untempted* Fair, are little capable of judging her Distress, and will be apt to say her *Misfortune* was no more than what her *Folly* merited: yet let those pitiless Deriders of her Frailty take care to fortify their Minds with *Virtue,* or they will but vainly depend on the Force of their own Resolution to defend them from the same Fate she mourn'd.

She now found that she had a greater Stock of Resentment in her Soul, than, till it was rouz'd by this Treatment, she could have believed; sooner would she have sent a Dagger to his Heart, than any way subjected herself to a second Insult, by inviting him to return, or testifying the least remains of Tenderness, had not the Condition she was in compell'd her to it, and forced her trembling Hand, in spite of Pride, to write him the following Epistle.

To the Ungrateful and Perfidious
MELLADORE.

Ill-treated, forsaken as I am, and scorned, perhaps the Remonstrances made you by my *Pen* may be more effectual than those of my *Tongue;* yet had you Love or Honour, Gratitude or Pity, they would be needless: To what purpose then, may you say, do I write?—I have indeed, but little hope of Success on a Man of the Disposition I now find you are, and would sooner chuse Death than the Obligation to you on my own account.—But Oh! there is a tender Part of both of us, which claims a Parent's care: That dear Unborn, that guiltless Consequence of our mutual Raptures, starting within me, makes me feel a Mother's Fondness, and a Mother's Duty:—Nature, Religion, Pity, and Love, all plead in its behalf, and bid me leave no Means untry'd to save its helpless Innocence from Shame and Want, and all the Miseries of an unfriending World;—be just then to your Vows—Remember you are mine as much in the Eye of Heaven, as if a thousand Witnesses had confirm'd our Contract: The Ceremony of the Church is but ordained to bind those Pairs, who of themselves want Constancy and Resolution to keep the Promise which Passion forms.—How often have you sworn I was your Wife, that you considered me as no other, nor would relinquish that right my Love had given you over me for all the World calls dear?—But you are altered since and I too sadly prove your boasted Virtue but Hypocrisy, a Feint to hire me to Destruction.— Ah! how inhuman, how barbarous has been your Usage of me! If with the loss of my expected Dower I also lost your Heart, why did you not then reveal it?—What Provocation had I e'er given you, that you should join with Fortune to undo me? *join,* did I say?—how infinitely inferior was my Unhappiness in being deprived of Wealth, when compared to those more valuable Treasures thy fatal Passion has robb'd me of.—My Innocence, my Reputation, and my Peace of Mind by thee destroy'd, no more to be retrieved!—tormenting Thought! Reflection all distracting! ease me of it, or to the Number of thy monstrous Actions add yet one more, and kill me; the worst of Deaths, is a mild Fate to what I now endure,—and will be a kind Cruelty not only to me, but to the little Wretch I bear:—Let the Sword finish that ruin which Deceit begun, and send us both from Shame, Reproach, and never-ending Woe.—Answer this not, till you have well weigh'd the Circumstances which compel me to write in a manner so vastly different from what I once believed I ever should have cause to do, and make me now subscribe my self no other than

> *Your most injured and*
> *afflicted* GLICERA.

This she ordered to be given into no Hand but his own, to the end that he might not have any pretence to avoid answering it: but being now wholly taken up with making himself appear as agreeable as he could in the Eyes of a fine Lady, who was represented to him as a great Fortune, he either forgot, or had not leisure to compassionate the Complaints of the undone *Glicera.*—For some days did she remain in expectation, but hearing nothing from him, all the little Remains of Patience which her Misfortunes had left her being exhausted, she urg'd a second time the Certainty of her Fate in these Lines.

To the unworthy
MELLADORE.

Tho' void of Hope, as thou art of all Sense of Honour, Gratitude, or Humanity, I once more dare thee to avow thy Purpose,—tell me at once what 'tis I must expect:—No longer seek by silence to skreen thy Perfidy, but boldly own the Fiends that lurk within thee;—what is there in me to awe thee, when Heaven has not the power to do it? Scarce is there a possibility that thou art not the vilest and most detestable of thy whole betraying Specie, yet is there something in my Heart which will not suffer me to assure my self thou art so, till thy own Words destroy Suspence, and put it past my power to make a doubt:—Still, therefore shall I persecute thee with Complaints,—still testify the Agonies of my distracted Soul, divided between *Love* and *Rage:*—Continue with alternate *Soothings* and *Revilings,* as either of the opposing Passions rise, to weary and *perplex* each future Moment of him, whose *Happiness* was once my only Care.—Ah! what a dreadful Revolution has thy Ingratitude caused within my Breast—my Thoughts before serene as an unruffled Sea, now toss'd and hurried by tumultuous Passions, o'erwhelm my Reason, and drive me into Madness.—I cannot live and bear it.—O that as I have heard, I could be certain also, that when supportless Injuries like mine distress the Soul, and drive it from its clayey Mansion, it still has power to wander and disturb the cruel Author of the Wrongs it suffers; how gladly would I welcome Death in hope of Vengeance, in horrid Shapes would I appear to thy affrighted Eyes, distract thy Dreams, and sleeping and waking be ever before thee!—O what a Whirl of wild Ideas possess my troubled Brain—the Tortures of the Damn'd exceed not what I feel;—thou Monster of thy Sex, thou wert not sure of Woman born, thy Mother's Softness must have given some Tincture of Good-nature to thee, but thou art savage all! The Cruelty of Tygers is within thee, and all the base Subtilty of the betraying Crocodile,[1]—Perdition seize thee: How canst thou, darest thou use me thus? Heaven will revenge my Wrongs, tho' it denies the Power to

The Miserable
GLICERA.

Whoever has the least Knowledge of the Temper of Mankind will believe a Letter of this sort would have but little Effect on the Person to whom it was sent. Instead of compassionating her Misfortunes, he took the Opportunity she gave him of reproaching him to come to a downright Quarrel; and having taken a little time for Consideration, answer'd her in these Terms.

To GLICERA.

I know not to what end you give yourself and me these needless Troubles: I thought you Mistress of a better Understanding than to imagine an Amour of the nature our's was, should last for ever:—'Tis not in Reason, 'tis not in Nature to retain perpetual Ardours for the same Object.—The very word *Desire* implies an Impossibility of continuing after the Enjoyment of that which first caused its being:— Those Longings, those Impatiences so pleasing to your Sex, cannot but be lost in Possession, for who can wish for what he has already?— Marriage, as you justly observe, obliges the Pair once united by those Tyes to wear a *Show* of Love; but where is the Man who has one Month become a Husband, that can with truth aver he feels the same, unbated Fondness for his Wife, as when her untasted Charms first won him to her Arms.—Had Circumstances concur'd, I could, however, have been content to drag those Chains with you, so uneasy to be borne, by most of those who wear them; but since Affairs have happened contrary to both our Expectations, lay the fault on Fate,

---

1. **Crocodile:** allusion to the fable from Greek and Egyptian folklore that crocodiles lure people to them with human-sounding, sad groans and moans, then devour them, shedding "crocodile tears" (hypocritical ones) over their prey.

and not on me, who would else have still avow'd my self to be what I once was,

Your most Affectionate
MELLADORE

P.-S. I would have you take notice that this is an Answer to the first of your Epistles;—the other I think not worthy of a serious Regard, and would advise you to send no more to me on any score, this being the last you will receive from me. And am still so much your Friend as to wish your Peace; which, if you really love me with that Ardour you pretend, you can never retrieve, till you resolve to think no more of what has past between us: there being a Necessity that we must part for ever.

It must be something more terrible than Storms or Whirl-winds, or the Roar of foaming Seas, which can describe the Hurricane of her outrageous Soul at reading this Letter:—Reason she had none, nor Reflection, but what served to bring a thousand direful Ideas of approaching Misery before her Eyes;—more than once did she in the first Gust of her Passion endeavour to lay violent Hands on her own Life, but was prevented by a Servant Maid, in whose presence she received these stabbing Lines. The unusual Force of those Emotions with which she was agitated, threw her into a Mother's Pangs long before the time prefix'd by Nature; her Delivery was arriv'd, and by that means the Consequence of her too easy Love proved no more than an Abortion.—The Danger to which this Accident expos'd her, made her Life despair'd of by everybody about her; and in spite of the late Attempts she had made on herself, she no sooner found she was given over by the Skilful, than she verified that Saying of the Poets:

The Thoughts of Death
To one near Death are dreadful.[1]

---

1. **The Thoughts . . . dreadful:** quotation unidentified.

Tho' press'd with ills, which neither Philosophy nor Religion[1] can enable us to sustain with Patience, and every Hour we wish to be no more, we fear to pass the Gates of Life, and travel that dark and unknown Road whence none return to tell what they have met. 'Tis in general so with us:—Some, indeed, may have a greater share of Fortitude than poor *Glicera*, but few there are who hear unmov'd the Warnings of their Fate, especially in Youth.

The extreme Fear she had of Death, in some measure contributed to prolong her Life; for all her Cares being buried in that superior one, the Distraction of her Mind abated:—To this may be also another Reason added, which was, that her desire of Living made her readily comply with every thing prescribed her by the Physicians; and their Skill and Care, join'd to her own strength of Nature, at last restor'd her to that Health, which none who saw her in her Illness imagined she ever would have enjoy'd again.

But while she languished in Pangs which were look'd on as the Harbingers of Death, was the perfidious *Melladore* triumphing in a Bridegroom's Joys. He was married to a young Maid call'd *Helena*, whose Father being lately dead, was reputed to be worth 5000 Crowns, and those were Charms which in his avaritious Eyes far exceeded those *Glicera* was possess'd of, and tho' infinitely inferior to her in every Perfection both of Mind and Body, was thought worthy his most tender Devoirs,[2] while the other unpitied, unregarded, was almost dying under the Miseries which he alone had brought upon her.

When she was told this last Proof of his remorseless Infidelity, the News was near throwing her into a Condition almost as dangerous as that which she had lately escap'd; her Passions, however, being much weaken'd by the decay of her bodily Strength, she fell not into those Ravings, which drove her almost to Madness as the first Causes she had to think him false: And in a few Months she not only regain'd her Health, but also a greater Tranquility of Mind than could be

---

1. **Philosophy nor Religion:** Eighteenth-century writers liked to compare and contrast the comfort religion and philosophy offered; Henry Fielding's *Joseph Andrews* includes a comic episode based on the contrasts.

2. **Devoirs:** attentions.

expected in a Condition such as her's.—The Memory of her Wrongs, however, left her not a Moment, and by degrees settled so implacable a hatred in her Nature; not only to *Melladore,* but to that whole undoing Sex, that she never rejoic'd so much as when she heard of the Misfortunes of any of them.

The Affair between her and *Melladore* being blaz'd abroad, was of too much Disadvantage to her Reputation, to suffer her to imagine she should be able to make her Fortune by Marriage, tho' several there were that addressed her in Terms which had the appearance of Honourable; but she had already experienced Mankind, and was not to be deceived again by the most specious Pretences: despising therefore the whole Sex, she resolved to behave to them in a manner which might advance both her Interest and Revenge; and as nothing is capable of giving more Vexation to a Lover, than a Disappointment when he thinks himself secure from the Fears of it, she gave Encouragement to the Hopes of as many as sollicited her.—She received their Treats and Presents, smil'd on all, tho' never so Old or Disagreeable; nor indeed was it a greater Task, to feign a Tenderness for the most *Ugly* than the *Loveliest* of Mankind—for all alike were hateful to her Thoughts.

Among the Number of those whom her Beauty attracted, and the hope of gaining her more firmly engaged, was an *Alderman,*[1] immensely Rich, but so Old that none who had beheld his wither'd Face, and shaking Limbs, would have believed that in those shrivell'd Veins there was a Warmth sufficient to maintain *Life,* much less to propagate *Desire.* His palsied Tongue, and toothless Gums, however, mumbled out a strange Fervency of Passion; and tho' it was scarce possible to refrain laughing in his Face, yet did she listen to him with a Seriousness which made him not doubt but that he should be in time as happy as he could wish. His Age and Dotage making her believe she should be able to profit herself more by him than any other of her Enamorato's,[2] induced her to treat him with a double Portion of seeming Kindness, nor did he fail to return the Favours she was pleased to grace him with; scarce ever did he visit her without testifying his Grat-

---

1. **Alderman:** member of the higher chamber of a borough or city government.

2. **Enamorato's:** enamoured ones, suitors.

itude for the deference she paid him in some fine Present.—She abounded in Rings, Toys for her Watch, Plate of all kinds,[1] and Jewels; but all these were no more than so many Earnests[2] of his future Zeal: —The last and greatest Favour was yet to come, and he assured her that there wanted only that to engage him to make her a Settlement,[3] which should support her in a manner as grand, as that in which the Wife of *Melladore* at present liv'd. But vastly different were the Designs which made her treat him in the sort she did; from those which he imagined them to be; and resolving to make the most of his Folly, she let into the Secret of her Thoughts a young Woman with whom she was exceeding intimate, called *Laphelia*. This Confidante, who had a ready Wit, to try the Force of this old Wretch's Love, was left sometimes to entertain him, while *Glicera* pretended to be engaged elsewhere on some extraordinary Business. And when he would be talking of her, and almost exhausting the little stock of Breath left him in Encomiums on the Beauty of his absent Mistress, in this fashion would the other reply to him: *Grubguard,* said she, (for that was the Name of this decrepid Lover,) I wonder not that you should be charm'd with *Glicera,* who is without exception the loveliest Woman in the World, but I am amaz'd that a Man of your Sense should go so wrong a way to work for your Designs:—Do you believe that she will ever be brought to like that formal Dress and Behaviour with which you accost her?—She that has a thousand young Noblemen dying at her Feet, each in the Habit of an *Adonis.*[4]—Embroidery, Powder, and Perfume[5] are infinitely taking to our Sex.—A very Angel of a Man with a Bob-wig,[6] a Hat uncock'd and flapping o'er his Eyes

---

1. **Toys for her watch:** charms and jewels to hang on her watch chain. **Plate:** silver or gold utensils and tableware of all kinds.

2. **Earnests:** promises or tokens of something to come or partial payments to bind a contract.

3. **Settlement:** contract providing an independent income or assuring a trust or income upon his death.

4. **Adonis:** epithet for masculine physical perfection, from Greek myth of the beautiful young man loved by Venus and Proserpina.

5. **Embroidery, Powder, and Perfume:** worn by both men and women in the eighteenth century; literature of the time frequently satirized those who did not wear them tastefully.

6. **Bob-wig:** a wig with the bottom locks turned up into curls.

like *Obadiah* in the Play,[1] no Sword, and a dirty Pair of Gloves, would be detestable in a Woman's Eyes. Humph, *reply'd the Dotard,* (after a little Pause) I took *Glicera* for a Person of more Understanding than to prefer an outward Finery to the intrinsick Virtues of her Lover.—My Passion for her is violent and strong, 'tis sincere without Dissimulation or Hypocrisy;—then for my Constancy, no Martyr would suffer more for fair *Glicera* than would her faithful *Grubguard.*—But if 'tis Dress must please her, I can afford to wear as fine Clothes as any Man, and, it may be, become them as well. Scarce could *Laphelia* contain her self from bursting into a loud Laughter at these Words; but she forbore till after he was gone, and relating the Discourse which had pass'd between them to *Glicera*, nothing could afford greater Diversion to them both, unless it were the sight of him the next Visit he made, wholly transform'd from what he had been.—Never was an Object of more Ridicule, and tho' they had form'd a most comical Idea in their Minds of what he would appear; for *Laphelia* was certain he would endeavour to ingratiate himself by this means, yet it was infinitely short of the Reality.—A white Perriwig with a huge Foretop,[2] Clothes trim'd with Silver, a long Sword with a brocaded Ribband hanging to it, and every Implement of the most perfect Beau, which, join'd to a diminutive Stature, small Face and Limbs, made him look exactly like one of those little Imitators of Humanity, which are carried about Streets to make Sport for Children.[3]

Nor was his Habit the greatest part of the Jest, his whole Deportment was also chang'd; the *Minuit* and *Boree* Steps[4] which he had learn'd about some sixty or seventy Years past, he now recalled to mind, and would now and then attempt to cut a Caper as he walk'd

---

1. **Obadiah . . . Play:** a character in Robert Howard's *The Committee* (1662) who became the symbol of the pompous, hypocritical Puritan; this play was a great favorite of Charles II.

2. **Perriwig with a huge foretop:** a full wig of the sort that British judges and barristers still wear; its spreading rather than bobbed curls and fore-top emphasized the diminutive size of the suitor.

3. **Imitators . . . Children:** monkeys.

4. **Minuit and Boree steps:** Both French, the minuet was a slow, stately dance popular at court, and the boree was a rustic dance.

cross the Room, to present his Snuff-box to the Ladies, cramb'd full of *Orangerée:*[1]—But in the midst of these fine Airs, Age unluckily expos'd itself, and down he fell at the Feet of his Mistress, more through Weakness than Excess of Passion.—This Accident, in spite of all they had resolv'd, made them burst into an immoderate Laughter, which had like to have spoil'd all; for the *Alderman*, too conscious of the just Cause he had given them for Mirth, was a little out of humour at it, and began to make an aukward Excuse, that having been at a Country-Dancing some time before, he had sprain'd his Ancle, which had ever since been weak. *Glicera*, vex'd that she had so far discovered[2] the contemptible Opinion she had of him, had her Face immediately cover'd with a Scarlet-blush; but having a vast deal of ready Wit, recovering herself from the Confusion she had been in, I beg a thousand Pardons, *said she,* for the Ill-manners I have doubtless seem'd guilty of by so untimely a Mirth: but I assure you, *Sir!* it was wholly my own Folly I was ridiculing; for having a desire that my Apartment should be particularly Nice to-day, I made my Maid scour the Floor with new Milk, and the Cream has occasion'd so great a Slipperiness in the Boards, that I have twice myself had the same Misfortune which has befallen you. She was just telling me the Story when you came in, *added Laphelia,* willing to second what she had said, and if my Mirth must have been fatal to me, I could not for my Soul have forborn it, to see the ill Success of my Friend's over-great Care to please. This Excuse passing for a current one, the transmografied Lover resum'd his good Humour, and continued his Grimaces and affected Manner of Behaviour to so extravagant a degree, that more than once the Ladies were in danger of relapsing into that Error which had lately cost their Invention some pains to extricate themselves from.

Laphelia, to carry on the Jest, did not fail however, the next time she had an Opportunity, to tell him that her fair Friend was wonderfully pleased with the Change she observ'd in him, and that she did not doubt but he would find the good Effects of it in a short time: But they having contrived together, how they might make a better

---

1. **Orangerée:** Snuff scented with orange blossom perfume.
2. **discovered:** revealed.

Advantage of this Infatuation than meerly Sport; she told him that as he had begun, he must also perfect himself in all the Accomplishments of the other End of the Town; he must carry them to the Play, the Opera, and Masquerades,[1] and after attending them Home, must sit down to Gaming. No Man ever gain'd his will on a fine Lady, *said she,* till he had first lost a good Sum to her at Cards;—nothing discovers the Passion of a Lover so much as parting freely with his Money, and there is no other way of doing it handsomely:—Besides, *continued she,* play will give you a thousand Opportunities of expressing your Love and Gallantry:—You forget what you are doing, throw down one Card instead of another, commit a thousand Errors in the Game, and all through excess of Passion;—you can think of nothing in the presence of your Mistress but herself:—In fine, there are so many pretty little Airs a Man may give himself this way, that 'tis impossible he should not be agreeable. *Grubguard* listened with a wonderful Attention to this Discourse, and having met with so encouraging a Reception from *Glicera,* that he had not doubted obtaining the last Favour; yet finding she still evaded the grant of it, he imagin'd indeed that there was something more she expected from him: He was not unacquainted with the loss of her Fortune, and her Sufferings on account of *Melladore,* and knew very well that she must want Money; it therefore seemed feasible to him that she had made *Laphelia,* who he knew was dearly beloved by her, to talk to him in this manner. Resolving therefore to comply with the Humour, he thank'd her for the Advice she had given him, and told her he would most certainly obey it.

Nor did he do any otherwise than he had said, there was not the least particular of the Injunction laid upon him that he did not observe, with all the Exactness imaginable; and the Sums which every Night he lost to *Glicera,* took from her in a very few Weeks all need of lamenting her want of Money.—In this manner did she continue

---

1. **Masquerades:** masked costume balls. At masquerades men and women in costume mingled more freely than at other kinds of parties and took advantage of being, or pretending to be, unrecognized. Public masquerades became the rage in the 1720s. Count Heidegger's at the Haymarket often attracted a thousand ticket purchasers.

to delude him for a considerable Time: a true *Lover* like a *Camelion* can subsist for a long while on Air,[1] and stedfastly believing that the Measures he took would certainly put him in possession of his Wishes in the end, he waited with Patience for the happy Minute.

But it was not on this old Dotard alone that *Glicera* had Power, a great Number of much younger and wittier *Men* gave her the Opportunity of revenging on that Sex the Injuries she had received from one of them; and having as large a Share of Sense as Beauty, knew so well how to manage the Conquests she gain'd that not one whose *Heart* confess'd the Triumph of her Eyes, but made a Sacrifice also of his *Purse.*—So magnificent was she in the Trophies of her Slaves, that few Court-*Beauties* appeared more ornamented then did this *City*-Belle, when ever she appeared in any publick Place; and never did a Woman passionately in love take greater Pains to captivate the ador'd Object of her Affections than did this fair *Jilt,* to appear amiable in the Eyes of Mankind. Tho' she had enough overcome all Thoughts of *Melladore,* not to languish for his Return, or even wish to see him; yet the Hatred which his Ingratitude had created in her Mind was so fix'd and rooted there, that it became part of her Nature, and she seem'd born only to give Torment to the whole Race of Man, nor did she know another Joy in Life. In this Position let us leave her for a while, each Day attracting to her worshipp'd Shrine some new Adorer, gay, pleas'd and vain in conquering Beauty and superior Charms, and see what Fate in the mean time attended the perfidious *Melladore,* whose cruel Treatment had first occasioned so strange a Change in her once gentle and unartful Soul.

In some few days after his Marriage with *Helena,* he went to receive her Fortune; but how terribly Just was his Disappointment, when the Banker in whose hands it was lodg'd, told him, that the Moment before he came he had receiv'd a *Caveat*[2] to put a stop to his Payment of the whole or any part of it, till a material Question should be decided between the Lawyers: Which was, that the next of Kin to the

---

1. **Camelion . . . air:** chameleons were thought to live on air.

2. **Caveat:** a formal notice filed in court asking for a stay until the case of an interested party is heard.

Father of *Helena,* objected that the Marriage Ceremony between that Gentleman and her Mother had never been perform'd, and dar'd the old Lady, who was still living, to the Proof. Full of the extremest Vexation did *Melladore* return home with this News; but *Helena,* who at the hearing it was not much less perplex'd, immediately sending for her Mother, they both grew more satisfied on her protesting that it was only a malicious Prosecution, and that nothing could be more easy than it was for her to prove her Marriage.

Now were the best Lawyers consulted, and the Suit on both sides carryed on with the utmost Vigour, the Gentlemen of the long Robe flattering their Clients of each Party with hopes of Success: The truth is, both made out their several Cases in so fair a manner, and had so great a Number of Evidences ready to attest the Truth of what they said, that they deceived themselves; which makes good the Proverb, that says, whoever conceals the truth of his *Distemper* from his *Physician,* or the *Cause* he would defend from his *Lawyer,* is sure of being worsted.[1] *Melladore* relying on the Assurances made him by his Mother-in-law, talk'd of nothing but the Damages he should recover of his Adversaries, and spent his Money freely in Treats and Fees for extraordinary Diligence, not doubting but that all would be returned to him with ample Interest. Thus did he exult till the Day appointed for the Tryal on the Examination of Witnesses: Those who appear'd for the Mother of *Helena* appear'd so distracted in their Evidences, contradicted each other, and committed so many Errors, that the Judge had good reason to believe they had been corrupted; therefore ordering them to be put apart, he questioned them one by one, on which they were easily detected of Perjury, and *Melladore, Helena,* and her Mother hiss'd out of Court with the utmost Derision; the whole Effects of the Deceas'd decreed to the young Gentleman who began the Process, and *Melladore,* for so ill defending it, condemn'd to pay the Expence.

What was now the Condition of this guilty and unhappy Man? He had now not only married a Wife without a Fortune, but also a

---

1. **whoever . . . worsted:** variant of the proverb, "Deceive not thy physician, confessor, nor lawyer, " George Herbert, *Jacula Prudentum* (1651), no. 105; Herbert's collections of proverbs were almost as well known as Aesop's fables.

Woman basely born, and in whose Disposition he had reason to believe there was some tincture of her Mother's Nature: Besides all this, the prodigious Charge he had been at, in carrying on the Law, had very much broke in upon his Stock, he was not only oblig'd to call in several Sums he had out at Interest, but was likewise compell'd to borrow: Yet did not the Pride and Extravagance of *Helena* abate, by these Mortifications; she would keep as many Servants as before, as good a Table, and wear as rich Clothes: this occasion'd many bitter Quarrels between them, which in a very little time intirely eras'd all the former Tenderness that either had for the other. He endeavour'd to exert the Authority of a Husband in restraining her Expenses; she show'd herself a very Wife in the worst Sense, and without any Consideration of the ill Circumstances to which they were in danger of being reduc'd by her riotous manner of Life, had no bounds to her Desires, but sought the immediate Gratification of them, let it cost what it would: And to what Extremes sometimes her Inclinations were capable of transporting her, he discover'd soon after the loss of the Law-Suit.

Happening to come into her Chamber on a sudden, he surpriz'd her with a Paper in her Hand, on which her eyes being intently fix'd, she saw him not till he was very near her; but as soon as she perceiv'd him, she attempted to put it in her Pocket. The Confusion which overspread her Face as she was about to do so, excited his Curiosity, and made him not doubt but that there was something extraordinary in it; he therefore demanded to see it, which she refusing, he went to seize by Force: they struggled for some time, but his Strength at last prevailing, he took it from her; and as if his Misfortunes were not already great enough, he found an Addition to them in the following Lines.

To the Lovely HELENA.

Bad as you believe your Husband's Circumstances, I can assure you they are infinitely worse than you imagine; his ready Money is not only gone, but he is about to mortgage those Acres which were design'd your Jointure,[1] in case Fortune had been as kind to you as your Virtues merited. I heard this account of him last Night from one perfectly acquainted with his Affairs:—I would, therefore, once more endeavour to persuade you, to save what you can out of that general Ruin in which you else will certainly, and shortly be involv'd.—The Ship I told you of, sets sail for *Holland* in a few days; pack up your Jewels, and what other valuable Things you have, with all possible expedition, and leave this unworthy Husband.—I have provided a Concealment for you till the departure of the Vessel begins the happy Æra of our Lives, and begins our Voyage to a Land where we may live, and love, uninterrupted by any jealous Eyes:—Let your Answer be left for me at the usual Place, if you cannot come abroad.—Farewell my Angel,—I long to feast on those luxurious Joys you have yet but permitted me to taste, and to prove the eternal Vigour of

> *My adorable* Helena's
> *most devoted Slave,*
> VILLAGNAN.

This *Villagnan* was a kind of a Merchant, one at least who by retailing some petty Commodities between *England* and *Holland*, assumed to himself that Name. *Melladore* knew him well, he had frequently bought such Goods of him as he dealt in, and it was by that means he had an Opportunity of conversing with *Helena*, and discovering enough of her Disposition to encourage him to make a Declaration of Love to her. But never was Surprize or Rage equal to the Force of both these Passions in the Soul of *Melladore* at reading this Letter; little could he have believ'd, without so convincing a Proof, that such a Man would have attempted the Honour of a Woman like *Helena*, much less that her Pride would have suffer'd her to have rewarded his Love, or even condescended to listen to any Discourses on that Subject from one so infinitely inferior to her in every Circumstance. He having never felt much more for her than an Indifference,

---

1. **Jointure:** provision of land or income for a widow; usually made as part of the marriage settlement.

which by his late Uneasiness on her account was grown into a kind of a distaste, now turn'd to a perfect loathing on the knowledge of her Falshood:—He upbraided her in terms which let her see there was not the least remains of Tenderness for her in his Heart;—if there had, *Grief* would have been mingled with his *Indignation*, and his *Sorrow* at the discovery that he had a Rival in her Love, been equal to the *Rage* which the Injury she had done his and her own Honour caused. But instead of that tender Concern which a truly affectionate Husband could not have avoided testifying even in the midst of his Reproaches; all his Looks and words denoted only Hate, inveterate Hate, and the most keen Disdain. She, on the other side, made show of as little Regret, neither denying, nor excusing the Crime she had been guilty of, but behaving with a haughty Sullenness: All the Answer he could be able to get from her, being only that the Usage she had of late received from him was sufficient to provoke any Woman. He so little endur'd her in his fight, that he was some time in debate with himself whether he should by confining her take care to prevent her from dishonouring him for the future; or by leaving her to her Liberty, suffer her to take the advice of her *Enamorato*, and by that means get rid of her. He now repented he had seen the Letter, which if he had not, she had infallibly been gone; but now to endure her leaving him in this manner, he thought would look too tame, and subject him to the ridicule of the World; not for any Love of her Society, therefore, but for the sake of his own Character, did he disappoint her Lover's Hopes, by locking her into a Garret, of which, suffering none but himself to keep the Key, nor to go in to carry her Food to sustain Life; he took from her all possibility of escaping, till he heard the Ship mention'd in the Letter had put out to Sea, and in it the Man so charming in *Helena's* Eyes. Then did he with an Air wholly compos'd of Scorn set open the Doors, and tell her she was free to go to her dear *Villagnan* if she could find the way to him; tho' he had taken care she should carry no more out of his House than she brought into it, having secur'd what Jewels and Plate had presented her with before and since she was his Wife, leaving at her disposal only a few Clothes, and not the best even of those.

But in this Kingdom how great is the Privilege of Wives! how dangerous is it for a Husband to irritate them, tho' on the most justifiable Provocation! and generally speaking, the most guilty, are the least able to endure Reproof, as a celebrated Poet justly observes;

> Forgiveness to the Injur'd does belong,
> But they ne'er pardon who have done the wrong.[1]

The Severity with which *Helena* found herself treated by *Melladore*, notwithstanding the Cause she had given him, rouz'd all that was vindictive in her Nature, and regarding him with equal Hate, meditated nothing but how she should be able to return the Indignities with which he us'd her: Nor was it long before she found the Means. She went to the House of a Woman who had been the Confidante of her Amour with *Villagnan*, and was a Person perfectly skill'd in all the little Artifices of the Town. By her advice she took up, on the Credit of her Husband, not only all manner of Apparel, Jewels, Plate, rich Furniture, but also several large sums of Money; *Melladore* retaining yet the Reputation of being able to discharge much greater Debts.

The Noise, however, of her being separated from her Husband, made every one bring in their Bills much sooner than otherwise they would have done; and 'tis hard to say, whether Astonishment, or Rage, was most predominant over the Soul of this unhappy Husband when he found what she had done. He could not have imagin'd, that considering the Disadvantages she already lay under in every Circumstance, she would have dared to have acted in this manner; but so he found it, to compleat his Ruin: nor was there any Possibility of evading the Payment of those Persons who had given her Credit.[2] How truly wretched now had a few Months made the once prosperous, rich, gay, haughty *Melladore;* and how severely did the unerring Hand of Providence revenge the Injuries he had done *Glicera!* Scarce could one think there was a Woe in store superior to those already named; yet did he

---

1. **Forgiveness . . . wrong:** John Dryden's *Conquest of Grenada, Part II,* 1.2.5–6. Zulema's speech opening the scene in which he reveals plans to deceive by first gaining trust.

2. **evading . . . Credit:** Husbands were legally responsible for the debts of their wives, even when the wives had independent means, as Helena does not.

hereafter meet with one, which when compar'd, all others seem'd light and insignificant.

The vast Expences which had attended the Law-Suit, the riotous Manner in which he liv'd after his Marriage with *Helena,* her Extravagancies at that time, and her Contrivances since her Elopement of undoing him, reduc'd him to mortgage the last Stake he now had left him; and so closely did avenging Fate pursue him, that as if it was not a sufficient Punishment for the Crime he had been guilty of, in breach of Vows, that he had met with those very Misfortunes in the Woman he made choice of, which to avoid, he had made himself that Criminal; he must also have the Person he had wrong'd, the Arbitratress of his Destiny, and become wholly in the power of one from whom he neither could, nor ought to hope for Mercy.

So was it order'd by the divine Dispensation, to render his Shame the greater, that Alderman *Grubguard* was the Person to whom he mortgag'd his Lands. Had he known the Attachments he was under to *Glicera*, or indeed that he had been of her Acquaintance, sooner would he have leap'd a Precipice, plung'd himself into outrageous Seas, done any thing rather than have suffer'd his Misfortunes to be known by one, who, in all probability would reveal them to her: But wholly ignorant of the Correspondence held between them, Fate it was that directed him to *Grubguard*, who no sooner had the Mortgage in his hands, than he came to *Glicera*, and rejoiced that he had News to tell her, in which he was very certain she would take delight. He immediately related to her the whole Story: She had before been inform'd of the Disappointment he had met with in his Wife's Affairs, the Law-Suit, how she had been prov'd in open Court Illegitimate, and her Elopement since; but now to be assur'd that he was also ruin'd in his own Fortune, inevitably undone, fill'd her with a Satisfaction so exquisite, that for a moment she thought it impossible it could be exceeded; but soon it gave way to an impatient Desire, which gave her an adequate Share of Disquiet.—She long'd to be the Mistress of that Writing which gave the Person who had it in possession, the Power of all that *Melladore* was now worth in the World, and the little probability there was that *Grubguard* would have Gallantry enough to make a Present of so much consequence, and what had cost him so great a

Sum of Money, spread through all her Soul so mortal a Bitter, that it empoison'd all the Sweets her Revenge had tasted at the first News of *Melladore's* Misfortunes. She appear'd in so ill a Humour all the time the *Alderman* stay'd with her, that he imagin'd she still loved that false Man, and that her melancholy proceeded from the Knowledge of his Ruin. This gave our old Enamorato as much Anxiety of Mind as he had Delicacy enough to be capable of; and he long'd for an Opportunity of communicating his Opinion to *Laphelia*, who he fancied was a very great Friend to him, since she had given him advice to new model his Dress and Behaviour.

Glicera was no less impatient to consult with that Confidante, and as soon as the Departure of the *Alderman* gave her liberty, she sent for her, and acquainted her with what he had related to her concerning *Melladore*, and the Uneasiness she was in to have the Mortgage of his Estate in her possession. *Laphelia* could not forbear chiding her for the exorbitancy of her Wishes:—I never heard of any thing so unreasonable in my Life, *said she*; is it not enough for your Revenge that the Man who has wrong'd you is undone in every Circumstance, without triumphing yourself in the ruin of his Fortune:—That Fortune, answer'd the other, ought to have been mine, had *Melladore* been just,—nor do I think it sufficient that he has lost it, without I also have gain'd it. How often has he sworn, that were he master of ten thousand Worlds, they all were mine:—With what a seeming Zeal and Sanctity, has he invok'd each Saint in Heaven a Witness of his Vows to me!—O never, never can the Breach of them be pardon'd, nor never shall I think of Wrongs repair'd, till I am in possession of my Right;—I mean, *continu'd she*, the *Estate* of *Melladore*; for his *Person*, were he in a Condition, is now become unworthy my Acceptance. *Laphelia* perceiving she was resolute, offer'd no more in contradiction to what she said, but told her that she thought there was little cause for her Uneasiness on the score she had named, for that she durst swear the *Alderman* had Love enough to give her the half of all he was worth, much less would he deny to make her a Present of this Mortgage. O my dear *Laphelia*, *cry'd she*, could we but bring that about, how happy should I be! Never doubt it, *Glicera*, *reply'd the other*, leave it to my Management; and as I have begun to instruct him in the

Rudiments of Gallantry, depend upon it I will make him perfectly accomplish'd for our Purpose before I have done with him. A vast deal of further Discourse, much to the same purpose, past between them; at the Conclusion of which, it was agreed that *Grubguard* should be invited the next day to play at *Ombre*[1] with them, and that *Glicera* should be call'd out of the Room, on some pretence that her assisting Friend might have an Opportunity of trying her Wit, and the power she had of deceiving handsomely; after which, Night being pretty well advanc'd, they took leave of each other, the one departed to perfect the Stratagem which as yet was but an Embrio[2] in her inventive Brain, and our fair *Jilt* to pray to all the Powers of Eloquence to assist her in her Designs.

Our old Beau, who had past the Night in Perplexities, equal with those *Glicera* sustain'd, was infinitely pleas'd at the Invitation made him next day, especially when he heard that *Laphelia* was to be there, not doubting but that he should be able to persuade her to let him into the secret of his Mistress's Chagrin; he therefore prevented the appointed Hour, in hope of getting some Opportunity of speaking to her alone: his Impatience, therefore, forwarding the Gratification of the other, soon after he came in, a Servant belonging to the House where *Glicera* lodg'd, told her there was one desir'd to speak with her. On which, after having made a short Apology for her absence, she went out of the Room, and left them together.

She was no sooner gone, than *Grubguard* unwilling to lose a Moment, drew his Chair near to that *Laphelia* was sitting in, and began to relate to her the Troubles of his Mind; but she no sooner heard what had occasion'd them, than to save him the labour of further Speech, she interrupted him in this manner: How ingeniously, *said she laughing*, does Love torment his Votaries!—The wanton God prides himself in your Pains, and finds out a thousand Ways to make you delay the Bliss for which you languish;—you are at this time the happiest Man in the World, and do not know it.—Fortune has put in

---

1. **Ombre:** card game for three players played with forty cards; it is featured in Alexander Pope's *Rape of the Lock.*

2. **Embrio:** embryo.

your power the only Means to gain *Glicera's* Favour; and I am certain
should the greatest Monarch on Earth become your Rival, he must
sue in vain, unless possess'd of one thing, which none but *Grubguard*
has the means of bestowing. You speak in Riddles, *Madam!* answer'd
the old Dotard, but if there be a possibility of my being happy, why
will you not let me know?—There is nothing I would not do to
express my Love for fair *Glicera,* nor to testify my Gratitude to you.
I have told her so, *resum'd the artful* Laphelia, I am certain you that
have given her so many Proofs of your unbounded Passion, would not
scruple to add one more, especially when it will be the last that will
be expected from you, and infallibly put you in immediate possession
of your Wishes. Ah! *cry'd he,* (in a Transport which was pretty near
depriving him of the small Stock of Breath which Nature had left him,
to keep the almost expiring Lamp of Life awake;) dear, dear, *Laphelia!*
inform me what it is, that I may fly to make this acceptable Offering
at the Shrine of my ador'd Goddess, and I will worship thee for the
kind Direction. How just was my Opinion of you, *said she,* and how
much has *Glicera* wrong'd your wondrous Passion, to imagine you
would think such a Trifle too great a Price for the purchase of her
Love. Ah the Cruel! (mumbled he out, with his toothless Gums,) but
when I get her once in my Possession, I will so revenge myself for all
her coyness.—But sweet Girl, *continued he,* let me know what it is she
expects or desires of me, before she resigns me her Paradise of Beauty.
Nothing, *reply'd she,* (who now thought he was sufficiently work'd up)
but to make her a Present of that Mortgage you received yesterday
from *Melladore.*—Here she stop'd, observing all the time his Countenance, in which she saw immediatley so great a Change, as made
her more than half afraid she had taken all this pains to no purpose;
and perceiving he continued in a profound Silence, Heavens! *resum'd*
she, has my Penetration deceiv'd me then!—do you hesitate if you
should accept so great a Blessing as *Glicera,* when offer'd you on Terms
so easy?—Is such a Sum to be valued in competition with the Enjoyment of so fine a woman?—You quite mistake my Thoughts, *answer'd*
he, 'tis not the Money I boggle at; were it twice as much, I could
afford to make a Sacrifice of it for my Pleasure:—But alack! I have no

Notion, that after all this, I shall be a jot the nearer to the Gratification of my Wishes:—To be plain, I am afraid she has still a kindness for that spendthrift, and aims to get the Writings out of my hands only to return them into his;—I should then, indeed, be finely fool'd.—O fye, Mr. *Alderman!* I am asham'd of your distrust, *cry'd she,* interrupting him; can you suspect her of so much Folly, or me of such an unexampled piece of Baseness, to persuade you to this Generosity, if I did not know you would find your account in it?—I assure you she hates *Melladore,* and so far from giving him up his Bond, she wishes to have it in her possession, for no other reason than to prosecute the Penalty of it with more Rigour than perhaps any other Person would do.—This I can aver to you is Truth, and durst pawn my Life on the Certainty of what I say:—But, *pursu'd she,* affecting to seem displeas'd, I shall trouble myself no farther between you,—'tis in vain to endeavour to make People happy, who are resolv'd to be the contrary:—I am only sorry I should say so much in your behalf last Night, since I find *Glicera* was in the right to believe you did not love her half so well as you pretended. She cannot be more belov'd than she is by me *resum'd the Dotard,* and I have spar'd no Expence either of Time or Money to convince her of it;—but as I know *Melladore* was once very dear to her, you cannot blame my Jealousy;—they say, old Love can never be forgot, and if she should lay this Stratagem to deliver him his Writings, my easy Nature would be the Jest of the whole Town. Not more than her's, good *Grubguard, reply'd* Laphelia, the Injuries she has received from *Melladore* are not of a nature to be pardoned, much less rewarded to the prejudice of another, as this would be to you.—Believe me, I am perfectly acquainted with her very Soul, and know that she has only the extremest Detestation for that unworthy Man; and if you require it, will give you my solemn Oath.—No, no, it needs not, *interrupted he,* let her put me in possession of her Charms, and I will put her in possession of the *Writing;*—this she will not scruple, if she really designs to make me happy. Bless me! *cry'd Laphelia,* with an air of Surprize, I would not have her hear you for the World;—are you mad?—For shame, *Alderman,* recant what you have said.—I wonder how you could forget yourself and her so far, as to be guilty of such a Thought:—you talk as if you were in *Change Alley*,[1] where they chaffer[2] one *Transfer* for another.—Is such a Woman as *Glicera* to be had by way of Bargain? Nothing could be more pleasant than the Figure he made at this moment. He stood with his Mouth half open, and his Eyes fix'd on her with an unmeaning Stare, all the time she was speaking; nor when she left off, could he either gather up his Countenance, or recollect his Spirits enough to make her any answer; and she went on in this manner: Is this, *said she*, the effect of all the pains I have taken to make you worthy of *Glicera*, and have you given her so many proofs of your Passion, to be found deficient at last, when she was on the very brink of yielding too?—Did she not say last Night, as we were walking together in the Garden, that she thought she had held out long enough against a Person of your Accomplishments and Gallantry, and that there wanted but this one Experiment more to be made of your Generosity, before she threw herself into your Arms.—With what an angelic Softness in her Voice and Eyes did she leaning on my Shoulder, ask me, if I did not think you the most agreeable Man breathing;—then sigh'd and blush'd:—but I will reveal no more, I will rather persuade her to call back her Heart.— As she was proceeding, the old Sinner, who by this Discourse imagin'd, indeed, that he was belov'd by her: Ah *Laphelia! cry'd he out*, do not be so unkind,—she shall have the Mortgage, and I will trust to her Goodness for the Recompence of my Passion; nor did I mean to offend her by those foolish Words, which I beseech you do not report to her, but tell me in what manner this Present will be most acceptable. That indeed requires some thought, *said Laphelia*; and the time you have lost in these idle Scruples, had much better have been employ'd in contriving this handsomely: The manner of conferring an Obligation, is often more than the Obligation itself.—If you give it to her in the fashion you have done a Ring, or Pair of Ear-rings, or some such trifle,

---

1. **Change Alley:** Exchange Alley runs between Lombard Street, the banking center of London since the twelfth century, and Cornhill, one of the streets giving entrance to the Royal Exchange.

2. **Chaffer:** trade, bargain.

I know not if her delicacy will accept it, on the account of the large Sum she knows you have paid down for it;—I would therefore have you do it in the same way as you have enforc'd her, as it were, to take your Money,—that is, lose it at play.—I will pretend to be a little indispos'd, and refuse the Cards:—do you two sit down to *Picquet*,[1] and after you have play'd three or four Games, you may say you have no more ready Money about you, but will set her this Bond against a Kiss, or some such Favour.—I do not know any thing that will be more truly Gallant, and testify you to have a greater Acquaintance with the *Beau Monde*,[2] than such a Behaviour.—I know you will not leave this Apartment without your Reward, and that I may be no obstacle to your Happiness—as soon as I see the Bond lost, still continuing my feign'd Illness, I will take my Leave, and give you the Liberty of playing on, or making what use you please of the Discovery I have made you after I am gone.

Scarce could the *Alderman* contain his Joy at this Assurance, and now not doubting but that a few Hours would put him in the full possession of what he had so long been labouring to obtain, would have fallen on his Knees to thank the obliging Contriver of his Happiness, if he had not known he must have put her to the trouble of helping him on his Legs again.—He utter'd a thousand Expressions of Friendship and Gratitude after his fashion, and affected to appear so florid, that it was a task more difficult than any she had yet gone through, for the Person to whom he addressed himself, to forbear laughing, and by an ill-tim'd Mirth destroy all she had been doing: but *Glicera*, who pitied the Constraint she was under, and had been all this while no farther than the next Room, which being parted from the other only by a thin Wainscot,[3] gave her the Opportunity of hearing all that had passed; no sooner found her Friend had succeeded in

---

1. **Picquet:** card game suited for two players, using a thirty-two-card deck consisting of cards numbered seven and above.

2. **Beau Monde:** literally, "beautiful world"; fashionable society; the only world worth belonging to.

3. **Wainscot:** paneling.

the Plot they had laid together, than she appear'd, making a formal Excuse[1] for having stay'd so long. After which the Cards were call'd for, and the *Ombre*-Table brought; but *Laphelia* cry'd her Head ach'd, and she could not play. Let us have a game at *Picquet* then, Madam, said the *Alderman*. With all my heart, *reply'd Glicera,* since that ill-natur'd Creature will not make one among us.

They play'd at first for small Stakes, but the *Alderman* observing Directions to a tittle, pretending he had no more Gold, pluck'd out the Writings of *Melladore's* Estate, and cry'd, Come Madam, will you venture a Kiss against this? Yes, answer'd *Glicera,* and so begun the Game; *Grubguard* every now and then looking on *Laphelia,* endeavouring to discover by her Countenance how she approv'd his Behaviour, to which she gave him an assenting Nod, and he play'd briskly on.—The Game was soon run off;—*Glicera* had *Point,* or *Quatorze*[2] almost every time,—and drew the wish'd for Stake; which, as soon as she had in her Hands, I know not, *said she,* if I have not been playing for nothing, I understand so little of Law, that I cannot be certain whether I can demand the Penalty mentioned in this Bond, without a farther power from you than the bare possession of it. No, fair *Glicera, reply'd the Alderman,* I will not cheat you, and as you have fairly won it, must also let you know, that before you can act as *Mortgagee,* there must be a Label annexed to the Writing, testifying that these Deeds are assign'd to you for a valuable Consideration receiv'd by me.—I will have a Lawyer then to do it immediately, *said she,* for I love not a Shadow without a Substance. Nor will you feed your Adorer with that airy Food I hope, *resum'd* Grubgard. No, *answer'd she,* to him who truly loves me, I would rather exceed than be any way deficient in the Gratitude I owe him. These words confirming him in the belief which *Laphelia* had before inspir'd him with, made him not in the least oppose her sending for a Lawyer, who happening to live in the same Street, came in a short time, and made *Glicera* as full a *Mortgagee* as if she had pay'd her Money down to *Melladore* for that power.

---

1. **formal Excuse:** polite excuse with no pretense of being the actual reason.

2. **Quartorze:** quatorze, four of a kind.

The Lawyer, as soon as he had done his Business, took his Leave, and *Laphelia*, who stay'd only to set her hand as a Witness, now retired, as she had promised the *Alderman* she would do. Scarce had she left the Room a moment, before the Dotard run to her as fast as Age and Weakness would permit, and began to testify by his Behaviour that he now look'd upon her as his own; but soon did she strike a damp on the Boldness of his aspiring Hopes, her very Looks were sufficient to have aw'd a Lover more emboldened:—Think not, *said she*, to treat me with any other Liberties than such as the chastest Vestal might approve.—It is not in the power of the loveliest, wittiest, and most engaging of all your Sex, to tempt me to an Act of Shame, much less in thine, thou Wretch! worn out with Diseases, bow'd down even to the Grave with Age:—Rather shouldst thou employ the remnant of thy Days in Penitence and Prayer for past Offences, than attempt new ones:—how canst thou, durst thou, think of Sin, when every moment thou hast before thy Eyes unceasing Monitors of thy aproaching Fate? Death and Futurity ought to be now the only Subjects of thy Care, and the vain Pleasures of this World seem odious even to Remembrance. And is it for this, *said he*, that I have parted with so much Money, and the Mortgage of *Melladore's* Estate!—Did you not tell me that you would not be ungrateful to the Man who truly lov'd you. Yes, *reply'd she*, nor would I be so, were Love and Honour to be found among you;—but you are Betrayers all;—vile Hypocrites! who feign a Tenderness only to undo us.—The Man who truly *Loves* would *Marry* me; that is not in thy power, already art thou wedded, then what pretence hast thou to a noble Passion:—If I encourag'd thy Addresses, or accepted thy Gifts, 'twas but to punish thy impudent Presumption.—I rais'd thy hopes to make thy Fall from them at once more shocking, and receiv'd thy Presents by way of Payment, for the pains I have taken to reform thee, which sure, if not incorrigible, this Treatment will.—Go home, therefore, and resolve if possible to be honest, and I will then esteem and thank thee for the Benefits thou hast conferr'd upon me; but till then, I look on them only as so many Baits to Shame, and given only to betray my Virtue.

'Twould be needless to say any thing of the Rage of this disappointed Lover, the Reader will easily believe it was excessive; 'tis certain never Man had a greater Shock, and he testifyed his Sense of it in the most bitter Expressions his Capacity would enable him to make; but all he said, having no effect on her, he fell into such railings and revilings, that she was oblig'd to bid him quit the House, and threaten'd that if he stay'd and continued his Incivilities, she would send for those should teach him better Manners.

Thus ended the Amour of old *Grubguard*, and 'tis highly probable that after this he made an attack on no other Woman; for the Mortification he had receiv'd in this, joining with his Age and Infirmities, in a short time sent him to answer in another World the Errors he had been guilty of in this.

Melladore, being in a little time inform'd that *Glicera* was now the *Mortgagee* of his Estate, made use of all the Interest he had in the World, to raise Money to pay it off, having heard too much of the hatred she bore him, and was too conscious of the just Cause he had given her for it, not to expect she would treat him with the utmost Severity. But alas! tho' he had many Relations and Acquaintance, who had it in their *Power* to have oblig'd him, he found none who had the *Will*, and was now by sad Experience convinced that the Unfortunate have few Friends.[1] All his endeavours proving unsuccessful, and his Wife still continuing her Extravagancies, drove him into the greatest Extremities to which a Man can be reduc'd.—He was obliged to live conceal'd in an obscure part of the Town to avoid being prosecuted for Debt;—he was in want of almost every Necessary of Life,— and what was more terrible than all besides, Remorse and late Repentance lash'd his tormented Soul with ever-during Stings: He was now sensible of, and acknowledged in Agonies not to be express'd, the Justice of the divine Power in subjecting him to one he had so greatly wrong'd; he saw the hand of Heaven was in it, and was so greatly humbled, that, as much enforc'd by his Griefs for the Baseness he had been guilty of, as by his Necessities, he writ the following Letter to *Glicera*.

---

1. **the Unfortunate have few friends:** perhaps a paraphrase of "The poor is hated even of his own neighbor: But the rich hath many friends" (Prov. 14:20).

To the most deserving, yet most injur'd
of her Sex, the Lovely GLICERA.

Let not the well-known Characters,[1] which compose this Epistle, I
conjure you, put a stop to your perusal of it.—Believe me, you will
find nothing in it of that Disposition which formerly made me blind
to my own Happiness, and throw from me a Treasure I ought rather
to have preserved at the hazard of my Life.—O *Glicera!* I have greatly
wrong'd you, I confess; nor do I well know whether my Sorrows for
the Treatment I have given you, or for the Misfortunes my Crime has
brought upon me, are the most prevailing in my Soul:—Like the
foolish *Indians,* I have barter'd *Gold* for *Glass,* exchang'd the *best* for
one of the *vilest* that ever disgraced the name of Woman—But I imagine not that my Condition is unknown to you;—the Pawn that you
have in your hands, and which gives you the power over the last Stake
of my ship-wreck'd Fortune, sufficiently informs you to what a
wretched State I am reduc'd.—I will not, therefore, trouble you with
a needless recital of my Misfortunes, my Business now is to implore
your Mercy.—Yet, Wretch that I am, how can I expect or hope for
pity from her who found it not from me.—But Heaven, whom daily
we offend, is mov'd by Penitence and Prayer; and *Glicera* had once so
much of the divine Nature in her, that were I not abandon'd to Despair, and self-condemn'd, I yet might have some hope in her excelling
Goodness.—I cannot among the great Number of my pretended
Friends raise Money to redeem the Mortgage, nor any part of it; and
I am constrain'd to beg you would be pleas'd to release so much of
the Land, as I can borrow on, a Sum sufficient to buy a Commission
in the Army,[2] and I will make over the Pay to be receiv'd by you till
the Debt be discharg'd.—I long to expiate in foreign Wars, the Crimes
I have been guilty of at home, and to leave a place in which I have
created to myself so much Misery.—I have nothing to urge in my

---

1. **Characters:** letters, his handwriting.

2. **buy . . . Army:** Men could purchase warrants that allowed them to recruit, equip, and
lead a group of soldiers or sailors in British wars.

Vindication, nor to move you to a Grant of my Request:—I can only say that I repent, am unhappy, and wholly throw myself on your Goodness, which alone can preserve from a miserable Death

The guilty and
undone
MELLADORE.

P.S. I entreat the favour of a speedy Answer; for if the hoped Relief arrives not soon, it will be too late to avert the impending and irretrievable Ruin which hangs over my Head.

What more could the most implacable Rage desire, than such a Humiliation! The utmost Malice of the wrong'd *Glicera* was now fully satiated; ample was the Recompence which Heaven allow'd her Injuries, and she acknowledged it, nor wish'd the Offender further Punishment. But tho' her Hatred ceas'd, she perserver'd in her Resolution, never to forgive the Treatment she had received from him any otherwise than Christian Charity oblig'd her to do; some of her weak Sex would have again received the Traitor into Favour, and relapsing into the former Fondness by which they had been undone, have thought his Penitence a sufficient Atonement for the Ruin he had caused; but *Glicera* was not of this Humour: Not his most earnest Entreaties, (for after this he sent her several Letters) could prevail on her ever to see him more; she consented however, to let him raise the Sum he requested, which he immediately laid out as he had design'd, and soon after was commanded abroad, whence he return'd no more, being mortally wounded in the first Engagement. *Glicera* being in a State of happy Indifference, heard the News of his Death without any Emotions either of Joy or Grief: And having now a sufficient Competency[1] to maintain her for her Life, gave over all Designs on the Men, publickly avowing her Aversion to that Sex; and admitting no Visits from any of them, but such as she was very certain had no Inclinations to make an amorous Declaration to her, either on honourable or dishonourable Terms.

---

1. **Competency:** income, estate, easy circumstances.

Laphelia, to whose Friendship and ready Wit she was cheifly indebted for her good Fortune, continued to live with her in a fine House, which formerly belong'd to *Melladore*, till the arrival of a young Gentleman to whom she had been a long time contracted, gave her a pleasing Opportunity of quitting her Society, and exchanging the Pleasures of a single Life, for the more careful ones of a married State. *Glicera* loaded her with Presents at her departure, and on all occasions since testifies a Joy, to express the Gratitude with which she regards her. Few Persons continue to live in greater Reputation, or more endeavour by good Actions to obliterate the memory of their past Mismanagement, than does this Fair Jilt; whose Artifices cannot but admit of some Excuse, when one considers the Necessities she was under, and the Provocations she receved from that ungrateful Sex.

FINIS.

THE
Mercenary Lover:

OR, THE

Unfortunate Heiresses.

Being a True,

Secret History

OF A

CITY AMOUR,

In a certain Island adjacent to the
KINGDOM OF UTOPIA.

Written by the Author of MEMOIRS *of*
the said Island[1]

Improperly we measure Life by Breath,
Those do not truly live who merit Death.[2]
Step. Juv.

LONDON:
Printed for *N. Dobb* in the *Strand:* And
sold by the Booksellers of *London* and
Westminster. MDCCXXVI.
[*Price* One Shiling.]

An approximation of the title page from the 1726 edition.

1. **Kingdom of Utopia . . . the said Island:** Haywood is invoking the title of her first political satire, *Memoirs of a Certain Island Adjacent to the Kingdom of Utopia* (1725), which had been a notorious success.

2. **Improperly we measure Life . . . Death:** From George Stepney's translation of Juvenal's Satire VIII in *The Satyrs of Decimus Junius Juvenalis*, trans. John Dryden and Several Other Eminent Hands (1697), 196. This was a popular, much-quoted translation, and Aphra Behn was one of the contributors.

THE
PREFACE

So many Stories, meerly the Effect of a good Invention,[1] *having been publish'd as real Facts, I think it proper to inform my Reader, that the following Pages are fill'd with a Sad, but true Account of the Misfortunes of a Family, living in the Metropolis of one of the finest Islands in the World; and happen'd in the Neighbourhood of a celebrated Church, in the sound of whose Bells the Inhabitants of that populous city think it an Honour to be born.*

The Character of the Mercenary Lover, *black and detestable as it is, wou'd yet have been more shocking, had I inserted some Passages of his former Life; but tho' the Baseness and Cruelty of his Disposition was not less conspicuous in some other of his Actions than in this last, of which I have made mention, yet the Persons ruin'd by him being of inferior Merit, I chose rather to confine my self to that, where neither the Tyes of Affinity, nor the Charms of Beauty, Innocence and Virtue, cou'd be a sufficient Protection from his destructive Artifices, than to run on with a long Detail of particular Vices which all seem complicated*[2] *in this one.*

---

1. **Invention:** contrivance, imagination.
2. **complicated:** mixed into, illustrated in.

The Mercenary Lover

or, The Unfortunate Heiress

How little are the ill judging Multitude capable of chusing for themselves! How far are Wealth and Beauty, the two great Idols of the admiring World, from being real Blessings to the Possessors of them! With what numberless Dangers are their Attractions accompanied! and into what fatal Inadvertancies do they frequently plunge those who place their Dependance on them.

In a little Town, more famous for the wholesomeness of its Air, than Magnificence of its Buildings, or any other remarkable Qualification, there liv'd two Sisters, Co-heiresses of a very plentiful Estate; the younger of them, whose Name was *Miranda*, being of an airy, gay Disposition, gave Way to the Addresses of as many as had any Pretentions to merit a favourable Reception: But *Althea* the Elder being naturally more reserv'd and grave, was extreamly cautious who she entertain'd; and as she seem'd little ambitious of creating Admiration, was also not very inclinable to pay it: Hope, being the chief Food of Love, (especially in an Age where few Men, like the Heros of Antiquity, can patiently submit to a seven Years Service,[1] before they receiv'd the Reward of a Kiss of the Hand) she afforded so little of that, that

---

1. **seven Years service:** Jacob contracted to work for Laban for seven years in exchange for marriage to his daughter Rachel; Laban tricked Jacob into marriage with his older daughter Leah, and Jacob worked an additional seven years for Rachel (Gen. 29:14–30).

she had but few of those who declar'd themselves her Lovers, in Comparison with the Number who watch'd the Smiles of the eternally gay *Miranda*.

Among those who endeavour'd at the Secret to please this celebrated Toast, none had more Reason to flatter himself with Hopes of Success than young *Clitander*, an Inhabitant of the Metropolitan City of this Island; and tho' of no higher Rank than a Trader, had a Paternal Estate, which, together with his great Business, made his Fortune on an Equivolent with that of *Miranda*: To add to this he had a very agreeable Person, and was Master of Accomplishments rare to be found in a Man of his Station: In fine, he was such as *Miranda* liked, and of the Multitude who address'd her, he alone had the Power of Inspiring her with a real Passion, all others who pretended to her serv'd but to amuse her Vanity, the trifling Divertors of her gayer Moments; but *Clitander* in a small Time became the solid Business of her most serious Inclinations; when present, she felt a Pain-mix'd-Pleasure; and when absent, an Uneasiness, a certain Restlessness of Mind, which is the infallible Demonstrative of Love. He was too well acquainted with the Symptoms of that Passion not to perceive he had inspir'd her with a Share of it, sufficient to encourage him to expect every thing from it which he could desire; and redoubling his Attacks, prest her in a Manner so undeniable, that he not only obtain'd from her a Promise of Marriage, but also saw, that as one Step towards the Performance of it, she banish'd all others who made Professions of the same Nature his was, from her House. It would be heedless to detain my Reader with an immaterial Repetition of the Acknowledgments he made for this Condescension, the Behaviour of a Lover in the like happy Circumstance, is too generally known to want an Information;[1] and if the Sequel of this Story should prove him not in Reality possest of the Passion he pretended, yet it will infer that he had Aims which were fully answer'd by the favourable Sentiments she had of him. I shall therefore pass over in Silence those Particulars, which without my Assistance may easily be guess'd at, and only say, That every Thing

---

1. **Information:** a legal statement of fact narrated or written and signed by the informant.

being agreed, and the Relations on both Sides perfectly satisfy'd as to Matters of Joynture and Settlements,[1] these seemingly happy Pair were in a short Time united by a Tye, which ought to be indissolvable but by Death. They were married and *Miranda* grew so perfectly fond of her agreeable Citizen, that in Conformity to the Notions and Behaviour of those she came to live among, she entirely threw off the gay Coquet, and began to dress, look, speak, and act in every Thing as became a Person of the Station she had taken on her. *Clitander* on the other Hand express'd the utmost Pleasure at this Alteration of her Conduct, appear'd the most indulging Husband, as she did the most obliging Wife, and they were look'd on by all who knew them, as the most exemplary Patterns of Conjugal Affection.

'Tis certain, indeed, that on one Side the Felicity was sincere and Compleat, *Miranda* truly lov'd, and believ'd herself as well belov'd; but alas! where is the Skill to trace, or Rules to reach the unfathomable Heart of artful Man, practis'd in Wiles, experienc'd in Deceit, amidst the many Turnings Search is lost; and the short sight of Femal Penetration strives but in vain to pierce the hidden Depth: If a long Series of continu'd Courtship, if Longings, Ardours, and Impatiencies before Possession, cou'd denote a true and perfect Passion, if the most eager Transports, oft repeated Vows, and tender Pressures afterwards, might evince the Person faithful, *Clitander* had been the most enamour'd and most constant Man on Earth, and *Miranda* been as blest in *Reality*, as he was now in *Imagination*. But his was not a Soul capable of being touch'd with the Charms either of the Body or the Mind; Beauty, Virtue, or good Humour, he look'd on as Things indifferent, and not at all essential to the Happiness of Life,—Money was the only Darling of his mercenary Wishes, and as the Estate of which *Miranda* was Coheiress, was the sole Inducement to his addressing and marying her; so by that Means being possest by that Moiety[2] of it which was her Proportion, he now began to grow anxious for the other also, and put

---

1. **Joynture and Settlements:** provision of land or income contracted in the marriage settlement for the wife should she survive her husband; some expired at the woman's death, but others were property she could bequeath.

2. **Moiety:** share.

Invention on a continual Rack for some Contrivance to bring the long'd for Aim about.

The serious and reserv'd Temper of *Althea* gave him Hopes that she would not very easily be brought to listen to any Proposals; but as averse as she had hitherto declar'd herself, he knew not how soon the Minute might arrive which might make an Alteration in her Sentiments in Favour of some Youth, who she might think worthy to create that Change: Love, he knew, was a Passion which comes swift and sudden on the Heart; his Business therefore was, to prevent as much as possible all Overtures of that Kind being made to her. To that End, under the Pretence of Affection to his Wife, he scarce ever suffer'd her to be from their House, and by a thousand Artifices, of which he was a perfect Master, so wound himself into her Esteem, that she thought there was not so excellent a Man on Earth: All he said she likened to as miraculous Truth, admir'd all he did, as the Effects of the strictest Honour, and most tender Friendship.

Having gain'd this Influence over her, there was little need to fear she would take any Affair in Hand, much less one of so great Consequence as Marriage was, without consulting him, and that it was now absolutely in his power to dissuade her from entertaining any Man, however agreeable in Person or in Fortune, who should make his Address to her on that Score; yet, notwithstanding he knew all this, nay, had heard her frequently declare, That to the Aversion she ever had for Marriage, she had now another Motive added, to induce her to continue in a single Life, which was, that she wou'd rather that Part of the Estate she was possest of shou'd at her Death descend to him and his Heirs, than any other Person in the World, all was not sufficient to content him,—there was a possibility that these fine Promises might one Day be broke,—*Althea* was beautiful as an Angel and very young, tho' one Year older than his Wife,—he knew there were a thousand dying for her, and cou'd not be easy when he reflected that there was any thing in the Power of Fate which cou'd put a Bar to his avaritious Views, which in a little Time he became so resolutely bent to compass, that he had recourse to Stratagems, the most inhumane and base, that ever enter'd into the Heart of Man. He was sometimes tempted to marry her to some indigent Wretch, who for a trifling Sum wou'd be glad to make over to him before-hand the Acres he should be Master of when made her Husband; at others, the *Demons*, whose Assistance he invok'd suggested to him to get her trappan'd[1] on board a Ship, and transported to some uninhabitable Shore, where she shou'd be left to perish on the Rocks, or be devour'd by the wild Denizons of the Woods and Mountains, but both these Designs were rejected, almost as soon as formed, not that to any relenting Thoughts they ow'd their Banishment, but there was Danger in them; he dreaded the discovery of the Villany he wish'd to practise, and for that Reason cou'd not resolve to take any Measures wherein a second Person must be consulted, who perhaps, might some Time or other, either through Remorse or Malice, betray the whole Affair, and expose him to the Censure and Punishment his Crime deserv'd. The base are always Cowards, the same Meaness of Spirit which makes them the one, inclines them to the other also; they are ever in Fear, and while there remains even the smallest Probability of Danger, Peace is a Stranger to their Minds. *Clitander* therefore resolved to trust no other but himself, in the Execution of whatever Project he shou'd put in Practise, and the Difficulty there was to find one, in which there was not an absolute Necessity for a Confederate, kept him for some Months in a Perplexity not to be conceiv'd.

Yet so admirable was he vers'd in the Art of Dissimulation, that tho' his Soul was full of the most poynant Anxiety, his Countenance was all serene and calm as an unruffled Sky; upon his oilly Tongue the most melting Accents in soft Persuasion hung, and Tenderness unspeakable languish'd in his Eyes; gay Smiles play'd round his Mouth in dimpl'd Graces, and his whole Air was Harmony and Love: None but the All-seeing Eye of Heaven cou'd penetrate into his Heart, or guess at the Perfidiousness that harbour'd there. Never did two Persons think themselves more happy than did *Miranda* and her amiable Sister, the one in being possest of the best of Men and Husbands, and the other in a most sincere Friend and disinterested Relation. A perfect Amity and uninterrupted Chearfulness, seem'd to reign throughout

---

1. **trappan'd:** trepanned, lured, tricked.

this little Family—They were the Envy of their Neighbours, the Delight of their Acquaintance, and the Pride of their Servants:—So much is the World, and even our selves deceiv'd by Appearances; and how little are we capable of distinguishing the real Felicity from the Shadow of one? Those who believ'd themselves, and were by all believ'd to be in a State of the most fixed Tranquility that could be, were in Effect on the Brink, and ready to plunge into a Gulph of Destruction, as much to be trembled at, as their imaginary Comfort was before to be desir'd and coveted.

The working Brain of the industriously mischievous *Clitander*, at last furnished him with a Design, in the Success of which he promis'd himself a double Pleasure: Tho' Avarice was his prevailing Vice, and the Love of Money had so entire a Possession of his Soul, that no other Charms had Power to inspire him with a real Passion, yet was he not without those Desires which are too frequently mistaken for the Influence of the god of tender Sighs: The Beauties of *Althea*, and the Freedoms he enjoy'd with her as a Brother, had sometimes given him Emotions, such as Lovers feel, tho' unaccompanied with that Respect and Tenderness which those who are truly worthy of that Name must pay to the ador'd Object,—With strong and vehement Desires he burn'd to enjoy her, and when in *Miranda's* Arms, languished to rifle the untasted Loveliness of her beauteous Sister.—He plotted therefore, how first to satiate this Passion, which, once obtain'd, he thought would be the most effectual Means to gratify the other also; and determin'd to make her guilty before he made her wretched: He soon began to put in Execution this most detestable Invention, by all those Artifices of which he was a perfect Master, and for which, indeed, he seem'd design'd by Nature, who had given him a Countenance and Manner of Behaviour so vastly distant from his sordid Disposition.

To corrupt a young Maid of *Althea's* reserv'd Humour, bred up in the strictest Principles of Virtue, and unacquainted even with an unchast Thought, would have seem'd a Task too difficult to be accomplish'd, and with Reason have deterr'd any other Man from an Attempt that Way: but *Clitander*, as he was not only possest of more bodily Perfections than the generality of his, so he had also been more successful with the Fair; seldom had he been repuls'd, but often a Conqueror over the most seemingly obdurate Hearts.—He knew the Influence he had gain'd over that of *Althea*, and tho' it was only contracted under the Notion of Friendship, that That Passion was a very good Preparative for the other which he aim'd to inspire.—The Name of Husband to her sister, was at first some little Impediment to his Hopes, but then the Consideration how many Opportunities that Title gave him, which were deny'd to all other Men, satisfy'd his Doubts, and made him not fear but that a little Time and Assiduity, might by Degrees steal into her Soul those Inclinations which wou'd give him the absolute Possession of his Wishes.

The first Step he made towards the Accomplishment of this barbarous Enterprize, was to redouble the Civilities and Tendernesses with which he had been accustom'd to treat *Althea*, and knowing she was naturally a great Lover of Reading, took Care to Bring her home every Day something new for her Amusement; I say Amusement, for I believe the Reader will easily imagine, the Books he desir'd she should peruse, were neither Religion, Philosophy, nor Morality; there are certain gay Treaties which insensibly melt down the Soul, and make it fit for amorous Impressions, such as the Works of *Ovid*,[1] the late celebrated *Rochester*,[2] and many other of more modern Date, and of this Kind it was that he furnish'd the Study of his intended Victim, to the two worst Passions of deprav'd Humanity.

The affairs of her Family often calling *Miranda* away, gave him, who now scarce ever stirr'd from home, many Opportunities of entertaining her alone: All which he imploy'd to the best Advantage for his Designs; not that he ever in the least declar'd himself a Lover, but artfully, and as tho' it were by Accident, introduc'd a Discourse on the Force of Love, always undertaking to prove, That whatever were the Consequences of that Passion they ought not to be condemn'd,

---

1. **Ovid:** Publius Ovidius Naso (43 B.C.–A.D. 17?), Roman poet who wrote the *Metamorphoses.*

2. **Rochester:** John Wilmot, second earl of Rochester, noted libertine and poet. In his youth he kidnapped an heiress and married her; until his death at thirty-three he was part of the glittering, immoral court circle.

because they were unavoidable,—Nay sometimes went so prophanely far, as to make Holy Writ the Dupe to his Designs, bringing Instances from that to argue, that Incest[1] was no Crime. Had the modest soul of *Althea* been in the least appriz'd of the Aim of these Conversations, so different from what she had ever been accustom'd to hear, the Shock of such a Discovery had at once stop'd her Ears from listning to Doctrine so pernicious, but as she was far from suspecting any Thing of his Inclinations, and took an infinite Pleasure in hearing him talk, by little and little the Poison of his Infectious Precepts gain'd Ground on her Belief; and finding herself wholly incapable of defending the Cause of Virtue against those Arguments which his superior Wit and Genius brought, began to think, indeed, that what he said was just, and that those Laws which prohibited a free Commerce between the Sexes; were only the Boundaries of Policy, invented to keep Mankind in Awe, and restrain the Sallies of Nature, which otherwise wou'd involve the World in a general Confusion.

Soon did he perceive the Ground he had gain'd, and exulted at the Success of his Insinuations: Not doubting now, but that he should be able to persuade her to any Thing, he began to appear more open, wou'd often take her Hand and kiss it with Raptures, such as, had she accustom'd herself to receive Addresses of that Nature, she wou'd have presently known to have been the Effects of that Passion which is commonly call'd Love.—When ever he look'd upon her, his well instructed Eyes seem'd to shoot Glances of an unuterable Tenderness,— whenever he spoke to her, it was in the fondest, most endearing Terms that Love and Wit cou'd form.—Yet so innocent, so unexperienc'd was she in the destructive Passion and the betraying Wiles of Man, that all these Symptoms were not sufficient to alarm, nor warn her of the Danger. Unknowing, therefore, what was doing in her own Soul, she gave Way to all the Liberties he took, and became all disolv'd, lost in a Tide of Love before she imagin'd herself threaten'd by even its most distant Approaches.

But it was not so with him, he read the State of her Mind in the

---

1. **Incest:** Marriage between sisters and brothers-in-law were within the degrees defined as incest and prohibited in the Bible and in the laws of England.

soft Languishments of her shining Eyes, and in her balmy Sighs, when presuming on the Authority of a Brother, he sometimes took her in his Arms, felt the Alteration he had made, and was too well convinc'd that his Work was compleated; and he had nothing now to do, but to declare himself, and boldly seize his Wishes.

Since the fatal Discovery of her Sentiments some Days elaps'd, without giving him any Opportunity for the Accomplishment of his Designs; but at length Fortune, hitherto too much a Friend to this Traitor to all Honour and Fidelity, afforded him one as ample as he cou'd have wish'd. *Miranda* went to make a Visit to a Relation who liv'd at the Town where both she and *Althea* had receiv'd their Births and Education; she wou'd have persuaded her Sister to accompany her, but the ill Stars of that unfortunate Lady, wou'd not suffer her to comply with her Desires; and the other perceiving her refractory, wou'd not press her beyond her Inclination. The Distance between that Place to which she was gone, and the great City in which they liv'd being about three Miles, her perfidious Husband was secure that she wou'd not return till Night. And scarce ever had his Eyes beheld a Sight so joyful as the Departure of the Coach which bore away that Impediment to his Hopes, his Wife.

She was no sooner gone, than he ran up to the Chamber of *Althea*, where she happen'd to be sitting indulging her innocent Meditations, and altogether unsuspicious of approaching Ruin: After some previous Discourse on ordinary Subjects, he began to talk of Marriage and the Unhappiness of that State, when both the Parties so join'd were not content with their Lot.—"How much, my lovely Sister, shou'd I lament," said he, "shou'd I ever see you one of those complaining Wives, your Wit despis'd, your good Humour subservient to a lordly and imperious Husband's rule, your Beauty, all that inestimable Stock of Charms with which you are so divinely stor'd, unprais'd, unlov'd, and perhaps scorn'd even to your Face,—such a Behaviour is too frequent, and shou'd it be your Fate, O most adorable *Althea*," continu'd he, with a Voice which seem'd interrupted by his Sighs, "how very wretched, how accurst wou'd be *Clitander* to know and want the Power to ease your Mournings or revenge your Wrongs!" "Wou'd to Heaven," answer'd the unsuspecting Maid, "I cou'd as easily return the Obligations I have to your generous Care, as I can secure my self from all Apprehensions of those Miseries you so well describe,—the Merits of *Clitander* have freed me from the Danger of becoming an abandon'd Wife,—two such Husbands are not to be the Portion of one Family,—I despair to find a Man like him, and cannot submit to accept a Happiness inferior to that my Sister enjoys."

Tho' these Words were spoken with the most perfect Innocence, they were notwithstanding the Overflowings of a soul wholly devoted to him, and sincerely taken up with Tenderness, and Admiration of his imaginary Virtues; And well discerning from what Source they sprung, "Thou Angel of thy Sex," said he, taking her in his Arms, "how happy shou'd I think my self, cou'd I believe it was indeed, your good Opinion of me, which defended you from list'ning to the Insinuations of the less faithful Part of Mankind,—but alas!" pursu'd he, intently fixing his Eyes on hers, as tho' he wou'd look into her Soul, "I dare not flatter my fond Desires so far, and had I in *Miranda's* Stead address'd *Althea*, shou'd have been among the Number of those her Scorn has render'd miserable." "I must not then have known your Worth," resum'd she, "and if you think *Althea* as capable of judging what is truly valuable, as you have found *Miranda*, you must believe your Fate had been the same with one, as with the other Sister." "Had it been so," cry'd he, in a well acted Transport, "sure some kind spirit wou'd have warn'd me of the Blessing,—some Dream wou'd have convey'd to me the Knowledge of your Goodness, and instructed by my Guardian Angel what to do, I had not thus err'd in my mistaken Choice." These Expressions utter'd with the utmost Warmth, and accompany'd by an Embrace more strenuous than before this Moment he had ever ventur'd to clasp her with, gave her a little Surprize, and starting from his Arms, and looking on him with a kind of Confusion in her Eyes, "Do you not love *Miranda* then?" Said she. "Dear as my Life," reply'd he, who wanted not Presence of Mind to extricate himself out of the most puzzling Difficulties, "Never Man lov'd with a fonder, or more lasting Ardour than I my Wife,—but yet," continu'd he, with a Sigh, as if his Heart were bursting, "while my Heart avows the Merits of *Miranda*, it cannot be unjust to the infinitely superior ones *Althea* boasts:—Should *Miranda* forgetful of her Marriage Vows, and ungrateful to the Tenderness I bear her, relinquish me, and seek new Joys in any others Arms, my abused Affection and my wounded Honour wou'd give me Pains intollerable, but shou'd *Althea*,—O the thought is Hell,—shou'd the adorable *Althea*, tho' bound by no Obligements, admit to her Embraces some Youth, more happy than *Clitander*, how much beyond the Reach of Words wou'd be the Horror of my distracted State!—I cou'd not hear it, but should commit some wild Extravagance might plunge us all in Ruin.—O *Althea*," pursu'd he, taking Advantage of the Astonishment he saw her in, and which prevented her from interrupting him, "too lovely Maid pity your wretched Brother,—your Lover,—your Adorer;—the cold Returns of Friendship are Cordials too, too faint to keep the almost expiring Lamp of Life awake—O give me more, or withdraw them too, and kill me with your hate." He had no sooner pronounc'd these Words than he threw himself upon her Bosom, where, if the present Emotions of his Desires did not convulse him with real Agonies, he counterfeited them so well, that a Woman more experienc'd in those Racks of strugling Impatiencies than was *Althea*, might easily have mistaken them for Natural. But with what Words is it possible to represent the mingled Passions of *Althea's* Soul, now perfectly instructed in his Meaning; Fear, Shame, and Wonder combating with the softer Inclinations, made such a wild Confusion in her Mind, that as she was about to utter the Dictates of the one, the other rose with contradicting Force, and stop'd the Accents e're she cou'd form them into Speech; in broken Sentences she sometimes seem'd to favour, then to discourage his Attempts, but all dissolv'd and melted down by that superior Passion, of which herself till now was ignorant she had entertain'd, never had Courage to repel the growing Boldness, with which he every Moment encroach'd upon her Modesty, and when she most strove to say something which might dash his Hopes, cou'd bring forth no harsher Sounds than, "Forbear, forbear my dangerous, and too lovely Brother! cruel *Clitander*, wou'd you ruin me?" 'Tis easy to guess what the Consequences of such Sort of Repulses must be, and whether such a Behaviour wou'd not have been far from dissipating the Ardour of a Lover, less fiercely animated than was *Clitander*. He made but short

Replies to her Entreaties or Interrogatories, speaking to her only in
this Manner, "O permit me to secure the Blessing you have so often
promis'd,—let me assure my self you never will be another's—be
mine; and ease me of these Doubts Uncertainty creates."—Nor, indeed, wou'd it have been conformable to the rest of his Artifice to
have held a long Conversation, or given her Time for Thought or
Recollection, *Action* was now his Business, and in this Hurry of her
Spirits, all unprepar'd, incapable of Defence, half yielding, half reluctant, and scarce sensible of what she suffer'd, he bore her trembling
to the Bed, and perpetrated the cruel Purpose he had long since contriv'd.

The Scene of Ruin over, the barbarous Author of it, now began to
exert his utmost Wit and Eloquence to dry her Tears, and hush the
Remonstrances of violated Virtue; he enforc'd the Arguments she had
before too fatally given Ear to, That the Ties of Blood or Affinity were
but imaginary Bars to Love, pleaded the Violence of his Passion, and
the absolute Necessity it brought, either to enjoy his wish or dye; swore
ten thousand Oaths of an unalterable Constancy, and that the Secret
never should be divulg'd.—The natural Propensity which all People
have to listen to any Arguments which may serve to excuse the Errors
they commit, join'd to the Corruption which his Insinuations had
brought on her Principles, made her not aim at confuting any Thing
he urg'd, either in his, or her own Vindication; and of all the Passions
which had so lately ruffled her Soul, Love and Shame were only now
remaining: By repeated and endearing Familiarities he endeavour'd to
strengthen the one, and entirely dissipate the other; but the Confusion
of her Mind was so great, that tho' he stirr'd not from her the whole
Day, he found all his Efforts to compose her ineffectual; and at her
Sisters Return, the Sight of that wrong'd Lady overwhelm'd her with
a Disorder which had been sufficient to have made some Women
suspicious of the Truth. The villainous Occasion of it, apprehensive
of the Danger, and also to prevent any Notice being taken of his
having been all Day in the Chamber of *Althea*, if the Servants shou'd
happen to speak of it, with an unparallel'd Assurance, taking his Wife
in his Arms as soon as ever she enter'd the Room, "I am glad you are

come home my Dear," said he, "*Althea* is quite spoil'd with the Vapours,[1] and tho' I have been complaisant enough not to leave her a
Moment: since you went out, all I can do to bring her into good
Humour is but Labour thrown away;—she will, in spite of me, indulge
her Chagrin, and will give no other Reason for it, than that she had
an ugly Dream last Night." *Miranda* laugh'd at this idle Superstition
(as she call'd it) in her Sister, and began to rally her on the ill Effects
of a too thoughtful Disposition; till the other (who long'd to be alone,
to give a Loose to Reflection) answer'd her in so peevish a Maner, that
she seem'd in good Earnest affected with that Distemper *Clitander* had
accus'd her of; and what was really the Effects of Remorse might very
well be taken for ill Humour. *Miranda* continued her pleasantry for
some Time, but finding it of no Effect on her Sister, "Come my
Dear," said she, taking her Husband by the Hand, "let us leave her
to herself,—if we stay here much longer, we too shall catch the Con-
tagion."—As she spoke these Words they both quitted the Room.
Clitander as he was going out, turning back to make her a submissive
Bow, accompany'd with the most tender and endearing Air that Love
cou'd teach him to assume.

Althea now left to the Freedom of her Thoughts, felt a kind of
Pleasure, in giving Way to Pain; and in not checking the Struggles of
departing Virtue, found the Means to ease herself of its Remorse,—
She accus'd her easy Nature, wonder'd how she cou'd be so lost, so
abandon'd by all the Principles her Youth was taught, and curst the
Tenderness which had betray'd her,—the Wrong she had done her
Sister, the Dishonour she had brought on herself, the Crime she had
been guilty of to Heaven, all appear'd to her distracted Imagination
in their blackest and most damning Colours, and for some Moments
involv'd her in so terrible a Dispair, that she was almost ready to lay
desperate Hands on her own Life, thereby to put a Period to the
Shame of it. But as Things violent are seldom of any long Continuance, the Force of these Emotions in a few Moments were evaporated
and spent; and the Idea of *Clitander*, his Charms, his Fondness, and

---

1. **Vapours:** moodiness, especially depression; associated with nervous disorders, including
hypochrondia and hysteria.

imagin'd Honour and Sweetness of Disposition, took their Turn to triumph over the faint Remains of Modesty and Virtue; and the Felicity of being belov'd by a Man, whom she consider'd as the Wonder of his Sex, seem'd to her sufficient Reparation for that she had resign'd in the rewarding it; and the Gratitude she ow'd his Passion, an Excuse for the Crime her own had influenc'd her to commit. In fine, the Morning found her as calm and compos'd as she had been the Night before the contrary; and if there was left in her Soul any Tincture of her former Disquiet, the Endearments of *Clitander*, and the Arguments he made use of to reconcile her to what had past between them, entirely clear'd her of it, and made her willingly resign herself to frequent Repetitions of that guilty Joy, she had at first so much regretted.

In this Criminal Tranquility let us leave her for a while, and return to her Undoer: That cruel Brother, having thus satisfy'd the Cravings of his lawless Flame, and revell'd in the Spoils of violated Chastity, remain'd but a short Time contented with the Triumph he had gain'd, the Love of Money now resum'd its Empire in his sordid Soul; and as it was not so much the Possession of *Althea's* Person as her Estate, which had induc'd him to take this Pains, so having obtain'd the one, he now began to set his whole Wits at Work to become Master of the other also. 'Tis true, he was not in that Anxiety of Mind he had been, because having the free Possession of *Althea*, he was pretty secure from any Apprehensions of her marrying, at least while he continu'd to treat her with that Tenderness which had so fatally seduc'd her; but being in all his Passions, except Avarice, extreamly inconstant, he soon grew satiated with the unrestrain'd Enjoyment, and consequently weary of dissembling Ardours he cou'd no longer feel.—In those very Moments, when most he swore he lov'd, he curst her in his Heart; and with his Vows of everlasting Fondness, mix'd Imprecations and Wishes for her Death,—had the Means of it, without Danger of Discovery, been in his Power, 'tis certain she had not long surviv'd her Loss of Honour; but to the same Fears which had before Enjoyment been her Protection, was she still indebted to for her Safety; and tho' he was always contriving her Destruction, he cou'd not, with all the Invention he was Master of, find the Way to bring it about.

In this Dilemma he receiv'd a considerable Addition to the Perplexity he was before involv'd in, which was the Knowledge that *Althea* was with Child; the Dread which seiz'd his guilty Soul, whenever he consider'd how Difficult it would be to keep the incestuous Secret from Discovery, fill'd him with Horrour almost proportion'd to his Crime,—but so great a Master was he of Presence of Mind, that not all the Confusion of his Thoughts prevented him from prosecuting his Designs: He no sooner knew the Condition *Althea* was in, but to add to the Melancholy of it, he was continually filling her Ears with Stories of Women who had died in Child-birth, wou'd sometimes, in a well counterfeited Terrour tell her, he had heard a Weasel squeak,[1] at others, that a Raven[2] had perch'd upon the House, pretend some ominous Dream: In fine, scarce a Day pass'd over without his bringing her an account of some fabulous Prediction, till he wrought so far on the Weakness of her Sex, as to settle her in the Belief that she should not out-live the Time prefix'd by Nature for her being deliver'd of her Burthen. Having gain'd this Point, as he was sitting alone with her one Day, taking her by the Hand, and dissembling the most perfect Tenderness. "My most ador'd, my forever dear *Althea*," said he, "I have a Proposal to offer to you, which I have long wish'd to speak, but never had the Courage, fearing it shou'd encrease that Melancholly to which already you are but too much inclin'd,—but my Angel," continued he, "if you wou'd but make use of your good Sense to arm you against these womanish Apprehensions, you wou'd not think your self nearer to Death for being prepar'd for it." Here he paus'd, expecting she wou'd desire an Explanation of these Words, which she immediately did, not a little surpriz'd what it was he meant by them. "Since you command me," resum'd he, "I will no longer delay to reveal what for some Time has created me many Inquietudes.—Shou'd you," pursu'd he, with a Sigh, "which Heaven forbid, in giving Life to the dear Product of our Love, resign your own, the Estate you are possest of must, of Consequence, you dying without a *Will*, descend to your Sister, and the Children born of her become the Inheritors,—it

---

1. **Weasel squeak:** an omen of bad luck or, sometimes, death.

2. **Raven:** bird of bad omens, especially infection and death; the association began because ravens followed armies expecting dead bodies to feed on.

will not be in my Power to prevent it, and that most precious Pledge of the most fond Affection that ever fill'd the Heart of Man, must be a Beggar, a poor Dependant on an unhappy Father, who can do no more than make some mean Provision for it, as for the Child of some Acquaintance or remote Relation, while those begotten on *Miranda*, tho' far less dear, favour'd by Legitimacy, shall riot in the Plenty of your Lands, and look with Scorn on the wrong'd Babe, whose Birth-right makes them rich.—The Thought of this is worse than Death to me, and will be so to you, when once you come to know a Mother's Pangs, a Mother's Tenderness and Care;—I wou'd have you, therefore, to provide against it, and by a *Testament* legally drawn and sign'd by Witnesses, cut off *Miranda*, and secure your Child from all those Injuries which Want Occasions." "How can that be?" interrupted *Althea*, "we know not of what Sex the wretched Infant is, and in a *Will*, the Name, as well as Relative must punctually be set down." "For that I have laid a Scheme," reply'd he, rejoic'd to find her in so compliable a Disposition, "you shall bequeath your Lands, your Money, Jewels, and whatsoever valuable Goods you have to a fictitious Person—we may easily invent a Name;—and because it may be expected he should appear to claim the Benefit of the Will, I must be left *Trustee*, or if you please, his *Guardian*, and your *Executor*,—by this Means I shall have the Opportunity of doing Justice to my Child, since being my self, in Right of my Wife, next Heir, none has a Privilege to scrutinize into the Reasons of your having made so seemingly strange a *Will*; and thus will also, your Reputation, even after Death, remain unsully'd; and the worst the prying World can say, will be, that you were unnatural, and the Tenderness for that, which ought to be most dear, be taken for the Want of it, to your Sister." He said no more, nor indeed had he any Occasion for further Arguments, what he had already urg'd appear'd too reasonable for her to deny Assent: She very much approv'd, and thank'd his seeming Care, and the same Evening gave him Commission to go to a Lawyer, and have the *Will* drawn up according as he had advis'd.

Fortune, and the Credulity of the too fond *Althea* had hitherto crown'd all his Endeavours with Success, and he began now to think there was no Difficulty which his Genius, Resolution, and the Fertility of his Invention cou'd not surmount.—He was not however, of the Disposition of some People, who lull themselves too soon in an imaginary Security, and transported with what they have already obtain'd, sit down enjoying the Reflection, contented before their Work is done: With the same indefatigable Industry with which he commenc'd his Designs, did he proceed to the Accomplishment of them.—Early as the Day did he arise next Morning, and having given Directions to an able Attorney, what he would have done, in a small Time after, brought to *Althea* a Parchment, which he told her was the *Will*, but which was in Reality, a Deed of Gift to himself, of all the Estate she was at that Instant in Possession of. But because my Reader will doubtless be amaz'd for what Reason he went about to deceive her in this Manner, his Wife being the undoubted Heir, I must unravel the Bottom of his Aim, and set forth a Design so monstrous, as were there not too many whom the sad Catastrophe made acquainted with the Truth, wou'd scarce gain Belief in any Mind, less prone to Villany than that of *Clitander*. Fir'd as I have already said, with the repeated Possession of the Beauties of *Althea*, and burning with a yet unextinguish'd Passion for the Enjoyment of her Wealth, and to these two Motives for wishing her in another World being added, that of the Danger her Condition involv'd him in, of the Discovery of the Crime he had committed in debauching her, all together made him resolve to murder her, and to do it in such a Manner, as might have the Appearance of being acted by herself,—the Laws of the Nation depriving the Successors of Persons so desperate, of inheriting any Part of their Goods,[1] he contriv'd to secure himself by a Deed of Gift, drawn up, dated and sign'd before there was any Appearance of her laying Hands on her Life.

But here, Heaven was pleas'd to put a Stop to his Proceedings, and what he thought wou'd be the most certain Means to secure the Accomplishment of his Hopes, prov'd the Ruin of them.—He came to *Althea*, and in a great Hurry, as if he fear'd the coming in of some Person who might interrupt what he was about to say, show'd her the

---

1. **the Laws . . . Goods:** A suicide's property was forfeited to the state.

Parchment, and unfolding only that Part of it where she should set her Hand, desir'd her to sign. Chance, more than suspicion, made her desire to read it first; but that Demand a little alarming him, as not expecting she would scruple any Thing he requir'd, he was that Moment at a Stand how to reply, but recovering himself as well as he was able, told her there was no Occasion for her Perusal, for it was drawn up exactly as they had agreed, and that to look it over, wou'd take up more Time than she was aware of, and that probably her Sister, or some other of the Family might come up and catch her in that Employment. "There is no Haste then," said she, "for my signing it,—I shall scarce dye before to Morrow, and if you give it me, I will put it into my Cabinet, and read it when I am certain of no Interruption." Now was he indeed confounded, not all his Cunning or Assurance cou'd enable him presently to resolve what to do, in an Exigence so dangerous to all the Measures he had form'd; to leave it with her was to proclaim himself the Villain he was in Reality, and to refuse, was to give her Room to guess there was something in it of a different Kind from what he had made her believe: Making a virtue, therefore, of Necessity, after a Moment's Thought, "You do not consider," resum'd he, "of what ill Consequence it may be, to keep such a Thing by you,—it may be found,—some Accident may betray the Affair,—I wou'd have this Secret lodg'd beyond the Reach of Fate itself:—Remember," pursu'd he more eagerly, " 'tis for your Child you do it,— shou'd you neglect a Thing of so much Consequence to its Welfare; the unborn Babe may live to curse its too remiss and unkind Parent.— But," added he, perceiving she look'd amaz'd to hear him talk in this Manner, "if you imagine I have caus'd any Thing to be inserted there which you can scruple to approve, I will sit down and read it to you." "There may be more Danger in that," said she, "than can be reasonable apprehended from lying in my Cabinet,—but you shall have your Will." In speaking these Words she shut the Door, and prepar'd herself to listen to him. The grave and determin'd Air with which she spoke and mov'd, made him easily perceive she was not perfectly pleas'd with his Behaviour; his natural Boldness, however, enabling him to go on, he unfolded the Parchment, shadding as well as he cou'd, with his Hand the Top of it, on which was written, *The Deed of Gift*, and began not to read, but to speak such Words as were suitable to the Instrument for which she had given Orders, what he utter'd being altogether different from the real Contents. The Hesitation of his Accents, and the Confusion which he cou'd not keep from being visible in his Countenance, having created in her Suspicions, to which before her Heart was wholly a Stranger, with the utmost Watchfulness she observ'd his every Look and Motion, and taking Notice that he endeavour'd to conceal some Part of the Writing, and also glancing her Eyes over it, perceiving that his Tongue consulted his own Invention more than the Parchment, she was both convinc'd and shock'd at the Deceit with which he treated her; and nothing is more to be wonder'd at than, that she, so far from all Artifice herself, cou'd all at once have her eyes unseal'd to behold such monstruous Baseness and Hypocrisy in the Man, whose imaginary Honour and Fidelity she had forfeited all that was dear to her to reward, did not make her that Moment break out into some wild Extravagance of Rage, which shou'd have made him know his Wiles were now betray'd, and his deceiving Schemes no more cou'd boast their accustom'd Success.—Tis certain that her soul was all Surprize, Resentment and Confusion, yet did she bridle the rising Passions, and tho' half suffocated, restrain'd the swelling Sighs, forbid her Tears to flow, or Tongue to vent the smallest Tittle of her Discovery or Indignation, till having done reading, he once more entreated her to sign. "Yes," said she, "I will sign, but it shall be in Flames, as you hereafter must, for all the Miseries,—the eternal Ruin, your cursed Insinuations have brought on the undone *Althea.*" These Expressions were accompany'd with a Torrent of Tears and at the same Time snatching the Parchment from his Hand, she threw it into a great Fire, which, the Weather being very cold, was then burning in the Room, where it was immediately consum'd. The Amazement in which this Action invol'd the Soul of *Clitander*, is not to be express'd;—he saw he was detected, and had nothing to alledge in his Excuse or Vindication,—the projecting *Demons*, who had prompted him to this Villany, now refus'd him their Assistance,—his once ready Wit and Invention now forsook him,—all his Powers abandon'd him,—his Eyes and Tongue forgot their usual Artifice,—Fear, Shame and Horror sat on each unguarded Feature, and all the naked

Criminal appear'd in View;—with down-cast Looks a while he stood silent, revolving in his Mind a thousand black and terrible Ideas: And she recovering herself a little from that Excess of Passion, which had before stop'd the Uterance of her Words, went on in her Upbraidings in this Manner, "Ungenerous, mean Designer as thou art," said she, "how little didst thou know the lavish Fondness of *Althea's* Soul, or thy own Power?—had I been Mistress of all the Globe contains, and had been sensible *Clitander* wanted it, with Pleasure I shou'd have yielded the unvalu'd Treasure, and thought my self more rich in his Acceptance, than in any other Blessing that Heaven and Fortune cou'd endow me with,—to that Degree I lov'd you, Words cannot speak how much,—no Description,—nothing but my Infatuation can set forth the vast Extent of that transcendant Passion with which I was inspir'd;—but know, it was not to your lovely *Person* alone you were indebted for the Proofs I gave you of it,—I figur'd you out to my admiring Soul as the most perfect Pattern of Fidelity and Honour, and thought I never cou'd too much acknowledge the Beauty of your *Mind*,—O! how have I been deceiv'd," continu'd she, bursting a second Time into Tears, "how cruelly has my unwarry Innocence suffer'd itself to be impos'd on;—thou Monster of Hipocrisy, how wretched hast thou made me!" The struggling Passions of her Soul made her unable to utter more, but what her Tongue fail'd to express her streaming Eyes and agonizing Tremblings abundantly made up for. *Clitander* with much ado forcing himself to look upon her, demanded of her, but with a Voice wholly unassur'd and broken, What it was she meant? An Interrogatory of this Kind, appear'd to her to have so much Impudence in it, that it seem'd wholly to dissipate her Grief, to make Way for a more stormy Passion: Rage had now the whole Possession of her Breast, and she answer'd him in Terms which fully convinc'd him, if before he had any Doubt of it, that she had discover'd the Artifice of the pretended *Will*, and also that it would be no easy Matter to bring her to Moderation: He attempted it however as much as his Disorders wou'd give him Leave; but the more he aim'd to excuse what he had done, the more she grew incens'd; alledging, that tho' he had the highest Reasons for designing *a Deed of Gift* instead of a *Will*, which yet she cou'd not allow, she never cou'd forgive his Intention of deceiving her.—She told him, that since she found him capable of Artifice in one Thing, she doubted not but he had been so in all; and that she no more cou'd give Credit to any Thing that came from him.—All he cou'd say was ineffectual to move her from this Resolution, and he was oblig'd to leave her, having several Times been bid by her to leave the Room, without being able to work her to any Return of Softness, or even to look on him with less Resentment than that which both her Eyes and Tongue declar'd at the Time of her throwing the Parchment into the Fire.

It wou'd be as needless as impossible, to set forth, as it deserves, the distracted State in which this Night was past, both by *Clitander* and *Althea*, to be told what has happen'd between them, will better enable the Reader's Imagination to conceive their present Wretchedness than any Thing I am able to say.—The Deceiver and Deceiv'd felt equal Pains, the one in the Disappointment of his Designs, and Fears of something to ensue by this Discovery far worse: And the other, in Tenderness abus'd, and the Reflection on the irreparable[1] Ruin her Inadvertancy had brought upon her, the most poynant Remorse was now the Portion of her Soul; and Dread, and the sharpest Stings of Guilt and Horror his.

The Condition of the perfidious *Clitander* was so much the more perplex'd than that of *Althea*, by the Addition of Uncertainty in what Manner he should proceed; while that unhappy Lady, in the Midst of her Griefs found some little Ease in Resolution, and determin'd to quit a House which had been so fatal to her Virtue and her Peace; and justly detesting the Sight of her Undoer, as soon as she was inform'd *Miranda* was stirring, she sent to desire she would come into her Chamber, who immediately complying with her Request, she told her, That finding herself of late very much indispos'd she believ'd it owing to the Town Air, which by Reason she was not accustom'd to live in, did not agree with her Constitution, and that she would return to her Country Seat, at least, till she had recover'd her former Health.

---

1. **irreparable:** emended from "incomparable," based on the errata sheet in the first edition.

Her present Condition having render'd her Looks more pale and wan than ordinary, contributed to make this Excuse pass current;[1] and her Sister, tho' extreamly concern'd to loose the Pleasure of her Company, thought it would seem rather an Argument of Self-love than the contrary, to press her Stay.

While the two Sisters were engag'd in this Conversation, *Clitander*, who was alone in the Dining-room, was in all the Agonies which Guilt or Fear can inflict; he had heard *Althea's* Servant desire his Wife to come to her Mistress, and he knew not but the Violence of that Rage with which she was animated against him, might oblige her to relate the whole Story of their Intreague to her Sister. He was sensible, that Passion of what Kind soever, has finall Regard to Prudence; especially in a Female Mind, and began to accuse himself of Weakness, that he had not put an End to his Apprehensions, by depriving her of the Power of Complaining, "—with how much Ease," said he to himself, "might I have strangled or smother'd the fond Reproacher, as soon as I perceiv'd she took upon her to pry into my Meanings,—I might have left her breathless, to be found by the first comer into the Room,—the Act wou'd have appear'd her own,—No-body wou'd have suspected me,—perhaps my Wife might have made the first Discovery, and the Shock of such a Sight might have been fatal too to her, and I had been rid of both at once,—Fool that I was, and too, too careless of my own Safety, Interest, or Reputation,—shou'd her wild Rage disclose the fatal Secret, I am undone in all without Redemption, lost to all the Views of my aspiring Soul, nay pointed at, and hiss'd as I pass by the demure Inhabitants of this well-order'd City." In this Manner did he torment himself, till seeing the Servants run busily up and down the House, he call'd to know the Meaning of this unusual Hurry, and was by one of them inform'd, that *Althea*, being going out of Town, they were employ'd in packing up her Things, and preparing for her Departure. If he was before alarm'd, he now was much more so; this sudden Removal made him not doubt

---

1. **pass current:** be accepted, received as genuine.

but that she had betray'd every Thing, and unable to endure the just Upbraidings he expected to meet from both these injur'd Ladies, he flew out of the House immediately, resolving not to return till the Absence of one of them might the better encourage him to deny the whole Affair to the other.

He had been but just gone out, when *Miranda* came into the Room where she had left him, to acquaint him with her Sister's Resolution, and missing him, sent every where in Search of him, to take Leave of *Althea*: But he was no where to be found, he went a quite contrary Way from any Place where he cou'd be expected, and came not home till very late at Night.

The wretched *Althea* found a kind of gloomy Satisfaction, that she was not oblig'd to dissemble a Civility to the Author of her Ruin, and made what Haste she cou'd away, lest any of those sent to seek him shou'd succeed in their Endeavours: But he returning not till Night, was immediately eas'd of his Apprehensions, by the Person that open'd the Door, who acquainted him with the fruitless Search which had been made for him, and the Reason of it. A little more compos'd now in Mind, he had the Power of inventing an Excuse to his Wife for his running away in so abrupt a Manner, which she, wholly free from any Suspicion of the Truth, readily believ'd.

The villanously bent *Clitander* cou'd not, however, be satisfy'd while there remain'd even a Possibility of his Crime being made known; he resolv'd therefore, by some Means or other to put an End to *Althea*, whose Life he look'd on as a continual Danger; but as there was no Opportunity to compass this Design while they were at Variance, he endeavour'd by his former Artifices to gain a Reconciliation. She had not left his House three Days, before he sent her the following Letter.

> To the most Lovely, but too Rigorous
> *Althea*.

By this, I hope, Passion has had Time to cool, and Reason has got the Better of unjust Resentment,—Oh! cou'd I ere have thought *Althea*, who seem'd all heavenly Softness, wou'd have so far been deafned by her mistaken Rage, as not to hear *Clitander*;

her once lov'd *Clitander* plead!—I confess indeed, that I deceiv'd you as to the *Title* of the Instrument you had order'd me to get drawn up, but the *Design* was still the same; and it appear'd to me, and to the Lawyer; whose Advice I took, to be more firm and valid this Way than that other we had agreed on: The Motives which induc'd me to it are too long to be inserted here, but if you will permit a Visit from me, I can easily convince you that what I did was wholly owing to my Care to that dear Babe, which next to its charming Mother, must be most precious to my Soul.—Oh! my forever lov'd,—forever ador'd *Althea*, tho' I doubt not but I shall hear you own you have been to blame, and with your usual Softness avow *Clitander's* Truth, yet the Remembrance that I have been once suspected by you, will be an eternal Vulture to my aking Heart.—Confidence, as it is the greatest *Proof* of a perfect Passion, so it is also the highest *Blessing* of it; Resume it then thou dear, unjust Disturber of thy own Repose, and know *Clitander* better than to admit one Thought to the Prejudice of his Love or Honour; the inchanting Charms which dwell upon thy Mind and Person render it impossible for me to falsify the one, and the Principles in which my Youth was bred wou'd make me chuse Death rather than be guilty of sinning against the other;—how much then hast thou injur'd me, *Althea*!—what Torments has thy unkind Distrust inflicted on me!—My Soul, which flatter'd itself with the Belief it held so perfect an Intelligence with thine, that whatsoever pass'd in one Breast was to the other known, now starts with wild Amaze, and all its Faculties seem lost in Grief and Wonder.—O haste to cure the Wounds thy Cruelty has caus'd, and let the Balsom[1] of returning Love restore once more *Clitander* to himself,—for I am nothing, while depriv'd of thee, but a poor walking Statue, discover'd but by Dispair to have any Remains of Sense or Reason left.—Write to me some Lines of Comfort, and consent to receive once more into thy Esteem, into thy Sight, into thy Arms, the most ardent and sincerest Lover that ever own'd the Power of Beauty;—be doubly kind to make me Reparation for the Wrong thou hast done me, and know that it is the

---

1. **Balsom:** balsam; an aromatic healing, soothing balm made from the resin of balsam trees.

fix'd Determination of my Mind to dye if you persist in this Injustice, it being better not be at all, than not to be

The Divine *Althea's*
Clitander.

Whoever has been acquainted with the Force of Love, need not be told what kind of Emotions those are, which of Consequence swell the Bosom of a Person in the circumstances *Althea* was; never has Woman been possest of a more violent Passion than she was for *Clitander*, nor cou'd any Heart be capable of a greater Resentment than was hers, since the Discovery of his Deceit; she cou'd not read those tender Expressions he had made use of in his Letter, without a Flood of forgiving Softness pouring in upon her Soul; nor cou'd she reflect afterwards that 'twas possible they might be only owing to that Artifice, with which he had attempted to impose on her Credulity, without an Addition to the Rage she was before inspir'd with.—At some Times she was inclin'd to hear what he cou'd alledge in his Vindication, at others, not to admit of any Excuse; and what she endur'd in the Conflict, between Tenderness and Indignation, is not to be describ'd; the former, however, got at length the Victory; and the same fatal Softness which had at first betray'd her, now sway'd her Inclinations to a second yielding, and all the Remains of Severity she had left was, not to let him immediately be sensible of his Power and her own Weakness and Irresolution. "If not so guilty as I at first believ'd," said she to herself, "he yet has been to blame in endeavouring to deceive a Heart he might have persuaded.—He shall not, therefore, know my Easiness to pardon,—I will write to him with the same Rigour with which I spoke when last we parted: Nor can I err in this, if he be in Reality the true, the faithful Lover he pretends, his Constancy will abide this little Trial; and if, (as 'tis too possible, that he who cou'd be false in one thing may in others also) the seeming Softness of these Lines shou'd all be Counterfeit, and a second Imposition, I shall at least prevent him of the Triumph he expects." Thus did this unhappy victim of an ungovernable Passion, argue with herself, and fancy'd no-body cou'd arrive at a greater Height of Heroism than she was Mistress

of, in so far restraining the Dictates of her Tenderness, as to be able
to answer him in these Terms.

To the Thankless and Ungenerous
Clitander.

*If any Thing cou'd have added to the Astonishment which the Discovery
of your Perfidiousness created, it wou'd be to find you still entertain an
Opinion of me so contrary to what I am, or ought to be.—No, no* Clitander; *it is not in the Power of all your Artifices to deceive me twice;—to
know you have been false in one Thing, convinces me there is a Possibility
you may be so in all; and, as you too justly for your own Interest observe,*
Confidence *Alone makes* Love *a Blessing; as your Behaviour, therefore,
has taken from me the* one, *I must endeavour to expel the* other *also, or
be for ever wretched.—Am I not undone—ruin'd beyond Redemption—
by my unhappy Passion reduc'd to a Condition in which Life, Honour,
Reputation, every Thing that is dear must be expos'd to Dangers, infinite
and numberless; yet in this dreadful Hazard of my Soul what had I to
comfort me but thy believ'd Integrity, and that thou hast destroy'd; and I
am now all Misery and Despair, without one chearing Hope, one Dawn
of Consolation.—Oh why* Clitander *wou'd you abuse a Faith so entirely
dependant as was mine?—If there were Reasons for altering the intended*
Will *into a* Deed of Gift, *why was I not acquainted with them?—
Heavens! when I reflect with what a zealous Haste you press'd my tardy
Hand to sign that Writing, and with what a ready Cunning you turn'd
the Words so much the Reverse of what they were, it makes you seem, to
my distracted Thought, a Man long practis'd in Deceit, vers'd in Hypocrisy, and skill'd in every Wile of your betraying Sex.—Oh what a dismal
Change is this from that dear Character which won me first to Tenderness,
and made me think all Things a Virtue which thy Love requir'd.—But
to what End does my afflicted Soul thus pour forth her Complainings, if
thou art false, thou wilt but scorn my Griefs; if true, they are unjust;—
Oh that they were, and that indeed, I cou'd in the Assurance they were
so, confess I did amiss, and once more subscribe my self*

The too lovely Clitander's
Althea.

Having concluded this Epistle, she read it over, and thinking some Part of it express'd too great a Tenderness, to prevent him from entertaining any Hopes, which might be too presuming, she added a Postscript which contain'd these Words:

I wou'd not have you imagine, that because my Heart still avows some Softness at the Remembrance of our former Loves, that it can so much overpower my Reason as to sway me to any Thoughts of a Reconciliation, at least, as yet,—Time, and your future Behaviour can only decide what 'tis I ought to do.—Make no Endeavours therefore for an Interview, lest you should alarm a Resentment, which you deceive your self when you believe is lull'd asleep.

Farewell.

Clitander had too often experienc'd the Irresolution of a Female Mind when agitated by that undoing Passion, not to see *Althea* was as much his own as ever, and that there wanted but a few Oaths and tender Pressures to compleat what his Letter had begun: But as all the Ardours of Desire were now extinguish'd in him, and he no longer aim'd at the Enjoyment of her, he wou'd not seem too forward in his Hopes; his Design being only to keep her Mind in Play, till he shou'd get an Opportunity to rid himself at once of all his Fears, by making her away. Continuing therefore to counterfeit the despairing Lover, soon after the Receipt of hers he sent a second Billet, the contents whereof were as follows.

To the Dear, Unkind *Althea.*

If you had ever any Reason for Surprize in the Behaviour of *Clitander*, it is only now to find he is yet alive after so terrible a Testimony of your Indifference, as that your Letter gave me.—Yes, thou relentless, thou tyrannick Charmer, I yet survive the Loss of Love, but in a Condition, such as were there not a Power whose Indignation is more than even *Althea's* to be dreaded, wou'd make me gladly fly to Death for Ease.—Were I, indeed, the false, the perjur'd Wretch you think

me, how little Effect wou'd your Displeasure have!—Nay, how satisfy'd wou'd some inconsistent Lovers be of such a Pretence to part!—
but, Oh *Althea*! I am not of that Number, my Heart wholly made up
of Truth and Tenderness, disavows the Maxims of my Sex, and doats
upon thee, thou Soul of Pleasure, with the same unabated Fondness,
as when I first receiv'd the glorious Recompence of my Pains, and
triumph'd in Possession of thy Beauties.—How often have I thought
our Minds were pair'd by Heaven, and that we two were chose from
the unnumber'd Millions of Mankind to prove the Immortality of a
perfect Passion. No Woman sure, but my *Althea*, cou'd e'er inspire
such Raptures; no Man but her *Clitander* cou'd be so sensible of her
Power of charming.—Oh think upon the blissful Moments of our
Love!—bring back in Idea our past Endearments! remember to what
a vast Excess of unrestrain'd Delight we have been transported; and
while the extatick Image is in View, judge of the Fervour of *Clitander's*
Flame.—Didst thou deceive me with pretended Softness, and play the
Hypocrite in Pleasure? O no, thy Raptures were substantial and sincere; nor cou'd the Soul, when thus dissolv'd in Joy, find Room for
feigning.—Were mine so enervate, that thou canst doubt their
Truth?—thou dear, unjust Disturber! to thy own Heart let me appeal,
by that I will be acquitted or condemn'd.—Grant a speedy Answer
to my Prayers, but consider, that on what you write depends the Fate
of

Your Impatient Slave
Clitander.

What now became of *Althea's* Resolution! her Soul, unus'd to Artifice, no longer cou'd restrain its struggling Tenderness, each thrilling
Vein confest rekindled Passion; and the soft Fire diffus'd itself through
every glowing Fibre:—No more had she the Power to conceal Desire,
no more cou'd listen to the Dictates of Reason or Resentment, and
again melted by those destructive Languishments which had at first
betray'd her Virtue, she suffer'd her Pen to convince him of a Truth,
which before he had little Cause to doubt, and wholly forgetful of

all Considerations but those her Love inspir'd, answer'd him in this Manner.

To the too Charming *Clitander*.

By what magick Spells, thou dear Enchanter, dost thou work upon my Soul! how in a Moment is it in thy Power to reverse my most fix'd Resolves, new-form my Mind, and as thou pleasest tune every jarring Thought! in spite of all I had determin'd, in spite of the Suggestions of my Reason, which tell me, this second Folly is more shameful, even than the former, I confess the Prevalence of thy too fatal Charms, and once more own my self all thine.—O why Clitander! *dost thou alarm Reflection with the Remembrance of those ruinous Delights which I had sworn to take no more; am I not already too guilty without adding Perjury to the Number of my Offences?—will not all the Pleas of Love, and Nature, appear too weak to excuse my Crimes, and bribe the justice of that dread Tribunal, to which, perhaps, I shortly shall be summon'd!—O! exert thy utmost Wit and Eloquence to arm me against this Thought, and reconcile the two great Opposites,* Desire *and* Virtue,*—with healing Arguments, if possible, ease my Despair, and keep me, while on Earth, from sharing the Torments the Damn'd endure. But first, for O! there is no Hell like that of thy Perfidiousness, convince me that my Fears were groundless, and that there was, indeed, no other Motive but our common Interest for that Alteration in the intended Legacy, the sooner I hear your Reasons, the sooner my Inquietudes will cease; but be sure to come prepar'd with such as shall entirely banish all Distrust of their Validity; and give me no Pretence to be any other than what I wish my self.*

My Dear, Ador'd Clitander's
Althea.

If *Clitander's* Entreaty for a Reconciliation had sprung from a Desire of re-enjoying her, he had now sufficient to fit him for the utmost Transports; but alas! the Pleasure her Condescension yielded, was of a far different Kind from that which Love inspires: Her Death, which he now found was the only Means both to ease him of all his Fears of Discovery, and to give him the Possession of her Estate, was what he wanted; and the Opportunity her recover'd Kindness promis'd him of executing that horrid Purpose, spread a sullen Satisfaction over all his Soul: The Means he had projected to bring it about was in this Manner:

He had for a great while had an Intimacy with a neighbouring Apothecary, which he improv'd during the Time of his holding this distant Correspondence with *Althea*, but still preserving his old Maxim of depending only on himself, wou'd not let him into any Part of his Designs, but taking all Occasions of running into his Shop, and talking with him in a free Manner, wou'd sometimes ask him what was in one Drawer, and sometimes what was in another; which Intelligence,[1] join'd with his own Understanding in the *Latin* Tongue, made him perfectly acquainted with the Name and Nature of most of those Drugs which furnish out one of those Shops. Amongst the Number there was one, on which he kept a constant Eye; his Friend had told him, that it was a Poison of that deadly Quality, that without the Person who should take it, had very well prepar'd his Body by extraordinary Antidotes, all the Art in the World had not the Power to expel. This was a Dose proper for the Design of this remorseless Wretch, and he resolv'd to play the Thief for some Portion of it, the first Moment Fortune should present him with an Opportunity: According to his Desires he soon met one, the Apothecary happening to be abroad one Day when he came there, and no Person in the Shop but a young Aprentice, whom he sent out on some Pretence, he ran immediately to the Drawer, and taking out a sufficient Quantity of that fatal Drug, put it into a Piece of Paper, and conceal'd it in his Pocketbook.[2]

Being thus in Possession of the Treasure he so much coveted, he wanted nothing but the Means of applying it, which also he obtain'd in a short Time: The Anniversary of *Miranda's* Birth-day happening

---

1. **Intelligence:** information; the first intelligence, or national security, offices were funded in the late seventeenth century.

2. **Pocket-book:** a leather pouch, usually the size of a small book, sometimes with compartments for carrying papers, bank-notes, and small objects.

a Day or two after that, in which he had receiv'd that tender Letter from her Sister, he thought he cou'd not chuse a fitter Season for the Accomplishment of his cruel Aim: With a well counterfeited Tenderness, he therefore told that unsuspecting Wife, that he would keep that Day with a Solemnity proportionable to the Tenderness he had for her, and accordingly sent Invitations to all the Friends on both Sides, to come to his House and partake of an Entertainment he order'd to be provided in Honour of the Day: And at the same Time wrote a private Billet to *Althea*, conjuring her not to fail being there, telling her that if she attempted to evade it by any Excuse, it might create some Suspicion among the Relations, that there was not so good an Agreement between them as usual; and as there was a Time approaching in which she wou'd be oblig'd to abscond, it wou'd be best for her to appear as long as her Condition would permit; especially at a Time, when her Absence wou'd be look'd on as a Thing so particular, that every one wou'd be apt to enquire into the Cause. But he needed not have given himself the Trouble of urging so many Arguments, the Desire she had of seeing him again, was a sufficient Inducement of her coming, and now not doubting, because he had told her so, but that at their next private Meeting he wou'd be able to clear himself of every Thing she cou'd lay to his Charge, was easily persuaded to admit the Reconciliation, before she receiv'd the Reasons for it. In fine, the Day being arriv'd *Clitander* had the Pleasure of seeing his intended Prey readily fall into the Snare prepar'd for her; and the Success of his Designs made his Eyes sparkle with a Delight, which the deceiv'd *Althea* observing, imagin'd was owing to his Love and Tenderness. There was too much Company to give them any Opportunity for Conversation, but such as was general; but what was deny'd to their Tongues, their speaking Looks seem'd abundantly to make up for.— Unutterable Joy appear'd to revel amidst the soft Beseechings of his Glances, while her's stream'd with ten thousand nameless Languishments, the Badges of Desire, and Simptoms of a Soul dissolv'd.

After a magnificent Collation[1] they went to Country-dancing, where

---

1. **Collation:** light meal with delicacies.

this perfidious Wretch having *Althea* for his Partner, resolv'd no longer to delay the Execution of his abhorr'd Intent, and taking the Opportunity of being the lower Couple,[1] step'd to the *Beaufett*,[2] and filling out a Glass of Wine, drank to her, with these Words: "May this blest Moment," said he, "put an End to all distrust between us, and be the Beginning of an everlasting Peace to both." "With how much Joy I pledge that Health, Thou who knowest my Soul, be Judge," reply'd she; at the same Time looking on him with Eyes so sweetly languishing, that any Heart but his wou'd have relented and melted with Tenderness and Penitence: Yet was he all obdurate and unshock'd, no Starts, no Tremblings confess'd the guilty Secret, no Change of Countenance betray'd the horrid Purpose he was about to act, but keeping the cursed Drug conceal'd between his Thumb and Finger, as he was pouring out the Wine, dropt it into the Glass, unperceiv'd, unsuspected by the unhappy *Althea*, who took it from his remorseless Hand, and drank it to the Bottom.

They continued dancing a considerable Time, nor had the Company any Design of breaking up, when *Althea* finding herself extreamly disorder'd, surpriz'd them with taking a hasty Leave. *Miranda* perceiving she was indispos'd, wou'd have persuaded her to lye there, or to suffer some of her People to wait on her home; but she refus'd both, imagining that her Illness proceeded only from her being lac'd more strait[3] that Day than ordinary, to conceal the Alteration in her Shape, from giving any Suspicion of the Condition which had occasion'd it. Nobody looking on her Distemper as dangerous, they suffer'd her to depart, without giving any Interruption to the Gaiety, which *Clitander* took Care nothing shou'd be wanting to inspire among them.

But this abus'd Lady had not gone many Streets, before she found her Pains encrease in so terrible a Manner, that she was unable to

---

1. **lower Couple:** the last couple in a line of dances, therefore dropping out would not be disruptive.

2. **Beaufett:** buffet.

3. **lac'd more strait:** the drawstrings of her corset pulled and tied more tightly, thereby restricting her breathing.

sustain them, without endeavouring some Relief.—She knew there were many Months between that, and the Time in which she must expect those Agonies which all, in becoming Mothers, feel; and incapable of ascribing any Cause for what she endur'd, call'd out to the Coachman to stop at the House of an Apothecary, who on all Occasions was us'd to attend their Family, and liv'd in the Way she was to pass. Happening to find him at home, she suffer'd herself to be led into a Parlour, where she was no sooner set down, but she found herself grow worse; and in a few Moments swell'd to that prodigious Degree, that her Laceings burst, her Eyes seem'd to start out of her Head, and every Feature was distorted. The skillful Apothecary immediately cry'd out that she was poison'd, and ran to fetch Things proper to expel it, but the Malignity had spread it self too far, and all that he cou'd do was ineffectual: Fearing, however, to depend on his own Art, he sent for an Eminent Physician to come there, she now being in a Condition which would not admit of her being remov'd: But on the first Sight of her, he made no Scruple of revealing the sad Truth, That it was not in the Power of Art to save her. "Is it then certain," said she, "that I must dye?" "Nothing less than a Miracle can preserve you, Madam," answer'd he. These Words pronounc'd with a grave and assur'd Accent, join'd to the intollerable Pains which every Moment encreas'd upon her, made her not doubt, but that her Condition was desperate indeed; and in the Extremity of her Anguish, forgetful of all other Considerations but those which the Horrour of her Fate inspir'd, she cry'd aloud, that all in the House were Witnesses of the Exclamations, "Then I am poison'd by *Clitander*, that murderous Villain has kill'd both the Life and Honour of the lost *Althea*:— Oh! I am doubly damn'd first by the Crime he drew me to commit, and next by my Knowledge to what a Monster I have sacrific'd my Virtue."—Such Expressions seem'd to have a Meaning in 'em too dreadful not to make those who heard them press her to explain herself more fully; both the Doctor and Apothecary entreated she would give them the Particulars of what she seem'd to intimate, but cou'd get nothing from her but the same Words several Times repeated; perceiving that either her bodily Torments, or those of her Mind, had driven her into a kind of Despair, they ask'd her if she was not willing to consult a Spiritual Physician: To which she reply'd, That she was past all Hope of Relief, either in this World, or that to which she was going; and immediately fell into Ravings so horrible and shocking, that they imprinted a Terror on the Minds of those present, which for a great while they were not able to wear off. Never did the Idea of Futurity appear so dreadful, as that which her Behaviour inspir'd; nor never came Death accompany'd with Torments such as hers.—— The most guilty Wretch that suffers the Sentence of the Law has, with the Certainty of his Fate, a Time for Preparation for it allow'd him, but she had none, taken in the very Fulness of her Crimes; and by those racking Pains which every convuls'd Nerve, and starting Vein sustain'd, render'd incapable of Penitence, of Prayer, or Consolation. A Minister of that Religion she protest being sent for, he exhorted her by all the Admonitions he was capable of making, to endeavour to compose her Mind, and throw herself on the Mercy of all-gracious Heaven, but she wou'd not suffer him to speak on that Head. "—— Talk not of Mercy," said she, "I have sinn'd beyond the Reach of Pardon,—I am already damn'd," wou'd she sometimes roar out, "—— a Thousand Friends encompass me about,—they wait to seize my Soul;"—and then again, more wildly, "Now, now I burn," cry'd she, "now feel the Flames which are decreed for Adultery and Incest." In this Manner did she continue all that Night, and early in the Morning the Apothecary thinking it proper not to conceal the Condition she was in, sent a Person whom he cou'd confide in, to the House of *Clitander*, to acquaint *Miranda* with the fatal News.

That Lady being yet in Bed, the Messenger, who said he must needs speak to her that Moment, was order'd to come into her Chamber, where having told her in what Manner he left her Sister, and related some Part of those Expressions her Despair had made her utter, re-duc'd her to a Condition almost as pityable. She fainted away several Times while she was preparing to make herself ready to go; and indeed it is rather to be wonder'd at, that in so dreadful a Juncture, and in so unconceivably terrible a Surprize, that she retain'd Strength enough of Mind to bear the Sight of what she heard, than that she endur'd so much in the attempting it. She arriv'd not however at the Scene of Misery till her unhappy Sister was no more: The Moment of her

Entrance, was that in which the afflicted Soul forsook its wretched Mansion, leaving that once lovely and Desire-creating Form, the most terrible and ghastly Spectacle, that ever made the View of Death a Horror. *Miranda* was for some Time incapable either of making any Demands, or listning to any Informations, but as soon as she was in a Condition, receiv'd from the Mouths of the Divine, the Doctor, the Apothecary, and all his Family, a Confirmation of what the Messenger had said. The Reader's Imagination must here assist my Pen, or it will be impossible for him to form any just Notion of what she endur'd in the killing Repetition of so dreadful an Account. I shall only say, that she sustain'd it with Life, and that was all. It was the Opinion of every Body that *Althea* shou'd be open'd,[1] to which, it being propos'd to *Miranda*, she consented, nor wou'd leave the House till it was done, still hoping that the Surgeons who perform'd that Operation, might find some other Cause than Poison for her Death: But alas! how terrible a Surcharge to her Afflictions did she receive, when they acquainted her that That fair Unfortunate not only receiv'd her Death by those Means the Doctor and Apothecary had said, but also, that she was with Child; and to prove the Truth of what they told her, presented her with an Embrio of at least six Months Growth. This wretched, yet still tender Wife had now no Comfort left, but in the distant Possibility that her Husband might be wrong'd, and that in Spite of what the Deceas'd had declar'd, some other Man might have been the Father of the Child, and Author of this double Murder; but soon this Shadow of a Consolation fled, and she became all Misery and Despair: Remembring that when she first came into the Room, she saw a Pocket-Book of her Sister's lying on the Ground, she desir'd it might be search'd for, imagining that there might be something which wou'd give her a further Discovery of what she wish'd, yet dreaded to be assur'd. Accordingly it did, for it being immediately produc'd, she found, to the inexpressible Shock of all those Hopes with which she endeavoured to flatter herself, those two Letters before incerted here, and that last fatal one which drew her wretched Sister

---

1. **shou'd be open'd:** An autopsy should be performed.

to her Destiny.—Which, to satisfy the Curiosity of my Reader, and more to expose the monstruous Villany of the impious *Clitander*, I will also give a Copy of.

To the Most Excellent *Althea*.

With what Words, O thou Perfection of all Loveliness! Shall I make you sensible of the Ecstacies that fill'd my ravish'd Soul, at the forgiving Goodness of your last charming Letter;—sure I am, no Language can reach the vast Extent of Love and Joy like mine!—The unequall'd softness of thy own endearing Thoughts can best inform thee what thy *Clitander* feels in this Restoration of his long languishing, and almost expiring Hopes!—Desire, sunk to Despair, revives and gladens with redoubled Ardour!—O how I long to read in those dear Eyes the blest Confirmation of what thy Pen declares,—Soon wou'd I fly to seize the Transport, but that the Birth-day of *Miranda* being so near, I take the Opportunity, under the Pretence of Tenderness to her, to celebrate my Reconciliation with *Althea*.—O may that Day put a Period to all future Misunderstandings between us, and compleat *Clitander's* Happiness.—I beg you, by all the Tenderness you have profest, and which still sways your gentle Soul, to commiserate my Pains, not to fail blessing me with your Presence on that Day: You know, my Angel, that a Time will shortly arrive in which you must be oblig'd to shun the Converse of your Friends, and it will be of Service to your Retation, as well as to my eager Wishes, for you to appear as long as possible: Shou'd you be absent, not only your own distant Relations, but also *Miranda* herself wou'd be surpriz'd; and who knows on what Enquiries it might put some People? But that Motive, which I flatter my self will most induce you to comply is, that it is entreated by him, who I hope you soon will cease to doubt if he is

> The most adorable *Althea's*
> Truest and Everlasting Slave
> *Clitander.*

To know what kind of Emotions those were which swell'd the Breast of this distress'd Lady, at reading these Letters, which she too well knew were written by her Husband's Hand, one must be in the Circumstances she was; but it is notwithstanding very easy to guess her Agonies were the most terrible that Humanity cou'd support. She had lov'd him with too sincere a Tenderness for even this plain Detection of his Villany presently to obliterate, she cou'd not resolve to prosecute him in that Manner which his Crime deserv'd, yet was not so blinded by her Passion, as to forget what she ow'd to the Memory of her injur'd Sister, the Wrong he had done herself, and indeed the just Care of her own future Safety, as to think of living with a Monster, who she now found would scruple nothing. Making therefore very few Replies to the Invectives she heard utter'd against him, nor speaking any Thing of the Discovery which the Letters had made, she took her Leave of the Appothecary, telling him that he should hear further from her, and withdrew to the House of a Relation, who had formerly been her Guardian; whence she sent by a Porter the following Billet to her perfidious Husband.

I need not tell you that my Sister is no more, you know but too well that she cou'd not live, and doubtless are by this Time inform'd that I was sent for, to see the Last of that unhappy Wretch.—I believe you will scarce expect my Return to a Place, where I must every Day behold a Villain, who not content with murdering her Honour, took away also her Life, with that of the innocent Product of his incestuous Passion.—I wish to Heaven the dreadful Secret were only known to me, but in the Agonies of her departing Soul herself declar'd it to too many, for you, I fear, to escape the Punishment your Guilt deserves:— Take Care, therefore, of your self, for you will stand in need of all your Wit and Artifice to shield you from the Sword of Justice.—This Caution is the last Proof of Kindness you will ever receive from

Your Greatly Injur'd and
Unfortunate Wife
Miranda

Early as it was in the Morning, when the Person sent by the Appothecary came to *Miranda*, *Clitander* was uneasy till he knew the Consequence of last Night's Action, had forsook his Bed, and was gone to give a Loose to Thought in a retir'd Walk, which he very much frequented, but not being able to rest there, he went from Coffee-House to Coffee-House, endeavouring but in Vain, some Cessation of his perplex'd Imaginations; at length returning home, was told in what Manner *Miranda* had been call'd out, and the Condition she was in at some News brought her by the Person who came to her: This fill'd him with mortal Disquiets, which the Receipt of the forgoing Letter confirm'd. He had hop'd the Poison wou'd have taken Effect, and destroy'd her in a more sudden Manner, and began now to be apprehensive, that all the Secrecy he had made use of wou'd stand him but in little Stead.—As for his Wife's Resentment, it gave him but little Pain, since he perceiv'd she wou'd not appear as an Evidence against him; he thought it best however to take the Advice she gave him, and withdraw, till he should hear if any Thing was design'd against him or not, and accordingly went out of Town that very Night, entrusting no one with the Place of his Retirement, but a near Relation, to whom he also committed the Care of his House, and who sent him from Time to Time an Account of every Thing, and receiv'd his Instructions how to proceed.

Miranda declining the Prosecution of her Husband, those to whom *Althea* had declar'd the fatal Mistery of his Guilt, were the only Persons whom *Clitander* had Reason to fear; and on being inform'd that they talked pretty freely of the Affair, and mingled some Menaces with their Discourse of it, gave Orders to his Friend to act in this Manner: He went to each of them, and acquainting them with the Knowledge he had of their Suspicions and the Reasons they had for it, told them they ought not to judge by Appearances; that in Case *Clitander* were guilty, there was no Possibility of proving him so, the Lady who had accus'd him having been Lunatick for some time before her Death; and besides it was wholly inconsistant with Reason to believe him both her Lover and her Poisoner; it seem'd more probable, that being with Child, to conceal her Shame she had taken something to destroy it, which had work'd an Effect contrary to what she design'd, than that it should be given her by any other Person: And concluded these Arguments with a Remonstrance, that to go about to prosecute a Man for a Crime, of which at most he cou'd but be suppos'd guilty, wou'd only involve the Persons who did it, in a great deal of Trouble, and be of no Service either to restore the Life, or revenge the Death of the Person for whose Sake they undertook it. These Considerations, by Degrees made an Impression in the Minds of those to whom they were address'd, which, together with every one having Business which was more his own, join'd to make the Ghost of this wrong'd Lady remain yet unappeas'd, and the wicked *Clitander* triumph in the Belief, That neither Heaven nor Earth will take any further Notice of his Crimes.

For the Sake of his Reputation, however, he made use of all his Cunning to be reconcil'd to his Wife; and Might perhaps, have impos'd on her Belief as much as on that of others, had not the Letters found in the dead *Althea's* Pocket-Book, been an undeniable witness of his Guilt.—She keeps them by her, and daily reads them over, to preserve in Memory his Offences, and prevent his Artifices from the Success he aims at. The Knowledge how much he is in the Power of one he has so highly injur'd, is a perpetual Rack upon his Spirits, and in infinitely more reasonable Apprehensions of Danger on her Account, than ever he had on that of *Althea*; While *here*, he suffers a Taste of that Bitterness of Soul, which in greater Abundance he must *hereafter* swallow to all Eternity; having reap'd no other Advantage from all the monstruous Villanies he has acted, than an Augmentation of those Disquiets which an unsatiated Avarice creates.

FINIS.

THE
FRUITLESS ENQUIRY.

Being a

COLLECTION

Of several Entertaining

HISTORIES

And

OCCURRENCES,

Which
Fell under the Observation of a lady
in her Search after Happiness.

By Mrs. *E. HAYWOOD*,
Author of *L O V E* in Excess.

—*To the Mind's Eye Things well appear*
    At Distance, thro' an artful Glass;
    Bring but the flattering Object near,
    They're all a senseless gloomy Mass.
                                Prior.[1]

L O N D O N.

Printed for *J. S T E P H E N S,* at the
Bible, over-against the *Bear* and *Har-*
row-Tavern in the *Butcher-Row,* without *Temple-Bar.* MCDDXXVII.
[Price 2 *s.* 6 *d.*]

An approximation of the title page from the 1727 edition.

1. **Prior:** Matthew Prior, poet and diplomat, courted the favor of the great. These lines
appear in "To the Honourable Charles Montagu" published in *The Gentleman's Journal,*
February 1692, 5; the 1709 version reverses lines 1–2 and 3–4. Montagu was a schoolmate of
Prior's, a collaborator on the poem *The Hind and the Panther Traversed* (1687), and became
the earl of Halifax.

The Fruitless Enquiry

A Certain Nobleman of *Venice,* dying in the Prime of his Years, left behind him a Widow called *Miramillia,* justly esteemed one of the most lovely Women of the Age, and a little Son not exceeding six Years old; so dear to his Mother, that tho' her Beauty, Wealth, and Accomplishments, attracted the Love and Admirations of almost as many as beheld her, and the noblest Youth in the Republick desired her in Marriage: Yet did she decline all the Advantages offered her for this Darling of her Soul, and resolved to continue the Remainder of her Days in a single State, fearing that in bestowing her self, she should also be obliged to relinquish the Power she had of managing the Estate for him, to one who would less consult his Interest. Never was Mother more anxious for the Welfare of a Child, nor never did any Child seem more to deserve the Affections of a Parent; so greatly did he improve on the Education she allowed him, that his Behaviour was her Pride, as well as Pleasure: As he encreased in Years, he encreased also in every manly Grace; there was no Art,[1] no Science,[2] no Exercise, befitting his Quality, of which he was not a perfect Master, and in many of them he excelled those whose Profession it was to instruct.

Till he arriv'd at the Age of Twenty, did his happy Mother glory

---

1. **Art:** skill in matters of taste, such as in music, poetry, and dance.
2. **Science:** branch of knowledge.

in paternal Fondness; and was so far from believing she ever should have Reason to do otherwise, that she scarce knew how to pity the Misfortunes of those who lamented the Undutifulness, or ill Management of their Children: But alass! On how weak a Foundation do all humane[1] Joys depend, and how little ought we to triumph in the transient Blessings of Fate, which in a Moment may vanish, and in their Room as poynant Ills arise. In the Height of her Satisfaction, just when she had seen the promising Bloom of this young Man arrive at Maturity, and every Wish was to its Height completed; then all at once did Misery fall on her, and she became more wretched than ever she had been blest.

Early one Morning did this belov'd Son go out, as was frequently his Custom to indulge Meditation in a fine Wilderness adjacent to the Castle, but Night not bringing him Home, nor the ensuing Day, nor many others affording any Tidings of him; the Fears and Perplexities of a Mother so tenderly, fond as was his, are not to be conceiv'd. Through every Part of the City she sent in Search of him, but all her Messengers return'd without Success; he cou'd not be heard of, nor cou'd any Person be found that had seen him: Days, Weeks, and Months past on in this Manner, and quite raving with her Griefs, she fell into a Sort of superstious Credulity which before she had despis'd; it was that of applying to Fortune-Tellers, and a vain Expectation of knowing that from Man, which Heaven permits not the Discovery of, even to the Angels themselves. But her good Sense not suffering her to place any great Dependance on what they said, she no sooner heard the Predictions of one, than she went to another, comparing them together, believing that if they agreed, they might be worthy of Belief; but being different, one telling her, he would speedily return, another that he was dead, a third that he was married to a Woman unworthy of him; but a fourth wiser than the Rest, wou'd not pretend to give her any direct Account, but only told her, that to engage his Return, she shou'd procure a Shirt made for him by the Hands of a Person so compleatly contented in Mind, that there was no Wish but that she

---

1. **Humane:** frequent spelling of "human."

enjoy'd. "If you can prevail on such a Woman to undertake this little Piece of Work," said he, "before it be finished, you will infallibly hear News of your Son, but you must be certain," continued he, "that the Person you employ be perfectly at Ease; if the least anxious Thought, the most Minute Perplexity, Discontent, or Care, ruffles her Mind, or ever throws a Heaviness, upon her Spirits, the Work will be of no Effect." Tho' this afflicted Mother had too much good Sense to imagine such a Thing cou'd be of any Consequence to the obtaining her Desires, yet the Inchantment being of so innocent a Nature, she resolv'd to make the Experiment; and to that End, set her self to think which of her Acquaintance was the most qualified for this important Peice of Sempstry. One she knew had vast Possessions, all the Grandeur which the World idolizes, Beauty, Wit, Health, and a Sweetness of Disposition, which render'd her capable of enjoying those Blessings; but then she was married to a Man of so perverse a Nature, that it took up her whole Study to please him, and the little Success she had in that Endeavour, frequently gave her many bitter Perturbations. Another, in all Appearance was possest of every Thing that can be wish'd, a wealthy and good Husband, many fine Children, and the general Esteem and good Character of the World, but she had made this Lady the Confidant of her Passion for a young Gentleman, and in that criminal Inclination were all the Pleasures of her Life overwhelm'd and lost. One had an undutiful Son, another an unfortunate Daughter, a third an extravagant Husband, a fourth an unloving one, a fifth was distracted with a Step-Dame's[1] overlooking Eye; a sixth had married a Man whose Children by a former Venture, were an eternal Plague upon her Spirits; one had so much ready Cash that she was always in Care how to bestow it with the least Hazard, and most Advantage; another was perplex'd for the want of it, and the Exigencies to which Persons in that Misfortune are reduc'd. Few there were to whom she could apply with any Hope of Success, if it were realy Truth that the Predictor had endeavour'd to make her believe; but among the Number of those was a Lady whose Name was *Anziana,* she was married

---

1. **Step-Dame's:** stepmother's.

to one of the Chief of the Nobility, a Man scarce to be equal'd for his personal Charms, or the Improvements of Education, and one who both before, and after his Marriage, had given a thousand Testimonies of the most tender Regard for her, never did any Pair appear to live together in a more perfect Harmony; three fine Sons and two beautiful Daughters were the Product of their Loves, all lovely, all hopeful, and promising a future Age of Happiness to their glad Parents. Where cou'd Contentment dwell if not in such a Family, who can be compleatly blest if *Anziana* was not. To her therefore it was that she resolv'd to have Recourse, and doubted not but to receive from her Friendship, that Favour which she imagin'd was in her Power to grant.

In Pursuance of this Design, she again set her self at her long neglected Toylet,[1] and resum'd those Ornaments which till now she had not worn since the Loss of her dear Son; and when drest with all her former Exactness, went to the House of *Anziana*, where she was receiv'd by that Lady with all the Demonstrations, imaginable, of a sincere Friendship, but when she related to her the Errand on which she came, she look'd extreamly surpriz'd, and wou'd fain have perswaded her from giving any Adherence to Advice which seem'd so perfectly Chimerical;[2] but the other continuing to insist on it, and appearing some what Resentful that she should refuse so small a Trouble, when it wou'd do her so great a Peice of Service; at last she consented to make the Trial, on Condition she would remain in her House for the Space of eight Days: At the End of which Time, said she, If you perceive nothing which may render me incapable of serving you in the Way you mention, I shall willingly undertake it. The sorrowful Mother cou'd not but comply with so reasonable a Request, and in doing so, found every Thing agreeable to that Character of perfect Tranquility, to which the Prognosticator had directed her; she now no longer doubted but she shou'd be able to make the Experiment, if there were any Dependance to be plac'd in the Words of these Soothsayers. Never had she beheld a Family better manag'd, every

---

1. **Toylet:** dressing table; in the eighteenth century it was fashionable to entertain during the last stages of getting ready for the day.

2. **Chimerical:** fanciful.

Thing was done with that Ease, that Regularity, and Concord, that Business were a Pleasure: The Servants seem'd to obey more through Love than Fear, the Mistress had not the Trouble of commanding, so ready were they to observe her very Looks and Motions, that what she wou'd have done, was so before her Desire cou'd Form itself into Words: The Children, observ'd the same Decorum; but these were petty Felicities compared with that which flow'd from a conjugal Affection, so tender, so obliging, so ardent, and unchangable, as that appear'd to be between *Anziana* and her Husband Count *Caprera;* never were Endearments carried to a higher Pitch, nor had more the Look of Sincerity. In fine, all that can be conceiv'd of Felicity was theirs, and was thought an Exception to that general Rule, that perfect Happiness is not to be found on Earth.

The Time prefix'd by *Anziana* being elaps'd, her distrest Visitor entreated the Performance of her Promise; to which, the other in a melancholy Accent thus reply'd. "Alass!" said she, "how liable are we to be deceiv'd by Appearances! How little does the outward Show demonstrate, some times the real Disposition of the Heart! I, who seem the most Fortunate of my Sex, am indeed the most wretched, nor is it in the Power of Fate to load me with superior Ills. But to ease the Amazement in which my Words have involv'd you, follow me, and you shall be inform'd in Full of the whole dismal Cause." As she spoke this, she turn'd hastily towards the Door of the Chamber, and the other going after her as she had desir'd, they pass'd through several Rooms, till they came to a long Gallery, at the End of which was a Closet.[1] There *Anziana* stop'd, and taking a Key out of her Pocket open'd it, and went in, desiring the other to do the same: But with what Horror and Affright was her Soul invaded, when as soon as she enter'd; the first Object that presented itself to her, was the Skeleton of a Man, with Arms extended wide as if in Act to seize the adventurous Gazer, and on the Breast was fixed a Label; which, as soon as she was, enough, recover'd from that Terror which so unexpected, and so shocking a Sight had plung'd her in, to be able to look

---

1. **Closet:** inner chamber for privacy or retirement; small room.

upon it. *Anziana* took her by the Hand, and bringing her nearer, show'd it her, containing these Words, which to make them yet more dreadful, were writ in Blood.

"Remember *Anziana* it is for your Crime that I am thus, and let a just Contrition take up your ensuing Days, and Peace be ever a Stranger to your Soul, till you become as I am."

Let the Reader imagine himself in this Lady's Place, and he will then be able to conceive some Part of that Astonishment she was in at beholding an Object of this dire Nature, in a House where nothing but Mirth and Chearfulness appear'd to reign, to describe it, is not in the Power of Language; therefore, I shall only say, that it took from her the Power of Speech, and tho' she passionately long'd for the Explanation of so strange an Adventure, yet her Tongue refus'd to obey the Dictates of her Heart, and by the wild Confusion of her Looks, and Eyes half starting from their Spheres, alone it was, that she cou'd make known her Wonder! or her Curiosity: But *Anziana* perfectly understanding what it was she desir'd, made her turn from that ungrateful Object, and sit down by her on a Couch some Distance from it, where she began thus. Had I not been convinc'd of your Discretion, said she, I shou'd not have taken this Method to show how improper a Person I am to undertake the Task you came hither to employ me in: I will therefore exact no Promises from you of preserving my Secret, nor desire any other Security for it than your own Honour; but as I have begun with bringing you into this Closet, which since thus furnish'd, has never been enter'd by any but my self. I will proceed to reveal by what strange Means this dreadful Guest was harbour'd here, but because I cannot do it clearly, without going back to some Passages of the former Part of my Life, you must excuse the Length of my Narration, which will at least be of this Service to you, that your own Woes will sit more lightly on you, when you shall know how infinitely more heavy those are, under which I labour. These Words drew a Flood of Tears from her to whom they were address'd, as thinking it impossible for any Misfortune to exceed that which she sustained; but composing her self as well as she could, she prepared to give Attention to what the other was about to say, who immediately began the Relation she had promised in these Terms.

THE

OPERA of OPERAS;

OR

TOM THUMB the Great.

ALTER'D

From the LIFE and DEATH

OF

TOM THUMB the Great.[1]

AND

Set to *MUSICK after the* ITALIAN *Manner.*[2]

As it is Performing at the

NEW THEATRE in the *Hay-Market.*

════════════════

LONDON:

Printed for WILLIAM RAYNER.[3] Prisoner
in the KING'S-BENCH, and to be sold at the
THEATRE, and likewise at the Printing-Office
in *Marigold-Court*, over-against the *Fountain-*
Tavern in the *Strand*. MDCCXXXIII.
[Price One Shilling]

An approximation of the title page from the 1733 edition.

1. **Life and Death . . . the Great:** Haywood and collaborators altered Henry Fielding's *Tragedy of Tragedies* (1731), which was an alteration of his *Tom Thumb* (1730); *The Life and Death . . .* is the subtitle of *Tragedy of Tragedies.*

2. **Italian Manner:** opera.

3. **William Rayner . . . King's Bench: Rayner,** London printer and bookseller, was often interrogated and arrested for his political publications. **King's Bench:** prison that held, among others, those who offended the government.

THE ARGUMENT[1]

Tom Thumb was the Son of *Gaffer*[2] *Thumb,* tho' some Authors assert,
Thumb was not the Father's Name, but a Sir-name given the Son from
the Diminitiveness of his Stature, agreeable to a Wish his Parents
made, that they might have a Son and Heir, tho' he were no bigger
than their *Thumb.* Like another *Homer,*[3] his Birth is much contended,
and many claim the Honour of it. Some will have him of *German*
Extraction, Others of *French,* but the most received Opinion is, that
he was an *Englishman,* born of very honest, but simple Parents, living
in the Reign of King *Arthur,*[4] a *British* Monarch of the sixth Century,
who was Chief General against the *Saxons;* but whether ever *Arthur*
existed, is a Point much controverted.

However that be, *Tom Thumb* is the hero of the subsequent Opera,
and Favourite of *Arthur.* He returns about this Time from the Wars,
leading a Captive Giantess in Triumph. The King gives him a most
gracious Reception, and in Recompence of his signal Services, bestows
on him his Daughter the Princess *Huncamunca* in Marriage. At the
same Time, his Majesty conceives a violent Passion for the fair Captive
Glumdalca,[5] whose Heart is already devoted to *Tom Thumb.* The
Queen, who is likewise enamour'd of the Generalissimo *Thumb,* strenuously opposes the Match agreed to by the King, upon which a great

---

1. **The Argument:** a literary convention in which the author gives an abstract of the contents
or plot; more common in the seventeenth century than the eighteenth.

2. **Gaffer:** a form of respectful address to older men whose age, virtue, or qualities other
than elevated social class warranted the usage; common in rural areas.

3. **Homer:** the name given an unknown poet, or even a group of poets, to whom we assign
the *Iliad* and *Odyssey;* nothing is known of "his" birthplace or lineage.

4. **King Arthur:** hero of a cycle of Medieval romances. The legends are best known from
Thomas Malory's fifteenth-century *Morte d'Arthur,* but Haywood is correct to associate them
with the chieftain of the sixth-century Silures, a tribe of ancient Britons.

5. **Glumdalca:** the captive giantess queen, a character added to Henry Fielding's *Tragedy of
Tragedies* when it was expanded from *Tom Thumb.*

Quarrel arises between their Majesties.[1] On the other Hand, Lord *Grizzle,* a Courtier, is passionately fond of the Princess *Huncamunca,* whose Pretensions her Majesty seems to cherish, as a Means to frustrate the intended Nuptials, and thereby gratify her own Inclinations; but perceiving her Policy of espousing his Interest does not answer her Design, but on the contrary, adds Fewel[2] to the enflam'd *Grizzle,* and makes him breathe nothing but Destruction on his Rival, she immediately breaks with *Grizzle;* who, in Return, vows Revenge on *Thumb,* and also threatens to involve the Nation in the Disappointment of his Love.

Tom Thumb is not content to gain Glory only in the Field, but he likewise gives a singular Mark of Prowess, and Heroick Virture, soon after his Arrival; for his Friend *Noodle* being arrested, he gallantly assails the Bailiff,[3] and triumphant kills both him and his Follower.

Thumb's intended Spouse being of a Disposition, apt for the State of Matrimony, appears in a very sad, and languishing Condition, till the Proposition the King her Royal Father makes of a Husband, when her heavy Melancholy soon dissipates, and she is transported beyond Expression with the Idea of changing her Condition. Lord *Grizzle* paying his Respects at this Juncture, she faintly rejects his Suit, alledging her being promis'd to *Thumb;* and *Grizzle* using the Rhetorick of a slighted Lover, detracting from his Rival's merit, but above all urging his Insufficiency, she is overcome by his prevailing Arguments, and gives her Consent to marry him privately. Wing'd with the high Thoughts of Possession, *Grizzle* flies to fetch the Licence. In the mean Time *Tom Thumb* waits on the Princess to commence his Courtship. He makes some amorous Speeches, but is told by her Highness, that she is promis'd to another. *Glumdalca,* who thinks herself injur'd in her Love by *Huncamunca,* enters at this Crises, and a Scene of Con-

---

1. **Quarrel . . . Majesties:** In Restoration and late-seventeenth-century tragedies, scenes in which women engaged in heated verbal combat were very popular, almost conventional. Among the famous scenes are those between the queens in Nathaniel Lee's *The Rival Queens* (1677) and Cleopatra and Octavia in John Dryden's *All for Love* (1678). Haywood and Henry Fielding burlesque overused dramatic elements throughout their Tom Thumb plays.

2. **Fewel:** fuel.

3. **Bailiff:** an employee of one of the sheriffs of London; the equivalent of a modern policeman.

tention between the two fair Rivals ensues, but *Glumdalca* is defeated, *Tom* giving the Preference to *Huncamunca*. *Glumdalca* is left full of Fury and Resentment. The King, like a solitary Lover, throws himself in her Way, which occasions a Scene of Groans, finely wrought up.

Tom Thumb, who a little before found the Princess wavering in her Love, has now remov'd all her late Difficulties, and the Ceremony is perform'd, which puts an End to a Lover's Anxieties. *Huncamunca* soon after sees *Grizzle*, and tells him that, rather than incur his Displeasure, she will marry him likewise; but the incens'd *Grizzle* rejects the Proposal with the greatest Contempt, and vows Destruction on *Thumb*, and the whole Kingdom, which puts *Huncamunca* in a terrible Pannick.

The Ghost of Gaffer *Thumb* appears to *Arthur*, who is foretold of the Rebellion of *Grizzle*. The Queen having some Presage of this in her Sleep, quits her Bed in Search of *Arthur*, when a messenger arrives, who informs their Majesties, that *Grizzle* is in Arms. *Tom Thumb* is appointed to go against him. *Grizzle* with the Rebels appear. *Tom Thumb* marching in Pursuit of them, is told by *Merlin*[1] the Manner of his being begot, and withal shews him his Fate. The two Armies come to an Engagement. *Glumdalca* is slain by *Grizzle*, and he by *Tom Thumb*. The King causes Rejoicings to be made on this Success, but in the midst, a Messenger arrives, that brings Word of *Tom Thumb's* being devour'd by a huge Red Cow, as he was bearing off *Grizzle's* Head to his Majesty. This news puts a Damp on the King's Liberality, and he is much in Wrath. The Queen stabs the messenger,[2] and like Children at the Play of *Strike your next Neighbour, &c*,[3] they stab one another all around.

But this Scene of Horror is soon transform'd. *Tom Thumb* by Con-

---

1. **Merlin:** a Welsh or British poet who legends say became bard to King Arthur and went mad and died after the Britons lost a battle in A.D. 570; his story is often conflated with the stories about the great magician of Arthurian legends. This enchanter has different parentage and often appears in literary works, including Malory's *Morte d'Arthur* (1485) and Spenser's *Faerie Queene* (1590). He was a prominent figure in Queen Caroline's Richmond monument.

2. **stabs . . . messenger:** The idea that messengers bearing bad news were killed appears in literature from antiquity; "Don't kill the messenger" is a familiar saying and can be found in, for instance, Sophocles's *Oedipus Rex*.

3. **Strike your next Neighbor, &c:** quotation unidentified.

juration, is emitted from the Belly of the Cow, and all the rest are rais'd to Life again, by Virue of *Merlin's* Wand, in perfect Harmony with each other.

DRAMATIS PERSONÆ[1]

MEN

King Arthur[2]
Tom Thumb the Great[3]
Ghost of Gaffer Thumb[4]
Lord Grizzle[5]
Merlin[6]
Noodle[7] }
Doodle[8] } *Courtiers*

---

1. **Dramatis Personæ:** The following cast list comes from the June 1733 Haymarket performance, and only major characters are listed. I am grateful to Robert D. Hume for much of this information; he is correct to emphasize that the parts changed often and were played by people who were more freelancers than a company. I appreciate his sharing Judith Milhous and Robert D. Hume, "J. P. Lampe and English Opera at the Little Haymarket in 1732–33," *Music and Letters* 78 (1997): 502–31.

2. **King Arthur:** played by Thomas Mountier. Primarily a concert singer, Mountier played Arthur at the end of his first year in London; in the fall production at Drury Lane, he was demoted to Noodle but played a variety of other parts there. He had played Acis in Lampe's production of *Acis and Galatea* in May of that year.

3. **Tom Thumb:** played by Master Richard Arne, brother of Thomas Arne who composed the music for the Haymarket productions. He was fourteen and very small; the next year he played four Cupids and other parts calling for a tiny person.

4. **Ghost:** played by Gustavus Waltz, a bass and a member of John Frederick Lampe's opera productions and, beginning in the 1735–36 season, part of Handel's company at Covent Garden Theatre; in typical cast-doubling, he often played both Grizzle and the Ghost.

5. **Grizzle:** played by Gustavus Waltz.

6. **Merlin:** played by Mr. Davis, who played bit parts, such as the King of Fiddler in *Chrononhotonthologos* at the Haymarket.

7. **Noodle:** played by Mr. Snider, performer in Lampe's opera productions; he had debuted in *Amelia* and sang Liberty in *Britannia*. He, like Waltz, doubled, and played both Noodle and the Parson.

8. **Doodle:** played by William Mynitt, who performed in several of Lampe's operas; he spent most of his career in Dublin at the Smock Alley Theatre.

Foodle
Bailiff
Follower
Parson

WOMEN

Queen Dollalolla.[1]
Huncamunca, *her Daughter.*[2]
Glumdalca, *Captive Giantess.*[3]
Cleora, ⎫
Mustacha, ⎭ *Maids of Honour*

Courtiers, Guards, Rebels, Drums, Trumpets, Thunder and Lightning.
SCENE   The Court of KING ARTHUR, and a PLAIN thereabouts.

---

1. **Dollalolla:** played by Mrs. Jones (probably Jenny), an actress much in favor with Fielding; she played in his *Tom Thumb, The Lottery, The Welsh Opera,* and *The Mock Doctor,* among others, and appeared at his booth at Bartholomew Fair. She played the same part in the autumn Haymarket production. The great Kitty Clive performed the part at Drury Lane.

2. **Huncamunca:** played by Susanna Mason, another member of Lampe's opera productions; she played in both *Amelia* and *Britannia* and was a hit as Venus in *Cupid and Psyche*. Susanna Arne played the part in the fall at the Haymarket; she, like Waltz, went on to work with Handel, and, as Susanna Cibber, she became a successful leading actress.

3. **Glumdalca:** played by Camano, probably the bass Giovanni Giuseppe Commano cross-dressed as the giantess; he was on the list of salaried opera performers kept by Lampe's treasurer, Francis Martin.

The Opera of Operas

or, Tom Thumb the Great

ACT I. SCENE I

Scene, *The Palace.*

Enter Doodle, *and* Noodle.

RECITATIVO.

DOODLE. Sure, such a day was never seen!
The sun himself on this harmonious day,
Shines like a beau in a new birthday suit;
All nature wears one universal grin.[1]

NOODLE. This day, O *Doodle*! doubtless is a day,
A day we never saw before.
The mighty *Thumb,* call'd *Tom,* victorious comes;
Millions of *Giants,* like as many *Bees,*
Swarm round his chariot wheels,

---

1. **Sure . . . grin:** the opening lines of Fielding's *Tragedy of Tragedies*, slightly modified from his *Tom Thumb*. Here and throughout, Fielding's tongue-in-cheek notes to his plays are useful in reading Haywood's play.

Giants! to whom the *Giants* in *Guild Hall*[1]
Are fools, are infant dwarfs.
They frown, they foam, they roar, while *Tom,*
Regardless of their din, rides on.

AIR I.

So the Cock-Sparrow, *at barn-door,*
Huge flocks of Turkeys *hops before;*
The lubberd[2] Red-Heads *does despise,*
Nor at their noisy gugling[3] flies.

DOODLE. 'Tis whisper'd in the books of all our sages,
This mighty little hero,
By *Merlin's* art begot,
Has not a bone within his skin,
But is a lump of Gristle.

NOODLE. Then 'tis a gristle of no mortal kind!

DOODLE. Some god, O *Noodle!* stept into the place
Of Gaffer *Thumb,* and more than half begot
This matchless warriour *Tom.*

NOODLE. Sure he was sent express from Heav'n,
To be the pillar of our state
Tho' small his carcass be, so very small,

---

1. **Giants in Guild Hall:** Gog and Magog, legendary giants who led rival forces that led to the founding in 1000 B.C. of New Troy, Albion's capital. In another legend, they were the sole survivors of the terrible children of the thirty-three daughters of the Emperor Diocletian, who murdered their husbands, were exiled, and reached Albion. The children lost a battle to Brute, and Gog and Magog were taken to London in chains and forced to be porters at the royal palace, which was on the site of the present London Guildhall. Representations of them were paraded in pageants and processions at least from the time of Queen Mary I's entry into London in 1554. Their statues still preside over the Guildhall, and there is a legend that they will come down and fight should the City of London be endangered. The *Guildhall* is the imposing center of government and site of meetings, ceremonies, and official dinners for the city, the "one square mile" that is the original city within the Roman walls.

2. **lubberd:** lubbard; clumsy, loutish.

3. **gugling:** "guggling?; a sound like that of a liquid being poured from a small necked bottle.

A chairman's[1] Leg is more than twice as large,
Yet is his soul like any mountain big,
And as a mountain once brought forth a mouse,[2]
So does this mouse contain a mighty mountain.

DOODLE. Mountain indeed!

NOODLE. But hark!

Flourish.

Those trumpets speak the King's approach.

DOODLE. He comes most luckily for my petition.

Enter King, Queen, Grizzle, *and* Doodle.

KING. Let nothing but a face of joy appear;
The man who frowns this day shall lose his head,
That he may have no face to frown withal.
Smile *Dollalolla*—ha! what wrinkled sorrow
Hangs, sits, lies, frowns upon thy knitted brow.
Whence flow those tears fast down thy blubber'd cheeks,
Like a swoln gutter, gushing thro' the streets?

QUEEN. Excess of joy, folks say my lord,
Gives tears as certain as excess of grief.

KING. If it be so, let all men cry for joy,
'Till my whole Court be drown with tears,
Nay, till they overflow my utmost land,
And leave me nothing
But a sea of tears to rule.

DOODLE. My liege! I humbly petition—

---

1. **chairman:** men who carried chairs, little carriages on poles carried by two to four men; the equivalent of today's taxi.

2. **mountain . . . mouse:** a fable by Aesop, "A Mountain in Labour," in which a great mountain is rumored to be in labor; people come from all around to see what tremendous issue such a mother would bear but are disappointed when a mouse emerges.

Kneeling.

KING. Petition me no petitions, Sir, to day;
Let other hours be set apart for business;
To day it is our pleasure to be drunk,
And this our queen shall be as drunk as we.

QUEEN. Already I am half seas over,[1]
Yet let the cistern overflow
With good Rack punch[2]—'fore *George,* I'll see it out—
Of *Rum* and *Brandy* I'll not taste a drop.

KING. Tho' *Rack* in punch 10s. be a quart,
And *Rum* and *Brandy* be no more than six,
Rather than quarrel, you shall have your will.

AIR II.

When your dames of superior class,
    Submit to the pow'r of drams,[3]
This virtue attends the kind glass,
    It makes 'em as quiet as lambs.
If then without Brandy, *or* Rum,
    Your Wives will not study to please,
Let 'em swill till they're tight as a drum
    Or they'll live the longer to teaze.
But, ha! the warrior's come—the great *Tom Thumb*—

Trumpets.

The little hero—giant killing boy,
Preserver of my kingdom is arriv'd!

---

1. **half seas over:** halfway to the goal; thus, half drunk.

2. **Rack punch:** punch made with arrack, a strong alcoholic beverage originally from the Middle East and made from fermented rice, sugar, and coconut juice; with the rise in trade with the American sugar colonies, arrack was often made with molasses.

3. **drams:** small drinks; from the apothecary measure equal to sixty grains or one fluid ounce.

Enter Tom Thum.

With Officers, Prisoners, and Attendants.

O welcome! most welcome to my arms!
What gratitude can thank—away the debt,
Thy valour lays—upon me!

QUEEN. Oh! ye gods! [*Aside.*]

THUM. When I'm not thank'd at all, I'm thank'd enough;
I've done my duty, and I've done no more.

QUEEN. Was ever such a god-like creature seen! [*Aside.*]
KING. Thy modesty's a candle to thy merit;
It shines itself, and shews thy merit too—
But say, my Boy—
Where didst thou leave the *Giants?*

THUM. My liege, without[1] the castle gates,
The castle gates too low for their admittance.

KING. What look they like?

THUM. Like nothing but themselves.

QUEEN. And sure thou'rt like to nothing but thyself? [*Aside.*]

KING. Enough! the vast idea fills my soul.
I see them—yes, I see them before me—
The monstrous, ugly, barb'rous sons of whores!—
But, ha!
What finish'd piece of human nature strikes us!
Sure she was drawn by all the gods in council!
Who paus'd, and then cry'd out—this is a woman!

THUM. Then, were the gods mistaken—
She's not a woman, but a giantess,
A *High-German* Giantess.

---

1. **without:** outside.

GLUMDALCA. We yesterday were both a queen and wife;
One hundred thousand *Giants* own'd our sway,
Twenty whereof were marry'd to ourself.

QUEEN. Oh! happy state of giantism!

AIR III.

Our Passions are of Giant kind,
*   And have to th' full as large a sense;*
'Tis hard to one to be confin'd,
*   When with a score we could dispense.*

GLUM. But then to lose full twenty in one day!

QUEEN. Madam, believe,
I view your sorrows with a woman's eye,
But be as patient as you can,
To morrow we will have our Grenadiers
Drawn out before you, when you may chuse
What Husband you think fit.

GLUM. Madam, I am your most obedient Servant.

KING. Think, lovely princess, think this court your own,
Nor think my house an Inn, myself the landlord;
Call for whate'er you will, you'll nothing pay.
I feel a sudden pain within my breast;
Nor know I whether it proceeds from love,
Or only the wind-cholick[1]—time must shew,

[*Aside.*]

Oh! *Tom!* what do we thy valour owe?
Ask some reward, great as we can bestow.

THUM. I ask not kingdoms, I can conquer those;
I ask not money, money I've enough;

---

1. **wind-cholick:** gas, indigestion.

If what I've done be call'd a debt,
Take my receipt in full—I ask but this;
To sun myself in *Huncamunca's* Eyes.

KING. Prodigious bold request! }
                                    } [*Aside.*]
QUEEN. Be still my Soul!   }

THUM. My heart is at the threshold of your Mouth,
And waits it's answer there.

KING. It is resolv'd—the princess is your own.

THUM. Oh! happy, happy, happy *Thumb!*

QUEEN. Consider, Sir,—reward your Soldiers merit,
But give not *Huncamunca* to *Tom Thumb!*

KING. *Tom Thumb!*
Odzooks!¹ my wide extended Realm
Knows not a name so glorious as *Tom Thumb!*

AIR IV.

Your Alexander's,² Scipio's,³
        Inferior are to Tommy,
While others brag of Mac's *and* O's.⁴
        Let England *boast of* Thummy.

A Title is an empty name,
        Like many we have knighted;

---

1. **Odzooks:** "Godsooks," or usually "Godsookers"; an exclamation similar to "good grief" or "good gracious." The *Oxford English Dictionary* notes that "sookers" is meaningless or corrupt, but it is often expanded to "God's succour." Many writers used "Od" as a disguised form of "God" in attempts to avoid the Blasphemy Act of 1606 forbidding the use of holy names in stage plays.

2. **Alexander:** Alexander the Great, King of Macedonia, conqueror of most of Asia; Aristotle was his tutor. Alexander united Greece, which allowed his march through the Persian empire to what is now Afghanistan. Medieval romances celebrated his life, and plays about Alexander by Jean Racine and Nathaniel Lee (*The Rival Queens*) would have been familiar to Haywood.

3. **Scipio:** Roman general who conquered Carthage and defeated Hannibal.

4. **Mac's and O's:** Scottish and Irish heroes.

His merits bids us aid his fame,
 So Tom *shall not be slighted.*

QUEEN. Tho' greater yet his boasted merit was,
He shall not have my daughter, that is pos!

KING. Ha! sayst thou *Dollalolla?*

QUEEN. I say he shan't.

KING. Then, by our royal self we swear you lie

QUEEN. Who but a dog—who but a Dog
Wou'd use me thus?
But I will be reveng'd, or hang myself.

AIR V.

Then tremble all, who ever weddings made,
But tremble more, who did this match perswade;
For riding on a Cat,[1] *from high I'll fall,*
And squirt down royal vengance on you all.

Exit Queen.

DOODLE. Her majesty, the queen, is in a passion.

KING. Be she, or be she not—now, by ourself,
We were indeed a pretty king of clouts,[2]
To truckle to our consort's will,

AIR VI.

 We politic Kings,
  Know far better things
Than e'er to our consorts to stoop;

---

1. **Cat:** perhaps a vessel used to move coal and timber on the northeast coast of England (*OED*).

2. **king of clouts:** mere rag doll in the clothes of a king (idiom, *OED*).

For once you give way
To Petticoat sway,
You may for your Breeches go whoop.[1]

Come *Thumb*—I'll to the girl, and pave thy way.

Exeunt all but Grizzle.

GRIZ. Where are now thy glories, *Grizzle?*
Where the drums that waken'd thee to honour?
O, what art thou greatness!
A lac'd coat from *Monmouth-street,*[2]
Worn to day, put on anothers back to-morrow.
Yesterday as St. *Paul's*[3] high,
To day as *Fleet-ditch*[4] low.

Enter Queen.

QUEEN. Teach me to scold, oh, *Grizzle!*
Mountain of treason! ugly as the devil!
Teach this confounded mouth
To spout forth words might shame
All *Billingsgate*[5] to speak.

GRIZZLE. But first I beg to ask,
Wherefore my Queen wou'd scold?

---

1. **You . . . whoop:** play hide and seek for.

2. **Monmouth-street:** street running between Charing Cross Road and Broad Street and known throughout the century for old clothes shops.

3. **St. Paul's:** cathedral built by Christopher Wren; the first service was held in it in 1697. It was built on the site of the church destroyed in the Great Fire, which occupied a place where churches and temples had stood since the building of a temple to Diana. Important state ceremonies such as the celebration of the Duke of Marlborough's victory at Blenheim were held there in Haywood's lifetime.

4. **Fleet-ditch:** a sewer flowing beside Fleet Prison, between Fleet Street and Ludgate Hill and into the Thames.

5. **Billingsgate:** site of the fishmarket and renowned for foul language; one meaning of "Billingsgate" is "swearing and cursing."

QUEEN. Wherefore? oh, blood and thunder! han't you heard,
What ev'ry corner of the court resounds,
That little *Tom* will be a great man made?

GRIZZLE. I heard it, I confess.

QUEEN. Odsbobs![1] I have a mind to hang myself,
A grand-mother by such a rascal.
Sure, the King forgets
His mother put the bastard in a pudding,
And on a stile was drop'd?
O, good lord *Grizzle!* can I bear
To see him from a pudding mount the throne?
Or can my *Huncamunca* bear
To take a pudding's offspring to her arms?

GRIZZLE. Oh, horror! horror!

QUEEN. Then rouse thy spirit—we may yet prevent
This hated Match.

GRIZZLE. We will, in spite of fate.

AIR VII.

The Spaniel, when bid, does obey,
*   And twenty fine tricks shew with all;*
The Soldier's observant as Tray,[2]
*   And both will come to a call.*

The Lover's more fawning than these,
*   Or any Court Sycophant spark,*
He'll shoot, fetch, and carry to please,
*   And all for a touch in the dark.*

I'll tear the scoundrel into twenty pieces.
QUEEN. Oh, no! prevent the match, but hurt him not;

---

1. **Odsbobs:** variant of "Odsbods" or "God's bodikins"; originally "God's joke."
2. **Tray:** generic proper name for a dog.

For tho' I should not like him for a son,
Yet can we kill the man that kill'd the *Giants?*

GRIZZLE. I tell you, madam, it was all a trick;
He made the *Giants* first, and then he kill'd them.

QUEEN. How! have you seen no *Giants?* are there not
Now in the yard, ten thousand proper *Giants?*

GRIZZLE. I cannot positively tell,
But firmly do believe there is not one.

QUEEN. Hence! from my sight! thou traytor! hie away!
By all my stars! thou enviest *Tom Thumb.*
Go, sirrah! go! hie away! hie!
Thou art a setting dog![1] begone!

GRIZZLE. Madam, I go—
And *Thumb* shall feel the vengeance you have rais'd.

AIR VIII.

I'll roar, I'll rant, I'll rave;
    I'll ride on clouds; thro' seas I'll swim,
I'll for the nation dig a grave,
    And bury it for my whim

Exit Grizzle.

QUEEN. Alack-a-day! oh! whither shall I go?
I love *Tom Thumb,* but must not tell him so;
For what's a woman when her virtue's gone?
A coat that's got no lace—wig out of buckle—
A stocking with a hole in't—I can't live
Without my virtue, or *Tom Thumb:*
Then let me weigh them in two equal scales;
In this put virtue, that *Tom Thumb*—

---

1. **setting-dog:** a dog trained to "set" or point out game.

Alas! *Tom Thumb* is heavier than my virtue;
But hold!—cou'd I prevent the match,
And shou'd be left a widow,
Then *Tom Thumb* is mine.

AIR IX.

In that dear hope how many live?
I'm not the only one;
Oh! what wou'd some fine Ladies give
To have their husbands gone!
All things new,
Ever wanting;
Joys in view,
More enchanting;
'Tis the mode e'er husbands die,
To have another in one's Eye.

END OF THE FIRST ACT.

ACT II. SCENE I

Scene *The Street.*

Enter Bailiff *and* Follower.

RECITATIVO.

BAIL. Come, trusty follower, come on,
This day stand by me, and at night
Three double mugs of beer and beer expect—
This way must *Noodle* pass.

FOLL. No more, oh, *Bailiff!* ev'ry word

Inspires my soul with virtue.
Oh. I long to meet the fish, and nab him;
To lay arresting hands upon his back,
And nobly drag him to the spunging-house.[1]

BAIL. Oh! glorious thought!
But see our prey! let us retire—

They go aside.

Enter Tom Thumb, *and* Noodle.

THUM. O *Noodle!* I am wondrous sick;
For tho' I love the gentle *Huncamunca,*
Yet at the thought of marriage, I grow pale;
For oh!—

NOODLE. Oh! what?

THUM. My grand mamma hath often said,
Tom Thumb, beware of marriage!

NOODLE. Cou'd you indeed the princess gain without,
I would not have you marry,
But Sir, be jealous[2] of old women's sayings,
If they're against it, 'tis because they're past it.
Oh! think of all the joy your soul will have.
While on her panting breast, dissolv'd in bliss,
You pour out all *Tom Thumb* in every kiss.

THUM. Oh! friend! thou fir'st my eager soul;
Spight of my grand-mother, she shall be mine.

AIR X.

I'll hug, I'll eat her up with love,
  Whole days, and nights and years

---

1. **spunging-house:** a holding place run by the bailiff and under his absolute control; those arrested could be held there until indicted and even beyond. A meaning of "spung" is "to rob," and bailiffs often abused their power and made great personal profit from their spunging houses.

2. **jealous:** suspicious, skeptical.

Our Bed shall be a shady grove,
    A soft retreat from cares.

I will my loving gut so cram,
    I never will give o'er,
Like baby, who at breast of Mam,
    Tho' bursting, cries for more.

NOODLE. Oh, Sir! this purpose of your soul pursue.

BAIL. Oh, Sir! I have an action[1] against you.

NOODLE. At whose suit?

BAIL. At your *Taylor's* Sir.

THUM. Ha! dogs! arrest my friend before my face!
Take here your fees——[2]

Draws and stabs 'em both.

BAIL. Oh! I'm slain!

FOL. And I also.

NOODLE. Go both to hell like rascals as ye are.

THUMB. Thus perish all the bailiffs in the land.

AIR XI.

Come triumph, ye Debtors, a Bailiff, vile Foe,
I've genteely sent to th' Infernals below;
And tell me where else shou'd Bailiffs go,
    Who Fiendlike infest this great Town?

Let all such rank weeds of the State go to pot,
May stewing and boiling fall out to their lot;

---

1. **action:** legal writ, subpoena.

2. **fees:** money paid bailiffs and "messengers" for delivering writs and apprehending criminals.

Without more ado pluck 'em up by the root,
We cannot destroy them too soon.

Exeunt.

SCENE II.

Huncamunca's *Apartment.*

Huncamunca, Cleora, Mustacha.

HUNC. Give me some musick——see that it be sad.[1]

Solemn Musick.

Oh! Thumb! *Oh! wherefore art thou* Thumb?
Why not born of Royal Race?
Why had not mighty Bantam *been thy Father?*
Or else the King of Brentford, *Old, or New?*[2]
CLE. Madam, the King.

Enter the King.

KING. Let all but *Huncamunca* leave the room.

Exeunt Cleora *and* Must.

Daughter, I have observ'd of late,
Some Grief unusual in your Countenance.

---

1. **Give . . . sad:** Here and elsewhere Haywood (like Fielding before her) parodies popular plays, as this line does one in Shakespeare's *Twelfth Night* (2.1.1).

2. **Bantam . . . Brentford, Old, or New: Bantam** refers to a character in Henry Fielding's *Author's Farce;* the protagonist Luckless turns out to be the son of Henry I, King of Bantam. **Old Brentford** in Ealing parish and **New Brentford** in Hanwell parish, consolidated in 1875, were at a major crossing point on the Thames between London and Surrey. A battle between Edmund Ironside, king of the English, and Canute occurred there in 1016; in 1642 it was the site of one of the key battles of the Civil War.

Say, what's the Cause?
Ha'n't you enough of Meat and Drink?

HUNC. Alas! my Lord, I value not myself,
That once I ate two Fowls, and half a Pig;
Small is that Praise; but Oh! a Maid may want,
What she can neither eat or drink.

KING. What's that?

HUNC. O spare my Blushes; but I mean a Husband.

KING. If that be all, I have provided one;
A Husband great in Arms,
Whose Valour, Wisdom, Virtue, make a Noise,
Great as the Kettle-Drums of twenty Armies.

HUNC. Whom does my Royal Father mean?

KING. *Tom Thumb.*

HUNC. Is it possible? [*Smiling.*]

KING. A Country Dance of Joy is in your Face;
Your Eyes spit Fire, your Cheeks grow red as Beef.

HUNC. Yes, I will own, since licens'd by your Word,
I'll own *Tom Thumb* the Cause of all my Grief:
For him I've sigh'd. I've wept, I've gnaw'd my Sheets.

KING. Then thou shalt gnaw thy Holland-Sheets[1] no more,
A Husband thou shalt have to mumble now.

HUNC. O happy Sound.

AIR XII.

Long my Maiden head in keeping
    I have had against my Will;
It has cost me much sad weeping,
    Lest I should lead Apes in Hell.[2]

---

1. **Holland-Sheets:** linen sheets made in the province of Holland in the Netherlands; in the eighteenth century Holland cloths were prized for their high quality.

2. **Apes in Hell:** Medieval legend that women married neither to man nor God will be given to apes in the next world.

I thank my Stars that Fright is over,
    I shall try the Marriage-State;
Twenty sure deserves a Lover,
    Or too hard's a Princess' Fate.

Oh! I am over-joy'd.
KING. I see thou art.
This joyful news shall on our Tongue ride Post,[1]
And we ourself will bear it to *Tom Thumb.*

AIR XIII.

Yet you that take a Hero to your Arms,
Can't hope t'engross him always by soft Charms:
Various his Duty, various his Delight,
Now is his turn to kiss, and now to fight;
And now to kiss again—so mighty Jove,
When with excessive thundering tir'd above;
Comes down to Earth—and takes a Bit—and then
Flies to his Trade of thundering back again.[2]

Exit King.

Enter Grizzle.

GRIZ. Oh! *Huncamunca, Huncamunca,* Oh!
Thy Breasts, like Kettle-Drums of Brass,
Beat loud Alarms of Joy;
As bright as Brass they are, and Oh! as hard.
Oh! *Huncamunca! Huncamunca,* Oh!

---

1. **Post:** Men with horses were stationed along the postal routes to receive letters or packets and ride as fast as possible to the next station with them; some of these stations would furnish a change of horses to messengers.

2. **Jove . . . again:** Jove, or Jupiter, the supreme deity of Roman antiquity, father of gods and men. By the eighteenth century, his paternity, based on classical mythology, was something of a joke; he was, for instance, father of the Muses by Mnemosyne, of Apollo by Latona, of Mercury by Maia, of Hercules by Alcmena, and of Clytemnestra by Leda. In John Dryden's *Amphitryon* he takes Amphitryon's place and fathers Hercules; numerous jokes about his lasciviousness are part of the comedy (Bulfinch).

HUNC. Ha! what Boldness' this!

GRIZ. Yes, Princess, well I know your Rank;
But Love nor Meanness scorns, nor Grandeur dreads.
Love often Lords into the Cellar bears,
And bids as oft the Porter come up-stairs.
For what's too high for Love, or what too low?
Oh! *Huncamunca! Huncamunca,* Oh!

HUNC.

> But granting all you say is true,
> My Love, alas! is to another due.
> In vain you come,
> I'm promis'd to *Tom Thumb.*

GRIZ. And can you such a Durgen[1] wed?
One fitter for your Pocket than your Bed?
Oh! fie! the puny Baby shun,
Or you will ne'er be brought to Bed of one.

HUNC. If what you say be true,
This Instant I renounce my Promise.

AIR XIV.

By Promise I'm no longer bound;
The strongest Vows must fall,
When once a seeming Man is found,
In Fact, no Man at all.[2]

GRIZ. Ah! sing that o'er again——let the sweet Sound attend me as
I fly to *Doctor's Commons*[3] for a Licence.

---

1. **Durgen:** dwarf, undersized person.

2. **no Man at all:** Impotency was a cause sufficient for the legal annullment of a marriage.

3. **Doctor's Commons:** specifically the common table and dining hall in the College of Doctors of Civil Law, but usually a reference to the buildings occupied by the Society. Five courts were held there including the Court of Arches, the Prerogative Court of Canterbury, and the Consistory Courts, the courts having jurisdiction over ecclesiastical law, licenses for marriages, and petitions for legal separation.

HUNC. O no! lest some Disaster we shou'd meet,
'Twere better to be marry'd at the *Fleet*.[1]

GRIZ. Forbid it, all ye Powers!

AIR XV.

To gain the lov'd, the beauteous Fair,
What various Dangers Man will run!
But when for Love your Women dare,
How greatly is he then outdone?
Between two wide Extremes all Women move,
And more than man, they either hate or love.

They'll jump from Windows, run away,
They will employ their utmost Skill;
They'll marry, to prevent Delay,
Both when, and how, and where you will.
Between two wide Extremes all Women move,
And more than man, they either hate, or love.

Exit Grizzle.

Enter Tom Thumb.

THUM. Where's my Princess? where's my *Huncumunca?*
Where are those Eyes, those Card-matches of Love,
That light up all with Love my waxen Soul?

HUNC. Oh! what is Musick to the Ear that's deaf?
Or a Goose-Pye to him that has no Taste?
What are these Praises now to me,
Since I am promis'd to another?

THUMB. Ha! promis'd?

---

1. **Fleet:** Fleet marriages were usually performed by clergymen imprisoned for debt in Fleet Prison; rites were performed either in the prison itself or, when allowed "the liberty of the Fleet," in nearby taverns. Neither licenses nor bans were required, and, therefore, these marriages could be performed quickly; the Marriage Act of 1753 made them illegal.

HUNC. Too sure—'tis written in the Book of Fate.

THUMB. Then will I tear away the Leaf.

AIR XVI.

Fond to Madness,
    Up to the Ears in whining Sadness,
'Sdeath! what's Fate to him that doats!
    Pillag'd and robb'd,
    Of one we love fobb'd,[1]
I'd not be i' th' Filcher's[2] *Coats;*
    He that worships God of Love,
    Minds not the Decrees of Jove.

Enter Glumdalca.

GLUM. I need not ask if you are *Huncamunca*—

HUNC. I am a Princess—and Thou—

GLUM. A Giantess; the Queen of those,
Who made and unmade Queens.

HUNC. The Man, whose chief Ambition is to be
My Sweetheart, has destroy'd these mighty Giants.

GLUM. Your Sweetheart?
Think you the Man, who once hath worn
My easy Chains, will e'er wear thine?

HUNC. Well may your Chains be easy,
Since try'd on twenty Husbands;
The Glove and Boot, pull'd on so many times,
May well set easy on the Hand or Foot.

GLUM. I glory in the Number.

---

1. **fobb'd:** cheated.

2. **Filcher:** thief; often a petty or sneaky thief.

HUNC. Let me view nearer what this Beauty is,
That captivates the Hearts of Men by Scores.[1]

Holds a Candle to her Face.

O Heav'n! thou art ugly as the Devil.

GLUM. The best Shoes in your Shop you'd give
To be but half so handsome.

HUNC. Since you come to that,
I'll put my Beauty to the Test;
Tom Thumb, I'm thine, if thou wilt go with me.

GLUM. O! stay, and thou alone shalt fill
That Bed where twenty Giants us'd to lie.

THUMB. Alas! I ne'er can do the Work of twenty.

AIR XVII.

Madam, pray excuse the task,
Faith! I am unequal to't;
Some robuster Hero ask,
Who can better grant your Suit.

Exeunt Thumb *and* Huncamunca.

GLUM. What, left! scorn'd, loath'd for such a Chit!
I feel a Storm arising in my Mind;
Tempests and Whirlwinds rise, and rowl and roar;
I'm all a Hurricane, as if
The World's four Winds were pent within my Carkass.
Confusion! Horror! Murder! Guts and Death!

---

1. **That . . . Scores**: a line much of the audience would recognize as introducing one of the scenes of rivalry between women; see Dryden's *All for Love*, 3.1.416–19.

Enter the King.

KING. Sure never was so sad a King as I!
To love a Captive and a Giantess!
O Love! O Love! how great a King art thou!
O *Glumdalca!*

GLUM. What do I hear?

KING. What do I see?

GLUM. Oh!

KING. Ah!

GLUM. Ah! wretched Queen!

KING. Oh! wretched King!

GLUM. Ah!

KING. Oh!

Exeunt.

Enter Tom Thumb, Huncamunca, *and* Parson.

PARSON.

> Happy's the wooing
> That's not long a doing,
> And if I guess right,
> *Tom Thumb* this Night

Shall give a Being to a new *Tom Thumb.*

THUMB. It shall be my Endeavour so to do.

HUNC. Oh fye! I vow you make me blush.

THUMB. It is the Virgin's Sign, and suits you well.

AIR XVIII.

But Blushes, those crimson Invaders,
O strange! are now criminal thought;

In Scandal and Censure the Traders,
Bye and bye will call Bussing[1] a Fault.
An innocent Blush in us Lasses
Is Virtue but a second-hand;
If we blush, we are told by these Asses,
It is because we understand.

RECITATIVO.

PARSON. Long may ye live, and love, and propagate,
Till the whole Land be peopled with *Tom Thumbs.*

AIR XIX.

So when the Cheshire-*Cheese a Maggot breeds,*
Another and another still succeeds:
By thousands and ten thousands they increase,
Till one continu'd Maggot fills the rotten Cheese.

Enter Noodle.

NOOD. Never was Court more *Bedlam*-like,[2]
All Things are so confus'd! The King's in Love,
The Queen is drunk, the Princess marry'd is.

Enter Grizzle.

GRIZ. O *Noodle,* hast thou *Huncamunca* seen?

NOOD. I've seen a thousand Sights to-day:
The King, the Queen, and all the Court are Sights.

GRIZ. But what of *Huncamunca?*

NOODLE. By this time she is marry'd to *Tom Thumb*—

---

1. **Bussing:** kissing.

2. **Bedlam:** Bethlehem Hospital, the public hospital for the mentally ill.

GRIZ. My *Huncamunca*—
Tom's Huncamunca—Every Body's *Huncamunca*.

AIR XX.

Desp'rate is thy Case, I swear,
Women love not shill I, shall I;[1]
Ten to one you lose the Fair,
If in Love-Affairs you dally.

There's a Crisis, which, when over,
Makes you certain of their State;
They will take the next new Lover,
And cry, sneering—You're too late.

GRIZ. If this be true, all Womankind are damn'd.

NOOD. If she be not, may I be so myself.
And see she comes to prove I'm not a Lyar.

Enter Huncamunca.

GRIZ. Where has my *Huncamunca* been?
See here the Licence in my Hand!

HUNC. Alas! *Tom Thumb.*

GRIZ. Why do you mention him?

HUNC. Ah, me! *Tom Thumb.*—

GRIZ. Ah, me! I see you're false, and I am curs'd.

HUNC. O be not hasty to proclaim your Doom,
My ample Heart for more than one has Room;
A Maid like me Heav'n form'd at least for two;
I marry'd him, and now I'll marry you.

---

1. **shill I, shall I:** original form of "shilly-shally"; to vacillate, be indecisive.

AIR XXI.

Prithee no frowning——let's have no resenting,
For both I've enough, if all thou didst know;
A Day or two hence you wou'd be repenting,
And wish I had kept two Strings to my Bow:

GRIZ. Ha! do'st thou own thy Falshood to my Face?
Think'st thou I am so base to share thy Bed?

AIR XXII.

No,—no,—I will no Rival bear,
Nor unreveng'd the Willow¹ wear.
Where's the puny modern Beau,
Can such Legs and Shoulders shew?
Modish Dame, two Lovers take,
    I will have you all, or none,
But beware—the Court shall shake—
    So you may go pick that Bone.

Exit.

HUNC. O fatal Rashness! should his Fury slay
My hapless Bridegroom on his Wedding-Day,
I, who this Morn, of two chose which to wed,
May go again this Night alone to Bed.

AIR XXIII.

My Heart misgives me sadly!
    Some Lovers wo'n't be Fools;

---

1. **Willow:** traditional symbol of grief for an unrequited love or of mourning for a lost or dead lover; an allusion in numerous early ballads. English poets depicted Dido carrying a willow branch.

And Oh! I've acted madly,
  To fall between two Stools![1]
Oh! wretched Situation!
  By wishing more than one,
Oh! fatal Separation!
  I shall be left with none.

END OF THE SECOND ACT.

ACT III. SCENE I

Scene *Arthur's Palace.*

Ghost *solus.*[2]

RECITATIVO.

GHOST. Hail! ye black horrors of mid-night's mid-noon!
You *Fairies, Goblins, Bats,* and *Screech-owls* hail!
And oh! ye mortal watch-men, whose hoarse throats
Th' immortal ghosts dread croakings counterfeit,
All hail!

Enter King.

KING. What noise is this? what villain dares,
At this dread hour, disturb our royal walls?

GHOST. One who defies thy empty pow'r to hurt him.

KING. Presumptuous slave! thou diest!

---

1. **To . . . Stools:** failure brought on through indecision or the inability to choose between two courses of action.

2. **solus:** alone.

GHOST. Threat others with that word,
I am a *Ghost,* and am already dead.

KING. Have at thee Man, or *Ghost*—
Thou fly'st! 'tis well—

Ghost *retires.*

I thought what was the courage of a *Ghost!*
Yet dare not walk again within these walls
On pain of the *Red-Sea;*[1]
For if henceforth I ever find thee here,
Sure as a Gun[2] I'll have thee laid.

GHOST. Were the *Red-Sea,* and Sea of *Holland's-Gin,*[3]
The liquor, when alive, I did detest,
Yet for the sake of *Thomas Thumb,*
I wou'd be laid therein.

KING. Ha! said you?

GHOST. Yes, my liege, I said *Tom Thumb,*
Whose Father's Ghost I am,
Once not unknown to mighty *Arthur:*

AIR XXIV.

I am a civil, friendly sprite,
And come not hither to affright:
I throw not topsy-turvy chairs,
Nor tables rumbling down the stairs;
Nor yet behind the Wainscot rap,

---

1. **Red-Sea:** According to folk legends, ghosts could be drowned in the Red Sea, the sea that parted for Moses and the Israelites in the Old Testament (Ex. 14:21–27).

2. **Sure as a Gun:** to be dead certain.

3. **Holland's-Gin:** an inexpensive liquor made in Holland. Because Holland had most-favored-nation status, it was tax free; because it was an alcoholic drink made of grain and flavored with juniper berries, it was cheap.

Nor sudden make the casement flap:
The doors not jar, nor curtains spread,
Nor peep I in at feet of bed.

KING. 'Tis he—it is the honest Gaffer *Thumb,*
Oh! let me press thee in my eager arms,
Thou best of Ghosts! thou something more than Ghost!
But say, thou dearest air! oh! say, what dread
Important business sends thee back to earth?

GHOST. Oh! then prepare to hear—
Thy Subjects are in arms, by *Grizzle* led,
Intending to besiege thy royal palace.

KING. Thou ly'st, and thy intelligence[1] is false
Hence—or by all the torments of thy *Hell,*
I'll run thee thro' the body, tho' thou hast none.

GHOST. *Arthur,* beware!—I must this moment hence,
Not frighted by thy voice, but by the cocks.

AIR XXV.

Slight not the warnings of us rambling sprites,
Sent, for your good, thro' air, on dismal nights;
Strive to avert thy yet impending Fate;
For kill'd to day, to morrow, care's too late.

Ghost *exits.*

KING. Oh! stay! and leave me not 'twixt *Hawk* and *Buzzard.*

Enter Queen.

QUEEN. Oh! what's the cause, my *Arthur,* that you steal
Thus silently from *Dollalolla's* breast?

---

1. **intelligence:** information; the first intelligence, or national security, offices were funded in the late seventeenth century.

Why dost thou leave me in the dark alone,
When well thou know'st, I'm so afraid of *Sprites*,
I cannot sleep?

KING. Prithee, *Dollalolla*, do not blame me;
I hop'd the fumes of last night's punch had laid
Thy lovely eye-lids fast—but oh! I find
There is no pow'r in dreams to quiet wives.

QUEEN. Think, what must be thy wretched wife's surprise,
When, stretching—out her arms to hold thee fast,
She folds her useless Bolster in her arms.
Think! think on that! oh think! think well on that.

AIR XXVI.

In bed we often lie awake,
    We cannot always sleep;
When winds are high, and house does shake,
    We gladly closer creep.
We simple women, when alone,
    Are nat'rally afraid;
Least motion puts us in a swoon,
    Except when dear's in bed.

KING. Oh! didst thou know one quarter what I know,
Then wou'dst thou know—alas! what thou wou'dst know?

QUEEN. What can I gather hence? why dost thou speak
Like men who carry *Raree-shows*[1] about,
Now you shall see, gentlemen, what you shall see?
Oh, tell me more, or thou hast told too much.

Enter Noodle.

NOODLE. Long life attend your Majesties—
Lord *Grizzle,* with a bold, rebellious crowd,

---

1. **Raree-shows:** peep-shows, carried around in boxes.

Advances to the palace, storming loud,
Unless the princess be deliver'd strait,
And the victorious *Thumb,* without his pate,
They are resolv'd to batter down the gate.

Enter Huncamunca.

KING. See, where the princess comes! where is *Tom Thumb?*
HUNC. Oh! Sir, about an hour and a half ago,
He sallied out to fag[1] the Foe,
And swore upon his great, his warlike soul,
He'd make a Grizzle's Head a Nine-pin bowl.[2]
Come, *Dollalolla, Huncamunca,* come,
Within we'll wait securely for brave *Thumb.*
Tho' Men and Giants shou'd conspire with Gods,
Yet he alone is equal to those odds.

QUEEN. He is indeed a Helmet to us all,
While he supports, we need not fear to fall.

AIR XXVII.

His Life to us is what of yore.
  Was Pallas *to the* Trojan *Loons;*[3]
While that's preserv'd, the State may snore,
  And safely we may spend our Crowns.[4]
Best watch-men of a nodding State;
  In this a monarch's wisdom lies,

---

1. **fag:** beat.

2. **bowl:** ball used to knock down the pins in nine-pin bowling (in the United States ten pins are standard).

3. **Pallas . . . Loons:** Pallas is a name for Athena, the goddess of war and wisdom; the Trojans foolishly continued to worship her even though she clearly fought for their enemy, the Greeks, hence the term Trojan "loons" (idlers, sluggards, clowns).

4. **Crowns:** coins equal to about five shillings.

To chuse such servants as are great,
    And fit for ev'ry enterprise.

Exeunt.

SCENE II. A PLAIN.

Enter Lord Grizzle, Foodle, *and* Rebels.

GRIZ. Thus far our arms with victory are crown'd;
For tho' we have not fought, yet we have found
No enemy to fight withal.

FOODLE. And yet, methinks, we'd best avoid this day,
This first of *April* to engage our foes.

GRIZ. This day, of all the days of the year, I'd chuse;
God's? I will make *Tom Thumb* an *April* Fool.

FOODLE. I'm glad to find our army is so stout.

GRIZ. What friends we have, and how we came so strong.
I'll softly tell you as we march along.

Exeunt.

Thunder and *Lightning.*

Enter Tom Thumb, Glumdalca, *cum suis.*[1]

THUM. Is this the noise of thunder, or of coaches?

Merlin *calls from behind.* Hark!

MERLIN. *Tom Thumb!*

THUM. What voice is this I hear?

---

1. **cum suis:** with their companions or followers.

MERLIN. *Tom Thumb!*

THUM. Again it calls.

MERLIN. *Tom Thumb!*

THUM. Thrice I've heard my name.
Appear, whoe'er thou art, I fear thee not.

Enter Merlin.

MERLIN. Thou hast no cause to fear—I am thy friend—
Merlin by name, a conjuror by trade,
And to my art dost thy being owe.

THUM. How!

MERLIN. Hear then the mystick getting of *Tom Thumb.*

AIR XXVIII.

His Father was a ploughman plain,
 His mother milk'd the cow;
And yet the way to get a Son,
 This couple knew not how.

Until such time the good old Man,
 To learned Merlin *goes.*
And there to him in great distress,
 In secret manner shews;

How in his heart be wish'd to have
 A child, in time to come,
To be his heir, tho' it might be
 No bigger than his Thumb.

Of which old Merlin *was foretold,*
 That he his wish shou'd have;
And so a son of stature small,
 The charmer to him gave.

Thou'st heard the past, look,—up and see the future.

THUM. Ha! my sense is in a wood;
See there, *Glumdalca*, see another me.

GLUM. O sight of horror! see you are devour'd
By the expanded jaws of a *Red Cow*.

MERL. Be not dismay'd; for this heroic Act
Shall gain thee fame immortal;
Ages unborn shall warble this soft theme,
In tunefull Opera,
Exceeding far *Hydaspes*,[1] *Rosamond*,[2]
Camilla,[3] or *Arsinoe*.[4]

THUM. Enough—let ev'ry warlike music sound,
We fall contented if we fall renown'd.

AIR XXIX.

To have my Actions in soft musick told,
*   What greater renown can I crave?*
Oh! the pleasure will be, like the hero's of old.
*   To be ha, ha, ha'd, in my grave!*

Lords subscribing gold galore;
*   Oh what clapping will be there!*
Such a thundring loud Encore.
*   As will make a dead man stare!*

Enter Grizzle, Foodle, Rebels, *on the other side of the Stage.*

FOODLE. At length, the enemy advances nigh,
I hear them with my ear, and see them with my eye.

---

1. **Hydaspes:** opera by Francesco Mancini, performed in London in 1710.

2. **Rosamund:** *Rosamond*, opera by Joseph Addison with music by Thomas Clayton, performed at the Theatre Royal, Drury Lane, in March 1707.

3. **Camilla:** opera written by Antonio Maria Bononcini and supposedly translated by Owen Mac Swinny, with musical adaptations by Noccolo Haym, and performed at the Theatre Royal at Drury Lane in 1706.

4. **Arsinoe:** opera written by Thomas Clayton with a libretto by Tommaso Stanzani; performed at Drury Lane in 1705.

GRIZ. Draw all your swords—for Liberty we fight,
And Liberty the mustard is of life.

THUM. Are you the man, whom men fam'd *Grizzle* call?

GRIZ. Are you the much more fam'd *Tom Thumb?*

THUM. The same.

GRIZ. Come on—for Liberty I fight.

THUM. And I for Love.

[*A bloody engagement between the two armies here drums beating, trumpets sounding, thunder and lightning—they fight off and on several time—some fall—Grizzle and* Glumdalca *remain.*]

GLUM. Turn, coward, turn, nor from a woman fly.

GRIZ. Away—thou art not worthy of my arm.

GLUM. Have at thy heart then—

GRIZ. Nay, then I thrust at thine.

GLUM. Too well you thrust, you've run me thro' the Guts.
Oh! I'm dead, but not with joy—

GRIZ. Then, there's an end of one.

Re-enter Thumb, &c.

THUM. When thou art dead, then there's an end of two.
Villain!

GRIZ. *Tom Thumb!*

THUM. Rebel!

GRIZ. *Tom Thumb.*

THUM. Hell!

GRIZ. *Huncamunca!*

THUM. Thou hast it there.

GRIZ. Too sure I have.

THUM. To hell, thou rebel!

GRIZ. Triumph not, *Thumb,* nor think thou shalt enjoy
Thy *Huncamunca* undisturb'd—I'll send
My Ghost to fetch her to the other world;
It shall but bait at heav'n, and then return.
But ha! I feel death rummaging my spirits.

AIR XXX.

My body's like a bankrupt's shop,
  My creditor is cruel death,
Who puts to trade of life a stop.
    And will be paid with this last breath;
      Oh!

Groans and dies.

THUM. With those last words he vomited his soul,
Which he hath voided in the devil's close-stool—[1]
Bear off the body, and cut off the head,
For me to lug in triumph to the King—
Rebellion's dead, and now I'll go to break-fast.

AIR XXXI.

An artist who has overcome.
    Antagonist at skittle-ground,[2]
Withdraws unto some private room,
    And smokes, and hands the full pot round.

We must take breath in all we do,
    An interval whets appetite;

---

1. **close-stool:** a chamber pot enclosed in a stool, box, or chair.

2. **skittle-ground:** the playing field for skittles, a game with nine pins set in a square on a wooden frame; each player tries to knock the pins down in as few throws as possible.

Unless we eat and drink, you know,
  We cannot either love, or fight.

Enter King, Queen, Huncamunca, *and* Courtiers.

KING. Open the prisons, set the wretched free,
And bid our Treasurer disburse six pounds
To pay their debts—come, sit we down;
Here seated let us view the dancers sports—
Bid them advance—this is the wedding-day,
Of Princess *Huncamunca,* and *Tom Thumb;*
Tom Thumb! who wins two victories to-day,
And this way marches, bearing *Grizzle*'s head.

A Dance here.

Enter Noodle.

NOODLE. Oh! monstrous! dreadful! terrible! oh! oh!
Deaf be my ears, for ever blind my eyes!
Dumb be my tongue! feet lame! all senses lost!
Howl Wolves! grunt Bears! hiss Snakes!
Shriek all ye Ghosts!

KING. What does the blockhead mean?

NOODLE. Only to grace my tale with decent horror:
Whilst from my garret, twice two stories high,
I look abroad to take the air,
I saw *Tom Thumb* attended by a mob;
Twice twenty shoe-boys,[1] twice two dozen links,[2]
Chairmen and porters, hackney-coachmen[3]—whores,

---

1. **shoe-boys:** those who clean boots and shoes for a living; also called shoe-blacks.

2. **links:** boys who carried torches to light people's travel through the streets at night.

3. **hackney-coachmen:** the men who operated three kinds of eighteenth-century for-hire transportation.

Aloft he bore the grizly head of *Grizzle,*
When on a sudden thro' the streets there came
A *Cow,* much larger than the usual size,
And in a moment—Oh! guess the rest
And in a moment, swallow'd up *Tom Thumb.*

KING. Shut up again the prisons—bid my treasurer
Not give three farthings out—hang all the *Culprits,*
Guilty, or not,—no matter—ravish virgins—
Go bid the school-masters whip all their boys;
Let lawyers, parsons, and physicians loose
To rob, impose on, and to kill the world.

NOODLE. Her Majesty the Queen is in a swoon.

QUEEN. Not so much in a swoon, but I have still
Strength to reward the messenger of ill news.

Stabs him.

NOODLE. Oh! I am slain.

CLEORA. My lover's kill'd, and I revenge him so.

Stabs the Queen.

HUNC. My mamma kill'd! vile murtheress! there.

Stabs Cleora.

DOODLE. This for an old grudge, to thy heart.

Stabs Huncamunca.

MUSTASHA. And this I drive to thine,
O *Doodle* for a new one.

Stabs Doodle.

KING. Ha! murderess vile! take that

Stabs Mustacha.

And take thou this—

Kills himself and falls.

AIR XXXII.

A monarch, when his people's gone,
Wou'd look but aukward on a throne.
With pleasure then resign thy crown,
Since all thy subjects are o'er thrown.
What signifies it to survive,
When only thou art left alive?
So!
Oh!

Dies.

Enter Sir Crit-Operatical *and* Modely.

MOD. Well, Sir *Crit-Operatical,* how like you the Entertainment so far?

SIR CRIT. Faith, Sir, 'tis as pretty a Banquet of dead Bodies as a Sexton could wish, and Variety—but I hope Mr. *Modely* has a better Opinion of the Tenderness, as well as Regularity of my musical Disposition, than to imagine I can see such a stupid, irregular, bloody, abominable Catastrophe, without Indignation.

MOD. Have Patience, till you see the Catastrophe.

SIR CRIT. I would be glad to know who ever saw an *Italian* Opera end tragically? By Gad, when we *English* initiate any Thing that's foreign, we do it so aukwardly! There's something of Whim in the Opera, but split me, this will infallibly damn it in the Eyes of all good Judges—I could almost cudgel the Rogue, that committed so unparallel'd a Blunder.

MOD. But good *Sir Crit,* keep your Temper till you see the Catastrophe.

SIR CRIT. Catastrophe! Why, the Actors are all dead, and unless the Author can give them a new Being, he will never be able to give his Opera another Ending.

MOD. But I hear they are not really dead.

SIR CRIT. How! not dead?

MOD. No, Sir; they are only inchanted; for you must know, *Merlin* interpos'd in their Fall, and intends, by Virtue of the same magick Art, to make them all rise again, in Order to give a happy Conclusion to the Opera. And see—he comes.

Enter Merlin.

RECITATIVO.

MERL. Sweet Goddess of inchanting Strains,
That steal'st, like Drink, into Men's Brains;
Great Trader in soft, melting, Wane;[1]
Thou best of Cradles to our Care,
Lend thy harmonious Aid to free
From magick Spell this Company.

Solemn Music.

And first arise, thou fell—thou hideous Brute—

Waves his wand.

Thou rav'nous Cow!——I do conjure thee to't.

---

1. **Wane:** woe; already obsolete usage in Haywood's time.

A Red Cow appears.

Curtain drops.

Now by emetick Power, Red Canibal,

Waves his Wand.

Cast up thy Pris'ner, *England's Hannibal.*[1]
Forth from her growling Guts brave Worthy, come,
And be thyself—the Little Great Tom Thumb.

He comes out of her Mouth, after which she disappears.

Now King, now Lords, now Commons, all arise;

Waves his Wand over each as he speaks.

Be loose your Tongues, and open all your Eyes;
Be chang'd from what ye were—let Faction cease,
And ev'ry one enjoy his Love in Peace.

They rise up.

SIR CRIT. Wond'rous, astonishing Plot! more sudden than the Reprieve in the *Beggars Opera*[2]—a Transformation exceeding all Transformation——even the Comical Transformation,[3] or any in *Ovid's Metamorphosis.*[4]

---

1. **Hannibal:** the Carthaginian general who invaded Italy by crossing the Alps on elephants; he threatened the city of Rome with his victory at Cannae but was defeated by Scipio Africanus and returned to Carthage.

2. **Reprieve ... Opera:** At the conclusion of John Gay's *Beggar's Opera* (1728), the beggar, whose play it allegedly is, steps forward and prevents the hanging of the hero.

3. **Comical Transformation:** In Thomas Jevon's farce *The Devil of a Wife; or a Comical Transformation* (1686), the wife of a gentleman and the wife of a cobbler are magically forced to exchange roles.

4. **Ovid's Metamorphosis:** The *Metamorphoses*, written by the Latin poet, Publius Ovidius Naso, is in fifteen "books" of classical legends in hexameter verse; it includes stories of the

Recitativo.

KING. O *Dollalolla!* O my Queen!
Thou only art my Queen!

QUEEN. O *Arthur!* O my King!
Thou only art my King!

HUNC. O TOM THUMB!

THUM. O *Huncamunca!*

GRIZ. Rub well thy Eyes, O *Grizzle,* to see clear!
Hast thou been in the Moon, or in a Sleep?
That matters not, but this I know,
I've slept myself into a better Mood.
Pardon my late Rebellion, good my Liege—
Tom Thumb, be happy in thy *Hunky's* Love—
O sweet *Glumdalca!* could'st thou be so with me,
But half a Giant, yet an able Man.

GLUM. The Offer's kind, and not to be rejected
By one in my sad Case—a Stranger here—
Some hundred thousand Leagues, or more,
From any of my Giant Country-men.

Air XXXIII.

Dimension, in Lovers, takes all knowing Lasses,
    From twenty to thirty, or more;
But little or great, no matter, he passes
    With longing Old maids of two Score.
For be he short, or be he tall,
    One's better, sure, than none at all.

THUM. Rebellion's dead, tho' we are all alive;
Cur'd by a Miracle, by giving Life,

---

transformations of gods into the shapes of men or animals and of humans transformed in
various ways.

While others heal by taking it away—
Inchantment happy! Conjuror most blest!
Among the Faculty of Quacks the best.

DUETTE.

THUM. Tell me, *Hunky,* without feigning,
Dost thou longer like abstaining?

HUNC. View my eyes, and know my meaning.

THUM. I see the lent of love is past;

HUNC. And yet I have not broke my fast;

THUM. But soon you shall—I'm in the fit—

HUNC. For what?

THUM. To love.

HUNC. Then, prithee humour it.

BOTH. Ay, prithee let us humour it.

HUNC. But dear *Tommy,* prithee say,
Wilt thou never go astray?

THUM. I'll be constant as times go;
I'll sup abroad a night or so.

HUNC. But what if I should do the same?

THUM. You'd only do like modish dame.

HUNC. Pshaw! rather let us faithful prove;
Who shares a lover, does not love.

BOTH. Who shares a lover does not love.

KING. *Bravo! Bravissimo!*
Thrice three! full nine times happy *Arthur!*
Shew me the King, who is so bless'd as I?
My Subjects now no longer by the ears,
But all shake hands, like friends, with one another.

CHORUS.

Let fierce animosities cease,
Let all marry'd couples agree,
Let each his own wife kiss in peace,
And end all their Cavils as we.

FINIS.

ADVENTURES

OF

E O V A A I,

PRINCESS of *Ijaveo.*

A

Pre-Adamitical HISTORY.

Interspersed with a great Number of
remarkable OCCURRENCES, which
happened, and may again happen, to
several EMPIRES, KINGDOMS, REPUB-
LICKS, and particular GREAT MEN.

With some Account of the RELIGION,
LAWS, CUSTOMS, and POLICIES of
those Times.

---

*Written originally in the Language of Nature
(of later Years but little understood.)*

First translated into *Chinese,* at the command of the
EMPEROR, by a Cabal of SEVENTY PHILOSO-
PHERS; and now retranslated into *English,* by the
Son of a MANDARIN, residing in *London.*

===

LONDON:

Printed for S. BAKER, at the *Angel* and *Crown* in
Russel-Street, Covent Garden. M.DCC.XXXVI.

An approximation of the title page of the 1736 edition.

Adventures of Eovaai,
Princess of Ijaveo

A Pre-Adamitical History

The Kingdom of *Ijaveo*[1] was once among the Number of the most rich and powerful of any that compose the sublunary Globe; almost impregnable by its Situation, and more so by the Bravery and Industry of the People.[2] The Earth Produced all kinds of Fruits and Flowers: the Rivers abounded with the most delicious Fish: the Air afforded a vast Variety of the feather'd Race, no less beautiful to the Eye, than exquisite to the Taste; and to crown all, the Climate was so perfectly wholesome, that the Inhabitants lived to an extreme old Age, without being afflicted with any Pain or Disease.

This happy Spot of Earth was govern'd by a King call'd *Eojaeu*,[3] in whose Family the Scepter had remain'd for upwards of 1500 Years, in all which Time no Wars with foreign Foes, nor home-bred Factions

---

1. **Ijaveo:** [Haywood's note]This Kingdom, according to a Map annexed to the History, was situated near the South Pole: if so, it must be, within a few Degrees, the Antipodes to England, and Part of that huge Continent, now call'd Terra Australis, or the unknown Land. The Cabal were of Opinion, that by the Name of *Ijaveo* is meant, Opulent and Magnaminous.

2. **The Kingdom . . . the People:** This description of England is nearly formulaic in political allegories, and readers would have immediately understood phrases within it. For instance, "nearly impregnable by its Situation" refers to its being an island; the English were more often praised for industry than any other single quality, and this characteristic would have been recognized even then as bearing imperialistic overtones.

3. **Eojaeu:** [Haywood's note] Father of the People.

had disturb'd the Land. So long a Series of Tranquility produced Blessings too valuable for a good Prince not to wish earnestly for the Continuance of them; and it was with an infinite Concern, the illustrious *Eojaeu* knew, by a Science[1] in which he was a perfect Master, that with his Life would end the Felicity of his Subjects, or at least suffer a long and terrible Interruption. As he had no Son, and was to be succeeded by an only Daughter, he took care to educate her in such a manner as he thought might most contribute to alleviate the Calamities, which he foresaw the Fates had decreed for her, and the Nation she was born to rule. He employed no Masters expert in the Arts of Singing, Dancing, Playing on the Musick, or any other the like Modes of accomplishing young Ladies; nor, indeed, was there the least Necessity for it, even had the Business of her Life been no more than to please; for she had a Mistress capable of instructing, or rather inspiring every thing becoming of her Sex and Rank: *Nature* had given so graceful, so enchanting an Air to all her Motions, and taught her Voice to issue in such harmonious and persuasive Accents, that any *studied Forms* must have diminished instead of adding to her Perfections; but there was nothing of which he so much endeavor'd to keep her in Ignorance as her own Charms. To this end, he suffer'd her to converse but little with her *own Sex*, and strictly forbad those of the *other*, to mention Beauty, or any Endowment of the *Body,* as things deserving Praise; the Virtues of the *Mind* were what he labour'd to inculcate, and therefore took all possible care to render amiable to her. *Pride* and *Avarice* he taught her to detest from her most early Years, as Vices the most shameful in a crown'd Head; and as her Understanding ripened, laid down to her those Precepts of Government, which no Prince, who does not punctually observe, can make his Subjects happy; or be long safe himself, from just Resentment. He represented to her, that the greatest Glory of a Monarch was the Liberty of the People,[2] his most

---

1. **Science:** [Haywood's note] Magick, of which the learned Commentator on the *Chinese* Translation observes, there were two kinds practiced by the People of those Days; the one had for its Patrons the *Genii*, or Good Powers; the other was Diabolical. The Conduct of *Eojaeu* proves the first of these to have been his study.

2. **Liberty of his People:** [Haywood's note] This implies, that the *Ijaveaus* were a free People, tho' under Monarchical Government.

valuable Treasures in *their* crowded Coffers, and his securest Guard in their *sincere Affection.*[1] "Take care, therefore," said he, "that you never suffer yourself to be ensnared by the false Lustre of *Arbitrary Power*; which, like those wandering Fires,[2] which mislead benighted Travellers to their Perdition, will, before you are aware, hurry you to Acts unworthy of your Place, and ruinous to yourself.—Remember, you are no less bound by *Laws,* than the meanest of your subjects; and that even *they* have a *Right* to call you to account for any Violation of them:—You must not imagine, that it is meerly for your *own Ease* you are seated on a throne; no, it is for the *Good* of the Multitudes beneath you; and when you cease to study *that*, you cease to have any *Claim* to their *Obedience.*—Let then your Ear be ever *open* to *Complaints;* your *Mind* inquisitive into the Ground of them and your *Eye* swift in seeing their *Redress*. But this will be impossible, if you suffer yourself to be engrossed by any *one Man*, or *Set of Men;* above all things, therefore, beware of *Favourites*, for Favour naturally implies *Partiality*, and *partiality* is but another name for *Injustice*. All Passions deceive us, but none more than the Goodwill we bear to such whose Sentiments seem to fall in with our own: we know not ourselves the wrong we do to others, by loving these too well, nor can ever be sufficiently assured, they really merit to be thus particularized.—'Tis a Fault to rely wholly on the most virtuous and approved Minister, because the best may err; but that Prince is unpardonable, who suffers himself to be guided in Matters of Government by one who has incurr'd the *general* Hatred.—The common and universal Voice of the People is seldom mistaken, and in all Affairs relating to the *Publick,* the publick *Opinion* ought to have some Weight."[3] He illustrated this

---

1. **He represented . . . sincere affection:** The king's speech summarizes the Revolution Settlement precepts as propagated by the Whigs; many of the precepts, such as government existing for the good of the subjects, are in John Locke's *Second Treatise on Civil Government* (1690).

2. **wandering Fires**: will o'the wisp or *ignis fatuus*; a phosphorescent light generated by swamp gases from rotting plants. The light flickers or hovers over the ground, luring travelers toward what they hope is a campfire or dwelling.

3. **Weight:** Whether associated with the Norman Yoke theory or Jrgen Habermas's authentic public sphere, in the eighteenth century public opinion came to be a force politicians solicited and took seriously.

truth by many Arguments, as well as by a great Number of Examples from the History of *past* Times, and his own Observation of the *present;* and that he said to her might be the more deeply imprinted on her Mind, he obliged her every day to repeat to him the Subject of their Conversation the preceding one, with what Remarks she had been able to make upon it.

This excellent Father having thus done everything in his power to form her Mind for governing in such a manner as shou'd render her Reign *glorious* for *herself,* and *fortunate* for her *Subjects,* his next Care was to instruct her in the Mysteries of *Religion* and *Philosophy,* that, whatever should befall she might have so just an Indifference for all terrestrial Things, and so entire a Dependance on her future Inheritance in that World above the Stars,[1] as neither to be too much elevated or dejected at any Accident below.

Eovaii[2] (for so was this young Princess named) profited so well by these Lessons, that, in a short time, she was look'd upon as a Prodigy of Wit and Learning; and her Beauty, tho' far superior to that of any Woman of her Time, was scarce ever mention'd, so greatly was the World taken up with admiring the more truly valuable Accomplishments of her Mind. But alas! the Precepts she received were yet green, there wanted Age to confirm and spread their Roots; so as to enable her to bring forth the Fruit expected from her; she was but in her fifteenth Year, when *Eojaeu* found himself summon'd by a Power whose Calls no Mortal can resist, and the only Excuse can be made for her Conduct after his Decease, is, that she became Mistress of herself too soon.

When this truly good and great King perceived his last Moment was approaching, he commanded her to kneel by him; and, having tenderly embraced her, I need not tell you, said he, how dear you are to me; my Behaviour to you, and the care I have taken to instruct you in such Things as alone can make you happy, by enabling you to

---

1. **Dependance . . . Stars:** [Haywood's note] This denotes the *Ijaveans* to have a Notion of Futurity, not much differing from what most Nations now agree in.

2. **Eovaai:** [Haywood's note] By Interpretation, *The delight of eyes.*

discharge the Duties of your Place with Dignity and Honour, has abundantly convinced you of my Paternal Affection: but because no human Guards are sufficient to ward against the Blows of Fate, receive from me a Jewel of more Worth than ten thousand Empires.—A Jewel made by the Hands of the divine *Aiou*,[1] the patron of our Family, and most powerful and beneficent of all the *Genii*. This, if you preserve entire, and in its present Purity and Brightness, will avert the most malevolent Aspect of the Stars,[2] and even in the inveterate and incessant Attempts of the fiery *Ypres*[3] themselves; and defend you, and the Nations under you, in all the Dangers with which you are threatened. In speaking these Words, he took off a Carcanet,[4] which he had constantly worn upon his Breast, and put it upon her's. "Let neither Force nor Fraud," resumed he, "deprive you of this sacred Treasure: Remember that what ought to be infinitely dearer to you than your Life, your eternal Fame, and the Happiness of all the Millions you are born to rule, depend on the Conservation of it." He cou'd no more; and perceiving his last Breath issuing from his Lips, he laid his Hands upon her Head, by way of enforcing the Command he had just given her, and graciously bowing his Body to the Nobility; who were weeping round his Couch, expired without any of those Agonies which make Death terrible.

Eovaii now assumed the Throne of her Ancestors, amidst the Acclamations of a shouting and almost adoring People: Novelty has in itself so many Charms for the Populace, that nothing is more common than to see all the Benefits of a deceased Prince, buried in the Hopes of greater from his Successor; and the unequalled Beauty, and

---

1. **Aiou:** [Haywood's note] The Cabal differ'd very much concerning the Signification of this Name, and at length left the Matter undetermined.

2. **Stars:** [Haywood's note] By this Passage it is evident, the *Ijaveans* had Skill in Astronomy, and depended on future Events from the Influence of the Stars; but the System by which they studied is now utterly lost.

3. **Ypres:** [Haywood's note] By what is said of them here, as well as in many other Places of this History, the *Ypres* are no other than Infernal Spirits, who are sometimes permitted to torment the People of the Earth, and are always at enmity with them.

4. **Carcanet:** a jeweled necklace, often a collar.

rare Qualifications of this young Queen, prepossessing even the most wise and penetrating in her favour, it's not to be wonder'd at, that *Eojeau* was soon forgot. It was, however, by regulating her Conduct after the Model of that illustrious Instructor, that she a while so fully answer'd all the great Expectations conceiv'd of her, that the *Ijaveons* had reason to think, no Addition cou'd be made to their Felicity, except that of seeing their excellent Sovereign married to a Prince worthy of her, and by whom she might have Children to inherit her Dignity and Virtues.

This was a Happiness to which several potent Princes, and other Great Men aspired, but whether it were, that she found no Inclinations in herself to Marriage, or that she thought none of the Alliances yet offer'd were for the interest of her Kingdom, she gave no ear to any Proposal of that kind.

[Eovaai rules well until she loses the magic stone from her necklace. A series of calamities, both personal and national, ensue, and she is kidnapped by Ochihatou and taken to an enchanted land where she learns to feel vanity, libertine sentiments, and ambition. He takes her to Hypotosa, the land he has ruled by enchanting King Oeros and alienating him from his son Adelhu; she escapes and travels. A series of experiences, visits by spirits, and long dialogues with characters such as an ancient, "republican" man educate her, often through dramatizations of the principles of government explained by her father.

Ochihatou recaptures her and locks her in a room, wherein she learns the story of one of his former loves whom he has turned into a monkey. She and the monkey-woman trick Ochihatou, and he turns the monkey-woman into a rat as punishment. His palace is surrounded by the populace enraged against him, and he flees with Eovaai. The rebellion in Hypotosa led by the Patriots succeeds in ridding the country of Ochihatou's supporters, and King Oeros locates Ochihatou and asks the king, a friend of Oeros's who is sheltering him, to return him for his just punishment. Ochihatou is warned that a messenger is on his way to the court, and Ochihatou needs to escape but wants to maintain a position of power.]

The Magician[1] having vented some part of his Rage in Exclamations, began to consider how he should avert the Evil which seem'd just ready to burst upon him; he found the Courier of *Oeros* would arrive at the Court of *Huzbib*, within eight and forty Hours, and that on the delivery of the Message he brought, he should be immediately secured and sent to *Hypotosa*. Some Asylum must therefore be thought upon, and what Place promised so secure a one, as the Kingdom of *Ijaveo?* He knew by his Art, that the People had sadly experienced the Effects of Rebellion and Anarchy, and wished earnestly for the Return of their lost Princess, whom, since her strange Departure from among them, had never been heard of. Could *Eovaai* be prevailed on to marry him, he saw no Difficulty of living and reigning there; so he set himself to put on all that might conduce to bring her to this Point; to which indeed the Modesty of his late Deportment seem'd not a little to contribute.

Early the next Morning, he sent a Messenger to entreat a private Audience in her Apartment. As he had not since their coming to *Huzbib* made the like Request, this a little alarmed her; but as she had always Attendants within Call she yielded to it with the less Scruple, and he approach'd her with an Air so perfectly submissive, as entirely banish'd all unquiet Apprehensions from her Bosom. Madam, said this Master of Dissimulation, I come now to give you an uncontestable Proof of the Purity of my Intentions towards you.—The *Ijaveans* repent their ill Treatment of so excellent a Queen.—Loyalty is rekindled in their Hearts.—A vacant Throne attends your Presence, and I should add to my past Offences a much greater yet, could I be capable of detaining you one moment from your impatient People. No, Madam, pursued he, I swear to you by the immortal Gods, I will defer my Longings to return to *Hypotosa*, and the Revenge due to my Perse-

---

1. **Magician**: Ochihatou, the Robert Walpole figure, who "ruled every thing in Hypotosa, tho' Oeros, the King thereof, was living." He is described by Haywood as deformed in body, a master of hypocrisy, diligent and successful in the study of the "pernicious Science" of evil magic, and devoted to the Ypres but able to use "soothing and insinuating Behaviour" to get his way; see "The History of Ochihatou, Prime Minister of Hypotosa," *Eovaai*, 18– 26 (omitted in the present edition).

cutors, till I have seen you re-established in all those Dignities you
were born to wear.—Be pleased then to permit me to exert that Science,[1] which I shall esteem more than ever, if servicable to you, for
your Conveyance hence; and before the Sun has passed half his Diurnal
Progress, you shall behold yourself in the confines of *Ijaveo.*

It was with an inexpressible Confusion of Ideas, that *Eovaai* heard
this Discourse: Wonder and Joy, and Hope and Fear, joined with a
certain Suspence proceeding from them all, left her not the Power of
making any immediate Answer. *Ochihatou* gave her some time to recover herself; and when he perceived she grew more composed, I
doubted not, Madam, resumed he, if the Tidings I brought would fill
you with the extremest Surprize; but then I expected it would be a
Surprize wholly made up of Transport,[2] nor can see any reason why
you should hesitate, even for a moment, to accept the Offer I make
of restoring you to your Kingdom, and by that means attoning for
some part of my past Conduct.

Before these last Words, the Princess of *Ijaveo* had brought herself
to resolve in what manner she should behave: She knew nothing of
what had happened in *Hypotosa* since their Departure from that Court,
and could not but look on his Desires of setting her on her Throne,
before his own Re-establishment, as the highest Testimony of an un-
feign'd Affection and Respect. She imagined indeed, that he was not
without some interested Designs, both on her Person and Kingdom;
but then she thought she should be much more secure from any thing
he should attempt amongst her own People than she could be in the
Court of *Oeros,* where everything had been so entirely at his Command, and she expected would be so again at His return to it. She
thought it therefore much better to agree to his Proposal, by which
she seem'd to hazard but little, in comparison with what she might be
exposed to, if carried back to *Hypotosa;* and perceiving he had done
speaking, and seem'd impatient for her Reply; To be told, said she,

---

1. **Science:** knowledge; in this case, of magic; see note 1, p. 224.

2. **Transport:** ecstasy, great joy.

that the unfortunate *Ijaveans* are at length sensible of their Faults, and willing to repair the Injuries done to me, their lawfull Queen, is a Blessing I so little expected, or even hoped, that it might well put all my Faculties to a stand: But since you have assured me of the Truth, I should be ungrateful to the relenting Gods, to neglect any possible means of laying hold on the Bounty they, thro' you, present. If I have therefore hesitated, it is only occasioned by an Unwillingness to abuse your Generosity, in suffering you to bestow any of those Labours for my Establishment, at a time when your own requires them all.

Ochihatou reply'd to this little Compliment, in Terms full of Respect; and when he found she was no less impatient for this Journey than himself, Madam, said he, as you have potent Enemies among the Stars, who are continually at war with those who would pour down auspicious Influences on your Head, it is not at all Times, nor by all Methods, you can possibly attain any good.—This present Hour is governed by the most benignant of all the shining Train that fill the great Expanse above us.—Let us not lose it.—The next perhaps may render all Endeavors Fruitless.—We must depart this moment; and to do it with safety, we must both of us exchange the Forms given us by Nature, for those of a less noble Part of the Creation.—Excuse me therefore, continued he, with a well-affected Modesty, and yield to the necessity of plucking off your Habit.—We must be free, entirely divested of all that Pride, or Luxury, or Convenience invented for us, before we can assume the Shape of those less guilty Animals, who content themselves with appearing such as they were born.

Here followed a long Debate: *Eovaai* could not think of being naked, without a Confusion, which made her look on all the Benefits she might receive as too little a Recompence for the Shame she must undergo; but *Ochihatou* having uttr'd unnumber'd Imprecations, that while she was undressing, he would not so much as turn his Eyes that way, she was at last prevailed on, and screening herself behind a Curtain, slowly pull'd one thing off, and then another; *Ochihatou* urging her all the time to be more speedy, by crying out, Dear Princess, the happy Moment is almost elaps'd. At last, she was wholly stript of every thing but the Shell, which had contain'd the mystic Jewel given her by *Eojaeu,* and the Perspective of *Halafamai;*[1] the last of which she carefully conceal'd in the Palm of her Hand, and the former being tied about her Neck, had never quitted her Breast; and tho' she thought it no Value, the Stone being lost, was now happily forgotten by her.

Having thus done what was required from her, she told him, with a faint Voice, that she was ready. His Clothes were immediately torn off; and when they were, he threw back the Curtain where *Eovaai* stood cow'ring down half dead with shame: but he forebore to add to it, and without seeming to be at all affected with her naked Charms, spoke some Words altogether unintelligible to her, and at the same time struck her on the Forehead with his magic Wand; on which she immediately became the most beautiful white Pigeon that ever was seen: That done, he gave a Blow to himself, and clapping the Wand between his Teeth, was turned into a huge Vulture; then seizing the Princess between his Talons, yet in such a manner, as not to hurt her tender Body, took his Flight with her out of the Window, which he before had opened for that purpose.

Full many a League thro' Air the Vulture, with unwearied Pinions, bore his lovely Prize, nor perch'd for Rest on any Pinnacle, or Cloud-topt Rock, till he had reached *Ijaveo;* the sight of whose well-remember'd Towers, gave a strange Flutter to the Heart of *Eovaai.*

It was in a lone and unfrequented Forest *Ochihatou* chose to alight, and as soon as he had eased himself of his fair Burthen, took between his Talons the Wand, which he had all this while held carefully in his Beak, and having smote himself with it, instantly recovered his former Shape; then doing the same to *Eovaai* she also saw herself as she was before: but tho' she was glad to have resumed Humanity, yet when she considered she was naked and in the presence of a Man, who was so too, she was ready to sink into the Earth. She ran behind a Tree to avoid looking on *Ochihatou,* or being looked upon by him, and cried out, "Oh, my Lord! what shall we do for Habits?—Why did you not rather conduct me, modestly array'd in Feathers, to some Place

---

1. **Perspective of Halafamai:** a sacred telescope that allows the viewer to see through all delusions; Haywood, *Eovaai* (London, 1736), 77 (omitted in the present edition).

where Conveniences might have been provided for us, the moment
we returned to ourselves, and so have spared this most undecent Act?"
"Call it not so, my dear *Eovaai,*" reply'd he, laughing, "as I flatter
myself you intended, when you accepted my Service, to reward it with
no less than your Person, I see no crime in anticipating my Happiness." "Oh, all ye Stars!" exclaimed the Princess, trembling, "What is
it you mean, my Lord?" "I mean," said he, "to make myself Master
of a Blessing, I have but too long waited for." With these Words he
catch'd her in his Arms; but perceiving that unable to sustain the
Shock of Shame and Fear, she was just fainting, he endeavor'd to
extinguish those Passions, so much Enemies to the Desires he aimed
to inspire, and far from proceeding to any greater Liberties than a Kiss,
"Be not alarm'd, my dear Princess," said he, "I have brought you to
Ijaveo, your native Climate, brought you to live and reign over a People, who long for nothing more than to testify their Submission to
you; but I will now avow the Truth: I did you not this Service, without
hope of a Recompence; and what other Recompence would be worthy
of me, but to share your Crown and Bed?—Yes, Madam, continued
he, you must make me King of *Ijaveo,* and your Husband." "Stay then
till I am Queen," answer'd she, a little more assured, "does this wild
Forest afford us Regal Ornaments? Where is my Throne, the State[1] I
should be treated with?" "Soon shall you find it all," resumed he; "but
tho' this Place has none of the Glare of Greatness, it may however
produce a more delightful Bridal Bed.—What can be sweeter or more
soft than this enamell'd Verdure beneath our Feet? What Canopy so
magnificent as the high Arch of Heaven, where the gorgeous Sun
embroiders with his Rays the pure Serene? What Musick more enchanting than the Birds, which, from the neighboring Thickets, attend
to chant our Nuptials in a thousand different Notes. Yield then, my
Love," added he, (now growing more vehement) "be mine—all Nature
joins with my fierce Desires to tempt you to be happy, and you
must"—Here grasping her more closely to his Bosom, he was about
to render all Denials fruitless; but *Eovaai* summoning all her strength,

---

1. **State:** pomp, ceremony.

both of Resolution and Limbs, broke from his Arms, and with a Tone of Voice, which had more in it of the commanding than beseeching, "Hold, I conjure you," cry'd she "if, as you would have me think, your Desires are legal, lose not the Merit of them by violating that Virtue it should be your Interest to preserve.—Let me be carried to my Palace, cloathed according to the Modesty of my Sex, and then when Marriage-Rites shall have made us one" "—No, Princess," interrupted *Ochihatou*, "I have already too much experienced the little Consideration you have for me, to flatter myself with any Gratification, which must depend upon your Choice; and therefore resolved to make sure of my Reward before my Service is compleated. Hear me then," continued he, with a stern and determined Air; "if you do not resign yourself willingly to my Embraces, I shall forgo all the Respect my foolish Passion has hitherto made me observe, and seize my Joy; which done, I shall despise and hate—give all my Soul up to revenge.—Yield then, and be a Queen, or by refusing, cease to be a Woman.—This Wand, whose Power you know, shall strait transform you to a Weazel's loathsome Form; under which you shall pass the whole Remainder of your wretched Days."

This Menace entirely destroyed all the Courage poor *Eovaai* had assumed, but not her Virtue, which never was more powerful in her than at this dreadful Moment—tho' nothing could be more terrible to her than the Thoughts of such a Transformation; tho' she doubted not but he would really inflict it on her, yet she resolved to hazard every thing, endure every thing, rather than consent to sacrifice her Chastity to the Enchanter's Will. The Distraction of her Thoughts keeping her from making any Answer to his last Words, he inferr'd from her Silence, that tho' she could not bring herself to tell him she would be devoted to him, she had at least given over all Resistance; and abating somewhat of his late Austerity, he again approach'd her, and taking her tenderly in his Arms, endeavour'd to dissipate her Tremblings with repeated Vows of making her Queen of *Ijaveo*, as soon as, by having possest her, he could assure himself she would suffer him to reign with her. But she, who abhorr'd a Throne with such a Partner, continued firm in her Resolution, and as he was about to perpetrate the Ruin he intended,[1] "O divine *Aiou*," cry'd she, "this once afford me Relief!—Let not the Remains of thy Favourite *Eojaeu* become the Prey of Lust, nor the Princess of *Ijaveo* be polluted in that Land which gave her Birth!"[2] In speaking these Words, she seemed inspir'd by the Power to whom they were address'd, she sprung a second time from the Arms of *Ochihatou,* in spite of his superior Strength; and seeing the dreadful Wand, Instrument of his Mischiefs, lying on the Grass, she ran to it, snatch'd it up, and broke it in sunder before his Face. The Suddenness with which she did this Action, left *Ochihatou* not the Power of preventing it; and he saw himself undone, before he had the least Thought of being so.

The Moment *Eovaai* had broke the inchanted Wand, a dark'ning Mist fell from the Regions of the Air, and huge Claps of Thunder rattled over their Heads, a thousand frightful *Ypres* kept in subjection by *Ochihatou's* Power, now freed, express'd their Joy in antick Skippings round him, then vanish'd; while he, loud as the Storm, blasphemed the Gods, and uttered such Impieties, as would be horrible repeated after him. What otherwise indeed could be expected from him? He had renounced Heaven and all the Powers of Goodness: his Crimes had render'd him detestable to Earth; and the *Ypres,* who for his Ruin had become his Servants, now deserted him; the magick Wand broken, his Spells no longer were of use; and all his Skill in Necromancy but made him know how accursed he was. He who so lately could command the Elements, convert the Moon to Blood, and even annoy the Celestial *Genii* in their starry Palaces, had now no means of procuring for himself or Lodging, Food, or Rayment, much less of executing that Revenge his Soul was big with. *Eovaai,* of all created Beings, seemed only in his power, and on her he resolved to inflict all the Torments he was able. That poor Princess had hoped to

---

1. **to perpetrate . . . intended:** [Haywood's note] The Commentator observes, that either *Ijaveo* must be a very warm Climate, or *Ochihatou* of an uncommon Constitution, to retain the Fury of his amorous Desires, considering the Position he was in.

2. **O divine Aiou . . . Birth!:** [Haywood's note] The same great Author also takes notice that since the Loss of her Jewel, this was the first time *Eovaai* had ever assumed Courage to offer up any Prayer to *Aiou*.

conceal herself from his Fury in a little Thicket; but he presently
discover'd, and dragg'd her forth, then tied her up by her delicate Hair
on one of the Boughs of a spreading Tree, where, as she was hanging,
he got Bundles of stinging Nettles, and sharp-pointed Thorns, with
which he intended to scourge and tear her tender Flesh, till Death
should ease her Anguish: but even of this Mischief, of which he
thought himself so sure, was he disappointed. Just as his Arm was
stretch'd for beginning the Execution of his barbarous Purpose, a
young Man, richly habited, and of a most majestic Form, rush'd forth
from the inner Part of the Forest, and seizing him by the Shoulders,
"Inhuman Monster!" said he, "what more than savage Fury has possest
thee, thus to abuse the fairest and most perfect of the Creation?"
Ochihatou was surprized at the nervous Gripe,[1] but much more so at
the Sight of the Person from whom he received it; he hung down his
Head, and now for the first time shewed some Marks of Shame. "Can
it be possible!" cry'd he, "have I been then betrayed, has *Hoban* too
deceived me!" "Oh Heaven!" said the other at the same time, "is it
then the Villain Ochihatou, whom indulgent Fate has put into my
power!—O for ever blessed be the Influence that directed my Steps
this Way, and made me the happy Avenger of my own and Country's
Wrongs." As he spoke this, he hastily plucked off a Gold and Crimson
Belt, with which he was girded, and bound the vainly struggling
Wretch fast to the Body of a huge Oak, near to that on which the
Princess was still hanging. "—There, most accursed of all that ever
bore the Shape of Man," resumed the brave Stranger, "recollect the
horrid Catalogue of thy enormous Crimes, and think what Tortures
Justice requires should be inflicted on thee." Then turning to *Eovaai*,
"Pardon, divinest Creature," continued he, "that I deferr'd releasing
you from a Condition so unworthy of your Sex and Beauty, till I had
secured that Traitor to all Goodness; for should he have escaped, nor
Heaven, nor Earth, nor you, ought to have forgiven my Remissness."
While he was speaking, he gently untwisted her Hair from the Bough,
and taking from his Shoulders an azure-colour'd Robe embroider'd

---

1. **nervous Gripe:** sinewy, muscular grip.

with Silver Stars, in part cover'd the blushing Charmer. The first Use she made of Liberty, was to cast herself at the Feet of her Deliverer; but he obliging her to rise, received such Testimonies of her Gratitude, as made him see it was a Person of no mean Condition, whom he had the good Fortune to preserve.

Many Compliments had not pass'd between them, before they were surrounded with a numerous Band of the *Ijaveon* Nobility, who expres'd the extremest Joy at seeing the gallant Stranger safe, having been separated from him in the late Storm and Darkness. They accosted him with such a Respect, as well as Love, that *Eovaai*, who very well knew them, and their Quality, was at a loss to guess of what Rank he must be, to whom they paid such Homage. Being unwilling to reveal herself till more ascertained how Affairs went in *Ijaveo*, she drew part of the Robe over her Face, while her Protector was informing the Company in what manner he found her. The Relation of this Adventure made every one turn with Eyes of Horror on *Ochihatou*, whose Character in the World yet they knew not, nor did the Deliverer of *Eovaai* acquaint them; contenting himself with saying, he would hereafter divulge a Secret concerning himself, as well as that Captive Villain, which would amaze them all. He then gave Orders, that he should be tied with cords to a Horse's Tail, and in that manner dragg'd to Prison, till he had consider'd of his Execution.

But the unavailing Rage of *Ochihatou* being now converted into the most horrible Despair, he no sooner found himself loosed from the Tree, than before the *Ijaveons* could fasten the Cords about him, in order to carry him, as they were commanded, he broke from the Hands which held him, and running furiously against a knotted Oak, dash'd out his Brains, and by that means shun'd the publick Shame design'd for him.

Thus ended the Life of this pernicious Man, to the great Satisfaction of *Eovaai*, who could not think herself safe while he was yet in Being; but her Defender could not forbear testifying some little Uneasiness, that he had thus escaped the Punishment of his Crimes, for the least of which he thought Death by far unequal. He seemed however entirely submitted to the Will of Heaven, and having commanded that the Chariots, which attended them, should be drawn as near as possible to the Edge of the Forest, in consideration of *Eovaai,* he put the Princess into that which belonged to himself, and being seated in it by her, "Madam," said he, "I look on it as an inexpressible Favour of the Gods, that they have ordain'd me the happy Instrument of delivering you from that dead Wretch's Cruelty; and the more so, that the Accident happen'd in a Place where, having the sole Command, 'tis in my power to accommodate you in such a fashion, as your Perfections seem to merit."

This Discourse, meant for a Comfort, was the severest Corrosive to the Heart of *Eovaai;* it seem'd to confirm what she before believed, that he was King of *Ijaveo;* but she made no shew of Discontent, and when they arrived at her own Palace, where he bid her welcome with the utmost Gallantry and Politeness, scarce could she refrain from bursting into Tears; and finding herself unable to return his Civilities in the manner she fancied he would expect, pretended a sudden Ilness came over her Spirits, and entreated she might be put to bed.

The late Fatigue and Terror he was Witness she had endured, made this Request not seem strange to him. Women-Attendants were therefore immediately called, and she was by them ushered into a very rich Apartment, where she had enough to exercise her utmost Wit to keep herself from their Knowledge. She was obliged to feign a Weakness in her Eyes, which would not bear the Light, to make them darken the Rooms so far as not to render her Features discoverable; and as they all of them had waited on her when Queen, and might easily remember her Voice, she spoke no more than she was compell'd to do, and that in such disguised Accents, that they had not the least Notion they now served a former Mistress.[1]

Being left to her Repose, a thousand sad Ideas ran through her troubled Mind, which at length burst out in these Complainings: "Are these," said she, "my promised Joys at my Return to *Ijaveo,* to find my Throne in the Possession of another?—And, wou'd cruel Heaven allow me no means of Preservation, but from the Usurper of my Dominions?"

---

1. **Mistress:** employer.

To render, as she thought, her Misfortunes compleat, and capable of no Addition, the Charms of her Deliverer, when in that dreadful Moment he rush'd between her and impending Fate, had taken such fast hold of her Heart, that she now in vain struggled to get free; and indeed never were there such seeming Causes for Love and Hate blended in one Object. She could not harbour a revengeful Thought against the Invader of her Right, without being guilty of Ingratitude to the Preserver of her Life. Reason, had she been more the Mistress of it, than she was at present, had not the power of extricating her from this Labyrinth of Perplexity.—She knew not what she ought to do; but found too well for her Peace of Mind what she must do:— She felt she loved, and loved to that degree, that to live without him would be a Misery greater than in all her Sufferings she had ever before had any notion of. The first moment she beheld him, she wished he might be of a Rank that might not disgrace her Choice in making him King of *Ijaveo;* but as she now believed him already so, the Pride of Blood and conscious Title made her disdain the Thought of reigning with him, if even, to sanctify his claim, he should make her that Offer, when who she was should be discovered.

The various Agitations of her Thoughts were such, as would permit no Sleep: she long'd for Morning; but when Morning came, was as dissatisfied, as disturbed as ever. The Women brought her Habits, not inferior in Magnificence to such as would have been presented had they known her for *Eovaai;* but she continuing resolute to conceal herself for a while, refused to rise, and desired they would leave the Chamber. When they were withdrawn, she quitted her Bed, drest herself, and watch'd at the Window, in hope of seeing a Lady, call'd *Emoe,* who had been formerly of her Bedchamber,[1] and who, of all her Women, she loved best, and could repose most Confidence in; to her alone she was willing to make herself known; and as she knew her Lodgings faced those she was in, was not without hope of an Opportunity of speaking to her. In this, her Conjectures deceived her not; *Emoe* at length appear'd, and she calling her by her Name, and shewing

---

1. **Bedchamber:** The Ladies of the Bedchamber were the highest ranking servants of the queens and princesses and were almost invariably noblewomen.

her Face to her, the other, full of Amazement, rather flew than ran cross the Court, and was in a moment at her Feet, crying, "Royal *Eovaai,* my dearest Queen, do I then live to see you!" *Eovaai* interrupted her Acclamations, by saying, "Ah *Emoe!* who is King?" "— King!" reply'd that Lady, "what means your Majesty by such an Interrogation? Heaven forbid the *Ijaveons* should have a King ungiven by you.—We indeed have a Protector, one who is truly worthy of that Name.—The Nobility, the Populace strove to outvye each other in laying waste this unhappy Land—all things were in Confusion, and to make perfect our Undoing, the offended Gods sent among us a dreadful Monster, who in a short space of time devour'd thousands of your wretched Subjects.—No mortal Courage or Strength, was thought capable of subduing him, and setting free the Country; but when our Hopes were at the lowest Ebb, and Despair began to invade every Heart, a gallant Stranger arrived, and with his single Arm laid dead this Terror of the Earth, as did his Wisdom afterward reconcile the jarring Factions, and what before was Discord converted into Harmony. Such Services well merited the Distinction paid him: he was unanimously chose Guardian of the Kingdom, in which high Station he has behaved with so much Justice, Prudence, and Humility, as has endeared him to all Degrees of People in such a manner, as, I am certain, they would exchange him only for yourself."

Thus ended *Emoe* her little Narrative, and returned to her former Demonstrations of Joy, for the sight of her Royal Mistress; but how impossible is it to describe the Transport with which her Words had fill'd the Soul of *Eovaai:* to find, in the Preserver of her Life, the Preserver of her whole People. Also, to have such infinite reason to love the Man, whom she cou'd not have avoided loving, had it been otherwise, was such a Surcharge of Felicity, as Sense cou'd hardly bear. While she was in this Flow of Spirits, a Page enter'd the Chamber, to let her know the Prince Protector desired leave to wait upon her: A more welcome Message cou'd not have been brought. Impatient now to see him, she immediately dispatched an Answer of Consent; and his Entrance on it was so sudden, that she had only time to command *Emoe,* as she withdrew out of respect, to keep the News of her Arrival entirely secret till farther Orders.

The Meeting of this illustrious Pair had something in it very peculiar: They stood for some moments gazing at each other at a distance; then bow'd and approach'd, but without speaking; the extraordinary Emotions which hurried thro' their Souls, (as they afterwards confess'd) kept both in a profound Silence. At length the Hero recover'd himself; and, with an Air full of Respect, address'd her in these terms: "Madam," said he, "the Service I had the Honour to render to you yesterday, would be uncompleat, without taking care to have you conducted to some Place where you may promise yourself a safe Retreat: Therefore, as I shall quit this Kingdom in a few hours, and cannot answer for any thing after my departure, entreat you will accept of a Guard before I go, to wait you to whatever Residence you intend to bless."

[Adelhu, her rescuer, tells Eovaai that he intends to leave the country and goes to make arrangements. She decides to offer him "her Crown and Person," but first she asks for his life story, and he explains that he is the only son of Oeros, King of Hypotosa. He narrates a tale of wandering, the result of Ochihatou's treachery, which turned his father against him. He describes misgovernment, political intrigue, and turmoil in the lands he passed through. In the Desert of Bamre, an Apparition appeared, gave him Eovaai's jewel, and commanded him to protect it until he finds the "Virgin who has the Case. . . . 'Tis she alone is destin'd to make your Happiness, and that of Thousands yet unborn."[1] They marry, he is reconciled with his father, and the two kingdoms are united.]

---

1. **In the desert . . . unborn:** This story of the lost jewel has many similarities to the popular reworkings of the Indian legend *Sakuntala* by the Sanskrit poet Kalidasa.

THE

Invisible Spy.

BY

EXPLORALIBUS.

In FOUR VOLUMES.

VOL. I.

****

L O N D O N :

Printed for T. GARDNER, at *Cowley's* Head,[1]
near St. *Clement's* Church in the *Strand.*

M,D,CC,LV.

An approximation of the title page of the 1755 edition.

1. **Cowley's Head:** In addition to using a sign with Abraham Cowley's head as his address, Gardner printed his ornate figure with an identified portrait of Cowley in the classic poet's pose (head and draped shoulders) in the center above the legend "Printed by T. Gardner." Identifying himself with the poet was a political as well as literary gesture, for the innovative Cowley had suffered for his politics and was for Haywood's generation the great poet of his period. Among his contributions to English poetry were new ways of inserting political material in traditional verse forms. At one time, his *Davideis* was ranked with John Milton's *Paradise Lost.*

The Invisible Spy

VOL. I.
BOOK I.

CHAP. I.
INTRODUCTION.

To the PUBLIC

I Have observed that when a new book begins to make any noise in the world, as I am pretty certain this will do, every one is desirous of becoming acquainted with the author; and this impatience increases the more, the more he endeavours to conceal himself.—I expect to hear an hundred different names inscribed to the Invisible,—some of which I should, perhaps, be proud of, others as much ashamed to own.—Some will doubtless take me for a philosopher,—others for a fool;—with some I shall pass for a man of pleasure,—with others for a stoic;—some will look upon me as a courtier,—others as a patriot;[1]

---

1. **courtier . . . patriot:** At the time Haywood wrote this piece, courtiers were supporters of the king and Walpole, and those in Opposition to the ruling ministry styled themselves patriots.

—but whether I am any one of these, or whether I am even a man or a woman, they will find it, after all their conjectures, as difficult to discover as the longitude.[1]

I think it therefore a duty incumbent on my good-nature to put an early stop to such fruitless inquisitions, and also at the same time to satisfy, in some measure, the curiosity of the public, by giving an account of the means by which I attained the Gift of Invisibility I possess.

Know then, gentle reader, that in the former part of my life it was my good fortune to do a signal service to a certain venerable person since dead:—he was descended from the ancient Magi of the Chaldeans,[2] inherited their wisdom, and was well versed in all the mystic secrets of their art:—besides his gratitude for the good office I had done him, he seem'd to have found something in my humour and manner of behaviour that extremely pleased him;—he would often have me with him, and entertain'd me with discourses on things which otherwise I should not have had the least idea of.

But it was not long that I enjoy'd this benefit;—he sent for me one day to let me know he was much indisposed, and desired I would come immediately to him:—I went, and found him not as I expected, in bed, but sitting in an easy chair;—after the first salutations were over, and I had placed myself pretty near him;—"My good friend," said he, taking hold of my hand, "I feel that I must shortly quit this busy world;—the silver cord is loosen'd,—the golden bowl is bro-

---

1. **discover . . . longitude:** Ptolemy plotted latitude and longitude on his atlas, but his prime meridian, the zero-degree longitude line, was moved numerous times; map-makers located it in Rome, St. Petersburg, Paris, London, and even Philadelphia before it was officially fixed on Greenwich (1884). Latitude is easily calculated by the sun or stars, but longitude cannot be so determined regardless of where the zero degree is placed. The Longitude Act of 1714 offered the enormous prize of £20,000, for the person who figured out a "practical" way to calculate longitude within half a degree of the great circle (and a sliding scale down to £10,000 for within one degree). John Harrison, an English watchmaker, succeeded in 1735. A controversy broke out, but in 1773 he was finally awarded the prize he deserved. Haywood, who had a long-standing interest in science, probably followed this quest with interest; certainly the size of the prize would have attracted her attention. Tests of his instrument made news from 1735 through the next decades. See Dava Sobel, *Longitude* (New York: Walker, 1995).

2. **Chaldeans:** The study of astronomy and astrology developed and flourished in the period when the Chaldeans ruled Babylon. **Magi** is literally "wise men," and **chaldean** became a synonym for "astrologer."

ken,—every thing within me hastens to a speedy dissolution; and I was willing to see you once more before I set out on my journey to that land of shades,—as Hamlet truly says,

> *That undiscover'd country, from whose bourn*
> *No traveller returns.*[1]

As the remembrance of you, continued he, will certainly accompany me beyond the grave, I would wish, me thinks, to hold some place in yours while you remain on earth, to the end that I may not be quite a stranger to you when we meet in eternity.—I have no land,— nor tenements,[2]—nor gold nor silver to bequeath, yet am not destitute of something which may be equally worthy your acceptance."

Then, after a little pause,—"Take this," added he, giving me a key, "it will admit you into a closet[3] which no one but myself has ever enter'd;—I call it my Cabinet of Curiosities, and I believe you will find such things there as will deserve that name;—chuse from among them any one that most suits your fancy, and accept it as a token of my love."

He said no more, but rung his bell for a servant, who, by his orders, conducted me by a narrow winding staircase to the top of the house, and left me at a little door, which I open'd with the key that had been given me, and found myself in a small square room, built after the manner of a turret:—all the furniture was an old wicker chair, with a piece of blanket thrown carelessly over it, I suppose to defend the Sage from the air when he sat there to study;—near it was placed a table, not less antiquated, with two globes;—a standish[4] with some paper, and several books in manuscript; but wrote in characters too unintelligible for me to comprehend any part of what they contain'd:—just in the middle of the ceiling hung a pretty large chrystal ball, filled with a shining yellowish powder, and this inscription pasted on it:

---

1. **That . . . returns:** a part of Hamlet's "To be or not to be" speech in William Shakespeare, *Hamlet*, 3.1.78–79.

2. **tenements:** land or rental property.

3. **Closet:** small, private room, usually attached to a bedroom.

4. **standish:** inkstand or a stand containing ink, pens, and other writing materials.

THE ILLUSIVE POWDER

A small quantity of this powder, blown thro' the quill of a porcupine when the Moon is in Aries, raises splendid visions in the people's eyes; and, if apply'd when the same planet is in Cancer, spreads universal terror and dismay.

I easily perceived that this was one of the curiosities my friend had mentioned, and a great one indeed it was; but as I had neither interest nor inclination to impose upon my fellow creatures, I judged it fitter for the possession of some one or other of the mighty rulers of the earth.

I then turn'd towards the walls, which were all hung round with tellescopes,—horoscopes,—microscopes,—talismans,—multipliers,—magnifiers of all degrees and sizes,—loadstones cut in various forms, and great numbers of mathematical instruments;—but these, as I was altogether ignorant of their uses, I pass'd slightly over, 'till I came to a hand-bell, which having the appearance of no other than such as I had ordinarily seen at a lady's tea-table, I should have taken no notice of, but for a label prefixed to it, on which I found these words:

THE SIMPATHETIC BELL

The least tincle of which not only sets all the bells of the whole country, be it of ever so large extent, in motion, without the help of men to pluck the ropes, but also makes them play whatever changes the party is pleased to nominate.

Tho' I thought art could produce no greater wonder than this bell, yet I felt no strong desire of becoming the master of it; but proceeded to examine what farther rarities this extraordinary cabinet would present.—The next I took notice of was a phial, not much unlike those which are commonly sold in the shops with French hungary-water;[1]—it had this inscription:

SALTS OF MEDITATION

Which held close to the nostrils, for the space of three seconds and a half, corrects all vague and wandering thoughts,—fixes the mind,

---

1. **French hungary-water:** spirit of wine distilled with rosemary flowers.

and enables it to ponder justly on any subject that requires deliberation.

This beneficial secret I also rejected, through a mere point of conscience, as thinking it would be a much better service to mankind if in the possession of the divines,—lawyers,—politicians, or physicians, especially the two last mentioned, as it might prevent the one from engaging in any enterprize they have not abilities or courage to go through with, and the other from falling into those gross mistakes they are frequently guilty of in relation to the case of the diseased.

I should have ruminated much longer than I did on the excellence of these wonderful salts, if another object had not suddenly catched my sight;—it had the form of a skull-cap, or such a coif as serjeants at law[1] wear when a new one is called up:—what it was made out of I know not, for I am certain it was neither of the silk, woollen, or linnen manufactory;—it was, however, of so light and thin a texture, that as it hung at some distance from the wall the least breath of air gave it motion,—it was fasten'd by a single thread to the ceiling, to which also was fixed a slip of paper, which contain'd these words:

THE SHRINKING CAP

Which put upon the head immediately contracts all the muscles and sinews of the whole body, so as to render the person who wears it small enough to enter into the mouth of a lady's tea-pot, or a quart bottle; but great care must be taken no accident happens to the vehicle while he is in it; for if it breaks during that time, the man will never more recover his former dimensions.

I hesitated not a moment to reject this, as it seemed calculated for no other purpose than merely to amuse and astonish, and could be of no real service, either to myself or any body else:—I should, perhaps, not even have thought of it more, if an accident had not brought it fresh into my head:—my readers can scarce have forgot, that about some four or five years ago the town was invited, in a very pompous manner, to see a man jump into a quart bottle on the stage of the little theatre

---

1. **serjeants at law:** title given high-ranking lawyers from which Court of Common Law judges were selected.

in the Hay-market;[1]—on the sight of the bills I presently concluded that the person who was to exhibit this wonderful performance must certainly be in possession of my friend's shrinking cap; nor was at a loss afterwards to guess, why so illustrious and numerous an assembly, as came to be spectators, were disappointed in their expectations:—I doubted not, but second thoughts had reminded the man of the danger his bottle would be in from the waggish humour of some among the audience, and that an apple, or orange or even a hazle-nut,[2] darted from a judicious hand, might give a sudden crack to the brittle vessel, and so he would be compelled to continue a lilliputian[3] for his whole life.

The next, and indeed the first thing that raised in me any covetous emotions, was the apparatus of a belt, but seemed no more than a collection of attoms gathered together in that form and playing in the sun-beams.—I could not persuade myself it was a real substance, till I took it down, and then found it so light, that if I shut my eyes I knew not that I had any thing in my hand.—The label annexed to it had these words:

THE BELT OF INVISIBILITY
Which, fasten'd round the body, next the skin, no sooner becomes warm than it renders the party invisible to all human eyes.

A little farther, on the same side of the wall, was placed a Tablet, or Pocket book; which, on examining, I found was composed of a clear glassy substance, firm, yet thin as the bubbles which we sometimes see rise on the surface of the waters;—it was malleable, and doubled in many foldings, so that, when shut, it seemed very small; but when extended was more long and broad than any sheet I ever saw of imperial paper;—its uses were decipher'd in the following inscription:

---

1. **a man jump . . . Hay-market:** On 16 January 1749 a crowd filled the theater to witness a man jump into a wine bottle. The performer never appeared, but someone hidden behind the curtain informed the crowd that if they came back the next night at double the prices the performer would jump into a pint bottle. The crowd rioted, and the Haymarket was virtually destroyed.

2. **apple . . . hazle-nut:** objects sometimes thrown by eighteenth-century audiences, who were notorious for throwing things at the players.

3. **lilliputian:** the tiny people on Lilliput in Jonathan Swift's *Gulliver's Travels*.

THE WONDERFUL TABLET

Which, in whatever place it is spread open, receives the impression of every word that is spoken, in as distinct a manner as if engrav'd; and can no way be expunged, but by the breath of a virgin, of so pure an innocence as not to have even thought on the difference of sexes;—after such a one, if such a one is to be found, has blown pretty hard upon it for the space of seven seconds and three quarters, she must wipe it gently with the first down under the left wing of an unfledg'd swan, pluck'd when the moon is in the three degrees of Virgo;—this done, the Tablet will be entirely free from all former memorandums, and fit to take a new impression.

Note, That the virgin must exceed twelve years of age.

I was very much divided between these two;—the Belt of Invisibility put a thousand rambles into my head, which promised discoveries highly flattering to the inquisitiveness of my humor;[1] but then the Tablet, recording every thing I should hear spoken, which I confess my memory is too defective to retain, fill'd me with the most ardent desire of becoming master of so inestimable a treasure:—in fine,—I wanted both;—so encroaching is the temper of mankind, that the grant of one favour generally paves the way for solliciting a second.

While I was in this dilemma a stratagem occurr'd, which I hesitated not to put in practice, and it answer to my wishes;—I took both the Belt and Tablet in my hand; and, having carefully lock'd the door of the cabinet, returned to the Adept;[2]—he saw the Belt, which being long, hung over my wrist, but not perceiving I had the Tablet,—"The choice you have made," said he with a smile, "confirms the truth of what I always believed, that curiosity is the most prevailing passion of human mind."

"However just that position may be," reply'd I, "that propensity is not strong enough in me, to make me able to decide between the wonderful Tablet, and the no less wonderful Belt;—they appear to me of such equal estimation, that whenever I would fix on the one, the

---

1. **humor:** temperament, personality, inclinations.

2. **the Adept:** alchemists who professed to have attained the Great Secret or, less specifically, who were thoroughly proficient.

benefits of the other rise up in opposition to my choice; and I know not which of the two I should receive with most pleasure, or leave with the least regret;—I have therefore brought both down to you, and intreat you will determine for me."

I soon perceived he understood my meaning perfectly well; for, after a little pause,—"When I made you the offer," said he, "of whatever you liked best among my collection of curiosities, I intended not that your acceptance of one thing should render you unhappy through the want of another;—take then, I beseech you, both the Belt and the Tablet,—you shall leave neither of them behind you;—nor do I wonder you should desire to unite them;—they are, in a manner, concomitant; and the satisfaction that either of them would be able to procure, would be incompleat without the assistance of the other."

Thus was I put in possession of a treasure, which I thought the more valuable, as I was pretty certain no other person, in this kingdom at least, enjoy'd the like;—after making proper acknowledgements to the obliging donor, I took my leave and returned home with a heart overflowing with delight.

I was not long before I made trial of my Belt, and found the effects as the label had described; I also open'd my Tablet,—spoke, and saw my words immediately imprinted on it;—I then procured some Swans-down, according to direction, and intreated several young ladies to breathe upon it one after another; but tho' I dare answer for their virtue, the favour they did me was in vain,—the impression remain'd still indelible.

Indeed, when I began to consider maturely on the conditions prescrib'd in the label of the Tablet, I was sensible that it was not enough for a virgin to be perfectly innocent, she must also be equally ignorant, to be qualified for the performance of the task requir'd; and not to have once thought on the difference of sexes, seem'd a thing scarce possible after six or seven years of age at most, and would have been as great a prodigy[1] as either of those had been bestow'd upon me by the Adept.

---

1. **prodigy:** a wonder, a marvel, an astonishing thing.

What would I not have given for such a one as Dorinda in Shakespear's Inchanted Island;[1] but such a hope being vain I was extremely puzzled, and knew not what to do;—at last, however, a lucky thought got me over the difficulty;—it was this:—I prevail'd, for a small sum of money, with a very poor widow, who had several children, to let me have a girl, of about three years old, to bring up and educate as I judged proper;—I then committed my little purchase to the care of an elderly woman, whose discretion I had experienced;—I communicated to her the whole of my design, and instructed her how to proceed in order to render it effectual.

The little creature was kept in an upper room, which had no window in it but a sky-light in the roof of the house, so could be witness of nothing that pass'd below;—her diet was thin and very sparing;— she was not permitted to sleep above half the time generally allow'd for repose, and saw no living thing but the old woman who lay with her, gave her food, and did all that was necessary about her.

I frequently visited them in my Invisibility, and was highly pleased and diverted with the diligence of my good old woman;—she not only obey'd my orders with the utmost punctuality, but did many things of her own accord, which, though very requisite, I had not thought of.—To prevent her young charge from falling into any of those distempers which the want of exercise sometimes occasions, she contrived to make a swing for her across the room, taught her to play at batteldor and shittlecock,[2]—to toss the ball and catch it at the rebound, and such like childish gambols, which both delighted her mind and kept her limbs in a continual motion.

This conduct, and this regimen constantly observed, maintain'd my virgin's purity inviolate, as I did not fail to make an essay[3] in a few days after she enter'd into her thirteenth year, and the success of my

---

1. **Dorinda . . . Island:** In William Davenant's 1674 adaptation of Shakespeare's *The Tempest*, titled *The Tempest, or, The Enchanted Island*, Dorinda appears as Miranda's sister and is reputed to have never seen a man.

2. **batteldor and shittlecock:** popular game played by two people with the rackets, or battledores, and shuttlecocks; "shittlecock" is colloquial.

3. **essay:** attempt, a test.

endeavours made me not regret the pains I had been at for such a length of time.

Now it runs in my head that some people will not give credit to one word of all this; for as there are many who believe too much, there are yet many more who will believe nothing at all but what their own shallow reason enables them to comprehend:—well then,— let them judge as they think fit,—let them puzzle their wise noddles 'till they ake,—I shall sit snug in my Invisibility while they lose half the pleasure; and, it may be, all the improvement of my lucubrations.

But those who resolve to pursue me through the following pages, with an ingenuous candour, I flatter myself will lose nothing by the chace;—they will find me in various places, though not in so many as perhaps they may expect;—they would in vain seek me at court-balls,—city-feasts,[1]—the halls of justice, or meetings for elections;— nor do I much haunt the opera or play-houses:—in fine,—I avoid all crouds,—all mix'd assemblies, except the masquerade[2] and Venetian balls.[3]—I am a member of the establish'd church; but as I am not asham'd of appearing at divine worship, never put on my Invisible Belt when I go there.—I revere regal authority, but seldom visit the cabinet of princes; because they are generally so filled with a thick fog, that the christaline texture of my Tablets could not receive what was said there, so as to be read distinctly;—nor do I much care to venture myself among their ministers of state, or any of their under-working tools;[4] the floors of their rooms, in which their cabals are held, are composed of such slippery materials that the least, *faux pas* might endanger my Invisibility, if not my neck.—I should be more frequently with the military gentlemen, but that they are so apt to draw

---

1. **city-feasts:** formal dinners on such occasions as the election of the Lord Mayor.

2. **masquerade:** masked ball. At masquerades men and women in costume mingled more freely than at other kinds of parties and took advantage of being, or pretending to be, unrecognized. Public masquerades became the rage in the 1720s. Count Heidegger's at the Haymarket often attracted a thousand ticket purchases.

3. **Venetian ball:** masked ball at which guests wear dominos, loose-hooded cloaks with a small mask covering the top half of the face, rather than costumes.

4. **under-working tools:** the people who carry out their schemes.

their swords without occasion, that while they think they are fencing in the air they might chance to cut my Belt in sunder;—and what a figure I should make, when one half of me was discover'd and the other was concealed.—I will not mention the consequences such a sight might produce in some of them.

But it would be of little importance to the public to be told where I am not, unless they also know where I am:—have patience then, good people, and you shall be satisfied.

Sometimes I step in at one or other of those gaming-houses, which are above law, by being under the protection of the great; but I seldom stay long in any of them, as I can see nothing there but what I have seen an hundred times before in those lesser assemblies of the same kind that have been so justly put down by authority.[1]

Sometimes I peep into the closet of an antiquarian, where I find matter enough to excite both my pity and contempt.—What greater instance can we have of the depravity of human nature than in a rich curmudgeon, who, while he grumbles to allow his family necessary food, chearfully unties his bags and pours out fifty, or it may be an hundred guineas, for the purchase of a bit of old copper,—only because a fellow of more wit than honesty tells him it was found under the ruins of an ancient wall, where it had been buried ever since the time of Julius Cæsar[2] or Severus?[3]

Sometimes too I amuse myself with turning over the collection of a virtuoso,[4] where I am always filled with the utmost astonishment, at finding sums sufficient to endow an hospital lavish'd in the purchase of wings of butterflies,—the shells of fishes,—dried reptiles,—the paw

---

1. **Sometimes . . . authority:** Around this time, Susan, countess of Cassilis; Thomas, Lord Archer of Humberslade; Mary, baroness of Mordington; and other members of the nobility held highly profitable assemblies and claimed the "Privileges of Peers and Peeress" to be summoned and tried by the House of Lords alone. Now and then the House of Lords denied their appeals, but they were largely free from prosecution.

2. **Julius Cæsar:** Roman general (100–44 b.c.) who defeated Pompey and ruled the Roman world until he was assassinated.

3. **Severus:** Roman emperor who took Byzantium; in a.d. 208 he went to Britain and, among other things, repaired Hadrian's Wall.

4. **virtuoso:** learned person, connoisseur; often a figure of fun because of pretentious displays of arcane knowledge.

of some exotic animal, and such like baubles, neither pleasing in their prospect, nor useful in their natures.

Sometimes I make one at the levee[1] of a rich heir, just arrived from his travels to the possession of an overgrown estate; where I cannot help trembling for the future fate of the poor youth, on seeing him besieged with a crowd of marriage-brokers,—pleasure-brokers,—exchange-brokers,—lawyers,—gamesters,—French taylors,—Dresden-milliners,—petitioning harlots,—congratulating poets;—in fine, with sharpers, flatterers and sycophants of every kind.

Sometimes I mingle in the route[2] of a woman of quality,[3]—see who wins,—who loses at play,[4] and in what manner ladies are frequently obliged to pay their debts of honour.[5]

When I have nothing better to employ my time, I loyter away some hours in St. James's-park, Kensington-gardens, or at Vaux-hall, Rane-lagh, and Mary-le-bon,[6] and am often witness of some scenes exciting present mirth and future reflection.

---

1. **levee:** early-morning reception for visitors; the pretense of holding it just upon rising from bed in informal "undress" and with breakfast was popular.

2. **route:** rout; a fashionable social event usually featuring cards as well as other amusements.

3. **woman of quality:** fashionable woman; often a euphemism for upperclass women with dubious reputations.

4. **at play:** gambling at cards or, less often, other games of chance.

5. **debts of honour:** Plays and novels of the period often depicted gambling women as in danger of having to discharge their debts with sex.

6. **St. James's . . . Mary-le-bon:** These fashionable places to see and be seen are mentioned in many of Haywood's works. **St. James** is the oldest London park, and the Mall, which is its northern boundary, was an especially popular place to ride or walk about; the park was also a frequent place for duels and prostitutes' solicitations. George II began the custom of opening **Kensington Gardens** to "respectably dressed people" on Saturdays, and the Broad Walk became as popular as the Mall; William IV opened the gardens to the public all year. Until 1750, **Vauxhall,** often called New Spring Garden, could be reached only by water. It was free, and the intricate walks were lit at night but infamous as places for couples' meetings and sexual adventures. Supper boxes, a music room, and other rooms were added in the early 1750s. **Ranelagh Gardens** in Chelsea opened in 1742; for twelve pence, people could crowd around the central rotunda, eat, drink, and listen to an orchestra. A Chinese pavilion had been built by the artificial lake in 1750. **Mary-le-bon Gardens,** or "Marylebone," a surprising addition to this list, was a different kind of meeting place. Many of the same people frequented it as the other places, but it was known as a haunt of rich gamblers. In the early eighteenth century there was an amphitheatre there in which both men and women boxed and in which cockfights and bear-baitings were held (*London Encyclopedia*).

But my chief delight is in the drawing-room of some celebrated toasts,[1] whence I often steal into their bed-chambers;—but don't be frighted, ladies,—I never carry my inspections farther than the *ruelle*.[2]

These are some few particulars of the tour I have made;—to give the whole detail would be too tedious,—I shall therefore only say, that wherever I am found, I shall always be found a lover of morality, and no enemy to religion, or any of its worthy professors, of what sect or denomination soever.

And now, reader, having let thee into the secret of my history, as far as it is convenient for me to reveal, I shall leave thee to enjoy the advantage of those discoveries my Invisibility enabled me to make.

* * *

Chap VI.

Shews, that tho' a remissness of care in the bringing up of children, can scarce fail of being attended with very bad consequences; yet that an over exact circumspection, in minute things, may sometimes prove equally pernicious to their future welfare.[3]

Various were the reports concerning Alinda, both while she was alive and after her decease; but all the world could say with any certainty, either of her affairs or conduct, might be compriz'd in the following articles:

That she was the only child of a very eminent and wealthy merchant in the city, who, on the death of his wife, left off business, and having purchased an estate of near a thousand pounds a year in the country,

---

1. **toasts:** women toasted by groups of men, some of whom may know these women only by their reputed beauty, and featured in witty poems and broadsides.

2. **ruelle:** a space between the bed and a wall.

3. **Shews . . . welfare:** the chapter's "Argument." A number of writers before the modern period prefaced sections of their work with "Arguments," concise summaries of the content of the section; John Milton's *Paradise Lost* is a well-known example.

retired thither to pass the remainder of his days, taking Alinda with him, at that time about ten years of age.

That through some peculiarities in his temper she was educated in a very odd fashion,—secluded from all conversation with the neighbouring gentry, and scarce suffer'd to speak to any one out of their own family.

That after his death, which happen'd in her seventeenth year, she return'd, with the consent of her guardians, to London,—lived in a manner suitable to her fortune, and had many advantageous offers of marriage, all which she rejected without giving any reason for doing so.

That at one and twenty she fell into a wasting disorder, which was judged to proceed rather from some inward grief preying upon her spirits, than from any distemper of the body;—it baffled, however, all the skill of the physicians, and she expired after a tedious languishment of near three years, leaving the possession of her estate to a nephew of her father's, who was the next of kin.

All these things, I say, were public;—but as to the motive which made her avoid listening to any proposals for changing her condition, or the cause of that melancholy which brought on her death, every one spoke of them as they thought proper, and according as the dispositions of their own hearts inclined them to judge.

Few, however, were charitable enough to put the best construction on her conduct;—some said she was a man-hater;—others, that loving the sex too well she could not think of entering into a state which must confine her to one alone:—those who entertain'd the most favourable opinion, imagined she had unhappily engaged her heart where there was no possibility of a return:—this last conjecture seem'd, indeed, most probable, and gain'd ground after she fell into that heavy languor which excluded her from all those pleasures she had been accustom'd to partake, and at length deprived her of life;—but all this, to make use of the vulgar adage, was speaking without book,[1]—my

---

1. **speaking without book:** speaking without authority.

Gift of Invisibility gave me alone the means of penetrating into the mystery.

As I had been acquainted with her, and visited her while she continued to see company, I frequently sent, or call'd, to enquire after her health;—one day when I did so, a servant belonging to her kinsman and heir at law, came to the door at the same time, and we both received for answer, that she expired the night before.

The fellow ran directly to inform his master, to whom these tidings would probably be not unwelcome; and I went home, clapp'd on my Belt of Invisibility, and return'd in a short time to the house of Alinda; —the reader will perhaps wonder for what reason, and it is not fit I should keep him in ignorance.

There was a clergyman lived in the house with her, and perform'd the office of a chaplain;[1]—he was a person who her father having conceived a high opinion of had taken into his family, and set over her in the manner of a preceptor, and he had ever since continued with her; I had several times dined with him at her table, and perceived he professed an extraordinary sanctity and the extremest regard for the welfare of his fair patroness;—and this it was that made me desirous of seeing in what manner he would behave upon her death.

I expected to have found him either in his own chamber, bewailing the early fate of so beneficent a friend, or sitting by her corpse religiously moralizing on the shadowy happiness of this transitory world; but after seeking him in vain, in these and several other rooms, at last I discover'd him in a closet,[2] where I knew she reposited her things of greatest value;—he was busily employ'd in rummaging her buroe, from the little cell of which I saw him convey, as near as I could guess, between two and three hundred pieces of gold, and several bank bills[3] to a much greater amount;—he then pull'd out a drawer which con-

---

1. **office of chaplain:** Many families kept private chaplains, and the aristocracy built chapels as part of their houses or grounds.

2. **closet:** inner chamber for privacy or retirement; small room.

3. **Bank-bills:** bank notes drawn by one bank on another, payable after a specified date or on demand; they often drew interest.

tain'd her jewels;—he first took up one,—then another,—survey'd them with a greedy eye, but laid them down again and shut the drawer; but, after a moment's pause, open'd it a second time and took out a ring set round with large brilliants,—"I may keep this," cry'd he. "It will scarce be miss'd;—or if it be, I can pretend she made me a present of it in her lifetime, and nobody will suspect the contrary."—Here he gave over his search, lock'd the buroe, put the key into his pocket, and went into his own room.

It would be hard for me to determine, whether astonishment or indignation was most predominant in me at this sight;—I wish'd never to have beheld it, or that I had been at liberty to pluck the sacred robe from off the back of that vile prophaner of his order;—I was going away with a mind more troubled than I can well express, when one of Alinda's maids came running into the room with a seal'd packet in her hand, and deliver'd it to this disciple of Judas Iscariot,[1] telling him at the same time, that it had been found under her mistress's pillow just after her death; but that she had forgot in the hurry to bring it to him before.

He reply'd, with an affected indifference, that it was very well;— that he would look over the papers and take care that whatever injunctions they contain'd should be fulfill'd,—and with these words dismiss'd her.

The superscription on the cover of this packet was to a lady with whom Alinda had been extremely intimate, but had not seen for a considerable time, she being excluded, as well as the rest of her acquaintance, after she fell into that deep melancholy which ended her days;—the priest immediately broke the seal, and found a little letter to the above mention'd lady,—the contents whereof were as follow:

DEAR MADAM,

That I have not seen you so long has not been owing to want of friendship, but to a resolution of depriving myself of every thing that

---

1. **Judas Iscariot:** betrayer of Jesus Christ.

was agreeable to me in life; and that I do not now, in these last moments of my life, ask to see you is only because I would not tax your pity with the sight of so sad an object;—I am blasted, my dear friend, wither'd in my bloom, and scarce the shadow of what I was; the enclosed memoirs will inform you of the cruel cause, which I entreat you will publish to the world after my decease;—the shocking tale may perhaps be a serviceable warning to some parents as well as children:—I have given my cousin ****** orders concerning some things I would have done, among the number of which is, that he will present you with my hoop diamond ring;—I beg you will accept and wear it in remembrance of

Your dying friend,
ALINDA.

He started,—bent his brows, turn'd pale and red by turns, and seem'd in great confusion while looking over this little epistle; but all his emotions were very much increased on examining the papers that accompany'd it;—still as he read he tore the leaves asunder and threw them on the fire, which happening not to burn very fiercely, I was quick enough to snatch from the intended devastation and convey into my pocket, while he was taken up with the remaining pages, thought himself secure by the tale of his misdeeds being extinct in all devouring flames.

He had but just finished, when a servant came running into the room, and told him that mr. ***** was below, and having been informed that Alinda's keys had been deliver'd to him, demanded to speak with him immediately;—on this the artful hypocrite composed his countenance, drew every feature into the attitude of solemn sadness, and holding a white handkerchief to his eyes, went down to act the part he thought would best become him before the kinsman of Alinda.

I follow'd close at his heels into the parlour, where mr. ***** and two other persons waited for him;—he began, with well dissembled grief, to expatiate on the loss the world had in so excellent a lady as Alinda: and fail'd not, in his harangue, artfully to intermix some praises on himself, for the good principles his precepts had ingrafted on her mind.

Mr. ***** seem'd to take very little notice of all he said on this occasion, and prevented him from going so far as perhaps he otherwise would have done, by telling him, in a very grave and reserv'd tone, that he was in great haste at present;—that he came thither only to give the necessary orders concerning his cousin's funeral; and that till the melancholy ceremony was over, he should put a friend in possession of the house, and whatever effects it contain'd; therefore expected the keys of every thing should be immediately deliver'd.

To this the parson reply'd,—that he had got them into his hands with no other view than to secure them for him, who had the undoubted right to all which his dear benefactress had been mistress of;—"For indeed," continued he, "I apprehended some foul play might have been attempted, as at the hour of her decease she had none but servants about her, some of whom had been too lately taken into the family to have given any great proofs of their integrity."

After this they went through every room, examining what was to be found; all which scrutiny, as yet, afforded the heir no reason for complain:—on opening the abovemention'd buroe, and looking over Alinda's jewels, he miss'd not the ring he had been defrauded of, but when the other private drawers presented him so little of what he expected, he could not forbear discovering some suspicion, as it must be own'd he had sufficient cause; for the person who had been beforehand with him in the search, had left no more than eight guineas and one six-and-thirty piece in specie,[1] with three or four bills of an inconsiderable value.

"I am surprised," said mr. *****, "that a woman of my cousin's fortune should leave herself so bare of cash; and cannot imagine by what means she dissipated so large a yearly income."—"Alas, sir," reply'd the pretended zealot, with his hands and eyes lifted up to heaven,—"it ought not to appear strange to you, that a lady of your excellent kinswoman's charitable and benevolent disposition should

---

1. **specie:** coin, minted money.

refuse nothing in her power, when the cries of distress and the moans of affliction call'd for her assistance.—If you would know in what manner she disposed of her money, enquire of hospitals, the prisons, and the necessitous petitioners that every day received their sustenance from her bounty, and you will find an easy account of her expences in her large and numerous donations."

Mr. ***** only answer'd sullenly, that he should be better able to judge how he ought to think of the affair after he had spoke to her steward; on which the other clapping his hand upon his breast, was beginning to make many asseverations,[1] that till that moment he never knew what sum or sums the lady had by her when she died, or had ever look'd, nor even entertain'd a thought of looking into any place where it might be supposed she kept her money.—I staid not, however, to hear what effect his hypocrisy produced, but went home, being impatient to see the contents of Alinda's manuscript.

CHAP. VII.

Will Fully Satisfy all the curiosity the former may have excited.

The haste I made in snatching the following papers from the flames, happily preserv'd them so entirely from the destruction to which they had been destin'd, that tho' the edges were in many places much scorch'd, yet not a single word throughout the whole was any way damaged; and the reader may depend on having the story as perfect as if he saw it in the heroine's own hand.

Memoirs of the unfortunate Alinda, wrote by herself, and faithfully transcrib'd from the original copy

I am sensible that many people have been very busy with my fame while living, nor do I expect to be treated with less severity after I am dead;—I cannot, however, think of an eternal separation from this

---

1. **asseverations:** earnest, emphatic assertions.

world, without leaving something behind me which may serve to clear up those passages in my conduct, which by their being mysterious have given room for censure; and I do not this with any view of softening the asperity of the ill-natured for the errors I have been guilty of, or of exciting compassion in the more generous and gentle for my misfortunes; but merely to the end that if I am condemn'd, I may be condemn'd for real, not imaginary facts.

Sorry am I to accuse a father who so tenderly loved me; yet certain it is, that his over anxiety for my welfare had been the primary source of every woe my heart has labour'd under; and that by his mistaken endeavours to make me great and happy, I have been render'd the most miserable of created beings.

The fortune I was born to be possess'd of, and some natural endowments his affection fancy'd in me, made him flatter himself with the hopes of seeing me one day blaze forth in all the pomp of quality; nor could he endure the thoughts of marrying me to any man beneath the rank of right honourable; and for fear any partial inclination of my own should disappoint these high raised expectations, he kept me from the conversation of every one whom he thought capable of attracting a heart unbyass'd by interest, and unambitious of grandeur.

Soon after my mother's death he quitted business, and retir'd to an estate he had some time before purchased in the country:—when we removed, I was too young to have any taste for the pleasures of the town, and regretted only the want of those play-fellows I had left behind;—indeed I wonder that I was not quite moped;[1] I was suffer'd to go to no school, tho' there was a great one very near us;—never stirr'd beyond the precincts of our garden walls;—went not to church, because there it would have been impossible for me not to see and be seen;—no company visited us; for my father deprived himself of the pleasure of conversing with any of the neighbouring gentry, for fear that, as I grew up, I might take a liking to some one or other of their sons, none of whom he thought a match good enough for me, as they were not dignified with titles:—I had learn'd writing and dancing, but

---

1. **moped:** dejected, depressed, affected with ennui.

was far from being perfect in either; and my father, being unwilling I should be without these accomplishments, took the pains himself to set me copies to improve me in the one, and at length provided a master, too old and too ugly to give him any apprehensions, to instruct me in the other;—besides these two avocations, I had no amusement except reading, which, as I much delighted in, my father constantly supply'd me with such books as he thought proper for my sex and age.

Excepting some treatises of divinity, the subjects of my entertainment afforded little improvement to my understanding, they consisting only of romances, and some few very old plays; so that the ideas they inspired me with were as antiquated as the habits worn in the days of queen Elizabeth,[1] and I was utterly ignorant of the modes, manners and customs of the age I lived in.

In this stupid[2] and dispiriting situation did I pass full nineteen months; about the expiration of which time my father happen'd into company with a person who wears the sacred appearance of an Ecclesiastic; but is in reality one of those mention'd in holy writ by the name of wolves in sheeps cloathing;[3]—his outward behaviour seems directed by the ministers of grace and goodness, while in his treacherous heart a thousand fiends lie in wait to bring ruin and destruction on the credulous listner to his wiles;—but before I proced in my unhappy story, it is fit I should give a more particular character of the wretch who has so great a share in it.

First for his extraction:—his father was a frenchman, servant to a person of distinction in Normandy; but having more ambition than honesty, found means to rob his master of a considerable sum and came over to England, where he set up for a gentleman and a most zealous protestant, told a long plausible story of the great hardships he had sustain'd on the score of religion, and found here the same pity

---

1. **queen Elizabeth:** Elizabeth I ruled from 1533 to 1603; her reign was seen as a golden age of commerce, arts, and military success by Haywood and her contemporaries.

2. **stupid:** mind-numbing.

3. **wolves . . . clothing:** "Beware of false prophets, which come to you in sheep's clothing, but inwardly they are ravening wolves" (Matt. 7:15).

and encouragement as many others had done who fly here[1] for an asylum on the same pretences.

Soon after his arrival he married a Dutchwoman, by whom he had a son who inherits all his father's virtues, and is the person whose story is unhappily interwoven with my own.

Young Le Bris, for that is the name of this worthy family, discover'd in his youth some indications of a good capacity for learning, insomuch that a certain lord taking a great fancy to him, sent him to Westmister school,[2] and afterwards to the University, in order to qualify him for the pulpit, assuring him that he should not be without a handsome benefice[3] as soon as he should be fit to receive it.

But he had scarce completed his studies for that purpose, when all his present support and future expectations vanish'd on the sudden death of his noble patron, which was follow'd in a few months after by that of his father, so that he was left entirely destitute, his mother not being able to afford him the least assistance.

After many long and fruitless solicitations for a living, he was glad to accept of a small curacy in one of the remotest counties in England, where he resided several years; but was at last turned out on account of neglect of duty, and other misbehaviour;—he then came back to London,—gave out printed bills for teaching French and Latin at very low rates; but finding little encouragement that way turn'd Fleet-parson[4] earn'd a precarious sustanance by clandestine marriages.

It was in these wretched circumstances that my father met with him, being in town on some business, and being told by some one, who it is likely knew no more of him than what he was pleased to say of himself, that he was a very worthy, tho' distress'd clergyman, made

---

1. **zealous protestant . . . fly here:** Protestant refugees such as the French Hugenots from Catholic countries found refuge in England throughout the first half of the century.

2. **Westmister school:** probably a printing error for Westminster School, the famous boys' school dating from Medieval times to which Ben Jonson, Christopher Wren, John Dryden, Edward Gibbon and, in our time, Andrew Lloyd Webber went.

3. **Benefice:** a church living; a guaranteed endowment given to a clergyman.

4. **Fleet-parson:** one of the many disreputable clergymen around and even in Fleet Prison who were willing to perform secret marriages without bans (public announcements from a pulpit) or licenses.

him the offer of a handsome sallary to come into his family, by way of chaplain; and, withal, to instruct me in the French language, and whatever else was fit for me to learn, or he was capable of teaching;—he readily embraced the proposal, and on my father's return came down with him.

My father presented him to me as a kind of Tutor, or Preceptor;—told me I must submit myself to his directions,—be attentive to all he said to me, and in every thing treat him with the greatest respect and reverence;—"For," added he, "it is by the lessons he is capable of giving you, that you alone can make any shining figure in the station wherein I hope to see you placed."

It will, perhaps, afford some matter of surprise that my father, who had hitherto preserved such an extreme caution in preventing my having the least conversation with any man, should now so strenuously recommend this parson to me; but it must be consider'd, that he was no less than six or seven and forty years of age;—that tho' not de-form'd was far from handsome; and, besides, had a certain austerity in his manners which could not be thought would be very agreeable to youth.

It was, indeed, some time before I could be contented with the dominion given him over me; but my obedience to my father obliging me to behave towards him with esteem, custom[1] at last converted that complaisance, which at first was no more than feign'd, into sincere:—a kind of affection, by degrees, mingled itself with the reverence I was bid to pay him;—I was never so happy as in the hours set apart for receiving his instructions; and the thoughts of the benefits that might be supposed to accrue from them afforded me less pleasure than the praises I was always certain he would bestow on my docility.—In fine, I not only lov'd the Teacher for the Precept's sake; but, as the poet says,

I lov'd the Precepts for the Teacher's sake.[2]

Nor is it to be wonder'd at that I tasted more satisfaction in his

---

1. **custom:** habit.

2. **I loved . . . sake:** Sir Harry Wildair in the final speech in George Farquhar's *The Constant Couple* (1699), 5.3.277.

society than I had ever known before;—I wanted not ideas, tho' hitherto I had nothing to improve them:—I had been allow'd to converse with none but the servants, who could only divert me with idle tales of thieves, apparitions, and haunted houses;—my tutor, after having finish'd his graver lessons, would frequently entertain me with some extraordinary incident or other, either taken from history or romance; but, whether real or fictitious, I had sense enough to know were such as enlarg'd my understanding as well as charm'd my ears.

It is certain, indeed, that he spar'd no pains to insinuate himself into my good graces; and no less certain also that the ungrateful design he had in doing so succeeded to the utter destruction of the whole happiness of my future life; and, at last, of my life itself, as will appear by these memoirs, which, while I am writing, I know not whether I shall have strength to finish.

I shall therefore reduce my unhappy story into as short a compass as I can:—in spite of the little amiableness this Tutor had in his person;—in spite of the vast disparity of years between us, I conceived the most tender affection for him;—alas I was then too young,—too innocent, to know what was meant by the word love, any farther than that love which we naturally bear to a father, brother, or some other near relation,—and thought not that what I felt for him was any more, or would be attended with any other consequences; and, as I apprehended no shame or danger in the kindness I had for him, endeavour'd not to put a stop to the growth of it, nor even to conceal it.

But Le Bris saw much better into my heart than I did myself, and dreading lest my father should be alarm'd at the too open fondness of my behaviour to him, began to treat me with less familiarity, and exerted the master much more than he had done;—this change both surprised and griev'd me;—I bore it, however, for two whole days, without seeming to take any notice of it; but on the third, being alone with him in his closet, where I constantly went every morning to receive my lessons,—"What is the matter with you, my dear Tutor," said I, "I hope I have done nothing to offend you?—I am sure I would not willingly be guilty of deserving that you should frown upon me."—"No, my precious charge," reply'd he after a pause, "it is not in your nature to give offence; but I would not incur your father's displeasure either towards you or me;—men are apt to be jealous of the affections of their children, and I am sometimes afraid that he should think you love me almost as well as you do him."—"Indeed I do so,—quite as well," cry'd I eagerly. "But why should he be angry at that, when he bid me use you with the same love and respect as I did himself?"

"People on some occasions," answer'd he, "will be displeased at a too exact performance of their own commands; and if my worthy Patron, your father, should happen to be of this opinion, the consequence would infallibly be an eternal separation between us;—he would drive me from his house, and I should never see my pretty charge again."

"If you think so," return'd I, "though I hate all kind of dissimulation, I will make him believe I am weary of learning of you, and that I cannot abide you."—"Dear pretty angel," cry'd he, tenderly taking me in his arms; "there is no need of going to such extremes;—I would only have you behave with more distance towards me than you have done of late; and it will not be amiss if you sometimes complain that I set you too hard lessons; because if you should seem to learn too fast, he may begin to think there will soon be no occasion for a Tutor."—"Well," said I, "I will do every thing you bid me; for indeed it would almost break my heart to part with you."—Here he kiss'd off the tears that fell from my eyes in speaking these last words, and I return'd all his endearments with the same affection as the fondest child would do those of the most-indulgent parent.

It will, perhaps, seem a little strange that a girl turn'd of thirteen, as I then was, should think or act in the manner I did; but the way in which I had been brought up left me in the same ignorance and innocence as others of six or seven years old.

I obey'd his instructions with so much exactness, that my father was far from suspecting either my folly or the baseness of the person he had set over me:—the rest of the family were no more quick-sighted, nor it could not be expected they should be so,—our house-keeper, tho' a very good, was a silly old woman, and knew nothing beyond the œconomy of those affairs committed to her charge;—the maid who waited on me was her daughter, and had been bred to think every man who wore the habit of a Parson was to be worship'd; and the other servants were too seldom with us to have any opportunity of making discoveries.

I arriv'd at my fourteenth year,—my father kept my birth-day so far as to order something better than ordinary for dinner, and drank my health several times at table;—among other discourse concerning me, he said to Le Bris,—"Well, Doctor, your pupil will now begin to think herself a woman, and I must find a husband for her who will be able to reward the care you have taken of her with a good fat Benefice." To which the fawning hypocrite reply'd,—That the pleasure of seeing his worthy patron's daughter happy, would be to him the best benefice he could obtain.

Nothing farther pass'd at this time on the same subject; but the next morning, when I was alone with my Tutor in his closet, "Do you remember, my dear miss," cry'd he, with a very melancholy air, "what your father said yesterday?—you will be marry'd soon, and I shall lose you for ever."—"Do not talk so," reply'd I hastily, "I do not want to be married; but if my father should compel me to it, all the husbands in the world should not make me forget my dear Tutor; —no, you shall always live with me;—I would not part from you to be a dutchess or a lady mayoress."[1]—"Nor would I part from you," said he, taking me in his arms, "for an archbishopric;—and to be plain," continued he, "I have received letters since I have been here, with the offers of several great livings; but I have refused them all rather than quit my dear pupil."—"Have you indeed," return'd I hanging fondly on him?—"oh how kind you have been!—I should be the most ungrateful creature upon earth if I did not love you dearly for it."—" But will you always keep me with you," cry'd he?—"As long as I live," answer'd I—"Will you swear it," rejoin'd he?—"Yes," answer'd I, "a thousand and a thousand times over, if you desire it."

The wretch did not fail to take me at my word:—I bound myself, by the most solemn imprecations that words could form, that when I

---

1. **lady mayoress:** The Lady Mayoress was the wife of the Lord Mayor of the City of London; although prominent, the position did not compare to being a duchess.

became mistress of my actions he should always live with me.—After this, the hours we pass'd together were employ'd more in improving the foolish affection I had for him, than in any lessons for improving my understanding.—My father imputed the slow progress I made in my studies not to any want of ability in my teacher, but to my own neglect, and often chid me for it, which I bore patiently, as I believed it the surest means of keeping my dear Tutor with me:—this he took so kindly, that he told me one day, he flatter'd himself I lov'd him almost as well as I did my father. "I hope it is no sin," cry'd I childishly, "if I love you quite as well?"—"Far from it," answer'd he, "you are only his daughter by nature, but you are mine by affection;—you are the child of my soul, and therefore ought to love me better."—"I am glad of that," rejoin'd I, "for indeed I do love you a great deal better,—I am sure I do; for I don't feel half the pleasure when he kisses me as when you do;—and when you take me in your arms my heart beats as if it would come out."—It will scarce be doubted but that he now bestow'd upon me those endearments I had declar'd myself so well satisfied with; and some minutes after, as I had turn'd to a looking-glass to adjust some disorder in my head-dress, he pull'd me to him, and making me sit upon his knee,—"You are very pretty, my dear miss," said he, "and have no defect in your shape, but being a little too flat before;"—with these words he thrust one of his hands within my stays, telling me that handling my breasts would make them grow, and I should then be a perfect beauty.

Not conscious of any guilt I was ignorant of shame; and thinking every thing he did was right, made not the least resistance; but suffer'd him, by degrees, to proceed to liberties, which, had I known the meaning of, I should have stabb'd him for attempting; but, as I have somewhere read,

> *By no example warn'd how to beware,*
> *My very innocence became my snare.*[1]

---

1. **By . . . snare:** quotation unidentified.

It will, perhaps, be supposed that the perfidious man did not stop here, but proceeded yet farther, to the utter completion of my dishonour; but I shall do him the justice to say he never offer'd any such thing; though I have good reasons to believe he was prevented only by his fears of the consequences that might have attended it, to the ruin of a design which promised him more satisfaction than the enjoyment of my person.

In the ridiculous way I have been describing did we continue 'till I was in my seventeenth year, about which time my father being obliged to go to London on a law affair, he left the sole management of the family, as well as of myself, to his favourite chaplain, 'till he should return, which he expected to do in two months.

He had not been gone full three weeks before a stranger came to our house on a visit to my Tutor;—he received him with great marks of civility, and told me afterwards that he was the land-steward of a nobleman who had sent him on purpose to court his acceptance of a benefice worth near eight hundred pounds per annum:—as I suspected not the truth of this I was terribly frighten'd and cry'd out,—"Then you will leave me at last!"—"It would be with an extreme reluctance I should do so," reply'd he; "but what can I do?—If I should hereafter be exposed to any misfortunes, how would the world blame me for having refused such an offer?"—"What misfortunes," said I, "have you to fear?—I shall always have enough to support my dear Tutor."

"My dear child," resum'd he, "you forget that when once you are married there will be nothing in your power,—all will be your husband's, who may take it into his head to turn me out of door directly."—"No such matter," reply'd I hastily, "for I will make him promise and swear beforehand to keep you always in the family."—"Few men," said he, "pay any regard, after they become husbands, to the promises and vows they made when they were lovers.—In fine, my little angel," continued he, taking me tenderly in his arms, "there is but one way to secure our lasting happiness, to which if you agree I will immediately refuse the great offer now made me, with all my future hopes of rising in the church, and devote myself eternally to you."

These last words I thought so highly obliging to me, that I hung about his neck, kiss'd his cheek, and cry'd, I would do every thing he would have me;—he then told me that a writing should be drawn up between us, by which we should mutually bind ourselves, under the penalty of the half of what either should be possess'd of, never to separate.

On my ready compliance with this proposal, he ventured to make a second, even more impudent than the first;—after seeming to consider a little within himself.—"I have been thinking," said he, "that if the person you shall marry should happen to be of a cross, perverse nature, tho' for his own sake he will not drive me from his house, yet he may use me so ill as to compel me to go out of it of my own accord,—suppose, therefore, you should bind yourself by the writing I have mention'd, and under the same penalty, never to marry any man without my consent."

"Bless me," cry'd I, a little surprised, "how can I do this!—you know I must obey my father."—"Heaven forbid you should do otherwise," rejoin'd the artful hypocrite,—"you may be sure I shall never oppose either his will, or your own inclination, in the choice of a husband;—what I speak of is only a thing of form, which, when shewn to your husband, will oblige him to treat me with gratitude and respect."

I was entirely satisfy'd with this, and reply'd, I would do what he desir'd as soon as he pleased;—on which,—"It happens luckily," said he, "that the gentleman who came here on the business I told you of was bred to the law,—I will let him know as much as is necessary of our affair, and get him to draw up a proper instrument."[1]—In speaking these words he left me and went in search of his friend, who at that time was walking in the garden, waiting, no doubt, his coming.

I had little time allow'd me to reflect on what I was about to do,— Le Bris immediately return'd, bringing the lawyer with him,—the latter of whom desir'd to receive instructions from my own mouth for what he was to write, and accordingly I repeated the sense of the obligation I was to lay myself under, leaving it to him to put it in

---

1. **instrument:** formal legal document whereby a right is created or confirmed.

such words as he should find proper;—if I had been mistress of the least share of common reason, I must have seen that all this scheme was a thing previously concerted between these two villains; for the Lawyer immediately pull'd out of his pocket a large parchment, with seals fix'd to it, and every thing requisite to make the instrument firm and valid;—but I was infatuated,—all my little understanding was subjected to the will of this wicked Tutor;—I gave an implicit faith to all he said, and paid an implicit obedience to all his dictates.

The lawyer took his leave next day, and nothing material happen'd till within a week of the time my father was expected home, when, instead of himself came the melancholy account that he had been seiz'd with an apoplectic fit,[1] and tho' he recover'd from it, expired within two hours after;—he had made his will about a year before, by which he left me sole heir of every thing he was in possession of, except a few legacies, and in case his demise should happen before I was married, or of age, appointed two gentlemen for his executors and my guardians;—they both wrote to me, as did also my cousin ******, acquainting me that it was necessary I should come to London directly on this occasion, and each inviting me to their respective houses, which as they lived in different parts of the town, I was at liberty to chuse which I liked best.

My Tutor, however, dissuaded me from accepting any of their offers, and told me he would write to a friend in London to provide a ready-furnish'd house for my reception, till things were settled, and I should resolve whether I would reside in town or country;—accordingly he did so, and when we came within ten miles of London we were met on the road by the lawyer, who, as I have since discover'd, was his chief agent in every thing;—he conducted us to a house in Jermin-Street,[2] which was indeed very neat and commodious.

It was late when we arriv'd, but I did not fail to send the next morning to my two Guardians and cousin ****, who all came to see me the same day, and express'd themselves in very affectionate terms;

---

1. **apoplectic fit:** stroke.

2. **Jermin-Street:** a fashionable street near St. James developed by Henry Jermyn after the land was given him by Charles II.

—I presented my Tutor to them, as a person for whom my father had a high esteem, on which they treated him with that respect they supposed him to deserve.

I now enter'd into a scene of life altogether new to me;—several distant relations, whom I knew only by their names; and many other gentlemen and ladies, who had been acquainted with my mother, came to pay their respects to me;—all my mornings were taken up with messages and compliments, and all my afternoons with receiving and returning visits.—How strange was the transition?—from being confined to the narrow precincts of a lone country mansion, I had now the whole metropolis to range in;—instead of the grave lessons of two old men, my ears were now continually fill'd with the flattering praises of addressing beaus;[1]—instead of having nothing to amuse my hours, new diversions,—new entertainments, crowded upon each moment, and I was incessantly hurried from one pleasure to another, till my head grew giddy with the whirl of promiscuous delights.

As I was young, not ugly, and look'd upon as a rich heiress, proposals of marriage were every day made to me, all which I communicated to my Tutor; but tho' many of them were much to my advantage, he always found some pretence or other for refusing his consent, and I accordingly rejected them, to the surprise of all who knew me, and the great dissatisfaction of my best friends.

He was not, however, half pleased with the gay manner in which I lived, and as soon as the affairs relating to my estate were settled, would fain[2] have prevail'd upon me to return into the country; but I had too high a relish for the diversions of the town to pay that regard to his advice I had formerly done; and, instead of complying with it, quitted the house I was in, hired another upon lease, and furnish'd it in the most elegant manner I could:—he grew very grave on my behaviour; but as I kept firm to both the engagements I had made with him, he had no pretence to complain of my actions in other matters.

For a time, indeed, my head was not the least turn'd towards mar-

---

1. **beaus:** flirtatious men excessively concerned with fashionable, courtly conduct.
2. **fain:** gladly.

riage;—I thought no farther of the men than to be vain and delighted
with their flatteries;—happy would it have been for me had I continued always in this mind; but my ill fate too soon, alas, presented me
with an object which convinced me, that all the joys of public admiration are nothing, when compared to one soft hour with the youth
we love, and by whom we think we are beloved.

I believe there is little need for me to say that this object, so enchanting to my senses, was the young, the handsome, the accomplish'd
Amasis:—the world, whom he made no secret of the passion he pro-
fess'd for me, was also witness in what manner I received it;—we
appear'd together in all public places;—I treated him in all companies
with a difference which shew'd the esteem I had for him:—my friends
approved my choice, and the union between us was look'd upon as a
thing so absolutely determined, that many believed the ceremony was
already over, when, to their great surprise, they saw at once that we
were utterly broke off, and in a very short time after, the ungrateful
Amasis become the husband of another.

My tutor, on perceiving me inclined to favour Amasis more than I
had ever done any of those who had hitherto address'd me, began to
rail at him, and tell me a thousand ridiculous stories he pretended to
have heard in relation to his conduct;—I still retained too much reverence for this wicked man to contradict what he said, but not enough
to enable me to conquer my new passion;—I loved Amasis, and continued to give him daily proofs of it;—this so incensed him, that he
told me one day,—that he wonder'd I would encourage the courtship
of a man whom I must never expect to marry.—"Why not, sir,"
answer'd I, "neither his birth nor fortune are inferior to mine."—
"Suppose them so," rejoin'd he, "the most material thing is wanting,
which is my consent."—"When I gave you that power over me," said
I, "you promised never to thwart my inclination." "I did so," reply'd
he; "but, to be plain with you, I then expected all your inclination
would be in favour of myself." "—Yourself!" cry'd I, more surprised
than words can describe.—"Yes, Alinda," resumed he, "methinks the
thing should not appear so odd to you;—call back to your remembrance the familiarities that have pass'd between us, and then justify,

if you can, to virtue or to modesty, the least desire of giving yourself to any other man."

Rage,—astonishment, and shame, for the folly I had been guilty of, so overwhelm'd my heart at this reproach, that I had not power to speak one word, but stood looking on him with a countenance which, I believe, sufficiently express'd all those passions, while he went on in these terms: "How often," continued he, "have you hung about my neck whole hours together, and by the warmest fondness tempted me to take every freedom with you but the last, which if I had not been possess'd of more honour than you now shew of constancy, I also should have seiz'd, and left you nothing to bestow upon a rival?"

The storm which had been gathering in my breast all the time he was speaking, now burst out with the extremest violence;—I raved, and loaded him with epithets not very becoming in me to make use of, yet not worse than he deserved;—he heard me with a sullen silence; but when I mention'd the cruelty and baseness of upbraiding me with the follies of my childish innocence, he told me, with a sneer, that he would advise me not to put that among my catalogue of complaints.— "For," said he, "the world will scarce believe, that a lady of fourteen, fifteen, and sixteen, had the same inclinations in toying with a gentleman as a baby has with its nurse."

I would have reply'd, that the manner in which I was educated kept me in the same ignorance as a baby; but something within rose in my throat, stopping the passage of my breath, and I sunk fainting in the chair where I was sitting:—whether he was really moved with this sight, or only affected to be so, I know not; but he ran to me, used proper means to bring me to myself, and on my recovery I found myself prest very tenderly within his arms:—his touch was now grown odious to me,—I struggled to get loose;—"Be not thus unkind," cry'd he, holding me still faster, "you once took pleasure in my embraces, you have confess'd you did;—oh then recall those soft ideas, and we shall both be happy."

"No," answered I, breaking forcibly from him, "what then was the effect of too much innocence, would be now a guilt for which I should detest myself as much as I do you."—"I still love you," said he.—

"Prove it then," cry'd I fiercely, "by giving me up that writing which your artifices ensnared me to sign, and cease to oppose my marriage with Amasis."—"No, madam," reply'd he, "if you persist in the resolution of marrying Amasis, half your estate would be a small consolation to me for the loss of you; and you cannot sure imagine me weak enough to resign my claim to the one, after being deprived of the other."

I had not patience to continue this discourse, but retired to my chamber, where, throwing myself upon the bed, I vented some part of the anguish of my mind in a flood of tears; after which, finding some little ease, I began to reflect, that tormenting myself in this manner would avail nothing, and that I ought rather to try if any possible means could be found for extricating me from the labyrinth I was entangled in.

Accordingly I arose,—muffled myself up as well as I could to prevent being known,—took a hackney-coach,[1] and went to the chambers of an eminent lawyer;—I related to him all the circumstances of my unhappy case, concealing only the names of the persons concern'd in it;—he listen'd attentively to what I said, and when I had done, ask'd me of what age I was when I enter'd into that engagement I now wanted to be freed from; which question I answering with sincerity, he shook his head, and told me that he was sorry to assure me I could have no relief from law, and that the best, and indeed the only method I could take, was to endeavour to compromise the affair with the gentleman.

I return'd home very disconsolate, and was above a week without being able to resolve on any thing; but my impatience to be united to the man I loved, and at the same time eased of the presence of the man I hated, at last determined me to follow the lawyer's advice;—I sent for my wicked tutor into my chamber,—talked to him in more obliging terms than I had done since the first discovery of his designs upon me; but represented to him the absurdity of thinking of marrying me himself;—and concluded with telling him, that if he would cancel

---

1. **hackney-coach:** coach for hire; the equivalent of a modern taxi cab.

the engagement between us I would make him a gratuity of a thousand pounds, and also be ready to do him any other service in my power.

He rejected this proposal with the greatest contempt.—"You are certainly mad, Alinda," said he, "or take me to be so;—a thousand pounds would be a fine equivalent, indeed, for the half of your estate, jewels, rich furniture, plate, and whatever else you are in possession of; to all which your marriage will give me an undoubted claim, and I accordingly shall seize."—"Suppose I never marry," cry'd I. "Be it so," answer'd he, "I must still continue to live with you; and what you offer for my quitting you does not amount to five years purchase of my sallary and board as your chaplain."

These words making me imagine his chief objection was to the smallness of the sum, I told him I would double, nay even treble it, for the purchase of my liberty; but he told me it would be in vain for me to tempt him with any offers of that kind;—that no consideration whatever should prevail with him to depart from the agreement between us, and he would always hold me to my bargain.

The determined air with which he spoke this, made me think it best not to urge him any farther at that time;—the next day, however, and several succeeding ones, I fail'd not to renew the discourse; but tho' I made use of every argument my reason could supply me with,—tho' I wept, pray'd, rav'd,—by turns cajol'd and threaten'd, all I could say,—all I could do was ineffectual, and the more I labour'd to bring him to compliance, the more stubborn his obstinacy grew.

To make any one sensible what it was I suffer'd in this cruel dilemma, they must also be made sensible to what an infinite degree I loved the man whom it was now impossible for me to be happy with, and both these are inexpressible;—I shall therefore only say, that I was very near being totally deprived of that little share of reason heaven had bestowed upon me.

Amasis, to whom I had confess'd the tenderness I had for him, was all this while continually solliciting me to complete our union;—one day, when he was more than ordinarily pressing on this occasion, and my heart being very full, I cry'd out, almost without knowing what I said,—"Oh, Amasis, you know not what you ask, when you ask me to marry you!"—This exclamation surpris'd him; but having begun, I now went on.—"You expect," said I, "an estate of twelve hundred pounds a year; but I will not deceive you, you find me worth only the half of what you have been made to hope."—"When I made my addresses to the lovely Alinda," answer'd he, "I had no eye to the fortune she might bring me;—but wherefore this fruitless trial of my love?—your guardians have shewn me the writings of your estate, and I know to a single hundred what you are possess'd of."—"Suppose," rejoin'd I, "that I should have previously disposed of the one half of what otherwise our marriage would have given you?"—"I will suppose no such thing," reply'd he, "it cannot be."—"It both can and is," said I, bursting into tears, "I have unwarily enter'd into an engagement, by which I forfeit the moiety[1] of all I am mistress of, even to my very jewels, if ever I marry any man, except on certain conditions, which condition I am now well assur'd I never can obtain."

"Death and hell," cry'd he, starting up in a fury!—"What condition,—when,—where,—to whom, on what account was this engagement made!"—Shame would not let me answer to these interrogatories, and I remain'd in a kind of stupid silence.—"If by any artifices," pursued he, "you have been seduced to sign a compact of this wild nature, unfold the whole of the affair, and depend that either the laws or this avenging arm shall do you justice."—I now repented that I had so rashly divulged any part of this fatal secret,—not but I should have been glad to have seen my wicked tutor punish'd; but I knew that on the least attempt made for my redress, he would infallibly expose the follies I had been guilty of in regard to him; and when compared to that the loss of Amasis,—my fortune, or even my life itself, seem'd a less terrible misfortune;—for this reason, therefore, I refused the entreaties of a beloved lover, and screen'd the villainy of a wretch who most my soul abhorr'd.

In fine, I would reveal no more than I had done,—Amasis left me in a very ill humour, and the next morning I received a billet from him containing these stabbing lines:

---

1. **moiety:** share.

To miss Alinda*****.

MADAM,

I Have been considering on the amazing account you gave me last night; and as you refuse to discover either the person with whom you made this engagement, or the motives which induced you to it, can look on it as no other than a contract with some gentleman, once happy in your affections;—a second-hand passion neither suits with the delicacy of my humour, nor to encroach upon the rights of another with my honour:—I shall therefore desist troubling you with any future visits, but shall be always glad to hear of your welfare, which I despair of doing till you prevail upon yourself to be just to your first vows; sacrifice the affection you have for me to the obligations you are under to my rival;—I yield to his prior title all the late glorious hopes I had conceived, and wish you more happy with him than it is now in your power to make

Your humble servant,
AMASIS.

Here ended all my hopes of happiness;—all the soft ideas of love and marriage vanish'd for ever from my breast, and were succeeded by others of the most dreadful nature:—for several weeks I abandon'd myself to grief and to despair; but pride at length got the better of these passions; and, to conceal the real situation of my heart from the enquiring world, I all at once affected to be madly gay, and ran into such extravagancies, as, without being criminal in fact, justly drew upon me the severest censures.

But nature will not bear a perpetual violence,—grief and despair were the strongest passions in me;—in the midst of dancing, drinking, revelling, tears were ready to start from my eyes, and sighs from my bosom, which, when I endeavour'd to suppress, recoil'd upon my heart, and shook my whole frame with the most terrible revulsions;— the marriage of Amasis seconded the blow our parting had given;—I could no longer dissemble what I felt,—no longer appear the giddy thoughtless libertine, but flew from one extreme to the other;—I now would see no company, shut myself up in my chamber, denied access to my best friends, and never went abroad but to visit the hospitals and prisons:—I never suffer'd Le Bris to come into my presence; and I believe, perceiving me so resolute, he would now have accepted of a sum of money to have quitted my house entirely; but I had now done with the world,—had lost in Amasis all I valued in it, and would not give the monster, whom I justly look'd upon as the source of all my misfortunes, any more than I was compell'd to do,—his bare board and sallary.

Behold, by these memoirs, the beginning and progress of my miseries,—the end is near at hand,—death is already busy at my heart, and allows no time to apologize for the errors of my conduct;—pity is all my ashes can expect.

* * *

CHAP. VIII.

Contains a very brief account of some passages subsequent to the foregoing story, with the author's remarks upon the whole.

As I know very well that solidity has but a small share in the composition of the lady whom Alinda had intended to entrust with the publication of her memoirs, I thought the surest way of having the will of the deceas'd perform'd, was not to trouble a person of her character with the perusal of them, but to take the opportunity of my Invisibility-ship to present them to the world myself, which I accordingly have done.

And now, as I doubt not but the reader will be glad of being inform'd of somewhat farther concerning Le Bris, I shall relate such particulars as have come to my knowledge.

It must be concluded that this unworthy preceptor, in looking over the papers of Alinda, had either not observed, or afterwards forgot, that the ring he had just taken from among her other jewels was the very same mention'd in her letter to her friend, otherwise he would certainly have had cunning enough to have replaced it where he found it.

Mr. ****** soon recollecting what his cousin had said to him in regard of this little legacy, and missing it from her other trinkets, made a strict enquiry what was become of it:—Le Bris, having had her keys in his possession, was one of the first interrogated, and on being so, boldly reply'd, that such a ring had been bestow'd upon him by Alinda.—"How can that be," cry'd the other,—"when but three days before her death she bequeath'd it to a lady of her acquaintance, and insisted on my promise of delivering it to her?"—"She must then be delirious" said the parson; "but however that might be, heaven forbid I should detain what is even suspected to be the right of another;" and with these words presented the ring to mr. *****, who received it from him without the least ceremony.

This affair, notwithstanding the hypocritical manner in which the ring was return'd, gave mr. ***** room to imagine there had been some foul play in relation to Alinda's effects;—the steward prov'd, by his books, that he had paid into her hands, a week before her death, two hundred and fifty pounds in specie, and more than twice that sum in Bank-bills, being arrears he had receiv'd from the tenants;—it seem'd unlikely to them that she could have disposed of the money, much less have had any occasion to change the bills in so short a time; —orders were therefore sent to the Bank to stop the payment of such numbers till further notice; but the precaution came too late,—the person who had secreted them had been already there, and converted all his paper into cash.

The heir, however, was confident that he had been defrauded;—he consulted council upon it, who all advised him to have recourse to equity:[1]—whether Le Bris had any hint given him of what was in-

---

1. **recourse to equity:** the "natural justice" courts, which in England (and the United States) co-exist with the common and statute law and, when in conflict with them, supersede them. In Haywood's time, this court was the Court of Chancery, and it was understood to be the place to go when the other courts could not provide adequate remedy or might have been unjust because neither precedent nor statute seemed as good as natural, "common-sense" judgment.

tended to be done against him, or whether his own guilty conscience made him only apprehend it, is uncertain; but be that as it may, he had not courage to stand the test of examination,—he fled the kingdom, after having thrown aside that robe, which, had he been known for what he truly was, would long before have been stripp'd from off his sacrilegious shoulders.

But Providence would not permit him to enjoy his ill-got spoils, nor a life he had devoted to such wicked purposes;—designing to turn trader at Jamaica he embark'd for that place;—but the vessel being overtaken by a storm, was lost almost in sight of shore, and he with many other, perhaps less guilty persons, perish'd in the wreck:—this last piece of intelligence I received from his mother, who, tho' he had supported during the life of Alinda, to prevent being exposed by her clamours, he now left pennyless, destitute and starving, in an extreme old age.

Thus did the vengeance of heaven at last overtake the wretch, who, besides his other impieties, had been guilty of the most cruel ingratitude and breach of trust, in imposing upon the simplicity of a young creature committed to his care, and utterly destroying all the views of his generous Patron and Benefactor.

As for the unfortunate Alinda, tho' it is certain her conduct cannot be wholly justify'd, yet, according to my opinion, neither ought it to be wholly condemned;—it would be passing too severe a judgment, to impute the fondness she express'd for her wicked tutor to a wanton inclination:—if we consider the various arts of her seducer,—the commands laid on her by her father to love and obey him as himself;—the manner in which she was brought up;—the perfect ignorance she was kept in of the customs of the world, and how other young ladies behaved, we shall find that these are all of them very strong pleas in her defence, and not forbear pitying the mistakes of such artless innocence.

I wish as much could be alledg'd in her behalf on the score of her behaviour after breaking off with Amasis;—the excesses into which she ran, in order to conceal the disquiets of her mind for the loss of that favourite lover, too evidently shew that she sacrificed two of the most valuable characteristics of womanhood,—her prudence and her modesty, to one of the very worst,—her pride.

Nor can I offer any thing in vindication of the last stages of her life,—if convinced of her error, in being perpetually among a promiscuous unselected company, it was flying to an almost as inexcusable extreme, to shut herself from her best friends, and avoid the society of those whose conversation might have dissipated her chagrin, and at the same time improved her understanding;—to do this seems to me, I must confess, to have more the favour of despair, than of virtue or true fortitude.

There was, doubtless, a certain giddy propensity in her nature, which wanted to be corrected by reason,—example,—precept,—authority, and the rudiments of a good education, all which she was deny'd; and it must therefore be acknowleged, that both her faults and misfortunes were entirely owing to the caprice and credulity of her father, and the base designs of the person appointed to be her governor and instructor.

END OF THE FIRST BOOK

* * *

VOL. III.
BOOK V.

CHAP. I.

The author's introduction to this volume consists only of an apology for making no introduction at all, and his reasons for that omission.

Since my setting about this work, I have seen several late treatises that are half taken up with introductory Prefaces to the publick:—on a serious examination to what end those long discourses were penn'd, they seem to me to have been occasioned either by one or the other of the following motives:

First, That an author having contracted with his bookseller for a certain number of sheets,[1] without having well consider'd whether his head be stored with subject matter to make good his engagement, finds himself under a necessity of filling up the vacant pages by saying something by way of an introduction, preface, or advertisement to the reader.

Or, secondly, That fearing the eyes of the public will not be sufficiently open to the merit of his performance; or, perhaps, not have the curiosity even to look into it at all, he thinks proper to bespeak their favour by a pompous prelude, and sounds his own praises, like a trumpet at the door of a Puppet-shew.

Now I am too great a lover of liberty ever to bind myself by any such slavish agreement; the first of these incentives is quite out of the question, and cannot possibly have any weight with me.

And as to the second,—As a more perfect knowledge of myself, than I perceive some others have, will not permit me to be over vain in any thing I do, so the indolence of my nature will not permit me to be over anxious for the success.

Besides not having the temptation of the motives aforesaid, I have more adventures to relate than can be easily crowded into this volume, therefore have neither time nor paper to spare for an address, which would afford so little satisfaction to myself in the writing, and perhaps less to my reader in the perusing.

It may, indeed, be said, that as I gave some account of myself in the beginning of this work, it would be no more than good-manners to take a decent leave of the public at the end of it; but to this I must have leave to reply, that there is a wide difference between coming and going:—when a man intrudes himself into strange company, it certainly behoves him to tell the business that brought him there; but when he has done that, and has no more to say, I believe every one will allow that it is the best good-breeding to quit the place without ceremony, as I shall do.

---

1. **sheets:** pages.

VOL. IV.

CHAP. II.

Relates some farther incidents of a pretty particular nature, which fell under the Author's observation in the same evening's Invisible progression.

. . . I had the curiosity to call in at another great coffee-house, hoping I should find there something to give a turn to the present disposition of my mind.

But I found that the remains of my ill-humour were not to be so soon dissipated as I had imagined.—Here was indeed a vast deal of company,—clerks in public offices,—lawyers,—physicians,—trades-men, and some few divines, composed the promiscuous assembly; but all were engag'd on the same dirty draggle-tail subject, as one of our newswriters justly terms it, the names of Betty Canning, the Gipsey, and mother Wells,[1] resounded from each quarter of the crouded room, and the cause then depending between these creatures made the whole conversation at every table.

Here I would not be at the trouble of opening my Tablets, easily perceiving that nothing worthy of being recorded in them, or of com-municating to the public, was likely to ensue; and also that the smallest part of time I should waste in this company would be paying too dear for any discourses I should hear from them.

---

1. **Betty Canning, the Gipsey, and mother Wells:** Like so much eighteenth-century fiction, topical news events and crimes that attracted public notice find their way into Haywood's work. **Elizabeth Canning**'s was the most famous case brought before Henry Fielding when he was a Bow Street magistrate. Canning, an eighteen-year-old servant girl, had disappeared on her way home from visiting an aunt. Four weeks later (29 January 1753), she came home "emaciated, filthy, blue with the cold, and too weak to stand." She said she had been robbed, beaten, and imprisoned in an effort to make her become a prostitute. **Susannah Wells** was identified as the proprietor of the place she had been imprisoned, and the "Gypsy" was Mary Squires. See Introduction; Judith Moore, *The Appearance of Truth* (Newark: Univ. of Delaware Press, 1994); and Martin Battestin, *Henry Fielding: A Life* (London: Routledge, 1989), 570–76.

Accordingly I left the house after having staid there about seven minutes; but had not reach'd the next street before a confused noise behind obliged me to stand up in the porch of a door 'till the hubbub was pass'd by.

The occasion of this uproar presently appear'd;—it was a poor fellow carried on a bier,[1] with very little signs of life in him,—his face cover'd with blood which issued from his nose and mouth,—his cloaths torn that the naked flesh appear'd in many places; but so deform'd with bruises that it could scarce be known for what it was;—a mix'd rabble of men, women and children follow'd, shouting, hallooing, and crying,—it was good enough for him,—and that they were glad he had got his reward.

I was startled at so much inhumanity, for I thought nothing could excuse such cruel treatment, though I doubted not but the fellow had been guilty of some atrocious crime;—but I was soon undeceived in this point, and let into the whole affair.

A tradesman who happen'd to be standing at his shop door, just opposite to the place where I had taken shelter, stepp'd forward and ask'd what was the matter,—and by what accident the poor man on the bier was reduced to that condition he saw him in;—on this several of the mob gather'd about him, and answer'd his interrogatories in these terms:

FIRST MOB. Ah, sir, he is as arrant[2] a rogue as ever you heard on in your life.

SECOND MOB. Aye, 'twere no matter if he had been kill'd outright.

THIRD MOB. No, no, 'tis much better as it is,—I hope to make a holiday to see him hang'd.[3]

SHOPKEEPER. But what has he done?

---

1. **bier:** a stretcher, litter, or hastily constructed frame.

2. **arrant:** notorious, shameless.

3. **holiday . . . hang'd:** Because watching hangings and other punishments was considered instructive and a deterrant to crime, apprentices and other workers were usually given holidays to attend them.

FOURTH MOB. Done, sir, you will bless yourself to hear it;—he said that poor Betty Canning was a perjur'd[1] slut ;—that all she had sworn to was lyes;—and that she deserv'd to be whipp'd at the cart's tail, or pillory'd, or transported to the plantations;[2]—and a great deal more.

FIRST MOB. Nay, he was beginning to say worse things of her than all this, if his mouth had not been stopp'd.

SHOPKEEPER. Then I suppose he has been fighting?

SECOND MOB. No hang him,—I don't believe he has courage enough to fight; but he would have run his game[3] on Betty Canning 'till now, for any thing I know, if a brewer's servant and an honest slaughter-man in Fore-street, and three or four neighbours of ours in Norton-Falgate,[4] had not all at once fallen upon him and beat the words down his throat.

SHOPKEEPER. But was not so many to one odds at football?[5]

THIRD MOB. There is no minding fair play with such a rascal;—

---

1. **perjur'd:** guilty of perjuring herself. On 7 May 1754, over fourteen months after the conviction of Squires and Wells, Canning was convicted of perjury and sentenced to transportation—deportation—to the American colonies.

2. **whipp'd . . . plantations:** standard punishments intended to stigmatize and discredit people convicted of such offenses as perjury. When **whipped** at the cart's tail, criminals were stripped to the waist, their hands tied together and attached with a rope to a cart, and lashed with a whip by the hangman for the number of city blocks or miles proscribed by their sentence. The **pillory** was a wooden frame in which miscreants' heads and wrists were locked; **plantations** at that time meant a settlement of those "planting," or starting, a colony.

3. **run his game:** ridiculed; made fun of to his heart's content.

4. **Fore-street . . . Norton-Falgate:** inner-city London streets; both near Moorfields.

5. **odds at football:** Football was outlawed in the reign of Edward IV in the fifteenth century until 1845 but continued to be played, especially among the common people. Deaths from injury were recorded almost every year. Played by crowds of men sometimes as large as two hundred, even in narrow city streets, it resembled a melée more than a game with formal rules. In fact, each area tended to develop its own rules. The game began with two roughly equal sides lined up; an "indifferent spectator" threw the ball into the center, and each side attempted to move the ball past a goal line. Although rugby is the modern sport, the eighteenth-century game was more like "kill the man with the ball." Thus, the "**odds at football**" for the ball carrier, like the chances for the man who insulted Canning, were very poor. From at least the sixteenth century, football was the source of many metaphors of chance and experience, such as "we are but footballs to be kickt and spurned." Joseph Strutt, *The Sports and Pastimes of the People of England* (London, 1801), and Morris Marples, *A History of Football* (London: Secker & Warburg, 1954).

abuse poor Betty Canning;—why he deserves to have his house pull'd down about his ears.

FOURTH MOB. Aye, and so it should, if it were not for his wife and five small children.

The tradesman said no more but turn'd back into his shop, lifting up his hands and eyes in token of amazement, and the rabble ran to rejoin their companions, who I could hear still continued insulting and vilifying the poor maim'd wretch, who was altogether unable to return any part of their abuse.

This shopkeeper appear'd to me to be a more reasonable creature than most of those I had lately been among; and I should have been glad to have had some discourse with him concerning this adventure; —but that being impracticable, as I had no opportunity at present of shaking off my Invisibility, I was obliged to content myself and proceed in my progression.

I had now no design in my head,—no particular course to steer; but as I was entirely free from any engagement that evening, and thought it too soon to go home, I rambled from one street to another for a considerable time, yet without meeting any one thing sufficient to tempt my curiosity to make a farther enquiry into.

Any observing reader may reasonably imagine, that the little satisfaction I had been able to reap in the visits I had made at the two coffee-houses I had been already in, would have hinder'd me from going into another, and indeed I was of that opinion myself;—I soon found I was mistaken however,—and so will he;—I really ventured into a third; but the motive which excited me to do so was this:

As I was passing by I perceived thro' the windows, for then the candles within were lighted up, several gentlemen with news-papers before them, on which they seem'd to be discoursing with each other with a great deal of seriousness and gravity:—as I have naturally an extreme passion for knowing the affairs of the world,[1] those of Europe especially,

---

1. **As . . . world:** Many historians and critics have recognized the eighteenth-century obsession with news; coffeehouses supplied free newspapers, delivered hot off the press, and were, therefore, popular gathering spots.

I thought it highly eligible[1] in me to hear what was said upon them by persons who had the appearance of some understanding in them.

At the first table I came to were six or seven gentlemen, most of whom were some way or other concerned in the British Herring-fishery; but though they talk'd very learnedly on the subject, it suited not my taste, so staid not long with them, but adjourn'd to the next company.

These were merchants, who I found were greatly disconcerted at an article they had been just reading in relation to the strict engagements the French had enter'd into with the Indians, and the daily incursions those miscall'd friends and allies made on the English colonies;[2]—but as I cannot pretend to any skill in commerce, I did not spread my Tablets to receive the impression of their discourse; so can only say in general, that they made very heavy complaints, and cry'd out, that if speedy care were not taken to put a stop to those proceedings, trade must be ruin'd, and our settlements in that part of the world utterly destroy'd.

The third table was fill'd with persons who seem'd to be of no avocation, nor at all interested in any branch of business or public affairs; but talk'd of every thing they had been reading merely as things which afforded matter for conversation.—On my joining them, the magnanimity of the Prussian monarch[3] was the topic;—they extoll'd his wisdom, his bravery, his temperance, his clemency, the encourage-ment he gave to merit wheresoever he found it, and all unanimously agreed that he was the father of his people,—a blessing to the land he govern'd,—and a pattern to his fellow rulers of the earth.

---

1. **eligible:** fit or deserving to be chosen or done.

2. **engagements . . . colonies:** The Seven Years, or French and Indian, War began in late spring 1754 over a dispute between the English and French over the occupation of the Forks of the Ohio, the junction of the Allegheny and Monongahela Rivers, where both wanted to establish a fort. A mixed force of French and Indians defeated a mixed force of British and colonial troops at the Battle of the Wilderness on 9 July 1755. The French and Indians were defeated at the Battle of Lake George on 8 September, and so news of the war continued. Among the results of this war was the expulsion of the Acadians from Nova Scotia.

3. **Prussian monarch:** Largely out of fear of Russia, King Frederick II of Prussia, known as "Frederick the Great," had recently led his country to be an ally of Great Britain instead of France.

The just admiration I ever had of this truly great and most amiable prince,—exclusive of that regard due to him as so near a relation to our gracious sovereign,[1] would certainly have kept me at that table as long as the company had continued speaking on so agreeable a subject, if I had not been hurried from it by a propensity, I believe, more or less natural to all mankind, that of being most eager to explore what is hid from us with most care.

I observed at a little table, which was placed at one corner of the room, a good distance from the others, two elderly persons, who seem'd very earnest in discourse on some important and secret affair;—by the winks, the nods, and other significant gestures which accompanied the motion of their lips, I doubted not but that they were profound politicians, and were discussing some extraordinary transaction of the cabinet.

Their heads were pretty close together, and they spoke in so low a voice as to render it impossible to be heard by any one except by each other;—but this precaution had no efficacy when once my wonderful Tablets were display'd, which had this excellent property of receiving the impression of whatever was said within the distance of nine yards, tho' utter'd in the most soft whisper.

On my drawing near to them they seem'd a little impatient for the coming of a person who they expected, and who presently after appear'd;—as soon as he had seated himself the following dialogue ensued:

FIRST MAN. Oh, mr. Slycraft, I am glad you are come;—we were beginning to think you long,

SLYCRAFT. I am somewhat beyond my hour, indeed; but I assure you nothing could have made me so but the good of the cause.

SECOND MAN. Your zeal and diligence are not to be doubted;—but let us hear what success have your endeavours met with.

SLYCRAFT. Truly not so much as I hoped;—I do not think there is

---

1. **our gracious sovereign:** George II, uncle of Frederick the Great.

a more difficult thing in the world than getting people to subscribe;[1]—
I have been half the town over and have been able to procure no more
than three.

FIRST MAN. Then I hope they are fat ones.

SLYCRAFT. Pretty well, as times go;—Credulous Woodcock, Esq; has
set his name for twenty guineas.

FIRST MAN. Very handsome;—five or six hundred such as he would
do the business.

SLYCRAFT. Aye, but where shall we find them?

SECOND MAN. Well, but who are the others?

SLYCRAFT. Why there is mr. Nathaniel Vaingood,—twelve guineas.

FIRST MAN. We must take the will for the deed;—he has not above
sixty or seventy pounds a year to live upon.

SLYCRAFT. Then there is mr. Simon Goosly, the haberdasher,—ten
guineas, but has promis'd to prevail on some friends of his to set their
names very generously.

SECOND MAN. I dare say he will do all he can.—But have you seen
mrs. Waver?

SLYCRAFT. Yes, but she still desires a little more time to consider;—
says, she will enquire farther into the affair, and hear what her friends
think of it; and all I could get from her was an assurance, that if she
found it proper to subscribe at all she would not set her name for less
than an hundred pieces.

FIRST MAN. Then we may be pretty certain of her; for I know she
will be directed by mr. Cantwell, the Nonconformist preacher,[2] who
labours all he can to promote the cause in question.

---

1. **subscribe:** to put oneself down for a certain amount of money to support a cause, such
as the publication of a book or a charity. A number of subscriptions with varying degrees
of benevolence or opportunism were collected; see Moore, 216–17, and Zirker, xcviii, 293.

2. **Nonconformist preacher:** clergyman who was not a member of the Church of England;
Nonconformists, or Dissenters, were often objects of prejudice and slurs such as the one
that unfolds in this text.

SECOND MAN. Have you yet found an opportunity of talking with the Orator?[1]

SLYCRAFT. I was with him above an hour,[2] and when I had once convinced him that he should find his account in it, he gave me his word and honour that he would rant and roar 'till his chapel ecchoes in favour of the party.

FIRST MAN. That is well;—all engines must be set to work, or the town will grow cool on this business and begin to renew their clamour against Naturalization of the Jews[3] and Clandestine Marriage bills;[4]— the spirit of the people will have vent on something or another, and you know it behoves us to keep them silent on those scores,—nothing ever did it more effectually than this we are upon;—but it must be kept up for a time:—I could wish, methinks, we had the Westleys[5] on our side.

SECOND MAN. 'Tis a vain attempt,—they are now grown too rich to accept of a small gratuity; and I much question whether their exhortations would answer the expence.

SLYCRAFT. I am of your opinion;—besides, you know there is a person who can influence their congregations as much as any thing they can hear from the pulpit.—But I will tell you what I have done to

---

1. **Orator:** John "Orator Henley" had a chapel in Lincoln's Inn Fields where on Wednesdays and Sundays he performed orations and public disputes that he often advertised in the newspapers. Although ordained in the Church of England, he left its employment and began to lecture freely on nontheological as well as theological subjects.

2. **above an hour:** more than an hour.

3. **Naturalization of the Jews:** This act, which received the royal assent in May 1753, made it easier for Jews to apply for naturalization as citizens by dropping a few phrases from required oaths. An outcry and organized campaign resulted and the act was repealed.

4. **Clandestine Marriage bills:** The Clandestine Marriage Act became law in June 1753 and was intended to increase family control over marriage by requiring such provisions as parental consent before minors could marry, the establishment of residency, and required marriage registries. W. A. Speck, *Stability and Strife* (Cambridge: Harvard Univ. Press, 1979), 255–56.

5. **Westleys:** John and Charles Wesley, the famous evangelicals often credited with starting the Methodist Church; John especially was an inspiring preacher.

day,—I have engag'd a clergyman of the establish'd church[1] to write a pamphlet in behalf of the cause we have in hand.

FIRST MAN. A clergyman of the establish'd church employ his pen in behalf of such a cause!—Prithee, Slycraft, how did'st thou work upon him?—it must certainly be by some very extraordinary method.

SLYCRAFT. The promise of a small present at first wrought upon his necessities;—but on my telling him who and who were concerned in this business, and the motives which induced them to be so, the hopes of having the pitiful Curacy he now enjoys exchanged for a good fat living, made him wholly ours.

FIRST MAN. Admirable!

SECOND MAN. But may we depend upon his secrecy?

SLYCRAFT. Never doubt that, as his own interest is concern'd.

FIRST MAN. Hitherto things go pretty swimmingly on our side.—But let me see the subscription book;—I have received five guineas to-day from mr. Obadiah Prim,[2] and must insert his name.

'Till now I was at the greatest loss, as 'tis probable the reader will also be, to know what all this meant, or in whose favour or on what account the subscription they talk'd of was rais'd; but on mr. Slycraft's delivering the book to his friend, I look'd over the shoulder of the latter as he open'd it, and saw in the first leaf, by way of title page, these words wrote in a very fair hand:

A LIST of those worthy Persons

WHO

Have subscribed to the relief

OF

ELIZABETH CANNING.

---

1. **establish'd church:** the Church of England or Anglican Church; clergymen of all denominations wrote on the subject, including William Nicholls, the vicar of Canning's parish church, St. Giles Cripplegate, which was Anglican.

2. **Obadiah Prim:** a character in Robert Howard's *The Committee* (1662) who became the symbol of the pompous, hypocritical Puritan; this play was a great favorite of Charles II.

The names underwritten in this legend were too numerous to be inserted,—I shall therefore only say, that the sum of what was rais'd by their subscription amounted to little less than a thousand pounds;—Monstrous abuse of charity!—Preposterous benevolence! which will hereafter reflect more shame than honour on the bestowers.

My astonishment was greater than I can express; but I had not then time to indulge it.—The book being return'd to mr. Slycraft, he address'd his companions in these terms:

SLYCRAFT. You know, gentlemen, that though it is highly necessary a sum of money should be raised for this girl, to prevent her squeaking,[1] as Virtue Hall has done, yet the intent of those who set us to work was not to make her fortune, but by the strangeness of the story she tells to amuse the populace, and divert their attention from those things which they ought not to be too well acquainted with.[2]

FIRST MAN. Very true; and I think it answers the end.

SECOND MAN. Aye, and much better than could be expected.

SLYCRAFT. It has, indeed; but I have been thinking of ways and means to make it do so yet more;—suppose we advertise this subscription in the public papers;—I have drawn up something for that purpose, which I should be glad to have your approbation of?

FIRST MAN. By all means;—pray let us see it.

Mr. Slycraft then took a small piece of paper out of his pocket and read these lines:

SLYCRAFT. "Whereas many well-disposed and compassionate persons, in regard to the severe distresses, cruel usage, wonderful[3] preservation, and miraculous escape of that chaste maid Elizabeth Canning, are inclined to contribute towards her future relief, all such are

---

1. **squeaking:** informing on one's confederates. **Virtue Hall** had been identified as one of the women who watched Canning abused and jeered at her. Hall, however, was brought to Fielding and evidence taken that fully corroborated Canning's story. The evidence, however, was tainted in several ways, and she later recanted.

2. **amuse . . . with:** Here and elsewhere Haywood implies that unscrupulous men used the case to distract people from the substantive political and social issues then being debated.

3. **wonderful:** implies God's action; collections of "wonders" were once popular literature.

desired to send what sums they shall think fit to bestow to the following places."

SLYCRAFT. We shall easily find shops and coffee-houses where the money may be received, if any shall be sent, as doubtless there will by several persons who we have not an opportunity to address.—But that is the least part of the business;—these advertisements will reach the country,—the people there will be curious to know the story, which they shall be inform'd of by ballads and penny books sent down to them.—What do you think of it?

FIRST MAN. As of the most excellent stratagem I ever heard of in my life.

SECOND MAN. It is certainly a lucky thought;—the innocent country people will be quite alarm'd,—the young men will talk of nothing but Betty Canning to their sweethearts, and the old men think only to preserve their daughters from the danger she escaped;—all remembrance of what has been done by their superiors will be buried in oblivion, and elections may go how they will.[1]

SLYCRAFT. I wrote the advertisement in a hurry,—just as the thought started into my head,—I am sensible it will admit of some emendations.—Suppose we adjourn to a tavern, where we may consult farther upon it with more privacy than here?

FIRST MAN. With all my heart.

SECOND MAN. And mine, as all our expences on this occasion are sure to be reimbursed.

These brethren in iniquity went out of the coffee-house as the last repeated words were spoken, and I had not the least inclination to follow them, nor to hear what farther contrivances would be form'd to impose on the credulous, infatuated, deluded multitude:—indeed I was so thunder-struck at what I had already been witness of, that I

---

1. **all . . . will:** Sir Crisp Gascoyne, as Lord Mayor of London, presided over the trial of Wells and Squires. Gascoyne and many others believed that political opposition to him had become an important factor in the debate over Canning, and efforts to discredit him were escalating. He lost the election to represent Southwark in Parliament. The career of another Canning critic, John Hill, may have been negatively affected as well.

could scarce forbear bursting into exclamations, which if utter'd by an unseen mouth must needs have been very astonishing and terrifying to all who had heard them;—I therefore prudently withdrew, designing to attempt no future discoveries that night.

The mean artifices which I found some men, miscall'd the great, make no scruple of putting in practice to gain their ends, fill'd me with an equal share of indignation and contempt; but when I reflected how I had just now seen charity, the noblest of all virtues, perverted and prostituted to reward infamy and vileness, it struck me with a horror which forced from me these or the like words:

"Good God!" said I to myself, "in an age when numberless, nameless miseries abound,—when all our prisons labour with the weight of wretches confined within their walls, many for small debts which their necessities obliged them to contract, and some by unjust and malicious prosecutions,—while every parish, nay almost every street, affords objects of real distress,—while the remains of the most antient and honourable families are reduced by the fatal South-Sea scheme,[1] and other more latent public calamities, to the extreamest want, shall all these, or any of these, send unavailing petitions to those from whom they might expect redress, while a girl sprung from the lowest dregs of the people, bred up to toil, a drudge, one of the very meanest class of servants, receive donations which she as little knows how to make a proper use of as to deserve!—a girl, who if she had really suffer'd all she pretends to have done, would indeed have had a claim to justice against those who had wrong'd her, but none to the bounties so lavishly bestow'd upon her."

These kind of meditations would doubtless have accompany'd me to my own door, if they had not been interrupted, as well as my course towards home, by an unexpected accident, which the reader will find faithfully related in the succeeding chapter.

---

1. **South-Sea scheme:** The South Sea Company had been formed in 1711 to finance the War of Spanish Succession. The government guaranteed the Company a monopoly on English trade to the Spanish ports in South America and granted it an annuity. When new stock in the company began to be sold in April 1720, stock prices soared exorbitantly, abuses were rampant, and the South Sea "Bubble" burst in September 1720. Many individuals and companies suffered severely from this stock market crash, and a witch hunt for those at fault ensued.

THE

W I F E.

by *MIRA*,

One of the AUTHORS of The *Female
Spectator*, and *Epistles for Ladies.*

****

L O N D O N :

Printed for T . G A R D N E R , at *Cowley's Head,*[1]
facing *St. Clement's* Church in the *Strand.*

M,DCC,LVI.

An approximation of the title page from the 1756 edition.

1. **Cowley's Head:** In addition to using a sign with Abraham Cowley's head as his address, Gardner printed his ornate figure with an identified portrait of Cowley in the classic poet's pose (head and draped shoulders) in the center above the legend "Printed by T. Gardner." Identifying himself with the poet was a political as well as literary gesture, for the innovative Cowley had suffered for his politics and was for Haywood's generation the great poet of his period. Among his contributions to English poetry were new ways of inserting political material in traditional verse forms; at one time his *Davideis* was ranked with *Paradise Lost.*

The Wife

BOOK I
INTRODUCTION

Marriage was the first institution of the Great Author of nature, and intended to smooth the rugged ways of life;—the softner of the husband's cares;—the bulwark of the wife's innocence;—the cement of friendship between families, and the choicest blessing Heaven could bestow on mortals.

Who then can, unconcern'd, behold this glorious benefit perverted,—the blissful unison of hearts dissolv'd, and the hands, perhaps but lately join'd, struggling with the chains that bind them to each other;—discord and confusion, in the place of love and harmony;—and this too, not always occasion'd by the vices of either party,—(for I speak not to the profligate and abandon'd)—but by some unaccountable caprice,—some unguarded folly, which I should think those guilty of, need only be told of to reform!

The least disagreement between two persons, who ought to be actuated but by one soul, should be check'd in its very beginning; for if the perverse humour, of what kind soever it be, is once indulg'd, the breach will still grow wider, and must be of fatal consequence, not only to their peace, but also to their interest and reputation.

I shall not enter into any discussion whether, whenever contention happens between persons thus united, the husband or the wife will most frequently appear blameable;—but of this I am certain, that which soever of them begins the dispute, the other is equally culpable in continuing it.

Too many of both parties, indeed, stand in much need of admonition; but as law and custom have given the superiority to the men, it is doubtless the duty as well as interest of every wife, who would preserve the affection of her husband, to be constantly assiduous about two things:—first, by a prudent watchfulness over his temper and her own actions, to avoid whatever might create in him a disgust;—and secondly, to endeavour, by a soft and endearing behaviour, to win, and, as it were, steal him from those errors to which he may possibly be addicted, and which his pride, perhaps, would not suffer him to be reason'd out of.

I have therefore thrown together some few hints, which, if improved into practice, I think, cannot fail of restoring to marriage that true honour and felicity which reign'd in the first ages of the world; but has ever since been gradually decreasing, till so far deprav'd and lost as to render the sacred ordinance contemptible in the eyes of many, and enter'd into by most merely to gratify one or other of the two very worst passions that can actuate the human mind,—lust and avarice.

Some of my fair readers may perhaps imagine, that in some points I attempt to impose too hard a task upon them;—at first, indeed, it may appear so;—but let them reflect on the vast emolument,[1] the accumulated benefits, attending the performance;—a very small part of the time wasted by a woman of quality at her toylet,[2] or by those of the meaner class in a gossip's tale, if devoted to serious consideration, will be sufficient to convince their reason, and make them look on nothing as a difficulty that tends to the promoting the happiness of their whole lives, and that of the person to whom they are united.

I know it will be said by those who are no favourers of the sex, that, in an age like this, when modesty, with every native virtue of the

---

1. **emolument:** advantage, benefit, profit arising from a station.
2. **toylet:** dressing table.

female mind, is treated as ridiculous, and a bold licentious manner of behaviour is the chief requisite to constitute a reigning toast,[1] small encouragement will be given to a work of the nature I propose, and that one might as well expect to regain lost paradise on this side the grave, as to bring women back to the innocence and simplicity of former times;—yet, in spite of all these accusations, which I am sorry to say are, in the general, but too just, I hope, nay am confident, that there are a great many, a very great many, who will not suffer their reason to be totally swallow'd up in the torrent of fashion and example; and will be therefore thankful to any one who shall warn them against those mistakes into which they might otherwise fall thro' inadvertency.

As the workings of nature are the same in all degrees of people, and the method of attaining happiness may be as easily pursued in the cottage as the palace, in order to render this work of as general utility as possible, I have aim'd more at perspicuity than elegance of stile; chusing rather to confer some benefit on others, by my admonitions, than receive praises myself for the manner in which they are deliver'd.

SECT. III.

Difference of opinion in affairs of Government.

It seems to me, that a prudent wife will find it no hard matter to avoid entering into any disputes with her husband on the score of politics;—for, besides having it so little in her power to serve the cause she espouses, there are so few women qualified to talk on those affairs, that most of those that do would find it much more to the reputation of their understanding to be silent.

But supposing her to be endued with an uncommon genius,—a penetrating and sound judgment,—well vers'd in history and political tracts,—able not only to talk but also to reason well on the occasion, and have infinitely the advantage over her husband, will the secret

---

1. **reigning toast:** woman toasted by groups of men, some of whom may know her only by her reputed beauty, and featured in witty poems and broadsides.

heart-burnings, discontent, and ill-humour, which, in all probability, these debates may create in him, be atton'd for by the applauses her capacity may receive from others!

It is said by a very great and venerable author, that 'tis much better to be wise than witty;[1]—and sure there are none, who are in reality the former, will wish to purchase the reputation of the latter at so dear an expence as innate peace of mind:—a wife, above all others, is most concern'd to observe this maxim; for what satisfaction can she take in the empty compliments she receives from abroad, or the admiration of persons indifferent to her, when her own home rings with perpetual jars, and the man, in whose arms she lies, regrets the ceremony that has bound him to her?

If we give ourselves the trouble to examine into the latent sparks which kindle up this party[2] flame, we shall find that a very small number, in comparison of the whole that are actuated by a principle of conscience,—prejudice of education,—the prospect of some advantage to themselves or families,—a partial attachment to particular persons,—resentment for some disappointment,—the vanity of making a bustle in the world and being talk'd of, and often a mere spirit of contradiction makes a zealot, and equally influences both the courtier and the patriot;[3] and how vain is it to hope to make converts of such men, who refusing to take justice or reason for their guide, will not be convinced by either?

Women being excluded from all public offices and employments, the men are apt to look on any attempt made by that sex to intermeddle with affairs of state, as an encroachment on their prerogative; and, indeed, I think it must be allow'd, that she who busies herself too much that way, somewhat transgresses the bounds of her own sphere:—the unmarried, however, are at liberty to act as they please;

---

1. **'tis . . . witty:** reference to *Spectator* no. 568 (16 July 1714), by Joseph Addison; Addison's characters discuss the risks of political satire.

2. **party:** partisan; reference to political rivalry between the Whig and Tory parties, whose disagreements were sometimes violent and bitter.

3. **courtier and the patriot:** At the time Haywood wrote this piece "courtiers" were supporters of the king and Walpole, and those in Opposition to the ruling ministry styled themselves "patriots."

but certainly a wife will always find the best politics she can study, is how to merit and maintain the esteem and affection of her husband;— and this, with the management of her family, will be sufficient to take up her whole thoughts.

I hope to be forgiven for what I have said on this occasion, since I have so good an authority for it as the late ingenious Mr. Selden, who, though a great advocate for the ladies, and very much their favourite, in speaking of the duties of a wife, expresses himself in these terms:

> *Wives, like good subjects, who to tyrants bow,*
> *To husbands, tho' unjust, long patience owe;*
> *Reason itself, in them must not be bold,*
> *Nor decent custom be by wit control'd;*
> *On their own heads we desperately stray,*
> *And are still happiest in the vulgar way.*[1]

If a woman cannot bring herself to the same way of thinking as her husband, nor ought always to endeavour it, she has it nevertheless in her power to forbear thwarting his opinion; and how irksome soever such a restriction at first may seem to her, I am very well satisfied she will afterwards find her account in it.

A perfect concurrence of sentiment[2] between the persons united, is, without all question, one of the principal ingredients to make marriage happy;—I am therefore sorry when a too hasty entrance into that state hinders them from being well acquainted with the foibles, as well as virtues of each other; but as it is not the business of these sheets to prescribe what steps should be taken previous to the sacred ceremony, but what will, according to all probability, render both parties easy under their mutual engagements, I shall close this section with a little narrative, which may serve to shew the ill effects of obstinacy.

---

1. **Mr. Selden . . . vulgar way:** John Selden, a noted lawyer and scholar whose best-known work is probably his *Table Talk,* published posthumously in 1689. Source of quotation unidentified.

2. **sentiment:** opinion.

About the middle of last May were married a certain young couple of condition, whose names it is not necessary to mention;—the courtship between them had been very short,—they had seen and liked each other,—their fortunes were pretty equal,—the friends on both sides willing, and no impediment happen'd to retard the consummation of their mutual wishes. The first weeks of their marriage were pass'd in the fashion usual on such occasions,—feasting and visiting took up their days, and love engros'd their nights;—a more fair prospect of felicity could scarce present itself; but too soon, alas! the beauteous vision disappear'd,—black lowering clouds overspread their heaven of joy, and burst in storms, which, violent as they were, threaten'd to be no less lasting than their lives.

On the anniversary of that day which brought the unfortunate Chevalier St. George[1] into the world, three gentlemen in plaid[2] waistcoats, white roses in their button-holes,[3] and large oak branches in their hats,[4] stopp'd in a coach at their door, and were conducted in:—the lady, who is strongly attach'd to the present royal family, had a glimpse of these sparks as they pass'd to her husband's dressing-room, and easily perceiving what principles they were of—by their habits, was extremely disconcerted to think she was married to a man who kept such company.

But how much greater was the shock she receiv'd, when, in less than a quarter of an hour, she saw her husband enter the room where she was, accompany'd by his three friends, and in all points accoutred

---

1. **St. George:** St. George's Day, 23 April; St. George was adopted by Edward III as the patron saint of England by the middle of the fourteenth century. English troops sometimes fought with the battle cry "St. George!" The legend of slaying the dragon appears in many pieces of literature.

2. **plaid:** Many Scots, whose clans and fighting units wore plaids, had rebelled against the accession of George I in 1715.

3. **white roses ... button-holes:** In the War of the Roses (1455–1485), the house of York took as its symbol the white rose in its struggle for the crown of England against the house of Lancaster, which wore the red rose.

4. **oak branches ... hats:** Another sign of loyalty to the Stuart monarchy, the oak branches and leaves on a cavalier hat were the emblems of Charles II, who had survived the English Civil War by hiding in an oak tree on 3 September 1651. He and many other Englishmen cultivated oak trees from the acorns of that tree after Charles's Restoration in 1660.

like them in those flagrant marks of Jacobitism[1] above describ'd:—
after having given time to the gentlemen to make their compliments
to her, (which she could scarcely return with common civility) he said
to her,

> My dear, I am going with these gentlemen to meet some others that
> wait for us, in order to celebrate a day which we still live in hopes of
> seeing a joyful one;—so you must not expect me at home either to dine
> or sup.

He was in too much haste to go to the rendezvous to wait for any
reply, and they all went down stairs, leaving her in a consternation
not to be express'd.

This gentleman is one of those harmless Jacobites who will wear
plaid and white roses, swallow bumper after bumper, swear, and talk
loudly for the cause, but never contribute a single shilling for its support, much less run any risque of life or fortune.—He return'd not
till very late, and had toasted too many healths to render himself in a
fit condition either to sleep with his wife that night, or listen to the
reproaches she might otherwise have received him with.

The next day, being that which is celebrated for the anniversary of
his present majesty's accession to the throne, equipping herself to make
a loyal appearance at court, employ'd her thoughts and time the whole
morning:—her husband, who quitted not his bed till almost noon, on
his coming down found her dress'd in an orange-colour'd[2] suit of
cloaths,—a bunch of yellow[3] ribands on her head, and another on her
breast, on both which were stamp'd in silver these words:—King
GEORGE, and the Hanover succession for ever.

He gaz'd on her for some moments with an equal share of surprize
and contempt, and then cried out,—"Hey-day, madam,—what a fig-

---

1. **Jacobitism:** Jacobites, supporters of the claims to the throne of the children of James II,
could be prosecuted for treason.

2. **orange-colour'd:** From the time of William III, who was of the House of Orange, the
color has been associated with the Protestant cause; James and his heirs were Catholic and
excluded from the throne for that reason.

3. **yellow:** the color of the House of Hanover, to which George I belonged.

ure you make today!—You look all in flames,—orange and yellow is certainly the most odious mixture in the world.—Pray how came so odd a fancy into your head?"—To this she reply'd haughtily,

"Sir, It is a fancy which all good subjects and true protestants must approve; and I think you have no pretence to find fault with my fancy; —you, who yesterday thought yourself very fine, I suppose, in the livery of a highland ragamuffin, a silly flower with scarce any smell or taste, and a bundle of stinking leaves for a cockade!"[1]

"You talk impertinently, madam," said he.—"I have just the same opinion of you, sir," return'd she.—"If you had any regard for me," cry'd he somewhat angerly, "you would not endeavour to make yourself so disagreeable in my eyes by this ridiculous dress."—"I care not to whomsoever it is disagreeable," answer'd she, "I wear yellow in honour of our gracious sovereign, and orange to that of the immortal memory of our glorious deliverer king William, who bequeath'd us so valuable a legacy."

I forbear to repeat the reply he made to these words; because it is more than barely possible that some one or other, in this scrutinising age, might take it into his head to imagine that I was glad of an opportunity of venting my own sentiments through the mouth of a third person;—it will be sufficient to inform my readers, that one reflection drew on another, till the husband and the wife seem'd equally to have forgot all the regard due to decency and good manners.

This breach, however, was afterwards patch'd up, tho' not so well but it soon broke out again on every little occasion, and still grew wider than before;—each by turns endeavour'd to bring the other over to their own party; but that being a thing impracticable, created such inward discontents and heart-broilings, as well as open jars, that if they do not absolutely hate, they cannot be said to love;—a peevish thwarting each other even in matters of the most indifference to either, or a sullen silence are the least proofs of their mutual ill-humour:—in fine,

---

1. **cockade:** a rosette or cluster of ribbons worn on the hat as we might wear a button or pin declaring support for a cause.

the whole tenor of their behaviour affords too much reason to believe, that since they are not able to agree in one point, they are determin'd never to do so in any other.

* * *

Sect. XI.

Places of public Entertainment.

Among all public entertainments, those of the Theatre are justly allow'd to be the most innocent and improving.—I have heard many excellent men confess, that more may be learn'd from a good moral play, if well attended to, than from some discourses from the pulpit; and the former has this advantage of the latter, that the instruction it is capable of affording steals into the heart, and takes a deeper root by its being convey'd through the canal of pleasure.

There cannot certainly be an institution better calculated for the improvement of all moral virtues, and the putting vice and folly out of countenance, than that of the stage;—nothing has a greater effect upon us than the sight of those propensities which we feel within ourselves lively represented in the actions of another;—every man, in the persons of the drama, may see the form and turn of his own mind, as he does the features of his face in a mirror, and by that reflection will be taught how to add new graces to the good qualities he is possess'd of, and to rectify the bad.

Among the comedies, I am pretty sure the Careless Husband,[1] and the Journey to London,[2] have not been so often acted without making some proselytes both of husbands and wives; and as what I now write

1. **Careless Husband:** by Colley Cibber; the first production was in 1704, and the play remained a popular repertory piece with more than three hundred performances recorded by 1800.

2. **Journey to London:** Left unfinished by John Vanbrugh, revised and completed by Colley Cibber, it was first performed as *The Provok'd Husband; or, A Journey to London* in 1728.

is intended for the use of the latter, I would recommend it to all women the least addicted to coquetry, to take this lesson from the mouth of Lavinia in the Fair Penitent,[1] who, when her husband has been relating to her the vanity and inconstancy of some women, breaks out in this pathetic and tender exclamation:

> *Can there be such, and have they peace of mind!*
> *My little heart is satisfied with you;*
> *You take up all its room:—as in a cottage*
> *Which harbours some benighted princely*
> *stranger,*
> *Where the good man, proud of his hospitality,*
> *Gives all his homely lodging to his guest,*
> *And scarcely keeps a corner for himself.*[2]

I will not pretend to be so great an advocate for the stage, as to say that all pieces exhibited there have the same tendency, or are capable of producing the same happy effects, either through the author's want of abilities in the expression, or his not considering the true end of writing; but there are so many which have every requisite for this purpose, that none who are desirous of having their virtues heighten'd, or their faults corrected, need be at a loss for the means.

Though I am far from wishing to see any encouragement given to foreign performances, yet, as it is the property of music to tune and harmonize the hero's thoughts, and it has been the mode of late years, and is every day increasing, for ladies to go as far as they can out of their own sex, and assume the robust fierceness of the other, I cannot but approve of their going frequently to Operas, where the softness of the Italian airs may possibly contribute somewhat towards restoring them to their more natural sweetness of manners and behaviour.

Oratorios are endow'd with a yet greater and more peculiar advan-

---

1. **Fair Penitent:** by Nicholas Rowe. First performed in 1703, the play is notable for Calista's strong speeches against male tyranny and Altamont's willingness to forgive his wife for indiscretions. Lavina is the exemplary, virtuous wife.

2. **Can . . . himself:** from Rowe, *Fair Penitent*, 1.1.392–40.

tage; for being on divine subjects, and always perform'd in Lent, what can be more perfectly adapted to elevate the soul, and inspire proper ideas for the celebration of the approaching glorious festival?

Venetian, or Jubilee Balls,[1] Ridottos,[2] Assemblies[3] and Masquerades,[4] have not these pleas for favour; and I am always sincerely concern'd when I hear that any woman, who is suppos'd to have a just sense of honour and virtue, runs so eminent a hazard of both, as to suffer herself to be prevailed upon, either by her own curiosity or the perswasions of her more gay acquaintance, to make a party at any time in these dangerous, disorderly, miscall'd pleasures.

Vauxhall,[5] and Ranelagh-gardens,[6] are accounted very innocent recreation;—walking, they say, is a wholesome exercise, and music accompanying the promenade is extremely agreeable;—this must be allow'd,—but then it is no less true, than that the pleasure of this rural magnificence is in a great measure destroy'd by the vast numbers of people who crowd to be partakers of it; and that the late hours which some stay there cannot contribute much to their health or reputation.

Public breakfasting is an invention which the projectors[7] of time-killing methods have found out to rob husbands of their wives, chil-

---

1. **Jubilee Balls:** Pope Boniface VIII declared 1300 a year of remission from the penal consequences of sin if many acts of devotion (pilgrimages, fasts) were carried out. In England, the social events given this name played on the idea of freedom from the consequences of transgression.

2. **Ridottos:** fashionable social gatherings with music and dancing; the Haymarket Theatre held ridottos in the 1720s.

3. **Assemblies:** fashionable gatherings attended by both sexes for conversation, news, and cards.

4. **Masquerades:** masked balls. At masquerades men and women in costume mingled more freely than at other kinds of parties and took advantage of being, or pretending to be, unrecognized. Public masquerades became the rage in the 1720s. Count Heidegger's at the Haymarket often attracted a thousand ticket purchasers.

5. **Vauxhall:** free gardens that could be reached only by water until 1750; most of the walks were lighted at night, but there were also dark, mazelike paths that earned Vauxhall the reputation of being a place for intrigue, trysts, and even danger. By the time of Haywood's book, there was a shilling charge, but the crowd was still quite mixed. A music room and boxes for refreshments had been added.

6. **Ranelagh-gardens:** fashionable gathering spot for masquerades, garden walks, concerts, and fireworks.

7. **projectors:** devisers of plans, projects, or schemes; often to make money.

dren of their parents, and houses of their mistresses, nay Heaven too
of its due at those very hours in which their presence is most required;
—the husband would talk with his wife on some affairs of the preceding day, she cannot hear him then, she is going to breakfast at
Ruckholt[1] or Ranelagh;—the children crowd to ask a blessing of their
mamma, she scarce can stay to bestow it on them, the coach waits to
carry her to one of the aforesaid places; tradesmen bring their bills,
she is in too much hurry to look over them; the chapel bells ring to
call her to her usual devotion, she hears it not, but orders the coachman to drive away as fast as possible.—This public breakfasting is I
think, the youngest offspring of idleness and luxury,—a poor weakly
brat, and I hope will never arrive at maturity;—on this, however, we
may depend, that no wife, who has her own or family's interest at
heart, will ever join in its support, either by her purse or presence.

There is yet another grotesque figure, or rather shadow of an entertainment, which by starts makes its appearance, and catches the
unwarry, and capricious as they return from breakfasting, and engages
them till near the hours of dining.—I doubt not but I shall be easily
understood to mean those mimic scenes[2] which are sometimes presented at the Little Theatre in the Haymarket, wherein, as I have been
inform'd, not only the vices, but the imperfections which nature, age,
or misfortunes have inflicted on mankind, are exposed and ridicul'd
in as humourous a manner as the buffoon performers are capable of
doing.—Bless us!—what a strange revolution of sentiments, and manners has a few years produced!

This fantastic spirit has desisted his gambols for the present, and I
should heartily wish him to fly to some other quarter, and shew his
head no more in Britain, if I did not fear that some new, and if
possible, more enormous folly would rise up in his stead.

I think that I have now run through all the popular entertainments

---

1. **Ruckholt:** Also called Rookwood, this former residence at Leyton in Essex became a
fashionable public breakfasting house.

2. **mimic scenes:** It became fashionable for actors to imitate the habits or actions of well-
known living people; such mimicry was an important part of the political and social satire
of the Haymarket in the years immediately before the Licensing Act.

of this great town, and can find none, excepting Plays and Oratorios, worthy to employ much of the time and attention of a woman who aims to make her character as a wife perfect and compleat in all its branches:—even the very best among the others, which are call'd pleasures and diversions, should be used but sparingly, like rich cordials,[1] which, taken too frequently, and in large quantities, depress the spirits they were intended to exhilerate.

---

1. **cordials:** medicine, usually a liqueur, given to revive a person by stimulating the heart or circulation.